Dreamer in the North

Thomas S. Gough grew up in the suburbs of Manchester. He has a BA in Modern Languages from Durham University, with a focus on Chinese, Russian and French language, literature and culture. In 2019, he graduated from the University of Oxford with an MSc in Contemporary Chinese Studies, where his research focused on East Asian sexuality, gender and post-colonial migration patterns between China, Japan, Taiwan and South Korea. He currently works as a Research Analyst in London.

For my parents, grandparents, and all those who came before me; without their sacrifices, I would never have made it this far.

Dreamer in the North

T.S. Gough

© 2022 Thomas Sebastian Gough. All rights reserved.

Dreamer in the North

T.S. Gough

© 2022 Thomas Sebastian Gough. All rights reserved.

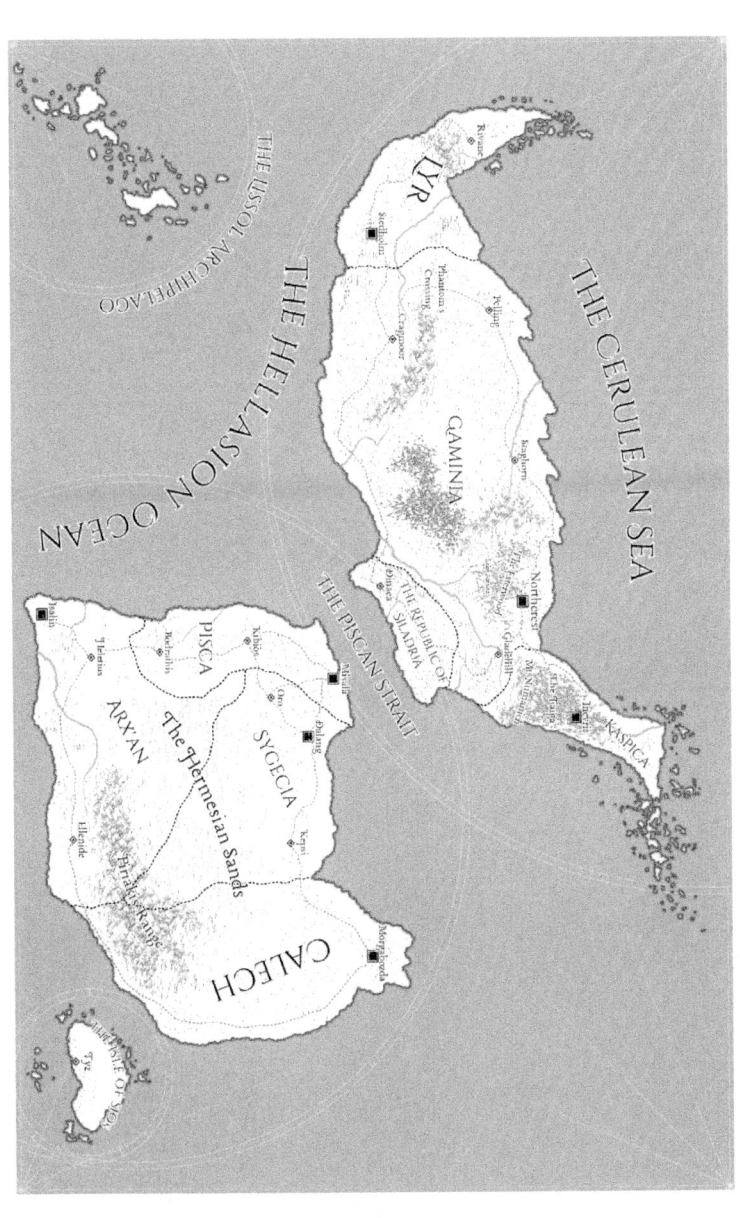

Chapter 1

Unexpected News

Aurelia had always preferred it here to the city. Above, the leaves of oak, elm and ash grew prolifically, spreading their green grasp till the sky was nearly invisible. Many wild flowers were in bloom; violets and yellows filled her periphery. This was the Esterwood, and since she was young, the lake had always been her favourite part of it. She often speculated whether its water held magical powers. Such possibilities fascinated her, and it was her unwavering, spiritual connection to life that kept her questioning Ysa's — the world's — mysteries. Here, she knew freedom from the city's many eyes, always staring and making judgements.

Sitting before the lake, she dipped her toes in and began to daydream. Small perch gathered nearby and flickered around her feet. In moments, she found herself transported into the water as one of its habitants, swimming freely among perch, bass and carp. Although the lake's water was far from limpid, Aurelia's sight was impeccable and air flowed through her gills effortlessly. Then, something began to tug on her; its touch was stern but not frightening.

Aurelia was pulled to the bottom of the lake, where she saw grasses and algae, stones and buried trinkets. Such out of body experiences were not unknown to her. She was calm, though the water's chilling touch bordered on unpleasant. Her vision grew sharper, and manifest before her was a mass of transparent bubbles, which on closer inspection, seemed to form the shape of a woman.

"Swimming again?" asked the watery shape.

"Who are you?" Aurelia was surprised at how natural it was to speak underwater.

"You've seen me in your dreams before. Or did you forget my warning so soon?"

Aurelia didn't know what to say. An invisible weight collapsed in on her chest. She fought hard in an attempt to break free, but the mass of bubbles seemed to reel her back and snare her.

"I remember. How can you be in the lake, and in my dreams?"

"I am not tied to any one place."

"Are you evil?"

"No, but it is coming."

"This is about the war with the Kaspicians again, isn't it?" asked Aurelia.

The bubbles collapsed into a fizzling sphere with a faint glow.

"You can't imagine how painful it is when one of those things burrows into your mind," said the watery shape.

"What things?"

"The ones who want you dead."

The lake spat her out. Like being smacked by a tidal wave, Aurelia crashed back into her body. It was like being riled from a deep and convoluted dream, suddenly to wake up dazed, head spinning. Gripping onto the grass, she grounded herself and took a slow breath. Something new stirred within her. She knew she was changing, but she wasn't afraid. She recognised that her dreams had begun to change. They were no longer whimsical displays of her childhood joys, nor did she stumble upon innocuous entities or ancient places of wisdom and learning out of curiosity. Visions of people she had never met were starting to speak to her. And they did not speak lightly.

Often, they came with grave warnings about wars to come and great devastation.

Aurelia was fortunate to have Mazin, her only friend. They'd first met during one of her games of hide and seek with her brother and sister in the woods. On that day, Aurelia had been lost, looking for her siblings, and stumbled upon Mazin, who calmed her down and helped her find Savas and Elfine. Despite their age difference, for a decade now they'd been friends, and had slowly formed a bond thanks to their shared interest in dreams.

Mazin's hut was conspicuously outside of the city limits, and decidedly unmodern in appearance — it suited his character well. There was a large black pot boiling away on a fire outside the hut producing an aroma of thyme and garlic.

After knocking a couple of times to no response, she let herself in, thinking that he must have gone out for just a moment. The hut's interior was decorated with an array of trinkets, some grotesque, others marvellous. There was a fireplace in the centre, and the mantelpiece was always covered in branches, leaves, stones, and other articles of questionable worth; red and gold woven tapestry hung above, one that Mazin said bore the crest of his people.

Aurelia heard Mazin lift the lid of the pot outside. She left the hut and saw him sitting down on a tree stump chair, stirring a handful of mushrooms into his stew.

Mazin had never told Aurelia where he was originally from, and even though his complexion was tree bark brown, he claimed he wasn't from the Southern Continent — the large island to the south of Gaminia across the Piscan Strait, comprised of four countries. The Hellasic people, as they were often known, were varied from olive-skinned to swarthy to dark, unlike Gaminians, who were all fair-skinned. Aurelia didn't doubt Mazin either: his sense of dress was completely unlike anyone she'd seen from either Continent. He was never seen without his nails, eyes and lips embossed with dyes fashioned from wild ingredients like berries and he preferred floor-length dresses to tunics and trousers. In a society of short-haired men, his long rope of black hair, which swayed along his back like a horse's tail, was also prominent.

"There you are! I was worried you'd left," Aurelia said.

He shot up quickly, dropping his ladle into the pot and splattering food on himself. "Oh! Aurelia! You startled me." He brushed off the hot stew from his tunic and arms. "I didn't know if you were coming back. I was picking mushrooms to the west. The boars keep eating them all on this side of the forest! Stay for lunch, if you like?"

"That's kind of you," Aurelia said, beaming. "I love your cooking. How is it called again?"

"*Vegetarian*," he enunciated each syllable.

Aurelia nodded, with a grin. "The food at home makes my stomach churn now," she added, sitting on the other tiny stool by the pot.

"I'm glad to have recruited you into my bizarre, cruelty-free cult!" He tittered. "And besides, I do so love to share my gastronomic endeavours."

"A good thing you know how to cook then," Aurelia continued. "Now that it's spring, great-aunt Melindra insists on having the servants prepare raw fish and oysters most afternoons. She says it keeps her skin fashionably pale. I don't touch the stuff."

"The Queen — Queen Consort, or whatever title she assumes these days — has always been a woman of peculiar tastes, as you describe her." Mazin smiled. "You were gone a while. Is everything alright?" He kept his eyes on the pot as he spoke, stirring vigorously. When the soup was ready, he ladled generous portions into two big wooden bowls and handed one to Aurelia along with a spoon. The contents quickly heated up the bowl and warmed her hands. Wild mushrooms, chunky beans and little fluffy dumplings bobbed in the broth.

"I think the lake spoke to me," Aurelia said.

Mazin slurped on the soup. "She is magical, after all."

"I'm inclined to believe you, given all that's been happening to me lately."

"What did she say, that old basin of souls and broken bones?"

"That the Kaspicians were coming." She paused. "And that they wanted me dead."

His eyes squinted as he contemplated the meaning and spooned a dumpling into his mouth. The moment of silence thereafter threatened to curdle. "It's curious that the lake brought this message to you in particular. I wonder if some part of you subconsciously wishes to communicate a message about who you are. You do know who you are, don't you?"

"What a peculiar question." She stirred her soup. "How could I not?"

"Ah, but you should ask, how *could* I? A strange spirit living in an even stranger lake consults you to warn you of something grave. Perhaps, this water-dwelling nymph knows you better than you know yourself. Many a bizarre thing has happened by that lake. One time I swam all the way to the bottom and found myself on dry land surrounded by fluorescent-eyed children with webbed hands eatin—"

"What?! You never told me this," Aurelia interrupted.

"I didn't think it was so interesting!" he replied. "You had a warning, nothing so important has ever come my way."

Mazin was a brilliant storyteller, though how much truth lived in his stories was questionable. His skills with food, however, were never in any doubt. Aurelia spooned the last mouthful of stew into her mouth. Satisfied, she then placed the empty bowl on the grass. "You really think this is important, don't you?"

"Have you ever known me to lie?"

"Just two seconds ago you spun a rather extraordinary tale." Aurelia squinted humorously at him. "But I'm not a real fighter. Not like Elfine."

"Neither am I, yet I battle with wild boar twice my size each day. I swear, all those giants do is eat, eat and eat!"

"Have you tried telling them to bore off?"

"Spoken like one who has never tried to wrest a prized truffle from the tusks of a potbellied sow!"

Aurelia giggled. He never got her dry jokes.

"Surely you've something more interesting planned for the rest of the day than nattering with me?"

"I'm having my first practical session with Healer Kistig today. He's asked me to help him treat a patient."

"Oh, how exciting for you! You must be his star pupil, what with all you've learned of pastes and poultices from me."

Aurelia looked at the ground. "Kistig is hard to impress," she murmured.

"I'm sure he'll recognise your talent soon, but you might want to get yourself cleaned up before going to the Academy," Mazin suggested.

Aurelia nodded, stiffly. She hated the public bathhouses, but Mazin had a point. "You're right. Anyway, I should be going." She got up and gave herself a perfunctory brush down.

"Will you be all right getting home this time?" He regarded her carefully.

"Oh, those bullies don't bother me anymore, Mazin." She gave a wan smile.

"Be careful, will you? I worry about these wicked harpies turning their beaks on you. Why do you think I live here in the woods?"

"Don't fret over me. I'm growing a tough shell," she stood up to leave. "I'll pop by again soon. Thanks for lunch."

The journey home required an uphill trudge through the woods to the main road. She hummed a tune from her childhood as she stepped onto the path. Between the trees she could see the imposing whiteness of the walls of her home in the distance. The sun beat down on the white stone, and the glare caused Aurelia to squint.

Outside the city gates, Northcrest was turbulent. The cries of merchants and roadside salesmen in their various accents were commonplace. Sellers from elsewhere, who chattered in various Southern, or Hellasic languages, peddled dainty parasols for the sun-loathing dame, purple tea leaves from the Empire of Yenhai, and a kaleidoscope of spices, all consummately arranged into cones. Another popular product as the days got hotter was orange juice mixed with salted water, a product said to reduce sweating. Drifting along the air was also the aroma of roasted melon seeds.

Travellers from the rest of the country arrived at the market in hordes, as did those hailing from the Southern Continent. Aurelia liked listening to their dialects and figuring out which part of Gaminia they came from, and testing her Piscanese as she heard their rapid, lilting speech. She envied the travellers. Even though Northcrest was Gaminia's capital and said to be its most exciting city, Aurelia often thought about leaving it behind. She had to rely on books and paintings to imagine what other places looked like.

As she neared the city, she was interrupted by a carriage racing past her straight towards the east gate, where it came to an uneasy halt.

The carriage driver dismounted before the gates and opened the doors for the passengers. Aurelia's curiosity was piqued: only someone with special cargo would stop here, but the two military types that then stepped out of the carriage confused her. Following behind them was an older looking man, dressed in navy and gold finery.

Aurelia stiffened when she realised that the man waiting to greet them inside Northcrest's walls was her own father, one of the King's most trusted advisors. As usual, he was in official dress, wearing the auburn tunic that fell to his ankles. The men proceeded to exchange minor pleasantries, but Aurelia couldn't think of anything worse than getting in the way of Father while he was with some dignitary. But she wasn't light on her feet, or adept at being inconspicuous, and she quickly made a fool of herself as a boy carrying a basket of broccoli ran into her.

"Aurelia?" Her father called, his jaw wobbling with embarrassment. "What are you doing here, all filthy like some urchin?" he hissed in a low voice.

"Sorry," mumbled the boy, who then collected all the broccoli off the ground and bolted.

The other man kept his back turned but his two guards sized her up with hungry eyes.

She froze with embarrassment, then bowed her head to her father, apologetically.

"Chancellor Rorstein, please, forgive my daughter for this untimely interruption," Father stammered.

The Chancellor turned around with an inscrutable emptiness etched upon his face. His silver stubble, intensely square jaw and large features were all the type considered very attractive in Northcrest's high society.

Aurelia got no warmth from him.

"Aurelia, this is Chancellor Rorstein of the Republic of Siladria." Father's eye movements were erratic as he spoke. "Don't dither over there, come and introduce yourself!" he barked.

"Chancellor Rorstein, it is a pleasure to meet you," Aurelia said, forcing a polite smile. "Please, excuse my sorry attire; had I known such esteemed visitors wer—"

"So, this is Thane Olsin's *other* daughter," the Chancellor interrupted, his voice an unenthused drawl.

Aurelia was used to her features provoking flared nostrils and tight-lipped scowls, especially from noble types, who so rarely had to deal with anyone who wasn't as pale as them.

Aurelia offered a blank expression to the Chancellor. "I hope that you enjoy your stay in Northcrest," she said.

"I won't be here long," said the Chancellor, who proceeded to walk away with the guards.

"Well, you must be busy. See you at Sunhold," Father said, hurrying off into the city.

Although Aurelia's father kept her in the dark when it came to his work, she knew that he had travelled to the Republic many times in the past months, despite King Thenris' famous hatred of the place. After all, Siladria, before it became a republic, used to be part of Gaminia, but it gained independence over a thousand years ago. Diplomacy has been scarce over the years, but Father, it seemed, had convinced the Chancellor to come to Northcrest. No Siladrian Chancellor had set foot in this city for centuries. And this was exactly why Father was so valued in Northcrest — he was a top graduate of the White Academy, Gaminia's prestigious breeding ground for politicians. Aurelia was glad that she'd never study there, since the White Academy only admitted boys.

Gathered in the bathhouse pool was a group of elderly Gaminian women, shrivelled and leathery like crocodiles. They stared at Aurelia as she scurried into the changing room. Undressing was the next thing to agitate her. She hated the feeling that people were watching her, examining the folds of her tanned belly, measuring the width of her feet or counting the thousands of twisting curls that gave form to her hair.

When she finally stepped into the water, she sighed as it enveloped her and muted her anxiety. Her body was hidden underwater, though she wrapped her arms around her chest out of habit. One moment later, something caught Aurelia's eye: a woman, entering the pool from the far side. Aurelia didn't recognise her. The woman's skin was like bronze, her face elongated and slender, with two eyes deeply sunken into her face like craters. She moved silently through the water then paused. She stared at Aurelia with clear eyes, their dark allure signalling urgency. She demanded Aurelia's attention, though she did not make a sound.

As the woman swam closer, it seemed that people's idle chatter began to dissipate into oblivion and Aurelia's vision blurred.

"You seem awfully calm," she said, suddenly right in Aurelia's ear.

Aurelia jumped, splashing a little water. "The water is relaxing, I suppose."

"It is a good place to be if you want to forget about important things," said the woman.

Aurelia laughed nervously.

The woman looked down and shook her head. "Are you afraid of this war, with the Kaspicians? Everyone's talking about it."

"I haven't really thought about what might happen," Aurelia replied.

"Don't you live in Sunhold, the King's castle? I would've thought you'd be very concerned by now."

"What makes you say that?"

"If the Kaspicians come, they'll come for you first." The woman submerged herself and swam back to the other side. Aurelia couldn't help but wonder if the woman had a point. Although she didn't think of herself as any sort of target, she was surrounded by all the people the Kaspicians would want to eliminate: the King, the Queen Consort and their advisers, the Myriad, which included her own father. At times, it was easy to forget about all the privileges of Sunhold and her social status; Aurelia tended to think of herself as a passive force in Northcrest, unnoticed by most, or ridiculed. Maybe that wasn't the case.

The woman exited the pool and disappeared into another room.

Aurelia got out, changed and made for the Academy.

The Academy was in Chapel Heights, the district where Northcrest's newly rich lived. Aurelia found the district dreary and pretentious. The people her age who occupied these gaudy properties rarely stepped out of their elitist circles, preferring to host extravagant parties to network and flaunt their questionably acquired riches. Along the way, Aurelia did enjoy looking in the windows of the fancy shops, which stocked such oddities as human-hair wigs, fur coats, frilled lace dresses, perfume bottles, and the latest fad — shoes made from cow hide. Another new phenomenon in Chapel Heights was the appearance of homeopathic clinics, which charged exorbitant sums of aurums to treat problems that didn't seem to bother the rest of Northcrest, like, wrinkly foreheads, digestive ailments, and of course, pipe cough.

On the Academy's grounds were various small clinics that helped to treat minor problems of local folk; Aurelia's supervisor awaited her in one of these rooms. Lost in thought as she meandered down the corridor, Aurelia didn't notice as she brushed by a girl, and accidentally caused her to tumble backwards. Tense, she bit her lip when she saw that the girl was Cornetta. She was exceptionally pale, like the petals of the white koondi flowers that grew in the mountains. She was with two friends, all of them pristinely dressed in frilled, lace couture.

"I'm sorry, Cornetta. I didn't see you," Aurelia said, offering a hand to help her up.

Cornetta scowled then swiped Aurelia's hand away. Her two friends quickly lifted her back on her feet, with the same contemptuous look on their faces.

"Desert-faced scab," hissed Cornetta. "Watch where you're going."

"Tell us Aurelia, was it mummy or daddy who rutted the Southern darkie?" taunted one of the other girls. In the next instant, the third girl was behind Aurelia, yanking on her curls. Cornetta, the ringleader, balled her hand into a fist and whacked Aurelia in the face.

Aurelia clutched the bridge. Fortunately, it wasn't bleeding. "You're horrible!"

"Indeed," said Cornetta, her chin tilted upwards as she smugly examined her fist. "And you look like a stray poodle. What ghastly curls! And that bog-brown skin! She belongs in Endvil with the other darkies, not Sunhold!" She shoved past Aurelia and strode off with her cronies, cackling off into the distance like a band of triumphant hyenas.

Aurelia checked her arms. Phew, she thought — still only lightly tanned, swarthy to some, perhaps, but not bog-brown. It was the same complexion as Mother, though a little darker than her brother and sister. But even that was enough of an affront to the milk-white Cornetta and her posse of perfect little imps, who could not contend with the fact that Aurelia and her family were not the castle's cleaners. Occurrences like these distanced Aurelia from life in Sunhold and her privileges, and ultimately, made her aware of how she did not fit in with Gaminian society.

To make matters worse, the only reason Aurelia had enrolled in the Academy of Healing Arts was because Cornetta and her friends had done so first. Cornetta was the exemplar that Aurelia's mother always compared her to. Being the same age, Aurelia and Cornetta had unfortunately interacted for many years, especially since the latter's family claimed to be distant cousins of King Thenris, though their application to reside in Sunhold remained pending. Cornetta's family, while not aristocracy by any means, were close to the top of Northcrest's upper echelon, living the narcissistic life of an old money family in King's Respite.

Aurelia actively resented her studies, especially on days where she ran into Cornetta. What good was it to train to be a healer? The healing arts had never piqued her interest, and the truth was she didn't have the best grasp of the subject either. What Aurelia loved was history and culture, reading about other people in faraway places, and most importantly, their languages. There were no careers for girls like Aurelia interested in such things. Only practical schools of thought were open to her, and training to be a healer was the best of a paltry selection of paths.

Stepping inside the usual room, Aurelia saw a lean woman with brown hair sitting upright on a wooden table. She looked to be around the same age as Aurelia, but something about her exterior was hard and her face was red and puffy. Beside her, a clumsy-looking, makeshift bow with a quiver of six arrows had been placed on the table.

"What happened to you?" the girl asked.

"Nothing," was Aurelia's response.

The girl scoffed.

"Good day, Healer Kistig," said Aurelia.

Aurelia's supervisor, Kistig, was fiddling with all sorts of strangely hued medicines and had barely noticed Aurelia come in. He turned around, revealing a cool and stern face. "You weren't bothering Cornetta again were you, Aurelia? I heard something out in the corridor." His voice was raspy; Kistig was a known pipe fanatic.

"No, Healer Kistig, Cornetta and I are getting on brilliantly these days," Aurelia said.

"Good," he smiled. "Now, pay attention." Turning to the patient, he said, "You didn't forget that one of my students was helping today, did you Temeka?"

Aurelia gave Temeka an encouraging nod.

Kistig looked at his notes, which were etched roughly on parchment. "Severe bruising on the arms and wrists. Several ribs likely cracked. Right middle-finger broken. Knife wound on the right cheek."

Temeka sighed, but said nothing.

"Don't worry Temeka — I won't ask what happened this time," continued Kistig. He had the patient lie prostrate whilst he prepared her arms, both of which were splotched with purple bruises. Aurelia watched intently and helped create a herbal paste to apply to Temeka's bruises. She bandaged Temeka up, trying her best not to cause the girl any discomfort.

Temeka paid in vee coins, which Aurelia guessed she'd earned as some kind of hunter considering the bow and arrows. Vee coins were a new currency awarded to labourers. They could use them to pay for medicine and consultations like this, as well as food and other necessities. Aurelia handed over a package that provided Temeka with enough of the herbal salve to last for a week.

Temeka looked to her first and said thanks, then gave Kistig a weak smile before leaving with her things.

Aurelia sat with Kistig in his office after the procedure. It was an airless space, overflowing with books, papers, journals, and all sorts of medical paraphernalia.

"Is it common procedure to not ask what happened to a patient?" asked Aurelia.

"It's better not to with girls of her... type."

Aurelia nodded, feigning to have understood his meaning.

"You did well today." He made no attempt to mask his surprise. "With all this talk of war and Kaspica, I wonder how much we'll see each other in the coming months." He was engrossed in his notes.

"Things are looking troubling, but I hope my studies will continue."

He continued perusing whatever document was in front of him, and she could not see his face. "You best get home," he said, "Not much of the day left."

Aurelia nodded. "Before I go, since you're in the Myriad now, I suppose you knew that the Chancellor of the Republic was in town?"

Kistig recoiled slightly. "You heard about that?"

"I've heard nothing, but I saw him with Father earlier," she replied.

He patted her on the shoulder with a frosty touch. "There's no harm in letting you know now then. The Chancellor is here for the royal wedding. He requested your sister in marriage for his son, and your father agreed."

Aurelia's whole body felt like it was suddenly shrinking. "What? An arranged marriage? How am I only just finding it now?"

"Wonderful, isn't it? We haven't had a royal wedding in decades." He looked far too pleased. She considered slapping the smile off his face, but it wasn't worth getting expelled.

"I thought Gaminia's biggest problem was this supposed war with Kaspica. Now we're having a random, royal wedding?"

"No one has forgotten the war. The Kaspicians remain the deadliest threat to life as we know it."

"So, my sister is to marry some boy that she's never met before. That's the sum of the Myriad's response to the threat?"

"Don't presume to know anything about politics; you're training to be a healer, not a leader."

"But you only trained as a healer, and now you've a seat in the Myriad. Perhaps politics isn't such a stretch of the imagination," she said.

He held her gaze for a stretched-out moment. "Speaking of the Myriad," he began, coldly, "We believe that the enemy has agents dotted about the city. Isn't that a grisly thought, that they could be walking among us and we haven't even noticed?"

A chill scraped Aurelia's spine. She thought back to the lake this morning, and the words she heard made an incision through her sudden dread: *You can't imagine how painful it is when one of those things burrows into your mind.*

She didn't doubt Kistig's words.

Chapter 2

A Dream Like No Other

King's Respite was the city's sovereign district, and it teemed with an eerie sense of power. At the end of any passageway, a gruesome end could be waiting. Cursed treasures were buried in people's gardens, and the eyes and mouths that gawped from the pastel green and blue balconies plotted nefariously. This was a place where people were prone to gossip. Everyone was observed and discussed here, whether they realised or not. Mysterious shadows lurked in ornate windows, strange shapes flickered about the alleys and licked at the walls like flames, footsteps seemed to follow one's every move, and whispers congregated around every corner.

Not everyone saw these things as plainly as Aurelia did. Sunhold was the unmistakable landmark of King's Respite. It was an emblem of power to outsiders, but to Aurelia, it was the house of a fractured and ailing King, whose influence did not extend beyond his bed-chamber.

Most who lived in King's Respite were nobility, but none were more influential than the Myriad. They were charged with seeing and documenting every happening in Northcrest, especially all that occurred on the King's doorstep. Even though her father was in the Myriad, Aurelia had always been sceptical of these self-serving politicians. The idea that her father had orchestrated some political marriage between Elfine and the son of the Chancellor, therefore, didn't come as a great surprise. Father was cold, ambitious and, it turned out, willing to do anything to propitiate his peers, even sacrificing his family.

Aurelia was close to home. The glare of the white buildings forced her to shield her eyes with her palm.

Many of the homes were draped in climbing ivy with diamond-shaped leaves. She heard cats meowing in pleasant conversation and the usual whispering down the darkening ginnels.

Sunhold lay at the end of a cobbled path, which was framed by a stretch of evergreen trees and flowering shrubs. The castle's chunks of sleek grey stone were threatening, and the facade had two tall towers that shot upwards like ashy candles, with burnt orange tiles flaring around them. The main towers formed part of a defensive wall around Sunhold, within which were more towers. Around the entrance, there were Protectors everywhere, some actively patrolling, others slacking off in little groups and bantering amongst themselves.

"Good day," Aurelia said quietly to two of them, as she passed through the gate and into the central bailey. This was the jewel of Sunhold, where the flowers of azalea bushes caught the light of the sun like coral stars; the scents of blossoming fig and apricot — the Queen's personal favourites — floated in the air.

Aurelia's room was as she left it. Tired from her long day out and lesson with Kistig, she collapsed on the bed, ready for a rest. At first, her thoughts refused to settle down. She wondered about Temeka and Kistig, and how she'd performed today, then about the lake and Mazin. Did she really have enemies to be afraid of? The thoughts sputtered through relentlessly, until her mind eventually wandered into the realm of light sleep.

"Aurelia!" She heard her sister's voice, followed by an urgent knocking. The voice was unnatural, as though Elfine was underwater. Aurelia approached the door cautiously.

"Elfine, I'm so glad you're—" She cut herself off mid-sentence when she realised that there was nobody there. The corridor was empty.

Aurelia dragged her feet as she returned to the foot of her bed. Glancing to her left, she noticed that neither her mirror nor her window was present. She was not in her room. Afraid, she turned again, to see that the door was also gone. In its place, a fluctuating disc of black, reminiscent of fire. Filling the entrance, it produced no sound, but rippled, like a puddle being whipped by hard rain.

The silence was unbearable. It dominated, desperate to be known. An inimical chill coiled around her bare arms. Her grip on reality dissipated and she felt her senses fade. A strange fuzziness around her prevented any possibility of moving. No air seemed to travel into her lungs.

The knocking came again and louder. A shadow of a person had stepped through the eerie, black maw. Sweat beaded upon her brow and the back of her neck itched with a profound heat. Why couldn't she move? She plummeted into a nightmarish abyss, fearing that the sensation of falling would last an eternity. But it came to an abrupt halt, and she found herself on her feet in a murky world, where cloying voices reached for her soul. It was a chilling void, lit barely by an indigo haze in a pale, sunless sky. She heard her name called by many different voices. Some were gentle whispers, others were urgent cries, others sounded of madness and desperation. The soil beneath her was rich but toxic at once; it housed memories, journeys of souls both lost and found, but also great sadness and emptiness.

Feeling returned to her feet, but it was onerous to move, as if she carried the weight of a huge sack of grain on her back. Her body shook with anxiety, terrified at the thought of these conspiring voices undressing her soul. Her breathing escalated, her heart thumped slowly, as if too terrified to draw attention to itself, and her nails dug into the flesh of her palms, inflicting a degree of pain she had never known in a dream before.

Yet she did not wake up. She only hurt herself trying to escape. The world she had entered could not be bent to her will, like in some dreams: was this a real place? It was void of life. It could not be real. But a fleeting flurry of crackles and hisses cut through the emptiness, shattering the illusion of solitude. A jolt roused her body. Something was changing. Her senses were fortified and she relished the sudden clarity she experienced. She could now clearly see the stars above her in the sky, and felt a certain warmth rally beside her. Her vision was overloaded with dazzling colours as a host of ghostly silhouettes emerged and formed a circle around her. They did not arrive with fear nor panic, but were free from emotion. Their shapes were difficult to discern, whether they were men, women, or something greater, was unclear.

Aurelia looked around and counted at least nine figures. She stood motionless waiting for them to speak. Their ethereal bodies flickered as if they were fire, but soon, their shapes stabilised. Although they remained immaterial, distant memories of what might have been their human bodies flashed sporadically, like a pair of eyes or thick curls of hair.

As though held at the centre of a whirlpool, Aurelia saw that she was surrounded by immense power. These creatures seemed timeless, potent and severe. Encircling Aurelia was ancient power and wisdom. The shape of one woman manifested itself in front of her; the woman-spirit stepped closer, examining and analysing Aurelia. Her expression flickered through different emotions, making it impossible to know the extent of her judgement.

"Do you hear us?" The woman's voice was muffled and barely audible. The shapes around her seemed disinterested and disappointed; their bodies flailed and shimmied with a sense of urgency. In the next instant, Aurelia heard their voices clearly.

"*Weak*. It neither hear nor see a ting," scoffed a second voice.

"Her magic recalcitrant. Perhaps she is too," a third voice commented.

"This Northcrester knows nothing of our burden," continued the second voice.

"You a great fool fi put we hopes inna dis white-people-loving sack of flesh," the third voice rumbled.

"Indeed! Must we entrust our struggle to one such as this? Our champion should not be this diluted, sullied pickny! How can she claim to be one of us, to stand amongst our people and know what the Eternal Wars have cost us?" The second voice barked.

"Eeedyat! You think she could claim anything else? That the snow-skins would ever see her as one of theirs?" Another voice said, then laughed.

"Stop your noise!" The woman who spoke first snapped. "She is my charge. I have reached her already."

A final voice joined in, sounding older and wiser than the others. "Expected. She carries you. You must bind yourself to her now." Their voices rang loudly in Aurelia's head and it became difficult to concentrate. A horrible tenseness took hold of her body, with a pain reminiscent of cramp rippling through her body.

Trying to speak proved futile. Her lips moved slower than ever before, and nothing came out. The spirits around showed little sign of disappointment that Aurelia could not utter a word. The woman-spirit in front, however, looked concerned. She grabbed Aurelia's arm, and the mere sensation of her touch alone inundated Aurelia's whole being with a feeling that was both ecstasy and fear. It was like being struck by lightning over and over again, only to keep coming back alive with more vigour each time.

A strange and unexpected connection between herself and this world started to form; everything around her grew common and familiar, as if she had traversed this place countless times. As she looked slowly around her, the feeling of having known this place was undeniable.

"Don't be afraid of my touch — you can trust me," the woman-spirit said, with a thin smile. "It is difficult to communicate between realms." Her voice was slow and deliberate. Aurelia was locked in time and space with this woman-spirit, who had stopped her from slipping back to reality too soon. She wanted to reply but still could not speak. "The Kaspicians are coming," the woman-spirit continued. "You must be prepared to face those who lead them. The serpent-jawed monsters and their leader. Aurelia — *awaken*." Indecipherable whispers ensued, enchanting and mesmerising. Deafening cymbals clattered and a lurid glare blazed like a sheet of white fire.

*

Aurelia's bedroom was lit faintly by a single lantern. She had been unconscious for some time. A while ago, her mother Trinne found her in this abnormal state. In a bout of worry, she immediately called Aurelia's servant, Mitenni, to prepare a special poultice. Trinne was perched on the bed, looking intently at her daughter. The sight of Aurelia unwell troubled her, but she was confident through her faith that Aurelia would be fine.

Mitenni busied herself by the desk crushing seeds, foul-smelling salts, and squeezing the juices of stems and leaves into a jar. Her brown face was small and round, and her black hair was tied neatly in a bun. As always, she wore a grey smock.

"Have you prepared the remedy with the exact measurements? There's no margin for error," said Trinne.

Mitenni nodded, trying to reassure her. She produced a clumpy, moss-green beverage, smelling of rotten fungus. Its colour seemed to grow brighter as she gently stirred it one final time. Proudly, she passed it to Trinne, who took a painstaking examination of the jar's contents.

Smiling with relief, Trinne murmured "Thank you Ishanaia, my wise goddess. You always answer our prayers."

Mitenni passed her a wooden spoon to administer the potion. With utmost care, Trinne spooned the liquid into her daughter's mouth as she slept and lifted her head to help her swallow it. Aurelia produced a cough and stirred slightly.

"Aurelia is fortunate to have one so devout as a mother," Mitenni said.

Trinne caressed her daughter's forehead and watched her for any signs of coming round. "My faith keeps my family alive, but we are grateful also to have been blessed with a servant so versed in the healing arts."

Mitenni tugged at her fingers. "Oh, you flatter me Lady Trinne, truly. In Sygecia, before I arrived here, my father taught me to treat many ailments."

"The Sygecian people are wiser than many here, despite the persistence of slavery in some parts," said Trinne.

Mitenni nodded. "I hope one day that problem will go away, Lady Trinne," she said.

The two didn't have a particularly strong relationship; Trinne's children knew Mitenni better, and they'd sung her praises. Trinne had never been to Sygecia either, but she knew Olsin, her husband, had been a couple of times, as had Elfine. Both had lamented the unbearably hot sun but confessed a certain fascination with the blistering heat and scarcity of life in the country's deserts, as well as the grand temples in the cities, filled daily with religious devotees.

"Aurelia said she had been eating less meat," Trinne mentioned, after a pause. "Thanks to your influence."

Mitenni nodded quickly. "Yes. Lady Aurelia doesn't like eating animals anymore."

"Is this behaviour common in Sygecia?"

"Lady Trinne, forgive me. I'm not sure what you mean."

"Do the people of your lands live like this, eating vegetables only?"

"There are those who live like this in Sygecia, and many who do not. It is my preference to eat like this; perhaps she was curious to try it for herself," Mitenni explained, fidgeting with her frock.

"I worry that it is making her unwell," Trinne fussed.

"Lady Trinne, many Sygecians adopt this diet and live heal—"

Trinne brusquely shushed her, watching Aurelia stir. She ran her hand lightly across her daughter's cheek, then tidied her disordered hair so that she could see her face clearly.

Aurelia's eyes opened. "Mother... I feel so tired," she said.

"Oh, thank Ishanaia. You're awake at last," cried Trinne. "Mitenni. I would like a moment alone with my daughter."

Mitenni bowed her head gracefully, and shuffled silently towards the door, sparing a parting smile for Aurelia.

"You must tell me everything. What happened?" asked Trinne.

With difficulty, Aurelia sat up on the bed cross-legged. "A dream, more lucid than any other." She rubbed her temples, hoping to squeeze the memory out of her head. "But there's a fog obscuring my mind."

"This is most unlike you. Normally, you recall everything with impeccable clarity. Something new is at work here," Mother said. She arose and floated towards the balcony, where she paused. Her pliant body folded over the balustrade, moving with a slow serenity.

"You're right." Aurelia joined her on the balcony. "Just as our nation prepares for the ultimate test."

"This war with Kaspica summons all manner of fear into our country's most agile minds. Yet you are the one who is peering through the veil, the one who is glimpsing the world of the dead. You don't seem afraid." Mother squinted upwards, hungry for Ishanaia — Mother's favoured deity, and one of three gods of the Yotanite faith — to pour forth knowledge from the skies.

"Maybe I am a fool to not be afraid, but I feel curiosity more than anything. I'm hungry for more."

Mother reached for Aurelia's hand and shut her eyes. "Then we pray."

"No, I don't think th—"

"Supernal Goddess, we seek your edifying wisdom, for you know the hearts of all men and the essence of all things. Strengthen us, Lady of Elements, so that we may know you in all things, be edified by your insight, and see—"

A rumble interrupted Mother, and Aurelia had to suppress a snicker. She hated prayer and thought it was a waste of time. What good had it ever done for them? The second peal of thunder deafened; Mother covered her ears. A blade of lightning split the black-blue sky in half for just a moment. Silvery sheets continued to rip through the mass of black clouds, suddenly pregnant with rain and shadows. They sprayed a heavy downpour onto Northcrest. Aurelia looked up and was relieved to remember that they were covered where they stood.

Mother looked rattled as she continued. "And we shall see clearly, not with our eyes, but with our eternal spirits, to whom no secret shall be withheld. Blessed be." She clamped Aurelia's hand tightly. "Say blessed be, or your prayer will go unheard."

"Blessed be," Aurelia mumbled, then pulled her hand away. She watched the rain and enjoyed the thick, heady smell of saturated stone. Petrichor, Tutor Fark had once called that scent.

"Ishanaia has heard us," Mother said, gesturing with open palms to the rainclouds. Most Yotanites worshipped the Three: Zerkal, Aseg and Ishanaia. Aurelia couldn't remember hearing her mother ever pray to Zerkal or Aseg — soldiers and fathers prayed to Zerkal; scholars preferred Aseg. Mother only cared for Ishanaia, though she almost never attended church services. Church folk irked her.

"You must tell me what you saw as soon as you remember," Mother went on. "It might be important for our whole family."

That word. *Family.* It made Aurelia shiver as she recalled her conversation with Kistig. "Is Elfine to be married to the Chancellor's son?"

Mother recoiled. "You heard..." she murmured, her voice barely audible amid rain and thunder. "It is true."

"Why didn't you say anything?" Aurelia asked, as they came back inside.

"I was sworn to secrecy," Mother replied. "Your father feared that if word got back to Elfine, she would not return for the wedding. You know how politics works — I have no power over these things."

"When will it be?"

"I believe the Myriad will meet tomorrow to decide, but I expect very soon."

"How could you be more loyal to Father than to us, to Elfine?" Aurelia pressed.

"Your father is unpredictable; I did not want to rouse his ire."

"I hate him."

Mother's head shook from side to side. "Let us not speak of this, Elfine has not returned home yet. She doesn't even know yet. You need to rest."

"I'm feeling much better already."

"Aurelia. Please. Your father simply would not have it any other way. I'm sorry, but I kept this secret to keep all of us safe."

"You think forcing Elfine to marry a stranger will keep us all *safe*?"

Mother strode up to Aurelia with a frown. "You are gifted. But you do not see things as clearly as I do because you lack faith."

"Faith!" Aurelia hissed. "What faith drove you to sell your child like this?"

"Would you rather go in her stead? Your father made his choice without me. But know this: when he asked me which of you to sacrifice, yes, I chose Elfine and not you. Do you know why? Because you are a foolish child, your sister is a warrior fiercer than any in this city. The cost of this weighs heavier on my heart than you will ever know, because you are not a mother. I'm going to bed — say your prayers and get some rest." She left.

Aurelia lay supine on her bed, staring up at the ceiling, wondering if Ishanaia truly cared about her dreams. A deity who actually cared about people should surely care more about Elfine, who was about to be flung into some awful, inescapable destiny. That was important, not hazy dreams and visions. At least, that was what Aurelia's heart told her to feel. She only had to tunnel deeper into her mind to realise that what she really cared about was her own future, not so much her sister's.

Chapter 3

An Urgent Message

Two cloaked figures approached Northcrest on horseback at the devil's hour — deep into the night, with dawn still distant. They left their horses in the care of a stablemaster just outside the city walls and paced through town urgently despite their exhaustion. The girl was lithe and moved with sophisticated poise despite her injury, and the boy had a determined stride. The two of them were not to be trifled with; they were deadly and powerful.

Their path illuminated by hanging lanterns, they advanced towards a secret location, known only to the Chicane: a small force of lethal experts, loyal to King Thenris. It was an abandoned house concealed in the crevices of Endvil: Northcrest's most sordid district, where the rule of crime and corruption reigned supreme. It was for this reason that Endvil became an excellent location for the Chicane, who, with little difficulty, disappeared into the perpetual dim and squalor.

The pair stole through a shadowy alley, where the voices of the unwell could be heard spluttering curses and invectives against the King. This alone deterred most, but the two continued, whilst footsteps without feet and bodiless growls sounded faintly in the background.

Upon entering the unremarkable structure, it seemed like no one lived here. The girl pushed through a hidden doorway in the wall. On the other side was a room steeped in a history of murder, theft and plotting. There was an aged feeling to the place, and the red-brown stains on the floor reminded the girl of how many throats had been slashed here.

A man and a woman were sitting around a circular wooden table. They were both older and more seasoned than the other two; the woman's complexion was red-brown, almost coppery, and her long and slender face bore the authoritative features of a leader. Several candles lit the room, and atop the table was a mess of papers. The new arrivals unveiled their heads and assumed their positions at the table. The elders maintained frosty expressions.

"We weren't expecting you back so soon," said the copper-skinned woman. Her expression was grave.

"Zatela, Rhyslan." The girl bowed her head with respect. "We left sooner than expected. There were... complications." She looked anxiously at her partner.

"The point of this organisation is to effectively handle such complications," Zatela replied. Her gaze focused on the young man, Lorcan, who began to shuffle uncomfortably in his seat.

"We did our best, Zatela," Lorcan said. "Our training was not sufficient, and—"

Zatela cut Lorcan off. "Where is Terig?"

Elfine's head sagged with guilt.

"Elfine," Zatela barked, "report, please."

"Our contact never showed in Minnet. He wasn't the first to go missing there either," Elfine started. Minnet was the northernmost township of Gaminia, situated right at the base of the perilous Numanich Mountains, beyond which was Kaspica. "There were numerous reports of disappearances, but the local leaders acted as though under a spell. They ignored the fears of their people." Elfine squeezed her thumb and forefinger together. She recalled the images of confused people, wandering about like they were daydreaming, unresponsive and unhelpful.

"It wouldn't be the first time we've dealt with something like that," Rhyslan added. He had served in the

Chicane for almost five years, making him the third most senior member of the group. A man of great intellect, he was an excellent fighter too, despite his wiry frame. The coruscant blade of unsullied silver in his scabbard had vanquished man and beast both in service to Gaminia.

"Vigilantes had assembled search parties to look for the missing residents, but the only thing they found was a... cellar," continued Elfine.

"What sort of cellar?" Zatela asked.

"There was a cauldron. Looked as though someone had been cooking human bodies in it," Lorcan supplied, at a stammer.

Elfine thanked Lorcan with a quick nod. "We set out towards the Numanich Mountains the next day and we encountered something."

Zatela's eyes widened. "*Something?*"

"We climbed through snow and hail for hours, and after hours of isolation, we heard voices behind us," Elfine continued. "We realised there were four enemy scouts on our tail. We separated and awaited them from stealth; Lorcan and Terig doubled back and prepared an ambush from the trees, and I climbed further up. The storm was so strong I could barely see anything." She paused, trying to recall every detail. "Then, two scouts appeared on my right and I launched two knives laced with poison as quick as I could; they both dropped in seconds."

"Terig and I handled the other two with a few arrows. But what came next wasn't human," Lorcan said.

"It was a steel colossus, taller than any man I'd ever seen, with a massive double-sided axe that looked able to cleave a human in two. It took its helmet off to frighten us, but its face was no different to an ordinary man's. When I saw it grip its weapon tighter, I hurled two poisoned knives at it, but the thing didn't even flinch."

"Perhaps its armour was too sturdy for your blades to penetrate the flesh?" Rhyslan suggested.

Elfine shook her head in doubt. "Didn't look like it. Lorcan fired two arrows at the thing as well, but it deflected them with its gauntlet. In the next instant, the thing was charging towards me like a raging bull. When it struck me with its fist, I flew back into a tree and was winded badly. Terig tried to strike the beast from behind, but it overpowered him straight away." Elfine shuddered. "The beast took him by the throat and kneed him in the stomach till he was spewing scarlet. Then, he dragged Terig into the mist. And we couldn't save him. We just ran."

Zatela folded her arms and sighed.

Rhyslan pinched the bridge of his nose.

"That is not what I was expecting to hear," Zatela said. She shot up from behind her seat and moved to leave, then nodded to Rhyslan. "You did well. I will see to it that the King hears of this."

Lorcan piped up, full of emotion. "Is that it? You're supposed to be our leader, and you're going to just leave us like that, with no explanation? We could easily have died out there."

Elfine and Rhyslan held their breath, tensely looking at the floor.

"You don't get to question my leadership," snarled Zatela. "*Mbwesi aku puro tom au'wa.*" She hurried to the door and left.

"What did she just say?" Lorcan whispered to Rhyslan.

"Juvenile, idiot, moron, disrespectful, snow-skin — some combination of those insults. My Sygecian is rusty, but don't worry about Zatela, she's always been fiery. You did well," Rhyslan said, encouragingly.

"We should've gone after Terig," Elfine said, full of regret.

"I wouldn't worry too much about that wily old fox. Even if Ysa split in half, he'd still survive," Rhyslan joked.

Lorcan seemed to consider a smile, then vacillated to a puckered brow. "Do you know what it could've been? Elfine's knives were coated in valitosin, even an ox couldn't have withstood poison that deadly," he said.

"Some enemies require special tactics. Perhaps, this one was resistant to valitosin," Rhyslan suggested.

"No human being is resistant to valitosin. That's why we use it. It kills everything," Elfine said curtly, remembering the words Zatela herself had once said.

"Perhaps what you encountered was not human at all then. We all have much to do it seems." Rhyslan smiled at the weary pair before him, then departed.

The meeting was over, and Elfine and Lorcan were left alone. Young and inexperienced as they were, it had been a sobering exchange, and the reality of a war against such an alien force struck a harsh note. Elfine did not know whether she envied or admired the level-headedness of Zatela and Rhyslan. Their manner did little to reassure her.

"I'm shocked neither of them seemed to care that Terig was battered and dragged into Kaspica before our eyes," Elfine said.

"Rhyslan's right. Terig isn't a fool. Maybe he knew what he was doing," Lorcan speculated.

Elfine sighed. "What should we do? We can do nothing here."

"I guess we'll have to wait and see what she decides to do next," he said. He paused and looked into her eyes. His eyes were a modest, greyish blue. Elfine sometimes found herself counting the specks of blue hugging his iris. "How's that injury coming along?" asked Lorcan.

"It's nothing; it's pretty much healed." She shrugged. "By the Three gods do I hate being back in Northcrest, but I need to head home."

"Aren't you at all excited to see Aurelia and Savas though?" asked Lorcan.

"My sister prefers the company of bees and Savas can't hold a conversation unless he's blind drunk."

Lorcan raised an eyebrow. "The luxuries of Sunhold surely excite you, then," he flashed a toothy grin.

"That stony heap of rubble?" she sneered.

Lorcan looked puzzled. "I never could understand what you hated so much about that Castle. Free meals, clothes, regular baths, servants... I used to love staying there."

"You loved my satin sheets more than you loved me, I think," she teased. "But Sunhold is so dull. I find everything about it meaningless. It was like a hotel, only the owners didn't really want you there. My family have never been considered worthy of being royalty, and over the years, people have made it clear that that's how most of the city's power-holders also feel."

"I never thought of it like that," he said, grinning. "Still, I wouldn't mind if you invited me again soon."

"Are you suggesting something?"

He blushed. "No. Why? Would you like me to?"

Elfine nibbled her bottom lip. She knew that whenever she did that, he found her irresistible. "I think I'll be too busy with my family to have you round anytime soon."

"Well, I won't wait forever."

She rolled her eyes. "Our love will have to wait," she said. "Zatela betrayed nothing, but I could tell she was alarmed. That's never happened before."

Lorcan nodded.

"Apart from that monster's size, it looked like an ordinary man in a fancy suit of armour. Zatela knows what it was. I can tell," said Elfine.

"You don't doubt her, do you?" asked Lorcan, leaning back into his chair.

"No, not like that," she said quickly. "She's done a lot for me. And you. But she's keeping something from us. Rhyslan is too."

"I want you to be wrong," he said, then frowned. "But you have a point. Spies, assassins, thieves — yes, we've both been all of these things, but we haven't been trained to hunt monsters. What's next, a wyrm, a cockatrice?"

"Maybe we haven't been paying enough attention," Elfine said. "Perhaps, the whole point of our training was to deal with monsters."

"Then we failed the first test," Lorcan said.

Elfine sighed. "There must be something about what we saw in the logs. Something we haven't been taught yet."

"It might be best to put our trust in Zatela for now."

"She almost got us killed. Doesn't seem like she's very prepared," said Elfine. "What if there's an invasion tomorrow?"

"An invasion?" Lorcan worried.

"That thing was on Kaspician soil," Elfine said. "There's a good chance it serves the enemy. Our people haven't waged war for centuries, nor does his majesty King Idle Bones make it his business to prepare his forces. The Protectors are good for nothing but making pointless arrests and aimlessly policing the downtrodden. That's our city's first line of defence — a bunch of lazy, metal-headed oafs who play cards and pick their arses all day. You and I are supposed to be the best, and we nearly got crushed."

Lorcan's expression turned dour. "A good thing there was only one of those monsters, then."

Chapter 4

Encounter with the Past

Aurelia could never figure out what was going on in her older brother's head. Rarely did Savas take care of her as an elder brother might, nor was he particularly protective, but they understood each other in some ways. They were able to laugh at similar sorts of jokes, thanks to their shared disdain for their mother's religious fixations and their father's political scheming.

Recently, Aurelia had hardly seen him. He was always slipping in and out of Sunhold at odd hours, and it was not unusual to catch him utterly intoxicated.

Having slept a little too late, Aurelia rushed to get dressed. She put on a loose-fitting robe that went down to her knees. She hesitated several times looking at her clothes, worried if she looked too curvy and overly concerned that no one else would be wearing the colour green. Trivial as it was, such was the effect of her social anxiety sometimes, and she often laboured over every outfit before going out. The idea of standing out in a crowd worried her.

Yesterday's experience left her groggy, but she pressed on as normal. Her memory of the events remained blurry, existing mainly as flashes of light and sound in her mind. Strange dreams were commonplace for her, but she sensed that this was no ordinary dream, just like she knew that the watery shape in the lake was not a trick of her imagination. One exceptional occurrence was acceptable, but now a second one, even stranger, was cause for concern.

As she passed through the bailey, she smiled and waved politely at the gardeners, even though her mind was grappling with all sorts of worries. The memories that came before her were equal parts dreams and nightmares, and she found herself unable to recall them entirely. All the same, they weighed heavily on her heart; something far beyond her comprehension tiptoed around at the back of her mind.

Vague visuals of her twilight dreamscape began to cluster as she walked. The occasional face, hushed voices of unknowable origin, and the memories of sounds never before heard were hard to comprehend. It felt like a realm wider and weirder than anywhere she'd ever known, forming a chain of broken images, and nothing of clarity emerged. The deluge of thoughts caused her head to swim, and though she seldom drank alcohol, the word hangover seemed apposite.

She headed down Fortune's Avenue, the famous stretch of mercantile territory that connected King's Respite to the district of Brighthaven. Here, buyers and sellers hailed from all over and a panoply of identities converged: Sygecians clad in vibrant garments, some with their hair expertly tied in a decorative headwrap; Piscanese, whose lilting chatter was quicker than birdsong; and Arx'ani, with their bronze skin and sinewy bodies allowed Aurelia to hide in the variety. Uppity nobles like Cornetta seldom braved the disarray of Fortune's Avenue.

Those who did come to trade manoeuvred with terrible urgency as that was the custom along this belt of bedlam. Voices cried and shouted with double the volume as elsewhere. People gushed forth from all directions at once, racing between every stall in search for the best prices. Aurelia had heard that it paled in comparison to similar bazaars across the sea in Pisca and Sygecia, but it was good enough for the Northcresters, who saw their city as the pinnacle of modern culture.

A large queue to her left gathered by a popular street food stall. A wizened lady whose family presumably had been in the trade for generations prepared the dish every day for hordes of urbanites. Her speciality was a kind of sweet pastry filled with orange and cinnamon custard, but she also served a savoury variety with cheese, cured sausage and beans cooked in a tomato sauce. Such food never made its way to Sunhold, where most of the dishes served had to reflect the Queen's so-called exquisite taste, like raw fish.

"Have I seen you getting your hair done at Nektaria's down Endvil?" asked a woman behind.

Aurelia jumped slightly, to which the woman smirked with good humour. "I've never been out to get my hair done."

The woman took a slight step back and appeared to examine Aurelia's hair with her eyes in a comical squint. "Oh. Right. By the way — are you queueing, or just browsing? I'm in a hurry."

"No," said Aurelia. "I'm not queueing."

Seeing the staring black and brown faces of the Hellasic people in the queue, Aurelia left, unsure whether she was more welcome in this territory or not. Families of similar status to her own derided her for her looks, but people from the Southern Continent seldom saw her as one of theirs either.

As usual, Aurelia's curiosity grew as she meandered through the soon-to-be gentrified streets of Brighthaven, where stylish eateries and pubs had begun to mushroom on every street. Endvil was too dirty, and Fortune's Avenue was too chaotic, but here, there was more balance. Locals were enamoured with the concept of eating out here. They liked to choose their wine from a long list, and they tended to opt for small plates of food and share them among their large group of acquaintances. Whilst they dined outside, they also smoked pipes and blew clouds of scented smoke into the air between raucous bouts of laughter that looked somehow affected for passers-by.

Savas' favourite part of Brighthaven was a stinky watering hole called the Angel's Hovel: one of a small number of not-so fashionable establishments in the area — Aurelia hated the dive. All the customers were middle-aged, white Northcrester men, most of whom were thick-bodied, hairy and reeked of ale. They regarded Aurelia with hostility as she dithered in the doorway, battling waves of anxious thoughts.

She saw her brother waving conspicuously, grinning ear to ear with an early morning tipple before him. Beside him, there was an unexpected guest: the girl from the clinic, Temeka. She had cut all her hair, leaving only a peppering of stubble behind. Contrary to yesterday, Temeka had a glow about her. The puffy-faced, bruised girl seemed to have been transformed overnight as though she had discovered a new holy scripture that affirmed all of her beliefs and desires.

Savas, as Mother often used to say, resembled a boy version of Aurelia. His hair wasn't as curly, but it was the same shade of brown, and he had the same sun-blushed skin and pale green eyes. Northcresters were more obstinate when it came to the demands made of women, however. Pale white skin, blonde hair and blue eyes remained the official gatekeepers of feminine beauty, yet Savas was often viewed as exotic and handsome.

"Is that a beer?" Aurelia asked, sitting in the chair opposite Savas.

"Good morning to you too," he said, jovial. "And you know I don't drink beer this early. It's apricot cider; the favourite fruit of our city."

Aurelia rolled her eyes. "I see you're still taking care of your health then."

He grinned. "This place will do, won't it? There aren't any birds for you to chit chat with, or trees to banter with."

Temeka looked at her feet as she broke into a light smile.

"This is Temek. I've been wanting you two to meet for a while." He looked endearingly between the two women.

Aurelia was astonished to see him with such a playful glee about him. She looked over to Temek politely. "As it happens, we crossed paths yesterday at the clinic. Only I thought your name was Temeka?" She examined the girl, deliberating whether she was her brother's friend or lover.

Temek reached for Savas' cider and took a swig; the intensity of her black eyes was unnerving. "It's Temek, not Temeka. Kistig refuses to say my name properly," she said, glancing at Savas. Now removed from the awkward company of Kistig, her voice had a cool confidence. Her arms and hands were covered; Aurelia was curious if they were healing or if they were in the same condition as before.

Savas hummed an upbeat tune, as though laughing at a secret joke. "Of all Kistig's students, Aurelia ended up being the one to treat you. Isn't that outrageous?" he grinned.

One corner of Temek's mouth crept upward into a non-committal kind of smile.

"Well anyway, you've met properly now and that's that. What did you want to talk about?" Savas asked.

"It's about Elfine." Aurelia inhaled sharply. "Apparently, she's going to be married off to the Chancellor of the Republic's son."

Savas arched an eyebrow. "And I thought I'd been having a hard time lately. Wish I could've given her a warning earlier."

"Has she returned home?" Aurelia asked, surprised.

"Oh, yeah, I guess you wouldn't have heard. She arrived late last night. I saw her this morning on my way out." Savas swirled the stein of cider around aimlessly.

"And she didn't come to see me?"

"Don't be like that, you're still her favourite," he teased. "Anyway, you seemed to be enjoying a lie-in."

Aurelia's face curled into a frown. "How was she?"

"She looked stressed. Said she saw something wicked." There was a tension rising around the table, like a veil of undue heat around their bodies or a rapping in their chests.

"Saw something?" Aurelia pressed for more.

"Not sure. She wasn't up to chewing the lard with her brother so early."

"Savas," Temek said suddenly. "I think we need to get going. Now." She stood up quickly, then gave Savas a look that was bursting with either desperation or dread.

"What's the hurry?" said Aurelia.

Savas looked all around, and judging by his blanched face, he'd seen the same terrifying thing as Temek. "I forgot about... something! Best be off yourself, yeah?" he said, with pleading eyes.

The two of them raced through the backdoor, not sparing a second glance back.

Looking over her shoulder, Aurelia met the unfeeling expression of a large man. The instinct to greet him, if only out of politeness, was instantly silenced. A menacing aura hovered around him, like some reaper with departed souls following in his wake. Death clung to him, and it stank so much that Aurelia's nose wrinkled. But he had no interest in her, it seemed. The man darted out the same door he'd come in. Aurelia wondered if there was something she ought to do, but what? Savas was about as likely to divulge a life-threatening secret as Mother was to forget her hourly prayers. Quickly, Aurelia made to leave and headed to Mazin's hut. Anxious as she was about her brother, she had her own troubles to deal with.

She walked through the woods and knocked on Mazin's door.

"Oh, it's you! I forgot you were coming today. Please, come in!"

"Hi Mazin," she said, then made for her usual spot — a seat made from a stump by the fireplace.

Aurelia bit her lip when she realised that Mazin had been in the middle of something. The table was a mess, strewn wildly with all sorts of bizarre items and trinkets. Open jars brimming with odd bits and pieces, some recently living, others long dead, crumpled bits of paper, charcoal for drawing and a large, violet crystal.

"Actually, we hadn't arranged to meet today," Aurelia said.

"Is that so? Let me make some tea anyway. What will you take? Dandelion, cinnamon, nettle? I might even have some mint somewhere."

"Dandelion has always been my favourite."

"Quite right." He leapt to the counter and began preparing the dandelions. With deft flourishes, he trimmed them and sliced them cleanly, and put them into a pot of water. He struck flint and tinder to get the fire going again and hung the teapot above the flames. His motions were fast and precise, and it seemed that mere seconds had passed before he appeared in the seat opposite Aurelia. They watched the pot eagerly, wondering who might speak first.

"If you weren't planning to come, then I guess something must be on your mind," he ventured.

"Something else happened last night. Mazin, is there anything beyond just dreaming?" She paused to gather her thoughts for clarity, and Mazin's interest was already piqued.

"The religions of antiquity spoke of priests and prophetesses who conjured visions," he said. "Others mentioned monks who wandered between worlds. Those who know the spiritual world as you — as we — do are gifted with sharper eyes and ears than most. Whether these things come from the gods or faith, I cannot say. Neither of us is religious, yet the doors to the other side are open to us. If your mother is right, then you are blessed by Ishanaia." Mazin tittered at this, then inertly inspected the cracks on his red fingernails.

"You told me once that the gods of our people only live in weathered tomes and boring sermons," she reminded him.

"Indeed! They've always been a tedious bunch. Too self-absorbed to bother interfering with the lives of mortals, but is it so preposterous to believe that they enhance certain mortals with, shall we say, *magic*?" He slipped out of sight behind an armoire in a dark corner and emerged with a tiny jute pouch. It emitted a potent, herbal fragrance. "I learned about this by way of an ancient sect who used it to voyage through the spirit world. None of them remains now, but I think it might help you find what you're looking for."

The tea began to bubble loudly. The hot vapours warmed Aurelia, and soon, a grassy smell overtook the room.

"How come you never told me about it before?" she asked.

"I didn't think you were ready for it before, but you'll be 19 soon." Mazin took the teapot off the heat and placed it in front of them. He retrieved two cups and filled them eagerly.

"What should I do with it?" She was tense but eager to experiment.

He beamed and giggled as if he was a child playing a trick on a friend. After untying the pouch, he sprinkled specks of the strange dust into her tea and invited her to drink.

Aurelia examined the contents of her cup. Floating atop the liquid was now a slowly dissolving powder. It merged with the tea and caused a fluorescent green arc to swirl around the cup.

"Are you afraid of the Kaspicians, Mazin?" she asked, the cup almost at her lips.

He raised his eyebrows at her, but they dipped back down as the question mulled in his thoughts. "As afraid as anyone is, I suppose; though I have less to lose than some."

"But they have magical powers, don't they? They want to steal into our minds and make us imagine things that aren't there."

Mazin seemed about to gasp but paused midway. "What on Ysa made you think they'd want to do that?"

"It *is* what they do, isn't it?"

"If you speak truly, then only the sword of vegetarianism will be strong enough to defeat them."

Aurelia smiled, then took a few sips of the piping hot brew. It was a strange feeling at first: her flesh tingled with a delicate warmth, but a less pleasant, stifling heat rose up her face. She felt like she was suffocating. Then, a heaviness fell on her, until she could no longer move. The cup blurred in her hand and she looked up to see the stillness of Mazin's frame opposite her. Was he speaking? His lips seemed to move, then he floated off like a cloud of sand. As he faded into nothing, so did the rest of her surroundings.

There was no falling this time, only a sudden awakening in an intense world. Above, streaks of purple lightning lit up a cloudy sky. Aurelia stood on a platform that was in the clouds, the lightning travelling to her left and right. The dais-like platform was fashioned from a smooth, black stone. Around the circular structure were dozens of tall columns, and between them, were thrones. Some were empty, while others were occupied with spiritual beings. Their forms came and went out of focus, as though stuck in limbo between one world and the next, unable to manifest the bodies that once contained them. Standing in the centre of the platform, Aurelia felt exposed.

"You've always been a fool Ylestra," said one of the women sitting on a throne. Her voice was deep and potent.

"The gall!" cried another woman, older than the first. "You want fi use our power to lock her up, and have we tied to that wicked duppy forever? A joke you must tell!"

"There is no other way!" retorted Ylestra.

Aurelia could hear the voice of Ylestra, but could not see her spirit form.

"Don't you see what it is she desires?" Ylestra went on.

"Hah! You gon' start talking about the demise of we people again? Don't bother mek we laugh," snorted a third voice, a man this time.

"Eehee... we people time soon come anyway. What this duppy child gonna do to make things worse fi we?"

"Just let my sister speak!" Shouted the woman who had spoken first, apparently Ylestra's sister.

"There is a book," Ylestra continued. "Written by... something more arcane than even us. I believe it is how they were made. You know of what I speak: those abominations skulking around the borders were not always there, and if my research is correct, this grimoire is capable of far greater atrocities than their creation. In enemy hands, the magic contained in this book could undo us entirely. We should be terrified."

"She just a child," said one of the women. "And nobody teaching her how to use any stupid old snow-skin book of spells."

"Her father nothing special too. Dem deh idiots only know what king be because of we," laughed another woman.

"This book," began Ylestra's sister. "How exactly did you come to know of it?"

"I have glimpsed it," answered Ylestra. "Here, in the Ankasa, the call of that book is loud to those with ears to hear. I am sure that the Kaspicians have it in their possession."

"A truth you tell?" said another of the women.

"We never hear nothing about no snow-skin book of doom," scoffed a man.

Just then, Ylestra appeared in the centre of the platform. Her skin was a lustrous ebony, darker even than the Sygecian people, and her black hair was plaited in thick braids, encircled by gold and silver patterned bangles. While she did not wear much in the way of armour, the sturdy, embellished breastplate she wore over her robes singled her out among this counsel as a warrior.

Something spectacular began to occur. Ylestra's body began to glow with a faint blue. Water appeared, as if the might of an ocean had erupted from someplace within her. She directed the waters to whip around her like a cyclone. The water took on a luminous quality.

"I have made myself strong, faced with what is to come," replied Ylestra. "And I have seen a great deal more than this."

Suddenly, the vision became unstable. Faces rushed before Aurelia. They were black, white, grey, silver and blue. Voices whispered, others threatened to scream and shout. Her heartbeat quickened and her breath was long and drawn out as she now found herself sliding down a lightless cavity. Submerged deeper into the dark of her subconscious, Aurelia was met with a cold, barren surface. When she saw that the sky above was a wild canvas of amethyst and turquoise, she realised she was in the same place as yesterday's nightmare.

"Dreamer," hissed an invisible spirit. "Are you foolish, or brave to tread on my land? I would have your head!" A grisly screech sounded. It certainly didn't sound like anything human. Aurelia was met with a pulsating shadow of black and red reeling towards her mid-air. Two eyes appeared, round and milky like the moon, and then, a massive maw that seemed like it could swallow her in one bite opened menacingly.

A hand reached for her from behind and Aurelia turned quickly to see a woman.

"*Ki sata wavesti!*" shouted the woman.

The flashing shade wailed, then dissipated into a pile of glowing blue ash.

The woman turned to Aurelia. It seemed like she was neither human nor spirit. Instead, she fluxed between the two: black skin, brown eyes, plaited black hair and a glowing topaz pendant were the markers of a forgotten humanity, overlayed by an immaterial body of pale-blue light. Aurelia felt a longing for this woman's presence, and wanted her to love her.

"What are you doing here, in the realm between realms?" the woman-spirit asked.

"You are the spirit from the lake, aren't you?" Aurelia asked. "The one I spoke to in my dreams."

"We have spoken across dimensions," answered the spirit. "But you should not be here. What fool snuck you into this place?"

"My friend, Mazin."

The woman-spirit produced a peculiar noise, as if Aurelia had unknowingly made a joke. "You shouldn't have come here like this."

"But I was here just yesterday, what changed?"

"Last time you were summoned here safely. You're lucky I found you in time: there are foul creatures that stalk this place, many of them would have you and me dead."

"Why would anything want me dead?"

"My enemies are your enemies. The reason for the hunt has not changed in the centuries that have passed. You saw something before, didn't you?"

"I witnessed a meeting. It seemed urgent, but that council would not listen," Aurelia said.

"A grave mistake," the woman-spirit said.

Aurelia heard a rumble, like a stampede of thousands of furious feet. A crack split the earth just a few paces ahead. A radiant glow erupted from out of the fissure as if the essence of a star were contained therein, but it was nothing so beautiful that came out. They were like men, but clearly, some species apart or victims of some transformation. They were emaciated, ashen things, skeletal and draped in a fine layer of skin. Their limbs jerked as they crawled out of the ground in odd, rapid movements. Where their eyes might have been were glowing gemstones, and their mouths were wide and ravenous. It was frightening, but this strange woman-spirit placed herself in front and shielded Aurelia.

"Perhaps now you will understand the severity of my warning," she said. "You must leave."

The last thing Aurelia saw was the spirit pointing three fingers at the sky and uttering some incantation. Her vision flooded purple, then a soft shade of blue.

She was back in Mazin's hut, and he was snoring loudly on the bed behind her. Daylight had nearly vanished. She got up and tapped him on the shoulder. "Mazin?"

Straight away, his eyes opened and he shot up. He blinked several times, and wiped his eyes; a purple smear of make-up rubbed onto the back of his hand. "How was it?"

Aurelia sat back down. "Edifying, as my mother would say. I saw a lot: a council of dark-skinned women, a bleak land with a purple sky, monsters rising out of the earth and a spirit: the same one from the lake, I think."

Mazin squinted. "If only there were a way to record what one had seen and show it to everyone else. I envy you. In my own experience, the other dimension is a den of riddles and enigmas; no two journeys are ever the same." He moved to the table and uncovered a pot of red liquid, which he began to paint onto his nails with a fine brush. "This spirit troubles me though. Such beings do not move between realms, they reside in specific places and have specific purposes. A spirit would certainly not latch itself onto you without you knowing. They are heavier than you might think."

"Spirits seem awfully complicated."

"In my experience, they are simple. Mortal creatures, however, weave confusing webs."

"I mentioned you to the spirit," Aurelia continued carefully. "I got the impression that she'd heard your name before."

Mazin stared at the drying paint on his nails for a long moment. A broad smile appeared on his face after a pause. "So, I am famous on the other side after all!" He laughed.

Aurelia giggled. "I hope for the right reasons."

"You know," he continued sharply, "This spirit doesn't sound like a spirit at all." Mazin smiled at the fresh coating of red on his nails, then stopped. "What did you say she looked like again?"

"At first, she was bright and spirit-like, but I saw glimpses of her body: she was blacker than anyone I've ever seen, with long, plaited hair. She wore a big, topaz pendant around her neck too."

"I should have told you that spirits don't tend to have bodies," Mazin said. "Even if they once did, they certainly wouldn't show you for no good reason."

"What kind of thing would have both a human and a spirit form then?"

"Simple," Mazin said. "A human."

"I don't understand. The power associated with the lake, and the person communicating with me is a human being?" Aurelia questioned.

"The lake, perhaps, served as a conduit for the two of you to meet. This particular entity is comfortable moving through water, I imagine."

"There was a woman-spirit called Ylestra at the council meeting I saw. She summoned a whirlpool around herself at one point."

Mazin's eyes widened. "What an odd name! But yes, perhaps she is the one who is communicating with you."

"There's no way she's an ordinary woman."

"Not all humans are the same. Did you yourself not just travel into another dimension, unknown to the majority of this country?"

"The Ankasa. That's what Ylestra called it."

Mazin tittered. "Fancy names in foreign languages don't change what it is: a realm of infinite possibility, and a place of horror, mystery, beauty and joy beyond what exists in our boring physical world. It is no place for ordinary people."

"What does that make me, some kind of freak?"

"Then we are both freaks in the eyes of the average Northcrester," he laughed. "There is power in being different and knowing who you are. I asked you once if you knew who you were, and perhaps now, you can answer that question differently. I do not claim to know the many secrets of Ysa, but I know that what you have with this being is special. You must listen to her and follow your intuitions carefully."

"You're right," she replied. "I've never felt more myself. Whatever is happening to me, it terrifies me. But I love it too. I wish I knew why this being came to me specifically."

Mazin beamed. "The two of you must be united by something indestructible," he said. "My own family never took an interest in me, but I can sense the bond of blood between you and this woman."

"The bond of blood?"

"She is your ancestor. The one from whom all your power stems."

Chapter 5

The Wraith

There was no masking the fear in Savas' step. For all his attempts to move smoothly, his erratic breathing and rapping heartbeat betrayed the dread he battled as he slunk through Endvil. The cloying dank of the air did little to alleviate his worries, but he advanced, undeterred. At this hour, few were about in Endvil, but he heard chilling ululations and whispers depart the tongues of those who dared to brave this capricious district by night. Many who passed through Endvil found fault: the structures were morose, remarkable only in that so many were lopsided and sinking. Most places were just one story tall, their wooden foundations long infested by rot. Some days, it seemed that the sun's light could not penetrate its barren depths. It was a realm of sufferance, but despite that, and for all its nefarious dealings, squalid streets and sullied faces, Savas loved how easy it was to disappear here. Nobody cared about who he was in Endvil, and although he was afraid, none remarked on his passage.

He headed down a narrow alleyway, flanked on either side by weed-choked concrete. Sitting on the pavement, a small girl was buried in a pile of rags; with her sandy complexion, pointy nose and straight black hair, she was obviously Piscanese. Her once yellow frock was muddied beyond repair, and she slumped by the wall, tormented by flies. With tired eyes, she stared longingly. Without saying a word, Savas placed a five aurum coin in her hand, enough for a couple of days' worth of food.

"*Kristo*. Thank you," she murmured.

Down a second alley, he spied two young men kissing in a rushed, passionate moment of forbidden eroticism in a city that was still recovering from the hangover of its puritanical past.

"Won't you join us?" one of them asked, his eyes glimmering seductively.

Savas ran away without response, though he found himself grinning. Coming to the end of the alley, he reached a ramshackle wooden house. The door was ajar already, but as he stepped closer, it edged itself further open so that he could step inside. A lone lantern hanging by the doorway's flame was a bewitching hue of red, surrounded by a fluttering cohort of angry moths. As he entered, the creak of the floorboards was unsettling. Two heavily built men were sitting at a wooden table; they glared frostily at Savas. The one on the left had fashioned his thick beard into a strikingly neat red plait, adorned with several tribal-looking rings around it. To his right, the other was clean-shaven, with long, matted dark hair clumsily arranged in a ponytail.

Yet it was not these two who intensified Savas' fear. A large wraithlike shadow scurried from behind the door where he had been skulking. The creature flitted towards the table like the insects around the lantern outside.

Temek had told Savas a little about this thing, whom she knew only as the Wraith. Now, Savas saw for himself why he was so named: he was a lifeless shell, whose arid and drawn flesh appeared to have been slapped over a skeleton and bereft of the flow of blood. His deeply sunken eyes, encircled by whorls of fine wrinkles, wan lips and prominent bones filled Savas with disquiet. Neither his tattered black robes nor his matted clumps of grey hair looked like they'd been washed in some time. Silently, this strange-looking thing beckoned Savas to sit down with an unnerving flourish of its hand.

"I knew you'd find your way here in time," croaked the Wraith. "You just needed a little nudge, is all." The creature's eyes began to spiral hypnotically.

Savas' lower jaw shook as he spoke, "I came on behalf of Temek. From now on, you deal with me, and you stop terrorising her."

The Wraith produced a grim smile, unveiling a set of crooked teeth, some black, others yellow. They were pointed like tiny stalactites, perfect for tearing flesh clean off the bone. "Oh. How my hopes plummet. Another princeling who makes outrageous demands. What else is new?" The Wraith looked to his two brutish companions and all three broke into mocking sniggers.

"I know what you want her to do. And I can do it much better," Savas countered.

The Wraith scratched its hairless chin, as though playing out some gruesome fantasy in his head. Sickening breaths escaped his mouth as he sneered. "I never liked Temeka, oh excuse me, Temek… whatever she wants to call herself. She was of minimal value and possessed few admirable qualities. Really, it's a wonder we let her carry on in the first place."

Savas' face soured when he remembered how dangerous this house was. But he wasn't going to show an inkling of weakness. "Compared to the two geniuses here, who I'm sure ooze competence."

The Wraith's lips formed the slightest smirk "Your status means nothing here, boy-lover. There's talk of a revolution, you know."

Boy-lover? Inside, Savas froze with humiliation, but he upheld his aura of courage. "Revolution?" he asked.

"Yes. It starts with that turgid carbuncle of a Castle you live in."

The trenchant voice made Savas recoil backwards, desperate to never see the beast before him again. His mind was briefly assaulted with the terrifying image of waking up in Sunhold, only to find it was burning to the ground. The tumbled towers and shattered stone were filled with the remains of everyone and everything he'd ever known.

"First I've heard of it. But what's that got to do with Temek? I want your word that you'll leave her alone," Savas tried to bring the discussion back to his purpose.

"I suppose you could be her replacement." The Wraith glided around the table towards Savas, his bony fingers sliding across the wood and then clasping Savas' shoulder with a horrid grip. The beast's dishevelled, greying hair tickled Savas' cheek, saturating his nose with the stench of rotting carrion. As it dawned on Savas that he was as close to the Nether Pits as he'd get in real life, face to face with one of its ugliest demons, his bravery began to wane.

"I could?" Savas squeaked.

The bearded man began to rummage through a bucket of sunflower seeds under the table and cracked them open, sending bits of shell across the table as he crunched on them. For a moment, those chewing noises were the only sounds that kept Savas from thinking he was no longer awake, but trapped in a nightmare with the Wraith.

"I could make all sorts of terrors come to life for you," rasped the Wraith. "But I will give you a chance. You will take the produce to Winnik, my associate, so that he may sell it."

The Wraith briefly let go of Savas and started sucking at his teeth and fidgeting around his mouth with his tongue. He paced around the room with his weak bony hands loosely joined behind its back. The tapping of his shoes against the creaky wooden floorboards almost seemed calculated, as though he moved in slow-motion on purpose.

Savas' mouth was so dry. He swallowed for what seemed like the first time in years.

After a deep inhalation, the Wraith disappeared in a flurry, and retrieved a large, intricate glass bottle from behind a shelf. A monstrous smile curled across his face as he handed it to Savas.

"It's called Viska, and strictly a cultivated man's drink." The Wraith attempted a wink, but the creature's taut flesh didn't quite allow it. "You've but one job, for now. There'll be plenty more if you want to pay off Temeka's debt."

The man with the ponytail glared cruelly at Savas, his cold eyes betraying every last one of his callous desires. Only then did Savas realise that the deadpan glaze of the man's eyes belonged to the same brute who had come into the tavern earlier.

"Doesn't sound like you're giving me many options."

The Wraith crept back up on Savas, teetering behind him. His rancid breath irritated the back of Savas' neck. "*Options*. What luxuries you have grown accustomed to in Sunhold!" The Wraith was grotesquely close to Savas' face. "You will find Winnik at the end of Ingly Lane, here in Endvil. Last house on the left."

Sparing not a second, Savas made for the exit with the bottle in hand.

The shadows over Endvil had darkened, as though suffused with the malcontent of its listless inhabitants. Savas turned down an alley where Temek had been waiting. She looked at him, her features softly illuminated by a lantern nearby. A tomcat darted past, clattering into a rubbish heap and frightening away a pack of hungry rats.

"Well? How did it go?" Her dark eyes throbbed with anticipation.

He embraced her tightly, but she recoiled. Savas had forgotten the pain of her bruises. "I'm just glad it's over."

Temek prudently watched for any sudden passers-by. "I'm proud of you. Did he give you the Viska?"

Savas nodded stiffly. "He wants it delivered to someone called Winnik."

Temek looked from side to side, as if pulling a dark memory from deep within. "Winnik... he used to come to me at the Parlour. He's the Wraith's main dealer?"

Savas gave a half-hearted nod. "Are you sure this is all because—"

She cut him off. "They could have done this to anyone else," said Temek, lifting up her shirt to show her bandaged chest. "They targeted me because I'd rather lie with women than them. You've got the same bullseye on your head, Savas."

Savas shuddered. "I just don't get why this Viska thing is so important to them. Why did they attack you just because you didn't want to deal their weird potion around the Parlour?"

Temek's face scrunched up as if she'd taken a swig of rancid milk. Savas hadn't known her too long, but he knew not to probe too deeply. He was only just coming to terms with his own sexuality and the difficulties it burgeoned, never mind hers.

"I have no idea, Savas," she said. "Whatever it is, they don't want the authorities knowing about it. That's why they kept coming to the Temptress' Parlour and forcing us to pass it on to clients. The Lady of the Parlour did nothing to protect me the night they chose to come to me. It was like she was under a spell."

"Did the other workers blindly accept the Wraith's terms each time he came?"

"Yeah. I was the first one who tried to resist," said Temek. "The only friend I had there quit shortly before the Wraith started showing up."

"Do you think he could help us somehow?" asked Savas.

"I-I... I don't know," Temek baulked. "Lei Jia is slippery. I doubt he'd want to get involved in this."

"There's more, isn't there? Tell me," Savas said.

Temek began to shake. "The Wraith... did something to me," she stammered.

Savas' eyes popped with concern, realising he might have triggered her.

"No, not like that," Temek said. "It was something unnatural, like he paralysed my mind and my body. Every passageway in my thoughts became wide open and he slithered around in there like a worm."

"Are you saying he has psychic powers?" Savas asked.

"I don't know," she said, confused. "He saw all my secrets, all my pain, and he mocked me. He laughed at me for being gay. Queer. Uncomfortable in my own body. He saw you as well Savas. He knows we're friends. That's when it stopped, when he saw my memories of you. Then he got his lackeys to beat me up."

He reached for her shoulder with a consolatory touch, but such actions had never come naturally to Savas. His hand trembled with its own unease as it met her agitated body. "But aren't there other queer people working in the Parlour?"

Slouched and amid a bout of tears, Temek said, "You weren't there — you should've seen the look on his face. He was disgusted." She shivered.

Savas tightened with distress. "I just don't understand why would he care about any of that."

Her composure regained, Temek stood tall again. "I remember something, actually. I heard him say something about a door. That's right. He was looking for a doorway."

"A doorway? What could be so special about a doorway?"

"I don't know. Guess it depends where it leads," she replied, half-heartedly.

"There's a lot we don't know, like this Viska stuff," said Savas.

Temek arched an eyebrow. "You don't really need me to tell you what that is, do you?"

"It can't be that bad," he laughed nervously.

"I'm a huntress. I know what blood and flesh smell like."

After a pause, Savas asked, "That's really what it is, isn't it?"

She nodded. "You said you'd help me get revenge, so let's kill him."

Chapter 6

Betrayal

Thoughts skittered through the ducts of Elfine's mind like centipedes. She wanted to devise war strategies, to see Lorcan, to practise combat and knife throwing. The beast in the mountains haunted her too. But she was expected in the Great Hall, and she was running late, on purpose. She had decided to turn up when she was mentally prepared, rather than when it suited the Chancellor, who her father had said would be present. In fact, she hoped that her lateness would annoy the Chancellor. As to what the agenda of today's meeting was, Elfine wasn't sure. She thought Zatela had promised to inform the Myriad of the mission in the mountains with Lorcan, but perhaps the Myriad wanted to speak to Elfine personally.

However, that did not explain why the Chancellor was here. It was around three months ago that Elfine travelled with her father to Dinaea, the seat of Chancellor Rorstein's power and capital of the Republic. That was her first and only encounter with him. Elfine feigned working as a diplomat to cover up her role in the Chicane, though she'd spent most of her time in Dinaea as a tourist. The Chancellor had left an atrocious impression, with his incessant scowling and rude manners.

Now, as she stepped into the Great Hall, she was greeted by stern glares. It was an unlikely gathering of Siladrians and Gaminians together. King Thenris and Queen Consort Melindra were also present. Most of the rest were strangers to her. Quickly, she surmised by the awkward glances from her parents that something was amiss.

She sat opposite the Chancellor, whose withering sneer threatened to turn her soul to ice; the taciturn Dame Leneare, with her mouse-like features, looked like a prosaic ornament perched next to him. Elfine had forgotten their son until that moment: Sigun, who looked several years younger than Aurelia. He was beaming at her with a set of neat, square teeth; Elfine couldn't recall seeing teeth so remarkable in Northcrest, or anywhere. The boy was young, but not in the sense of being eager or full of untapped potential and strength. Hidden behind the confident grin, slicked back hair and exuberant finery was a timid and weak thing. With flesh so pale the sun could roast it, and beady, columbine eyes, Sigun looked pitiable and insignificant next to his father.

"By Aseg's flaming breath, how late she is! What a poor show!" growled the Chancellor.

The room was strangely quiet, and Elfine suddenly wondered if perhaps there had been so little to discuss that everything important had already been said.

"The work of diplomacy is tiring and demanding of late." She stared intensely at the Chancellor, whose glower only worsened.

Father cleared his throat. "She's here now, that's what matters."

There was silence, punctuated only by the smug expression upon the Chancellor's face. Why did his son look so delighted?

"The leaders of Northcrest have come to a decision that will benefit the greater good of our people," said Father. "This is something to represent the first bridge of solidarity in centuries between ourselves and the Republic."

Suddenly, Elfine pondered the meaning behind all those trips her father made to Dinaea. The gestures that had seemed innocuous replayed in her mind — dinners together, clandestine meetings, a handshake. She remembered seeing it from the balcony of the room she'd stayed in the night before they returned home: her father and the Chancellor had come to some agreement.

"In exchange for the military and financial support of the Republic, you will marry Lord Sigun, the Chancellor's son," Father announced. "This will entitle their family to unfettered access to Gaminia's future support, and grant Sigun a seat in Northcrest's Myriad."

Breath escaped her mouth, but she didn't feel responsible for it. She felt as though she wasn't real, like she'd been ferried all the way to the bottom of the ocean, flattened by wave after wave until she was a helpless flounder. Her aspirations departed towards an unreachable depth. What role would she play in the war now? And what about the Chicane, would that all be over now?

Lorcan...

She couldn't look at Sigun. Marriage was something Elfine had never considered. Her path had already been laid out, hadn't it? She thought she had been saved from this tradition. Her life was supposed to be dedicated to being a secret agent — doing something meaningful. Not wasted alongside some foreign aristocrat she barely knew.

And at 20, wasn't she already past her peak? Aurelia was only a year younger, but Mother would've protected her; she still saw her as a baby. Besides, Aurelia's looks had always bothered Father: she was neither slim nor fair enough to have any value in this sort of deal.

So she had to be the sacrifice.

"Where was my say in all of this?" Elfine burst out. "How many times did you meet, and not once think to ask me my thoughts!?" Her face throbbed with fiery wrath.

Mother wiped away a tear with her hand.

"Elfine, I'm afraid that this isn't about individuals and their wishes," her father retorted icily. "War requires tremendous sacrifice, and really, getting married is hardly an egregious task."

"Well said, Thane Olsin," added the Chancellor, looking so smug Elfine could have stabbed him with a butter knife.

The usual exhaustion was apparent in the King's face: puffy eyes, ever-intensifying wrinkles and a wan countenance. Queen Consort Melindra stroked his arm, whispered things in his ears, and stared at him with her bug-like eyes.

"The crown remembers Elfine's place; she will not be forgotten for her services!" King Thenris addressed her directly, to everyone's surprise. It was so rare that the King had any input, most had grown accustomed to his silence.

"Oh, yes," the Queen stepped in. "We expect to make many sacrifices but few will be as noteworthy as yours. What an honour, Elfine! What a tremendous woman you are — Northcrest will never forget the girl who married Lord Sigun of the Republic." Her great-aunt's face looked like an old mare. There was a hint of something facetious in her grandiloquent way of speaking.

"And as you know, in accordance with our customs, we also expect that you will spend some time in Dinaea with Sigun's family," said Father.

In the tension of the moment, Elfine had not even considered the traditional customs of her people; a man of Sigun's status could not simply move in with his wife's family, would be considered a great shame to his family.

"Sigun and I will search for a place for the two of you to live in King's Respite when you return," Father continued.

Nobody present knew anything about Elfine's role in the Chicane, except her parents, and even they only knew a little. It seemed fitting that none of them understood her pain either; she couldn't bear the thought of her wings being clipped and living the same sort of life as Mother. But even Mother had suffered this treatment. Arranged marriages were still normal for women of status in Gaminia. Elfine knew that none of the women around her looked at her with sympathy; if anything, they thought it was a blessing. The thing that might rescue her from her tiresome life as a diplomat. How wrong they all were! She had no choice but to endure the arbitration of those gathered here. She knew she couldn't get out of this. "And when is this 'wedding' to take place?" she asked.

"Tomorrow, dear," announced the Queen. "The more time we have to prepare for the Kaspicians, the better."

"But surely there won't be enough time to get everything ready?" asked Elfine.

"This is politics Elfine," the Queen responded, with a patronising inflection. "You understand that, don't you? Really, we couldn't have hoped for a more auspicious, well-timed occasion."

Elfine put on her best stuck-up noble voice for the Queen and the whole room. "Yes, how opportune that the Chancellor and I arrived in Northcrest the same day. Fate must be on our side," she feigned a smile.

Sigun's eyes roved along her with a predatory appetite. She inspected him again and the absence of attraction towards him yawned back at her. The mere sight of him made her body recoil; he was nothing like Lorcan. Making love with Lorcan was intoxicating, but Sigun looked like a child. He was a child.

Mother regarded both the King and Father. "If I may, I believe that it would be better for me to discuss the necessary details with Elfine in private," she said.

King Thenris coughed loudly. "An excellent idea," he said.

The Queen beamed at her partner with all the sincerity of a targeted fart. "Shall we finish here then, my King?" she asked.

"Yes. Adjourned," he rasped. The monarchs were gone.

Elfine and her mother walked to the bridge that connected the main body of Sunhold to its tallest tower, which was the home of her parents. In the distance, she could see the crags of the mountains to the north.

They paused. Elfine watched the tiny, insignificant inhabitants of Northcrest scamper like ants. The urgency of tomorrow's affair was alleviated for a moment, and the refreshing breeze spoke only of peace.

The atmosphere made Elfine think that she was by the sea; with her eyes closed for just a brief instant, she could imagine the rocks and sand under her feet and the sound of the undulating waves bringing their force to bear on the beach. She recalled a similar feeling when she had been in Pisca, and it was all she could to try and distract herself from reality.

"It's a lovely place to get lost in your mind, isn't it?" Mother said. She smiled as she soaked up the fresh air. She was youthful and radiant still in many ways, but her years of servitude to Northcrest had gradually taken their toll. To the younger noble women of Northcrest, she was already ancient and rusted.

After a lengthy pause, Elfine asked "how long have you known about this and not once thought to tell me?"

"I tried to avoid it Elfine, honestly I did..." Mother fumbled over her words. "Your father only told me after you left on your last mission. He didn't want me knowing in case I told you and you ran off, or something. As soon as we received word that you were almost home, your father invited the Chancellor here. I'm sorry, but believe me when I say this: I have prayed for you every day and every night since you left, Ishanaia *must* have heard my prayers. Nothing bad will come of this."

Elfine scoffed. She was not a woman of faith; the trials and tribulations her mother endured in service to amorphous deities were meaningless to her. "You could have at least found a more interesting man. How old is the lifeless sap?"

Her mother looked too guilty to respond with laughter, but a weak smile crept across her face. "Sixteen, I believe."

"You and Father betrayed me," Elfine griped. "You would never have made Aurelia do this."

Mother winced, then reached out and put her hand on Elfine's shoulder. "This is not the end of life as you know it. The Chicane will still need you, as will your family. Just look at my aunt, the Queen. She is far from powerless at Thenris' side, and you are far stronger in body and mind than her." Usually, her words had strong conviction, but this time, Elfine only heard the stifled bleating of a doe caught in a trap. "And don't worry about the wedding. We've a splendid team arranging everything as we speak. There'll be delicious food to eat, and you'll have the finest raiment to wear."

Elfine knew that marriage meant little to her mother. That was probably why she didn't seem to care that much about having kept this a secret. Mother was happy to throw a banquet and stick a pretty dress on Elfine to make everything seem suitable. Marriage was political: her own marriage to Father had been similarly arranged.

"I know men of this echelon," Elfine said. "Power drives them, and it poisons them too. Look at Father; he's spent decades wheedling his way into King Thenris' pocket. Sigun will turn out just as sly."

"He is just a boy, not half as clever as you are. You will have no difficulty controlling him."

"I can try," Elfine said. United by an ominous silence, neither spoke for a while. Elfine sensed Mother had other fears buried deep down.

"Last night, your father stood here with several hooded figures," Mother spoke in a cautious tone. "I could've sworn I heard him say the word revolution."

The coolness of the breeze around them at once became harsh. It exposed Elfine, made her long to be hidden away inside. The once beautiful stone of the bridge no longer looked pleasant, but instead its burnt orange hue was lurid and obtrusive, and its stony touch unbearably coarse.

"He's one of the most valued advisors to King Thenris and Queen Consort Melindra now." Mother's tone spoke of fear.

Father had risen to such prestige in the political court, yet who really knew what deals and sacrifices he had made to get to where he was? In the back of Elfine's mind, clots of fear coagulated.

"Father has always been ruthless. You fear how far his ambition stretches, don't you?" Elfine gave her mother credit for having put up with Father. That took a great deal of patience and confidence.

"He is deeply withdrawn lately."

"Don't forget he went to the White Academy. Those elitist bastards hoard knowledge for sport, so who can say what he has withheld about Kaspica, or this war?"

Trinne slid into silent reverie. "Ishanaia speaks through you. Until you went to Kaspica, I forgot that it even existed. Yet now, we are told that they threaten our country with extinction, that they are slaves to avarice and seek bloodshed; to wage war simply because it is what they want, perhaps even because it is what they were made for. We live in fearful times. The gods cry out for our devotion more than ever."

Had Elfine asked enough questions about Kaspica when she stood on the border, in the Numanich Mountains? She'd blindly followed Chicane instructions, and never stopped to think about the history of the place, or its people. Mother's words ricocheted in her thoughts.

The image of her assailant in the mountains flashed through her mind. It appeared beside her, its breathing loud and raspy, leaving a sickly aroma to cloy and curdle. Embers of amethyst began to glimmer in the vacuous trenches that were its eyes. Elfine pinched her thigh. "I haven't asked enough questions," she said, hurriedly. "Think it's time that changed."

"The Three be praised. You're wising up," said Mother.

"Do the Yotanite scriptures speak of the supernatural at all?" Elfine asked.

Mother's eyebrows pinched together in a concerned squint. "The Nether Pits are said to house creatures of impure design. But dominion of that plane is Zerkal's; Ishanaia has no dealings with hell. Why do you ask this?"

"Don't know. Guess I'm just worried about my soul."

"I'm glad. My prayers can only do so much for you," Mother spoke solemnly.

"Right," Elfine said. "But are there monsters that live in the physical world as well, or just the Nether Pits?"

"On Ysa? I cannot say for certain, but knowledge of the Three did not originate in these lands. The liturgy is said to have come from a distant continent. It says that thousands of years ago, there were other powers at work in what we now call Gaminia: shamans and seers who worshipped twisted, old gods and brought devastation to the land. Ishanaia took their powers and created the Nether Pits as a prison for evil forces; Zerkal became the steward of the Nether Pits, and Aseg the gatekeeper to Heaven. The world was cleansed of sin before, though it is possible that Ishanaia's work could be undone over time by the evil of men."

"And dark powers could return to Ysa," Elfine murmured.

"Say your prayers, Elfine. Ishanaia will protect you."

"Is that all the advice you have, to pray?"

"What greater answer could there be? Seek your father's counsel if you desire, but I have no interest in the wisdom of men. The Goddess watches over you, Elfine."

Chapter 7
Logs of the Persecuted

Aurelia passed many days in the Northcrest City Library. It was majestic: a long set of stairs led to the grand entrance, embellished with twisting white columns that reached to the sky and an entablature adorned with the faces of the Three: Ishanaia, Aseg and Zerkal. It was around 400 years old, situated opposite the White Academy, where her father had once studied. The library was built during King Venelag the Open's reign, on the advice of a court astrologer, who was fabled to have wheedled her way into the King's breeches with an enchanted wheel of cheese. Aurelia had climbed to the sixth floor before, but knew it had several more; most women could not go beyond the seventh floor, which was where she was headed.

The seventh floor was so quiet Aurelia worried her footsteps, or even breath, would disturb the other attendants. There was a strong stench where ancient parchment gathered, and the smell of unwashed men wafted about the air with a rude liberty. Wizened academics with scraggy, grey beards, whose portly folds burst out of their seats, scowled at Aurelia. The recent amendment to allow women into libraries, enacted only a decade ago, remained contentious.

Aurelia peered at the spines of several tomes in a number of sections: ancient Gaminian history; Yotanite rites; and Hellasic traditions and culture. She picked a few up and flicked through some of the pages, but nothing seemed useful. As she meandered through the shelves, budding students appeared sporadically, vigorously rummaging through the articles of knowledge.

None of the books caught her eye at first, but that wasn't surprising — she only had a vague idea of what she was looking for. Anything that pertained to dreams, the spirit world, council meetings of black women with a strange accent, or information on the heinous book the spirits mentioned. After perusing for a while, one corner revealed a tome, weathered and dusty. As Aurelia reached out to touch it the air around became icy. There was an intense stillness. She felt removed from the rest of the library, as if this corner was a dimension outside of reality. The book had an allure that instantly drew Aurelia to it. She wanted it. Longed for it, even. Something about it whispered of power and knowledge: two things that she had never realised she cared about until now. Living in Northcrest had withered a part of her, she realised now; she had become irredeemably sick of her home, sick of the fact that Tutor Fark's lessons had ended because it was not within the royal budget to continue them, sick of being doubted and ridiculed. War, it seemed, was inevitable; Aurelia didn't want to be caught in the jaws of Kaspica when the enemy made its move. She would venture further down this path of dreams, spirits and monsters until she had the power to face them, and the wisdom to know who, or indeed, what.

The book was bound in black leather and a simple string to lock it. Dust particles on the surface went *pfff* as she blew them away. As she untied the string, she immediately sensed the years of history within. The crumpled pages, yellow with age and rot, had passed through generations of hands. There was no title anywhere, but inside the book was written *Castrellus' Journal*. Low voices seemed to whisper at the sound of the fluttering pages as she turned them. A strangely comforting emptiness overtook the space around her; the cold dark it proffered sent shivers of a sensual power throughout her. Just then, she caught a glimpse of her reflection in the window, but a sinewy and skeletal thing looked back at her, strapped in a layer of greying skin with its mandibles on show. The vision frightened her. Was it because she held the book that her reflection looked like a corpse? And then, there was a familiar noise, one that she had quite heard. It was the sound of the earth beneath her feet fissuring open like a yawning, black maw. Appearing to ascend out of the crack were those same grisly creatures that she had seen crawl out of the ground that the woman-spirit had protected her from. This time, they did not clamour out, all gangly and limby like ashy spiders; they leaped out, galloping across the bookshelves, leering at her from the ceiling, with those same tormented expressions.

"I wouldn't read that if I were you." A man's voice shattered the grisly hallucination.

Aurelia pivoted, alarmed, but saw no one.

"I'm over here." His voice diminished to a murmur.

Turning back around, she saw a man. His willowy form was accentuated by his slouching against the bookshelf. Something about him resembled a long, stretched-out crow. Aurelia wondered if he might sprout wings, caw and arc out of the window.

He examined her. "She doesn't look Gaminian," he said, but to whom?

Aurelia's cheeks went torrid with nerves. "Is there something wrong with this book?"

"Ain't nothing right with it," said the man. "Filthy hands done wrote it." He swivelled and crept towards the window in front. He leant forward for a moment, watching passers-by below. "*Filthy.*" The word echoed.

"He's right," a second voice cut through the quiet behind her.

She turned to see him, but there was nothing there. As she looked back to the window, the two of them were there, their expressions unreadable.

"Are you gonna turn into a monster, like all the others did?" sneered the first man.

Aurelia clenched her jaw. "Where did you two even come from?" A seething river came to life in her thoughts. It swelled with anger.

"What's she doing?" The second's voice asked.

"Dunno. Looks like she's getting mad."

"Are you upset, you silly, sorry little thing?"

Aurelia slammed the book shut. In the next instant, the two men dispersed into countless particles of yellow light. Her ears vibrated, as though she'd bellowed all the air out of her belly into a giant chasm. She looked around, questioning if anyone had noticed what happened. A dozen or so men were seated at a circular table behind her. They had all ceased their reading to stare in Aurelia's direction. They glowered, dispensing unknowable curses into the silence, never to be heard. It seemed they hadn't seen the men who disappeared; and after a moment, they returned to their studying.

Aurelia composed herself. Whatever had just happened wasn't going to get in the way of reading this book. She was drawn to it, and somehow, the fact that it came with a distinctly ominous warning made her all the more keen to unearth its knowledge. Quickly, she forgot all about the two vanishing doomsayers. "Anyway," she said quietly to herself, "only the books upstairs are off-limits."

She sat on the windowsill and opened the book again. It was a collection of diary entries, written by a certain Castrellus. He wrote in an ancient language; she believed it to be a long-outdated form of Gaminian, and although it took no extra effort to read it, she couldn't remember ever having seen the language before. Many of the pages had been damaged by damp and decay; others had been torn out. When she landed on a clear page, she straightaway began to read:

Sage Era 2384, 7th Moon, 13th Sun

I am leaving my home at last. I can take it no more. I have been hounded, vilified and persecuted across the continent. I fled my home after my community exiled me and stripped me of my rank, but now even the Calechians have discovered my secret. I can take no more of this war-torn country. The Calechians are intent on destroying everything. Many things are now illegal under their new laws — they have woven state and faith together and made a hideous thing. They call it the Vorician Codex, named after those Vorician hypocrites who spread their gospel of hatred constantly.

Under its law, my very existence is a crime here. I have made it to Pisca, the land of my birth, where even still I am hunted. The Codex's laws are spreading quickly across the whole Continent. I have no choice but to flee.

There is a land across the Piscanese Strait called Gaminia. I have never been to this place. The Northern Continent... It is the home of fair-skinned folk. It is said that they are milder, that they do not care so deeply about things as we from the South do. I have no choice but to go there, for my own people desire my death. I am drawn there by the promise of a new god, one who will embrace me and shield me from my past.

I have heard tales of the House of Noul, even in my country. His flock is diverse. My old god has left me, but I pray that I will find acceptance with this Noul. They say that he is the Groom of Whispers and he consumes our darkest secrets.

Tomorrow, I will hide on a cargo ship bound for Gladehill in the northeast of Gaminia. It is my intention to reach Northcrest, where I will begin anew. And I am taking this wretched book with me; it will be my Journal.

She flicked ahead in the Journal.

Sage Era 2386, 11th Moon, 1st Sun
It is my second year living in Gaminia. The followers of Noul call themselves Dreamists. They are so impressed with my progress; I am at peace! This is beyond anything I could ever have imagined. The Dreamists are tolerant and kind. They have looked favourably on me. This is a refuge for people like me.

Tonight, our leader will initiate me fully by way of an ancient rite. I must speak my darkest secret into the spirit fire of Noul, then, the Groom of Whispers and I will be bound. My prayers will reach his ears with ease, and he will grant me great power in the realm of spirits so that occult knowledge will reveal itself to me.

I expect the experience to be cathartic. After so many years of oppression and running, I want to be freed of my burden so that I may grow. Here, I can use my power for good. The Dreamists learn to heal and mend from the other side, to aid their flock with the old knowledge of herbs, roots, saps and stones. Not only that, Noul translates dreams and grants prophetic visions. I am in the right place at last. I will not be found or discovered here by people who wish me ill, nor do I need to hide any part of myself.

The head of this monastery has taken a liking to me too. He is not of fair-skinned descent like the Gaminians. I forget how great this secret of mine is at times. There is no way that anyone could know what it is I hide from them, what my crime really was.

And yet, sometimes, I catch him staring at me.

Aurelia's experiences with dreams, which came so frequently and so vividly, quickly led her to question whether this was something that pertained to her own identity. The book, unfortunately, did not answer as many questions as she wanted. As she inspected page after page, she realised many of them were destroyed, or irrelevant. She needed more time with the Journal.

The reception counter was piled high with papers and various books, and sitting behind it was a glowering man. Not just any glowering man, but the miserable goblin-looking thing that had worked there for as long as Aurelia could remember. Her every interaction with him had been unpleasant. As expected, he pretended not to notice her as she approached the desk, and instead feigned labouring over the mass of papers before him.

"Good day," she did her best to force a smile. "I'd like to withdraw this book."

He made a big effort to keep up his ruse of being busy, before looking up. His expression instantly soured when he saw her. His small, beady dark eyes held her gaze, deadpan. After a long silence, he frowned and put out his palm for the volume.

After a terse examination of the contents, he snapped, "this book is not from this library."

"I found it on the seventh floor," she said, wiping a layer of sweat from her brow.

He paused, if only to give her the full force of his glare. "It's not even in Standard Gaminian," he continued, returning the Journal to her.

"If it isn't in Gaminian, how do you believe I managed to read it?"

"Did you graduate from the Academy for Court Jesters, twirling around in front of the King with bells on your feet and head? You belong in a madhouse if *you* think you can read this; wise men in here thrice your age could barely translate this." Although he had tried to speak quietly, he ended up shouting, launching a barrage of spittle at her.

A small crowd of readers and scholars began to watch the spectacle.

Aurelia had had enough. "So rude," she uttered under her breath.

The librarian snorted with rage. "I heard that! You obnoxious child!" He stood up, livid.

"Isn't that girl part of the Queen's family?" Croaked a scholar, somewhere in the audience.

"I wouldn't talk to a highborn like that," another said.

The librarian scoffed. "*Highborn*. My family has lived in Northcrest for centuries, and no one who looks like *her* has ever set foot in Sunhold before that wasn't a cook or a cleaner!"

"Queen Janira, wife of King Venelag, was half Arx'ani. According to the portraits in your library, she and I looked quite similar. You don't know your history very well for a librarian, do you?" Aurelia retorted.

"If you don't leave now, I'll call the guards, and I think I know who they'll believe," the librarian said, his face compressed into a withering sneer.

As she turned to leave with the Journal in her hands, the mass of papers on his desk spiralled upwards into a vortex. Squinting from the doorway, Aurelia could've sworn the papers formed the shape of a woman. Was she laughing? The librarian gasped in fright then began to whimper like the morose hound that he was. The rest of the library attendants who had been watching the spectacle apparently could not see the feminine shape that Aurelia and the librarian saw.

She left. Looking at the grand centre of knowledge and learning from the outside, she sniggered. Something about the book she held made her feel victorious, as if she'd been waiting to find Castrellus' writings for years.

The book was hers now; the library had rejected it, and she could banquet on its secrets in peace.

*

Savas stood opposite Temek in a secluded alley just off Ingly lane, near where Winnik lived, as demanded by the Wraith. Festooned in the orange rays of light from a nearby tavern, Temek was striking, like a floating Will o' the Wisp. Even while she snacked on a stick of barbecued squirrel meat, spitting occasional bits of bone or hair on the ground, she had both a particular poise and the resting, stern expression of someone ready to fight for their life at any moment.

"Squirrel alright?" Chilly, he rubbed his hands together and blew air out of his cheeks.

"It always tastes better when you catch it yourself." She threw the stick on the ground after finishing it and sucked at her teeth. A dog was hiding in wait watching her eat, lolling its tongue desperate to salvage whatever scraps were left.

Savas had always been fascinated by animals, seeing as they were completely forbidden in Sunhold. The Queen's hatred of pets was famous, and rumours still circulated that she had King Thenris' eight royal hounds poisoned when she moved in. He knelt down to pet the dog, but it skirted out of reach, and looked up with suspicious eyes. Slowly, it reached for the skewer then ran off.

Savas sighed. "He's just around the corner. I'm nervous."

"Winnik is a freak, but he's not dangerous." She took hold of his hand. "We need to do this just once, otherwise the Wraith will get suspicious."

Remembering when he found her at the Temptress' Parlour, all cut up and bruised, Savas was determined. "You're right. It's just a delivery. I can do it."

He went off down the alley. It was an unassuming home, its inhabitant likely more affluent than the average Endvil resident, but certainly not wealthy.

Savas knocked and waited anxiously.

Rain began to fall. It was a welcome distraction amid the lingering quiet. Nobody came so he knocked again, louder this time. The door creaked open, and a shadowy face emerged in the crevice of light, illuminating only the barrenness of the hallway and the faintest glimpse of Winnik's ashen skin. The rest of his face was hidden in shadow.

Savas' nerves bubbled. "I was sent here to deliver this to you." He rearranged his hair, moving the damp ringlets off his wet face. He pulled out the bottle of Viska from his pocket and waited for Winnik to invite him inside, or respond.

Neither of these expectations came to pass. Instead, a gaunt hand, with javelin fingers emerged from the crevice at an unsettlingly quick speed, palm facing upwards.

"Oh, I see. I haven't done this before, I thought maybe we would chat first, or something," Savas stammered.

A murmur hovered in the atmosphere. It prickled Savas' flesh with cold, numbing needles. He was frozen in place. A horrible shiver scraped across his body. Savas couldn't remember how dark it had been when he first knocked; his vision descended into an absence of clarity. A glacial fog rushed at him. Teeth chattering, he placed the pouch in Winnik's hand. The door shut quietly, and Savas was left stunned in the rain.

Temek observed the ordeal from nearby. She hurried over to Savas, her head now covered with a hood. Her touch seemed to jolt him back to life.

"You're skragging frozen! Let's get away from this place." She ferried Savas away from Winnik's house to find shelter from the rain. They stood under the awning of a closed down restaurant on a quiet street, near the light of a few lanterns. "How did it go?"

"I don't know. He got what he wanted, and I'm fine."

Temek squinted, unconvinced. "You're shaking. Are you sure?"

"Yes. I just want to be done with this night."

The Wraith's door was ajar. Savas looked at Temek with concern, as she stood waiting under cover from the downpour. The place was the same as he had left it, though the two brutish bodyguards were gone.

The Wraith was seated behind the table, staring gleefully at Savas, baring his rotten teeth. His arms were folded expectantly, and the grey of its complexion masked any sense of his true emotions. His hands skittered along the table like two arachnids preparing an ambush.

"Take a seat," came the sickening croak of its voice.

Against his better judgement, Savas shuffled over to the table.

"Are you keeping well, Savas?"

"I've had better days. But you're looking healthy." He replied, feigning a smile.

"How delightful that you've noticed. Now, to business. Have you done as I asked and seen my friend Winnik?" His thin, bloodless lips moved as though controlled by a puppeteer.

Savas nodded eagerly. "I've done as you asked."

"Do you drink, Savas?" Asked the Wraith, its head cocked at an unnatural angle.

"I'd have wine with every meal if I could stop getting hangovers." Savas' levity was met with silence. That disarming aroma that reminded him of death returned. Savas had only seen dead bodies at funerals, and the Wraith looked and smelled far worse than any of those cadavers.

"Perhaps this occasion calls for a small toast," suggested the Wraith.

"A toast! Why not?" Savas' voice cracked.

The Wraith's gangly body rose behind the chair and twirled towards a nearby cabinet in a cyclone of hair, bones and smelly robes. In his hands were now two copper cups and a bottle of something that looked very old and dark in colour. Savas noted the location of the Viska.

Looks darker than any red wine I've ever seen.

"It's not red wine, as you might have assumed. I thought you should taste Viska for yourself." The Wraith moved back to his seat and began to open the bottle. Liberally, he filled two glasses of Viska. Immediately Savas was assaulted by the heady smell of the concoction. It had a sinister sort of sickliness to it that made the tiny hairs on his skin stand up.

As the Wraith decanted it, the thick, unctuous consistency somehow looked more unappetising than what it actually was. If Temek was to be believed, Viska was made of flesh and blood, though Savas did not know whether it was brewed with the remains of animals or humans. "Don't drink it all at once! A few sips and you'll be ecstatic."

Savas took one look at the Viska and knew that if he didn't drink it, the Wraith might suspect something. He searched the red liquid for some secret omen, or buried foresight to confirm that it should not be drunk. Had this particular batch expired, or was there some dead fly floating within? No — it was without a blemish, but surely, he couldn't imbibe this boiled down nectar of flesh and fingernails. The longer he stared, he began to imagine hairs, teeth and eyeballs bobbing up and down in the glass. He couldn't risk drinking a drop of the brew. Temek was no fool, and Savas didn't doubt her assessment of what Viska was.

The Wraith raised his glass and gestured to Savas to do the same. The clink of the cups reverberated around Savas' head for what seemed like an eternity, as if his head had been clobbered with a steel-tipped drumstick.

"You have much more to offer than Temeka did," said the Wraith. His eyes seemed mesmerised by the Viska. He seemed to thirst for it greatly.

"Temek," amended Savas.

The Wraith wafted his glass dramatically around his face, apparently soaking up the stench of the drink. He seemed to be waiting, and it occurred to Savas that perhaps the drink was poisoned. An eternity seemed to pass as the Wraith's eyes glared at Savas with macabre delight, but then, the Wraith gulped the entire drink in one. Savas brought the drink to his lips and feigned taking a sip, then produced a satisfied *ahhhh*.

"I have many jobs for someone like you. You are discreet. You move effortlessly. Untraceably." He filled a second cup and swirled it around, spilling droplets on the table and the floor. The Wraith shook slightly, like an addict.

"I agreed to help until Temek's debt was paid. That's all." He replied. The knowledge that he had no intention of ever repaying this imaginary debt made him just as confident as it did terrified. He hoped that the Wraith could not see through the plan he and Temek had hatched.

The Wraith downed the second cup of Viska and his skin appeared to take on a more human glow. "I've always hated her sort. Sapping young men like yourself of their potential." The Wraith huffed, then licked the rim of the glass. "Your next assignment is to make two deliveries. One to my friend Kistig, and one to my friend Benthrin no later than tomorrow at sundown." He placed two bottles of Viska on the table and pushed them towards Savas.

"You don't have any intention of letting Temek free, do you? This debt is endless, isn't it?"

The Wraith was in the middle of pouring a third cup, and a fierce glower overcame its face at the sound of Temek's name. "Temeka's debt will never be paid. Surely, she knew that. You'll be running errands forever, boy." The Wraith laughed menacingly, downing a third cup. "Temeka… What a foolish girl! She betrayed me, Savas. *Me.* She'll never get away with that."

"She didn't want to sell your stupid Viska — so what?!"

The Wraith reached for the Viska, which was almost empty. It finished the last few drops quickly, and scowled to itself. It no longer looked at Savas, but sat angrily, seething with rage.

Savas' nose quivered as the stench of decay in the room intensified. "And I already told you, her name is Temek. Why is that so hard to remember?" He wondered if he had gone too far.

"She's a whore, Savas. There's no coming back from that level of shame. But you know all this — I bet she tried to seduce you, didn't she? Hah. I can tell she's lacking in the thing that makes you stand to attention. You remind me of those fairies running rampant in the Parlour, diving onto their gaunt knees for every fat noble poofter with a few aurums bulging in his pockets. That's what she did for a living, for so many years. Where's the respect in that? I will continue to call her Temeka, and enjoy doing so."

Savas seethed with ice-cold rage. But he had never set out to change the Wraith's mind, only to murder him. "We'll never see eye to eye. This is the last errand, and then I'm done."

The Wraith arched an eyebrow, mockingly, then passed him two addresses written on parchment. Savas slipped the bottles into his pocket and left.

Temek waited loyally outside and Savas raced to her to avoid the rainfall. "What did he say this time?" She looked sticky in the humid rain.

"Kistig and Benthrin. They're next." Savas spoke pensively.

"Kistig?!" she exclaimed. "He's one of the physicians at the Academy. Your sister knows him too."

"Skrak. Are you sure?" Savas asked.

"Definitely. I don't recognise the other name, but it doesn't matter… we're not doing it anyway."

"You're right, and I finally have an idea. All we have to do is poison his Viska."

"Poison?" Temek sounded uncertain.

Savas nodded. "We break in and contaminate his personal supply."

"Doesn't that seem too simple?"

"If it doesn't work, I'll chop his head off."

Temek let loose a sceptical laugh. "Lei Jia, the boy I mentioned before, will know where to get poison."

"He will?"

She nodded. "There's something I should tell you. Come, let's go to my place and get out of this bloody weather."

*

It wasn't Savas' first time seeing where Temek lived, but he'd forgotten what her home looked like. She was fortunate to have a roof over her head, considering she was a vee coin labourer; they didn't even earn aurums, and instead sacrificed the majority of their coins to live in dilapidated shacks across Endvil. Temek's home was spartan. The floor was stone and two cloudy, dust-caked windows formed the only glimpse of the world outside. There was a stove, a couple of chairs and a scrawny table, a stone bed with a few blankets, a bathing tub and a few cupboards for storage. It was easy to forget that not everyone lived under the auspices of Sunhold's boundless privileges.

She took a jar of milk out and took a few liberal swigs before sitting at the table with Savas, who politely declined her offer of a sip.

"I've joined the revolution," Temek spoke quickly.

Savas was surprised. "You have? What is this revolution?"

She looked uncomfortable all of a sudden. "We call ourselves the North Wind. It's a movement to bring an end to the corrupt monarchy."

"What do you mean, 'an end to the corrupt monarchy'?" he asked.

"The revolutionaries want them gone. We want a fair system of governance, not this stupid hangover from the old days. Did you know that there's an archipelago somewhere far called Lissol where they have this thing called democracy? The people vote for their leaders."

"They have that in Siladria, and I don't know how well it works," Savas countered.

"That's not true. The Chancellor is elected by a handful of other politicians; most people don't have any say," she replied. "And considering he's been re-elected every year for nearly two decades, I'd hazard a guess that there's a fair bit of corruption involved."

Savas bit his bottom lip in thought.

"Our leader calls himself the Helm," Temek continued. "He says there's an army of little folk in Gaminia, you know, peasants, farmers, labourers, and the like, all willing to join his movement. And fight in the war with Kaspica."

"What about me? I live with the monarchs."

Temek giggled. "You'll be much better off without them and the Myriad."

"How did you get to join?" he asked.

"Lei Jia," she said. "He quit his life at the Parlour to do something about how crap everything was for people like us. I wasn't about to carry on rotting in the Parlour while he was out there putting his mind to work and doing something useful. I want to see change in my life, so I met with him and he was able to get me in."

"Such a shero," Savas grinned.

"Hero is fine," she amended, gently.

"As long as I'm not in Sunhold when you tear it down, I don't really care what you do to it."

Chapter 8

How to Slay a Monster

"You look radiant," said Mother.

Elfine shrugged. "It's just a dress." She took it off, got back into her usual clothes and sat on her bed. Her room had never looked like this. The platters and trays of food had become ubiquitous in the space of a few hours, specially prepared for her and Mother to enjoy as a pre-wedding treat. Earlier, Mitenni had also dropped off two pitchers of wine, but Elfine was not in the mood. Abundant as the room seemed, an emptiness inside Elfine had infected the room. She knew that Mother sensed it. All day, it had drained Elfine and left her shrivelled. Now, it sought new prey and lurked in the nebula of uncertainty that clung to Elfine, smothering every lengthy silence or sudden sound with the inexorable dread of tomorrow.

"I think this custard pie will be served tomorrow," Mother asked, in an annoying voice, desperate to make everything seem normal. She peered down at the leftover pie, hopeful. "You liked it, didn't you?"

Elfine nodded, though these things seemed unimportant.

"I thought about what you said the other day. About the supernatural. Something slipped my mind," Mother said.

Elfine looked up, her attention aroused.

"There is a passage towards the end of the scripture that speaks of a kind of entity," Mother continued. "The being is not discussed at length, nor does it appear anywhere else, so there is no name for that thing. But Ishanaia seemed to know whatever it was. She is said to have communed with a winged thing that descended from the skies."

Elfine lifted an eyebrow. "A winged thing?" she asked.

Mother nodded slowly. "Remember I told you she cleansed the old world of darkness? Well, this thing was not pleased with her for doing so. In fact, this is precisely how our scripture ends. It is said that while she did save humankind from destroying itself, the Three also had to work to keep other forces away from Ysa. Superstitious people might call such things demons, or spirits, though as you know, there are few in any Yotanite congregation who believe in such things. The Yotanites who go to church mostly sit there to reap the rewards of looking like good folk as they glare with contempt at the rest of us," she scoffed.

There were goosebumps on Elfine's arms. "I need to go," she said.

Mother started to say something, but Elfine was already in her cloak and out the door.

On her way to the Chicane meeting house, she flinched when she passed posters announcing the royal wedding. The streets would be filled with strangers, celebrating a pointless occasion. According to the posters, the King had decreed that the day of the wedding would be a holiday for all of Northcrest.

A holiday. Elfine wanted to gag.

Elfine stepped into the meeting house. Rhyslan was missing, but Zatela and Lorcan were present. Spread across the table were two sheets of parchment.

"Late," Zatela remarked.

Lorcan glanced at the ceiling, and spoke only when it was clear Zatela had nothing else to add. "It's from Terig," he said, passing the report to Elfine. There was something worrying about the way he looked at her. "It came earlier today, between the claws of a jay." Even the use of messenger pigeons and crows was a fading gift, but Terig always had an uncanny affinity for animals and particularly birds, which he used for communication purposes. It was for that reason that Zatela chose to send him to Kaspica in the first place — for reliable and regular updates on the enemy.

Elfine skimmed through the report, her irises sketching a zigzag, yet her excitement about Terig surviving was short-lived. "The Kaspicians have begun their descent into Gaminia," she said, flatly.

She read on. Their force numbered in the thousands. They were taller and broader than Gaminians: bearded giants scantily clad despite the cold, painted orange and black with tattoos that snaked around their thickly muscled bodies; men who marched side by side with grizzly bears garbed in steel, whose roars made the ground tremble; women who held clubs of animal bone in their hands, who would squish the men of Northcrest under their toes; and musicians of war who clobbered on drums and gurgled spells to control the tide of battle.

Elfine placed the parchment back on the table. "Northcrest isn't ready," she said. She wasn't either — she had a stupid wedding to deal with.

"There's more." Lorcan handed her a second piece of parchment.

Elfine read the addendum quickly. The letter spoke of not one, but three enormous warriors, enshrined in impenetrable steel. The leaders of the Kaspician army were those monsters; she had seen one in the mountains. Elfine's thoughts returned to the moment its metal gauntlet struck her in the gut and winded her.

"The monster that took Terig is one of their leaders?" asked Elfine.

Zatela's furrowed brow finally receded. "It seems so," she said.

"What happens now?" Lorcan asked.

"I need you to assassinate someone," Zatela said, coolly.

"In Northcrest?" Elfine was unable to mask her surprise.

"Yes. Benthrin is his name. I believe that he arrived with the Chancellor's Siladrian envoy. He is holed up in Endvil, of all places," Zatela said.

"An envoy of the Chancellor? Staying here, in Endvil? The others are all staying in luxury in King's Respite," Elfine said, shocked.

"Wait — the Chancellor of the Republic is in Northcrest?" Lorcan blurted out.

Zatela nodded.

"If he's in the Chancellor's party, he must be valuable. Killing him could be an act of war," Elfine worried.

"If my theory is correct, then we are already at war," Zatela continued. "There is something treacherous at work here. I've seen its effects taking toll first in Endvil, now in other parts of the city. A drug, of some sort, being pushed around Northcrest. I believe it is responsible for what you encountered in Minnet."

"Do you think it's something that can influence people's memory, like we saw in Minnet?" asked Elfine.

"More," said Zatela. "I think it can somehow control people entirely." For once, she looked scared.

"And Benthrin is connected to all of this?" asked Lorcan.

"Correct."

Lorcan's eyes bulged with excitement. "Where is he staying?"

"Close to the south gate, around Ingly Lane there is a house with boarded up windows and red markings on the door. You won't be able to miss it."

"Hold on," Elfine interjected. "Don't send us off with only half the story again. What else aren't you telling us?"

Zatela turned to Elfine, but resisted snapping at her. "I haven't been sharing as much as I should have with the two of you," she sighed. "And the truth is, I don't have all the answers myself. I don't want to frighten you with possibilities and maybes. What I do know is this: there is a lot more out there than I have prepared you for, and some time ago, I was faced with something I didn't understand. It went away, but I can feel it coming back. That thing you saw in the mountains, what you said about human flesh in the cauldrons, this drug. And now Benthrin."

Elfine had not known her heart to move in the way that it did at that moment. Whether it was unbridled dread, or something worse that she could not even name, she did not know. Its patter stalked her with movements that were subtle, yet terrifying. She didn't want to know more, or be pulled further into this enigma, but she had to. "Then start telling the truth. All of it. What exactly is Benthrin?"

"A Menyr. They are servants of a dark power, far stronger than any human. I know little else; I've only seen a few in the flesh." Zatela was solemn.

"Menyr," Lorcan parroted the word, getting a sense of its magnitude.

"I sent you to Minnet because I feared their involvement with the Kaspician forces, and sadly, you proved me correct."

"And what of Rhyslan?" Elfine asked.

"I've dispatched him south," Zatela answered. "I remembered an old lead about the Menyr. Could be some useful information there."

"If a Menyr is what we saw in the mountains, it wiped the floor with us. I'm assuming you aren't trying to send us to our deaths, again?" said Elfine.

Zatela got up and went into the back room, then came out with two swords, which she placed on the table.

"These look incredible," Lorcan said, eyeing up the glossy weapons.

"This is your advantage. I should've given them to you before, but I hoped I was wrong about the Menyr. That was my mistake, and I'm sorry. But these swords were made for killing Menyr," she said.

Elfine inspected the weapons, though she did not touch either of them. They certainly looked special enough to put an end to a supernatural threat. She'd never seen a sword with such magnetism. The glint of the blades, enhanced by the soft yellow of the flickering candles nearby, was mesmerising.

"Do we aim for the heart, or the head?" Lorcan asked, with a grin.

"With a weapon like this, you may aim wherever you please," Zatela replied. "There is powerful magic in these swords. Any strike will be fatal."

"Fine," Elfine said. "We will investigate this Benthrin, but with caution."

Zatela nodded. "Meet me here tomorrow night once the deed is done. Oh, and try to have fun tomorrow at your… party, Elfine," she said, wryly, then left.

"Some answers at last," said Lorcan, once Zatela was gone. He picked up the sword and unsheathed it; there were faint inscriptions along the blade and it glimmered in the low light. "I hope these actually can kill this Menyr thing. What's this party of yours anyway? Am I not invited?"

Elfine eyes drifted to the report again and she cleared her throat. Somehow, this conversation seemed more daunting than the one they'd just had. She couldn't meet his gaze, but felt it burning into her with those big, inquisitive eyes of his. "It's not that sort of party. My father agreed to pawn me off to the Chancellor's son as part of the negotiations between sides. I'm to marry him tomorrow."

Lorcan's smile scarpered. "What?"

"It's true. The Myriad can do whatever they want, it seems. I've decided to accept it."

"Elfine, I'm so sorry," he stammered.

"This will not get in the way of my duties to the Chicane. They plan to send me to Dinaea too. *In accordance with our custom,*" she mimicked her father's words. "But I won't go."

"I thought arranged marriages were dying out." He paused, still reeling.

Elfine snorted at his naïveté. "Really? You think we are living in some enlightened age here, where everyone is equal, and things simply aren't that bad? Please. I've seen more sophistication among the Desert Tribes of Arx'an. My father sold me because I am a *woman*, and that was the only value I had to him. My future and my feelings are meaningless, even in today's culture. Our work has taken us to strange places on many occasions and we have seen the workings of greedy and power-hungry crooks in backwater towns, yet our own home, with its supposed millennia of civilisation, is just as big of a skragging mess as anywhere else."

He gulped. "Where does that leave us?"

"Nowhere, for now."

"Your father is a swine," he said.

"And a fool. A fool to think that this marriage will change a thing. Perhaps, I'll slit my husband's throat in his sleep," she considered.

"Vicious, aren't you?" Lorcan teased. "What about Benthrin, will you still help me take him out?"

"I'm not about to let you walk in there and die alone." She smirked. "I'll come to Ingly lane, late, after the festivities."

He laughed in that boisterous way that people always noticed. "I don't want things to change between us."

Elfine looked away.

"But I'll still be here, whatever happens." He reached to hug her and his touch comforted her.

Elfine forgot about Sigun and the wedding, if only for a moment. It was so far from reality, but she pictured herself with Lorcan tomorrow instead, wearing that dress that she'd been so unenthused by before. Beside Lorcan, it was radiant. She dismissed the fantasy quickly; it'd never come to pass. The Chicane had taught her pragmatism. And yet, she yearned to stay in his arms a little longer. "I hope Zatela sends us away soon," Elfine said.

Lorcan's embrace tightened.

She pulled away and regarded him, bracing herself for the tears that should have come, but they did not. She did not want him to see her cry. She did not want him to know that she cared. Holding the tears back was easy; the Chicane had hardened her. Besides, their love was impossible. They could never be more than lovers, meeting in the shadows. Her family would never knowingly allow her to enter a relationship with someone like Lorcan. Her fears didn't stop her from leaning in to kiss him on the lips though. She hadn't done so for a while. His thin lips were always cool, like two slivers of spring water made hard.

"Surely it's inauspicious to kiss someone else on the eve of your wedding day," Lorcan teased.

"The wedding means nothing to me," she said. She pulled him closer to her by his collar; his breath tickled her cheek. With a practised touch, she kissed his supple neck. Memories flooded to the surface of their last time together.

Fate had conspired to separate them, and he'd never looked more enticing. He had a dense torso, square shoulders and strong jaw; even the tousled mop of brown hair aroused her. Gently, she reached for more and met his already throbbing crotch.

"One more time," she said. "Before everything changes."

*

Save for the hoot of a nearby owl and a chorus of chirping crickets, Elfine noticed nothing out of the ordinary as she journeyed back home. Not far from Sunhold, she suddenly heard someone stumble out of an alley behind her. There was something suspicious about this movement; it was languid and snail-paced, but she had the impression of being stalked. Elfine's reflexes stayed sharp since the incident on the mountain. Stealthily, she turned around several times but could not get a good look at whoever it was.

The next time she glanced backwards, a faint glimmer of yellow lit up her brother's face. Savas looked out of sorts.

She stopped and called out to him but he didn't notice. Instead, he continued to hobble forwards. After calling a second time, startled, he came to a halt and looked up.

Elfine snickered when she saw the state of him. The stench of alcohol was woefully apparent. In the dead of night, he belched so loud that Elfine jumped; overhead, the tawny owl flew off in a fright.

"Elfine? Is that you?" Savas' words oozed out slow and sticky, like tree sap.

"Let me help you home." She put his arm around his shoulder and together they walked towards Sunhold. For several years now, Elfine had been aware of Savas' drinking habit. She didn't like to think of it as a problem; thinking of Savas as an addict made her body go limp.

"What happened to you tonight?" She didn't expect much of an answer; Savas was good at stonewalling.

"Temek and I had quite a lot to drink."

"Temek? Is that your lover?" Elfine glanced at Savas with a playful suspicion.

"No, she's just my friend," he snapped.

Elfine flinched a little. "What were you two drinking for?" She adjusted her tone, hoping not to exasperate him.

"Just a little celebration. I've been helping her with something."

"Ever the people's little helper."

"Helping others is good…" He rationalised.

Elfine watched him swallow back his fear and wondered if she'd upset him. "Are you in trouble of some kind?"

"We'll be fine," he replied, then suppressed a cough.

She wasn't convinced. "What are you involved in now?" Just then, Elfine noticed that she could hear another set of footsteps further in the darkness behind. They were being followed.

"So nosy!" He cried, then grit his teeth. "Fine. I'll tell you. There's this crook called the Wraith. The man is so pale and wrinkly I don't even know if he's alive. He got his men to attack Temek when she refused to do his dirty work."

"It's noble of you to take up her cause, Savas. I hope that she'll be as good to you if the time comes. You've a habit of picking bad company." Elfine looked behind cautiously, then ushered Savas through the entrance quickly, where a pair of sentries let them by.

"I know, but Temek is different," said Savas, walking along the corridor, "and nobody seems to care about her fight. Is it abnormal to stand up for what should be right and oppose what is clearly wrong?"

This was a new Savas that Elfine had not known before. "You're right! But are you fighting her fight, or your own?"

He grunted, but gave no answer. "I'm speaking too freely. Too much to drink," he grouched. "What's new with you, anyway? You were all flustered when I saw you last."

She bit her lip, thinking back to the mountains again, and what was now required of her tomorrow. "I haven't figured it out yet, but that thing I saw was evil."

"Hope it doesn't end up here." He shot her a quick grin.

"Agreed." She laughed. She led him to his room and inside, saw that his wedding attire had been left neatly on the bed, probably by Mitenni. She propped him up beside the clothes.

"What's all this crap?" he asked, fiddling with the yellow, collared tunic.

"Oh. I must have forgotten to mention that I'm marrying the Chancellor's son tomorrow. You're looking at father's latest political ploy," she made a silly face as she pointed to herself.

"I'm busy tomorrow."

Elfine pretended to look slighted, then giggled. "You never have plans. Getting drunk again is not a plan."

"Oh, sorry Mrs I'm So Busy with My Wedding. Are you too good for a bev now that you're going to be a married lady?"

"Shut up," she said, smiling. "You've changed since I've been gone. It's because of Temek, isn't it?"

He nodded, slowly. "Do you know that feeling Elfine, when you meet someone who just gets you?"

She took a moment to think about the question. She and her brother and sister had led fairly sheltered lives as children. They had each other. And really, Lorcan was the closest she had to what Savas was describing. "I'm not sure… maybe Sigun will turn out to be my soulmate," she said drily.

"Sigun. Even the name makes me think of mushy cabbage. The kind that stinks out the kitchen."

Elfine laughed, then made for the door. "When have you ever been in a kitchen?" Her hand was on the doorknob, but then something halted her. "So, how are you going to do it?"

Savas hiccupped. "Do what?"

Elfine raised her eyebrow at Savas, though she wasn't sure what she intended to get out of him. "You are going to kill the Wraith. Aren't you?"

"Well, unless you want to do it for me," he said.

Elfine folded her arms, and regarded him sharply. "You were being followed earlier."

"It wouldn't be the first time the Wraith stalked me."

"You're acting like that's not frightening when you just admitted he's a criminal," Elfine said.

Savas shrugged. "He's the one who should be afraid. Temek and I are going to end him."

Elfine arched one eyebrow. "Just what did this Wraith do to you?"

"Not to me. To Temek. He's not human, so I have no qualms about murdering him. I won't let you talk me out of it either."

Elfine began to ball her fists. Her body bristled with some inscrutable form of fear. "Why don't you think he's human?"

"Because he got inside Temek's head, made her say things she didn't want to say. He and his thugs beat her up."

"I'm warning you: don't go after him. There are things going on that even in my line of work we don't yet understand. Be careful, Savas." She made for the door, ready for bed. "Don't forget the wedding. See you tomorrow."

Chapter 9
The Royal Wedding

Aurelia gazed at her reflection in front of the mirror. A different universe yawned back at her; she thought about jumping into it to avoid this day. She stared till her vision blurred, and she saw the dark-skinned woman of her dreams stare back at her, as if to question or accuse her of something.

Aurelia started. Her reflection communicated without words, arrested her gaze and sucked her into a fathomless universe. The dark pair of eyes transformed into hypnotic spirals that drew life into them like a vacuum.

"The only black girl in your life is your slave?" asked the woman-spirit, drily. Her lips were still, like a mahogany figurine.

Mitenni is my handmaid.

"Is that what you call her? How little times have changed," said the spirit.

What's that supposed to mean?

"All your education and you know nothing of the history of prejudice. Haven't you ever wondered why there are no people like me, or you, in King's Respite, or Sunhold? Or why there are none like me in the books you devoured with your wise tutor?"

Mitenni came into the room, unintentionally freeing Aurelia from her trance. "Lady Aurelia?" She called. "I have your outfit prepared for the wedding."

Aurelia could not find the words to answer straight away.

"Lady Aurelia, are you alright?"

She snapped out of it fully. "Sorry, I'm feeling distracted this morning."

Mitenni elegantly laid out a selection of jewels next to the dress, which had been sitting on the bed all morning. She always moved with an unpredictable rhythm, a kind of unself-conscious grace. That was typical of Sygecian people, Mitenni had once mentioned, who were said to produce both peerless warriors and dancers.

The sunlight seeped through the grand windows at that moment and elucidated the mirror with an ethereal glint. Aurelia heard it whisper to come back to it, but she resisted.

"Lady Aurelia, I don't want to rush you, but I think we are behind schedule," said Mitenni, hovering by the garment.

Aurelia's dress was made of blue silk from the distant Isle of Sios, the circular island southeast of the Southern Continent. The matching jewel was a silver bangle, fashioned in the form of an ivy plant. It had winding stems and leafy shapes, encrusted with several tiny diamonds. Lastly, she saw a pair of flat, leather shoes with a buckle inlaid with gold.

"Can you turn around?"

"Yes, Lady Aurelia," she replied, then also gave Aurelia some space.

Slipping into the outfit quickly, Aurelia moved to the mirror and made a cursory inspection. She knew that Mitenni had picked the outfit and didn't want to slight her by seeming too unenthusiastic. "Perfect. Thanks."

"Should I grease and run a hot comb through your hair to straighten it, Lady Aurelia? We must make you your most beautiful."

Aurelia inspected her curls in the mirror, wondering about that dark girl who asked her if she'd seen Aurelia getting her hair done at Nektaria's before. No one had ever done her hair apart from Mitenni, and on occasion, she had done it herself. But her hair was thicker and curlier than that of any other girl's living in Sunhold.

Aurelia looked at Mitenni's own hair, which was far bushier than her own. "Do you really think it's prettier if I straighten it?"

"That is just the style in Northcrest, Lady Aurelia. All the girls have straight hair."

"What about in Sygecia? Do you remember what the girls did with their hair when you were younger?"

"Oh, there are many things I have forgotten about my home. But not this. Our hair is very important to us. There are many styles. Some can take hours to do properly." Mitenni paused, nostalgic for home. "I would not straighten my own hair, if that is what you are asking," she said.

"Then let us leave it as it is today," Aurelia said, smiling.

"Knowing Lady Elfine, your hair will not matter much to her."

"That's because she's never had to worry about her looks," Aurelia said, rueful as she thought about how emotional this day could become. But her feelings didn't get the chance to sink deeper.

Savas marched into the room with a twirl. "I'm glad you look about as stupid as I do," he said. "*Norhiba*, Mitenni." He sounded drunk.

"*Norhiba*, hello, Lord Savas," she responded.

"*Untu ka masiti wope?*" continued Savas, asking Mitenni if she was keeping well.

Aurelia looked at her brother closely and saw his glassy eyes. "Tipsy. I shouldn't be surprised."

"Obviously. You're the only one who isn't!" He unveiled a small bottle from his pocket, unscrewed it and took a sip. The stench filled the whole room with something migraine-inducing.

"Fig tonic," Aurelia said, pretending to sound unamused.

"Triple distilled," he smirked.

"Utterly shameless," Aurelia said.

He took a second sip, closed the bottle, and burped.

Mitenni suppressed a snicker.

"Charming," Aurelia smiled.

His eyebrows shot up with a sarcastic grin. "Well don't dawdle all day — the carriage is waiting outside. Mother has already begged Ishanaia to ensure today runs smoothly; let's not weary her sanctimonious little heart any further."

"I didn't realise we were in a rush," Aurelia said, making for the door.

He grabbed her wrist as she passed him and made a terse inspection of her face. "Have you holes in that big brain of yours? Elfine — sister number one, is getting married to Simon of Siladria!" He put on a daft posh voice, like actors did when they made fun of the old aristocracy in the theatres.

She broke free of his grip. "What sort of made-up name is that? His name is Sigun."

"Sigun! That's it. You know, I could ask the Chancellor if Sigun has any friends. You should be thinking about marriage and children soon. Aren't you almost 19?"

She giggled. "When Father sells you, I hope he picks a bride from the Isle of Sios. That way, you'll be suitably far away from me."

"Are you sure you don't want a swig?" He grinned, offering her the bottle.

She swiped it out of the way, rolling her eyes, then turned to Mitenni. "We'll see you later, Mitenni. Three blessings."

Mitenni waved. "*Belisam.* Goodbye."

*

Elfine was bored. She had been ready for a while. Sigun was lagging in the chamber next door, though Elfine could hear him obsessing over every minute detail of his nuptial look. He was an insufferable nincompoop — an insult she'd never thought suited anyone prior to meeting Sigun. The way he lapped up all of the lies about her made-up diplomatic career astounded her. And he was going to work in the Myriad. It was absurd that he was so gullible. Why was it that the 16-year-old boy who had no experience, was the one who was offered the life-changing position? The exchange offered Elfine nothing of similar worth.

Wasn't the whole point to persuade the Chancellor to grant the King and the Myriad access to his military assets? Something didn't add up. Elfine was certain that more was at stake, but she was still blindfolded. The fact that the King didn't have the power to demand the Chancellor's support was already proof that things weren't as they seemed.

The Chancellor. He was no ordinary brute: there was something sinister about him. At least in that regard, Elfine was able to empathise with Sigun. Conniving, malicious fathers might have been the only thing they had in common. Her own father's betrayal was still raw and had her questioning her worth. She doubted all her contributions to the Chicane, now that it seemed as though her availability to wed was what made her most useful. Even Zatela had said nothing about the wedding. It was the way that no one really cared that bothered Elfine the most, and the fact that this task fell to her like people assumed it was always meant to be. It was like no one thought her to be worth anything more than just currency to be traded.

Elfine knew she was stronger than her brother and sister, tougher even than her parents. But she'd been trodden all over like some weakling, when she was a warrior. Her pride was bruised, and she couldn't escape thinking that Mother would never have allowed this to happen to her precious Aurelia, either. Elfine would've agreed to this if she'd been asked, but she hadn't. She'd been betrayed.

And then there was Lorcan. She'd allowed herself to believe that in some distant reality, she'd have the ending she longed for with him. Until now, she didn't even know how much she craved him. Did Sigun feel the same about someone else in his life? She knew how foolish that sounded; who could love such a naïve and ignorant boy? Sigun was jubilant about the wedding, while Elfine hated every part of it.

Like some puerile lord of the manor, Elfine heard him scolding the servants. *No, imbecile, more powder here. Ack! You greasy-pawed lout, apply it gently! This necklace is ghastly, you weren't expecting me to wear that, were you?* She already loathed his southern accent. The way his K's became guttural, phlegmy sounds and his R's were rolled out sounded like a woodpecker clobbering into a tree.

Elfine peered down from her balcony and watched the festivities. She watched the throngs of people trickling in and out of alehouses like schools of fish drunk on wine. She allowed her thoughts to roam.

Hand in hand with Lorcan, she raced through the city till they reached the south gate, only to be stopped by the Chancellor, her father and a troop of armed Protectors. Deftly, she engaged them in combat with her fluid form, evading their strikes and outmatching them with her swift, acrobatic style. Lorcan overpowered the remaining Protectors and barrelled into the Chancellor, sending him crashing onto his backside.

"I do," she imagined saying to Lorcan, in front of her father. Horses were conveniently waiting to take them out of the city, and she and Lorcan rode south, happy.

Her imagination led her to other, darker places: she contemplated a great dragon burning the city down. In her mind, the ceremony ended in cinders, along with much of the city. Chapel Heights crumbled into rubble and heaps of charred bodies were piled up, still smoking and stinking. Then, her thoughts were overtaken by a huge, furry, thick-legged spider with an abdomen the size of a cottage. It picked Sigun's limbs off one by one and ate them till all that remained was a sad little head attached to a puny body. Hundreds of baby arachnids hopped off of the spider queen's back and ravaged the leftovers, burrowing in and out of his eyes on a voracious rampage.

Rueful, she returned her attention to the spectacle through the window. The whooping and clanging and clinking and stomping magnified, as if Elfine was stood at the centre of it all. The cacophony crushed her, until an odd vision ensued, and everything seemed to stabilise. Between each body, Elfine saw threads of energy bounce throughout Northcrest. Like ephemeral strands of a glistening sky-blue, it shot up, down, left and right but harmed nothing it touched.

"What majestic clothes. Don't I look exquisite!" Without knocking, Sigun strode into the chamber in all his pretentious regalia, making Elfine jump. He twirled in front of the mirror and his robe traced a colourful flourish about him.

Elfine was glad to be freed from whatever dream or nightmare had her in its talons.

"Is *that* your outfit?" He went on.

Elfine turned around slowly from the balcony to face him. He was wearing a long, burgundy, velvet robe that had a white fur hem and collar, and was adorned with orange and yellow stitching around the shoulders, as well as some gold circles of thread around the base. The way he marvelled at his exorbitant garments in the mirror disturbed her.

"This is what I have been told to wear." She gave an unenthused flick of the wrist at her traditional garments: a navy and white dress with some gold stitching, which was much less extravagant than his costume. She wore a delicate tiara too, adorned with sapphires and coruscant diamonds. Mother had insisted she wear it.

"Traditional Northern garments. How quaint." His lip curled with a hint of derision.

"You know everyone will be looking at me, not you, don't you?" Elfine readjusted her tiara.

"Your hair might not be as wavy as your sister's, nor your skin as bronze, but you must be used to people staring. Rest assured my flower: no one will utter a word of injury at you. Not one! For indeed, who would dare insult the wife of a well-respected gentleman?"

They left the bed chamber. With each glance and step she took with Sigun, tighter and tighter did she imagine the rein around her to become. Politics was for buffoons like Sigun and schemers like her father and the rest of the Myriad. Elfine craved bloodshed and carnage; she wanted to be fighting the war with steel, not words.

Mother hinted that perhaps the best strategy was to have Sigun tied up, make him the one bound to a tether. How easy that already seemed. Walking beside him, his thoughts polluted the atmosphere like foul-smelling wind. Elfine's had trained her instincts over the years, and to tap into the surface thoughts of a weak mind was simple enough for her, especially so with Sigun. His fears, hopes and desires hung transparently around him. Like plucking out a child's tooth, Elfine saw that he craved the approval of his parents, longed to be recognised in the Myriad, where he could champion Siladrian affairs. He also wanted Elfine to love him. But there was nothing about the war, so she lacerated deeper, like a surgeon looking for a tumour. His mind was hers, so pliable. She saw random events from his childhood, hours spent reading law and history, always alone. There was a man and a woman too, more recently. A tall man with a raspy voice and long, clawed fingers. The woman looked Piscanese. The Chancellor and his wife were present too. She heard chanting, then nothing.

"Is something the matter, wife-to-be?" Sigun said, continuing along.

She squinted at him. "No."

They passed a grand set of windows and briefly stopped. She heard shouting and frolicking. Below, she saw the carriage waiting.

"It's great to know that we are already bringing such joy to the people, don't you think?" He said, exhaling a self-satisfied sigh.

"The joy they have today is nothing," Elfine replied. "Many of them might not even survive the coming months." She hoped that her comment made him squirm with fear inside. She sensed it coiling inside of him like a serpent made of blistering brimstone.

"Even if we go to war, the Kaspicians are barbarians, Elfine." He tapped her on the shoulder patronisingly. "Just oafs with hatchets and wooden clubs. There's no civilisation there. When you know the support my family can provide, you'll see things differently."

Elfine saw through his confidence. She was right to be so concerned — she'd seen the enemy general, he hadn't. "You sound so convinced; you speak as if you've seen the enemy in the flesh."

"I am a learned man. Perhaps we know more of Kaspica in the south. They are a dead civilisation. What sort of madness would drive people to scale those mountains and attempt to live in frozen wastelands?"

She let go of his hand, advancing through Sunhold. "Perhaps to them, we are also mad and living in desolation."

"Northern lasses aren't all as astute as you."

"We don't use the word lass as often as you think," Elfine retorted.

"My point remains. You are smart. And it's true: the Kaspicians must have many of their own reservations about us, if they are capable of such developed reasoning." He snickered under his breath. "You know Elfine, we can be more than the sum of our parents' ambitions. Have you considered that?"

Elfine faked a yawn. Her mind wandered to sketches of battle plans, reports in the claws of jays and axe-wielding monsters. After a pause, she mumbled, "What do you mean?"

"We could be a powerful couple. And perhaps eventually, you will fall in love with me." A dystopic vision entered her mind: the alternate future where they were happily married. A garish and exorbitant property in Dinaea, Sigun's parents constantly visiting, strange children that exactly resembled Sigun and spoke with his drawl.

A fleeting shiver passed over her spine. It was guilt, albeit a foggy kind. A sighing voice whispered that this was her destiny, that this was what Gaminia needed of her.

The Chicane would find new members. There would be others to fight the Kaspicians. Who else could marry Sigun today, if not her?

"I'm no prophet," she replied, "so I can't tell you what sort of life we'll have together. But my allegiance is to my home and to my people. As soon as my expertise demands me to travel elsewhere, be prepared that I will not remain where I am of no use." She stepped through the main gate of Sunhold into the bailey. As she inhaled the spring air, she searched amongst the grass for the Protectors, then signalled to the driver that they were ready to depart. A small escort arrived to accompany them through town.

In the distance, raucous cheering could be heard, and the citizens of Northcrest were eagerly waiting beyond Sunhold's grounds. The two beautiful black horses began to gently trot as the driver commenced. The patter of their hooves against the cobbled ground was hypnotic; it soothed Elfine's anxious spirit, but it was soon eclipsed by cheers and thunderous applause. The Protectors had cleared a path for the carriage to follow, making sure no one got too close.

The town became a jarring, lurid expanse: bright ribbons, colourful confetti and kites of yellow and red all soared above. Any other person on their wedding day might have found this to be a colourful dreamland. The cries of the intoxicated masses amplified the atmosphere as they sang, clinking their pints and splashing wine, beer and cider onto the streets.

Sigun appeared to be in his element. As Elfine stewed uneasily, he hurled waves and smiles to anyone willing to receive them, as if it were his coronation. He turned to face Elfine, and his hair had returned to its natural state of being: oily and clumpy, like black moss coated in dew. She wanted to chop it all off.

"We are changing the tide of this war before it is even begun." He beamed at the crowds.

Elfine feigned joy as she waved and smiled at passers-by. A little girl caught her eye and screeched to the heavens as she locked eyes with her, then disappeared into a cloud of pink confetti. Suddenly, a fistful of daisies landed on Elfine's lap and she tossed them behind her discreetly.

"Do you feel joy for nothing, Elfine?"

She did not reply.

The carriage came to a halt by the gardens. Ahead was an exuberant display of flowers, bunting and banners. They descended the carriage and Sigun slipped his arm through hers as they proceeded through the gardens. The Protectors closed the gate behind and spread out around the area.

In the sea of faces ahead, Elfine noticed her family, though she was unsettled by how many strangers were also present. Her parents had clearly gone to extra effort to make the event busy by inviting dignitaries, acquaintances, extended family and the like.

The setup included stone tables that were piled high with bouquets of flowers, ceramic vases filled with fine wines and other spirits, and sumptuous foods representing every shire. There were plaited nut breads, sticky sweet cakes, golden flaky pastries packed with dates and glazed apricots — all from Pelling, the shire to the northwest famous for its baked goods. Elfine looked on in awe of the rest of the feast: platters of roasted boar doused in orange and peppercorn jam; whole salmon grilled with fennel and turmeric — a northern staple. There were also bowls teeming with fruits, cold cucumber and smoked mackerel soup, almonds deep-fried in lard and tossed in garlic and paprika and hot pickled vegetables like cabbage, beetroot and peppers —food from the south.

Servants flitted about, gracefully filling the plates of greedy nobles and regional magnates with nibbles and keeping their drinks topped up. A band of musicians played a delicate melody with flutes, guitars and harps as a trio of singers warbled something soft and sensual.

As she and Sigun drew nearer, the cries and cheers of the Northcresters behind fell silent. Respectfully, her family enforced quiet as she approached. Only when she noticed Aurelia and Savas did the heaviness she battled evaporate.

The crowd of attendees returned to their seats and watched as the couple approached the centre. Two priests were waiting by a large altar, on top of which, Elfine identified a few trinkets associated with Ishanaia: a crescent-moon shaped knife, a gold figurine of the Mother Goddess, wooden prayer beads, and plenty of other trinkets she didn't recognise.

One of the priests was a tall, slender man with a gaunt face and fine grey hair neatly arranged with a silver circlet. The circlet bore an insignia on it that Elfine had never seen; a green semi-circle with three smaller white triangles above it. It must've been a Yotanite symbol. The other man was short and stout like a tankard, with a gruff, pig-like face and a fiery red beard. He wore the same circlet on his head.

The lanky, skeletal one started with an eerily smooth voice: "Welcome, Lady Elfine and Lord Sigun, to this very special moment in your lives, and the lives of the people of this country."

His tone unnerved her, making the hair on the back of her neck stand up. As much as she wanted to run away, she smiled amiably at the priests. Sigun bowed, showing great reverence to the priests.

"On this occasion, we celebrate the holy union of Lady Elfine Tillensis, great-niece of Queen Consort Melindra Helig, and Sigun Iderius, only son of the Chancellor of the Republic of Siladria, Rorstein Iderius and Dame Leneare Iderius," the plump priest said. His voice bore a deep, gurgling timbre that rumbled through the audience.

The tall priest fidgeted with various ornaments on the altar.

The plump priest continued: "We invite Ishanaia the Mother Goddess to oversee this occasion, as the patron of love, matrimony and fertility. We give thanks to Zerkal, Lord of the Skies, whose battle-ready brethren protect against all harm, and we honour our almighty Aseg, the fervent fire-bearer, and Son of Eternal Intellect, to bless this couple."

The plump priest lit the bundle of herbs and flowers with a candle atop the altar and blew some of the fumes towards the couple. The smoke was to cleanse and purify, and ward off dark powers, he claimed. To Elfine, it reeked, and it took all she had to suppress a coughing fit.

With his head bowed, the lanky priest then proceeded to say an incantation in one of the old religious tongues. The words that left his lips seemed to stick to Elfine, as if they were for her ears only, but she didn't understand a thing. For a second, she found herself thinking about that odd memory of the man and the woman she'd happened upon while perusing Sigun's thoughts.

There remained one final task before saying "I do" and the wedding process concluded: to drink from the sacred chalice. The priests uttered an incantation over a tea-coloured liquid and passed the chalice to Sigun.

Without hesitation, he took a large gulp and beamed, just like the infant he was.

Elfine hesitated, contemplating the meaning of all this ritual, and whether or not it would really change anything. She examined the ornate chalice. The liquid smelt worse the longer she held it in her hands. It seemed to sour before her very eyes. The expectant looks of the people watching made her take the sip and be done with it all. Those in the crowd who deeply believed in the significance of these ritual motions lapped up the spectacle.

"In the eyes of Ishanaia, the two of you are blessed," said the plump priest, "cleansed and promised eternal life. Your union is everlasting in the eyes of the gods. Will you promise to uphold the laws of the land, remain faithfully by each other's side and lead an upright life together in harmony?"

"I do," Sigun said, his excited eyes fixed on Elfine.

Elfine paused. Was now the time for her escape with Lorcan? He was not here. Maybe the fire-breathing dragon, or the great man-eating spider would save her? But neither came. The silence lingered. She knew all eyes were trained on her.

"I do," she said. There were cheers of joy from below, and people threw petals towards Elfine. Was there an odd moment of happiness, or was it because the day was soon over? The fear that she didn't truly belong here grabbed her by the throat.

With the ceremony finished, she dwelled on the rituals and the invocation of deities. Ishanaia, Zerkal and Aseg. Elfine rarely thought about the Three, even though she was well acquainted with them thanks to her mother.

Her dedication to the Chicane quickly overshadowed any thoughts about the Three. Today was the first day in years that she'd questioned whether they were real;

whether they were spying on her, or cared about her marriage to Sigun. She envisioned herself caught in a web she couldn't escape, now herself a victim of the spider she'd hoped would end Sigun. Something didn't feel right about the whole ordeal; the two priests and their strange incantations, drinking from the chalice were normal, but today, Elfine had the impression that she'd signed herself over to something that would be the death of her.

"Elfine!" called Mother, suddenly in front of her. "Let me hug you. I'm so happy."

Everything seemed so unbearably loud: people's laughter was like that of three-headed monsters, the filling of their cups like cresting waves. Elfine was desperate to escape. "I'm just glad it's over," she said, smiling thinly at Mother. Elfine and Mother went away to the sides and entertained various nobles and other self-interested bores for a while. At least there was freely flowing wine. A short moment soon became drawn out, and Elfine found that she had been stood drinking, talking and feigning smiles for several hours already until a man arrived.

"Lady Elfine," he spoke with mild urgency, "I have a message for your eyes only." He handed her a piece of parchment. "Have a blessed day," he said before disappearing quickly.

Elfine unfolded the tightly rolled parchment. It was a reminder from Lorcan. On the night of her wedding, she was still to take the new sword Zatela had given her and plunge it into Benthrin's heart.

Chapter 10
Call to Action

The last time Aurelia attended a royal wedding, it was when Prince Zander married Lady Felima, and Aurelia was only about five years old. Zander was the King's only son, and he tended to divide opinions. After his wedding, he took up residence in his wife's home in Staghorn, Gaminia's largest region, which was considered scandalous. According to Gaminian patrilocality, men should almost never move in with their wife's family. The King regularly disapproved of Zander and his wife. Only after close to a decade of the King's remonstrations did Zander return to live in Northcrest, though his wife chose to remain in Staghorn.

Liberal quantities of wine had been drunk and it was starting to show. People were in high spirits. Aurelia tried everything that didn't have meat or fish in it, and even the Piscanese wines, which, by way of the bombastic glutton sitting opposite her, she had recently learned were renowned for their notes of vanilla, clove and cherry. When she noticed that nobody else at the table was still eating, she quickly feigned disinterest in the food and put down her fork.

She'd been waiting for the right moment to catch Elfine, but Mother had remarked that Elfine needed to spend time mingling with Sigun and his family for a while. Watching Savas had proved quite entertaining, whilst Aurelia relaxed. He'd been skipping about merrily, emptying every unattended glass, bottle, cup or stein in sight. A moment ago, he'd returned to the table and sat back next to Aurelia.

"Have you tried these cakes?" Aurelia said to him. "One of Sunhold's bakers from Pelling made them, apparently. I think they have cranberry and pistachio in them. I've eaten far too many." She weighed up the costs of taking another bite. Savas hadn't noticed her, so she pushed the cake closer towards him.

His eyelids quivered for a moment, and then reopened as if he was taking his first glimpse of the world. With a fork, he pushed the cake around the plate a few times then frowned. "You think I keep this gleaming complexion by eating cake?" he sassed.

"Has Mitenni been teaching you Sygecian?" Aurelia asked. She gave in, and took another bite of the pastry.

"*Nim,* she has," replied Savas, in an annoying sort of way.

"You never paid attention when we studied languages with Tutor Fark."

"Tutor Fark *odi-odi.*"

"Calling an old man a buffoon when he isn't here. So tough, Savas." Aurelia simpered.

"Old? That's kind. The dithering fossil was old back when our troglodyte ancestors rutted in caves. He's ancient now. *Zazamani kekwe jua.*"

"As old as the sun," Aurelia translated, with a self-satisfied smirk. She doubted his Sygecian was as good as hers. "Your accent is a bit off."

"Aw, no one is as good as you, are they?" He sneered at her humorously, then arose from his stool and sauntered off.

Mother looked on, ashamed, as he stumbled away. Propriety was something that kept her awake till odd hours, and Savas' penchant for alcohol meant he regularly broke her sacred laws of decorum. "That one needs the Three more than any of us," she sighed, scratching her forehead. "Perhaps you can steer him to better faith, Aurelia. The gods have always listened to your prayers. Do you pray for your brother?" This was one of the first things Mother had said to Aurelia since arriving. She'd been so busy pretending to be interested in the big-bellied, noble guests.

"I sometimes wonder what I would be like if I drank so much," Aurelia said. "Once, our people had gods who encouraged drunkenness."

"Don't blaspheme! The rituals of our pagan ancestors are shameful. The Three have nothing to do with alcohol in any form; it is the work of sinful men to drink to excess. Perhaps if you *did* pray for your family, he would be better by now."

Father rolled his eyes. "Whatever deity you choose to throw yourself at, none of them will save Savas," he said. "Only he can rescue himself from whatever moral bankruptcy has left him so destitute. My only son, and he has spent his entire 21 years of life intoxicated and in the company of whores!"

Aurelia shuffled uncomfortably in her seat. She wished she'd left with her brother.

Father continued, "Does the idiot really think it's becoming for a *man* to behave like that? I'm sick of watching him prance around like some fairy with those girlish curls."

Nobody denied that Savas could be difficult, Aurelia least of all. But she hated to hear the way her father spoke about her brother. His fixation with things being a certain way and people living up to certain standards exhausted her. While she did find herself worrying about Savas from time to time, it was only because she wanted to be proud of him, to see him doing well, and not hemmed in by the obsolete notions of filial piety that their parents enforced. The thought crossed Aurelia's mind that Temek could be the one to help him grow, but it was soon truncated when she realised how little Mother and Father would approve of someone so unashamedly different to the sorts of noble girls they'd prefer at Savas' side. A life with someone like Temek would only rile them up even more. As for Aurelia herself — if her brother wanted to get married and have babies with Temek, who was she to judge?

"You are too strict sometimes Olsin, but not completely without reason," Mother said. "The gods hear every prayer, and no soul is beyond their redemption. Just keep your eyes on him Aurelia. Men can spend a lifetime seeking forgiveness."

King Thenris ceased shuffling his carrots around the plate; pierced a single pea with a fine-pronged fork, inspected it, then put it back down. He had, as usual, eaten a meal distinct to everyone else's, consisting of only unseasoned, steamed food, apparently for the benefit of his health. "The young men of today are a sorry bunch," he said, looking viciously across the table to his son, Prince Zander, who was paralysed with humiliation.

Zander sat without his wife, who had made some excuse not to attend the wedding. Aurelia didn't like the man, but she pitied him in that moment. She was thankful for the background noise, which overshadowed the King's injurious remarks.

"He allowed himself to be controlled by his wife for a decade before coming to his senses and returning to Northcrest!"

"At least the boy didn't end up with another man, my king," joked Father, collecting a few laughs from around the table.

"If that had been the case, I'd have had him castrated and shipped off to Yenhai to join the empress' famous eunuchs," continued King Thenris.

"Mind you don't tire yourself out with this banter, you've barely touched your steamed carrot," came the Queen's smothering contribution.

"A bit of banter won't hurt."

Aurelia shivered at the sound of Cornetta's toadying voice. Annoyingly confident, as always. How did she get away with marching into a conversion with the monarchy, when Aurelia had barely said a word all day? She'd forgotten that Cornetta and her family had been invited, seeing as they were exactly the sort the Queen kept in her back pocket: obedient sycophants who would tell her how fabulous she looked and how delicious the food was.

Cornetta appeared standing behind the table where Aurelia was seated, her mother and father on either side of her. "Did you manage to get your — what is it called again — vegetarian meal, Aurelia?" She simpered, the insincerity of her dimpled smile unbearable. "I'd be careful, King Thenris, she's been eyeing up your carrots all day, I bet."

As was expected, Cornetta's affected humour was met with the usual thin smiles and whispers of laughter that the rich preferred. The discussions became tedious. Aurelia could not sustain concentration on Cornetta's endless attempts to show off, the colourless chat her parents regurgitated about their latest business ventures and newly acquired summer homes along the south coast.

She escaped the monotonous conversations by thinking about Castrellus' Journal. The distraction invited all sorts of wild thoughts. Castrellus was a figure of paramount importance, as far as Aurelia saw. She envisaged him as a tall, powerful and compelling figure; a spiritual warrior, traversing the Ankasa, hunting for occult wisdom. He would speak with a rich, deep voice that reverberated about him, but not in a threatening way. I can teach you more than that crone in the mirror, he said, and Aurelia almost laughed out loud before the guilt stopped her. She loved the crone in the mirror too. They were both her keys. Keys to the supernatural world that would make her powerful and wise.

"May I be excused? I'd like to see Elfine." Aurelia looked to her mother for permission. A pack of Gaminian politicians snuck up on Father and he immediately turned to them and expressed his fakest, heartfelt greeting.

Her mother smiled. "Of course. Three blessings, darling."

Aurelia ambled towards her sister, with a cup of spiced apricot nectar in her hand, imagining that Cornetta was jabbing her in the back with that bladed glare of hers. Aurelia didn't care; she was glad to be free from her and the rest of the table.

Elfine's black hair billowed with each passing breeze, and her tall, slender figure left her enviably attractive in her traditional attire. Eyes slightly glassy, she managed to maintain an air of sobriety and engage in what appeared to be a deep conversation with Sigun and his father, Chancellor Rorstein. On closer inspection, Aurelia realised that her sister's blank expression made the explicit statement that she was approaching a boredom-induced coma.

At the sight of her sister, Elfine beamed, beckoning her over. She side-eyed the two men beside her then gave an acerbic roll of the eyes.

"I've commandeered the last jug of Piscanese plum wine, but I imagine you're happy with whatever presumably alcohol-free concoction is in that cup," she said, then took a big sip of wine and smiled, her teeth slightly purple.

Aurelia blinked, comically. She forgot about Elfine's proclivity for wine. "I like waking up with my memories intact."

"Hmph! You Tillensis ladies and your humour," Sigun said. He looked desperate to be included, hopping up and down on his tip-toes.

Elfine was wobbling like a willow in the wind, unsupported by Sigun. "My sister holds the prestigious award of 'Most Hilarious Woman in the North'," she said.

The Chancellor snorted. He folded his arms stiffly and sneered at Elfine as though he'd lain eyes on the most reprehensible creature under the sun. "Do take care of your woman, Sigun. They aren't supposed to drink — it reminds of whores."

"Yes father! Not to worry; she's in safe hands with me," came the boy's response.

Elfine could only hold her tongue for so long it seemed. "Chancellor. May I call you father now?" she asked.

"Not ev—"

"In any case, if you've got *whores* on your mind," she continued, "I'd be happy to point you towards some of Northcrest's best brothels."

Aurelia watched the creases in his face begin to produce a hideous scowl. His beady eyes shrivelled with frosty wrath. Inside, she was chortling at Elfine's comment. She wanted to clout the man round the ears with one of the silver platters, or melt his frosted glare by swilling him with her drink. "The last Chancellor from the Republic to arrive here came with a harem of thirteen," Aurelia said, insincere. "Did yours get lost on the way?"

Elfine fought back a giggle.

Sigun's cheeks flushed red.

The Chancellor's jaw dropped like that of a serpent about to swallow an egg. He raised his palm, then dropped it to his side when he saw Elfine glaring. To Aurelia, he said "You best watch what you say around me. If I need a whore, perhaps I'll come looking for you and that big mouth of yours." He stormed off towards the two priests who had conducted the ceremony. The three of them looked vexed, though their anger was discreet, and they did not shout or cry, but seemed to gripe to one another in low voices. The gaunt faced priest glanced over at Aurelia with a wily look about him.

The plump man, too, watched her conspicuously, his fiery red beard seemingly ready to ignite as he scowled in her direction.

"Was it something we said?" Aurelia said lightly.

"A foul stench in the air methinks," Elfine replied.

"You look stunning."

"I just randomly threw this together."

Before Aurelia could respond, Sigun butted in after slurping the dregs out of his wine cup. "I wouldn't speak to Father like that. King Thenris can't have what he wants without my father's support. If the King's concerns are true about Kaspica, then it's Siladria — *my father* — that will save this city from ruin." An air of smugness swirled around him.

Aurelia wondered if all men from the Republic had a superiority complex as great as Sigun's and his father's. "It was just the wine talking," she said, wanting to clear the atmosphere. "Let's forget about it."

"Fine," Sigun sighed. He tried to discreetly prise Elfine's wine cup from her delicate grip, but she deftly evaded his grasp and placed the cup on the table herself. Even when drunk, Elfine was too quick for him.

"Yes, yes… women and their place and all that," Elfine said drily. "We'll both be sure to offer Chancellor Rorstein our sincerest apologies." She went for a last gulp of wine theatrically, as if making a protest.

Sigun began to fidget with his robe and his eyes were shifting around the reception. The divide between Gaminia and the Republic would not heal in one day. "How about we go for a walk?" he suggested.

"A sobering stroll — how brilliantly your mind works, dear husband!" Elfine exclaimed.

"Will you join the evening feast in the hall tonight, Aurelia?" Sigun asked.

"I wouldn't miss it."

After a while, the merriment thawed. Aurelia looked around and realised no one that she cared for was still here. Most of the guests, tired from their drinking and feasting, were escorted back to King's Respite or Chapel Heights, where they would recover before returning to the Great Hall. Aurelia's parents left the reception a few moments earlier, and she decided to head home for a break as well. Having sobered up, she had no desire to interact with the crowds of drunkards cavorting through the streets, so she decided on a quiet route home through Chapel Heights.

The unwelcoming residents peered down at Aurelia from their balconies. A man with a coiffed blond wig sneered at her as he sipped a fluorescent green tonic out of a glass. Beside him was a woman with a broad sun hat, glaring down as she took a draught of a long pipe. She knew those two characters, though it wasn't until the third person, a girl all too familiar, bounced towards the balcony's edge, that Aurelia realised who they were.

"Careful you don't catch the sun any more you poodle-headed ogre," Cornetta said.

"Just my luck," Aurelia muttered to herself. "Twice in the space of a few hours." She stopped, wondering if she should run or engage with the girl, who was still clothed in her signature pink lace, waving mordantly with her white-gloved talons.

"Yuck! Don't talk to that sordid bimble-wimble," her mother hissed. "Yes — now that your family aren't here, I'll call you what I like. My little angel told me all about you knocking her over. Wretched fart-hole!" She puffed on her pipe again, then emitted a wheezing cough that sounded like it could've been her last breath.

Cornetta erupted into a high-pitch cackle, like the prejudiced little songbird she was. "Darling!" she cried. "A napkin for you. If you scrub hard enough, the extra *dirt* might come off."

The girl's mother was howling. "Brilliant, Cornetta! Oh, Lady Trinne certainly opened her drawers for something unsavoury, didn't she!"

"There's talk in my circle that she let a mad dog from Sygecia into her boudoir!" The father added, his voice as ugly as the mother's.

Aurelia reached to pick the napkin up. It was so soft and dainty it sickened Aurelia. She scowled at it, listening to the scornful cackles and guffaws from the two dragons on the balcony. She squeezed the napkin in her fist tightly, and anger overtook her. Blood infused into her saliva; she'd bitten her lip hard. Her vision blurred for a moment, till the napkin seemed to resemble the horrid girl's face. It began to contort unnaturally, writhing like a caterpillar held over an open flame.

A scream blared.

Tendrils of black ink erupted upon the napkin, like dozens of tainted veins. Aurelia looked back to the balcony and saw that the girl had projected a torrent of bile all down herself, and judging by the stink, something had erupted out of her backside too.

Her mother was whimpering like a dog trying to help her. "Cornetta! Get inside and get a wet cloth you rotten sewer!"

Aurelia dropped the tarnished napkin. As she watched it on the ground, it reverted back to its normal appearance.

Did I just do that? Confused and upset as she was, a trickle of excitement broke over her face. She set off at a dash and headed home.

Once she made it back to her room, Aurelia went straight to the Journal. It was the only place that offered some form of escape, and maybe the answers she needed. Opening it, she dove straight into a new entry.

Sage Era 2389, 2nd Moon, 18th Sun

A strange thing has befallen the House of Noul. We have found ourselves locked in a vicious battle against an unknown disease. The Dreamists are sick.

Our cries for help continue to go unheard. It is a dreadful time to be in this city. Chaos foments everywhere. The authorities wilfully neglect us, and indeed, it seems they harbour a terrible resentment towards us. It is the same resentment that catapulted me to this land many years ago. The House of Noul has been branded a wretched cesspool of depravity, but it is all lies. The Northcresters think that just because we open our doors to those the city chooses to abandon, we are a tainted lot, poor in spirit.

We remain faithful to Noul, the Mystic Voyager and the Groom of Whispers, and pray that a solution will come soon. Our leader is confident that things will improve. He has shared great knowledge with me. With his guidance, surely we will come out victorious. This is the hope that I cling to, because I believe that I know the cause of our suffering.

Deep within, I sense that my own transgressions are to blame for our plight. The others believe this to be divine punishment of sorts; they believe we have angered Noul, that we have become complacent in our faith.

But perhaps it was I who delved too deeply. The cursed magic of this tome is seductive. I opened a door to a plane far too deep on the other side. A creature found me. It called itself Onaxia. I should never have spoken to Onaxia, a being who was man and woman both. But I could not resist what it offered. It tempted my every desire, and the prized jewel it dangled before my eyes was too sumptuous.

Although Onaxia's power seemed but a ghostly whisper, it bewitched me instantly. The creature knew what I craved above all, and promised I would have it. It took the form of a comely man, and something was placed inside of me, a receptacle of magic, intended to transform me. Make me the person I'd always wanted to be. But nothing has changed. My desires torment me still.

It was only several days after that our leader summoned us for a group ceremony. We took the usual concoction, and together, travelled into the Ankasa, searching for what Dreamists have obsessed over for centuries: Noul himself. As always, our spirits were tethered to one another to anchor ourselves, but something dreadful occurred. Whatever Onaxia put inside of me, burst, and seeped into the other Dreamists' spirits.

Ever since, people have been dying.

Once, Aurelia never thought that gods, or anything lesser were real when she read about such entities. But now she knew that she had vivid dreams, and that spirits in the lake could come to life and haunt her. Her beliefs were changing. But a mystery illness, caused by a creature that could assume more than one form?

Who is Onaxia?

Aurelia pulled herself away from the Journal and crawled on top of her mattress. A nap was too good to resist. In a few moments, she drifted off into a quiet state of sleep. As the sensation in her limbs drifted farther and farther away from reality, her mind remained unnaturally alert. Her body however, seemed to have disconnected and she could no longer feel it. Soon, all that was left was the darkness of her mind, which could not even conjure the simplest image. In this expanse of emptiness and silence, her body remained asleep and her mind unable to break free.

She noticed a sudden coldness insinuate itself onto the back of her neck, her arms and her ankles. The way the chill moved across her body, as if spread by the breath of something insidious, made her think it wasn't natural.

I did shut the window, didn't I?

Aurelia heard a whisper, murmuring around her earlobes. She saw a mighty river. As its currents rose, the whisper grew louder, but it was unintelligible; a language not of the living. Streaks of a boundless form of energy palpitated throughout her.

The more she attempted to move, the more immobile she became. She tried to stop fighting. Focusing on the semblance of movement she detected in her chest as she breathed, she managed to ground herself. Not long thereafter, her spirit floated upwards of its own volition. She stayed calm, continuing to focus on her breathing.

As her body drifted towards the ceiling, she felt light beyond comprehension. The sensation was dizzying. She questioned whether she would shout for joy or cry with fear if she could, but her lips were sewn shut. There was no *bump* as she collided with the ceiling, instead, it seemed as though a hand reached to flip her over and pull her back to the floor. The sight of her sleeping body, so exposed, terrified her.

"There you are," came a whisper, sounding like it was formed on the slight mouth of a snake.

Where did this voice come from?

Aurelia exerted herself to her utmost to turn her neck. She moved as if her whole body was doused in honey. Fear wended through her spirit like a hellish river of bones and venom. And then she saw it.

A man. No — a crow. Both. Creeping in from the balcony, he must have climbed up Sunhold's walls. Shadows that could have been feathers receded behind and the large, black beak gave way to a human face as he stood up to full height. He was a skeletal looking thing, ensconced in black, hooded robes; Aurelia could not see the top half of his face. A few wisps of dark hair snuck out by his cheeks. His lips moved, but not as a normal man's might. Like two pale worms snaking through desecrated soil, they twisted.

Out of his mouth dribbled a primordial goo that looked like it was formed from the essence of the most heinous of demons. Something dead, drowned perhaps in the crow-man's stomach, landed on the floor. Many dead things. Bits and shards and legs and wings.

Bzzzzzzzzzzzzzzzzz.

The noise disarmed Aurelia. Flies. Or bees? No, wasps, perhaps. Tiny black things, winged and irate. Lots of them. Fat and strong from whatever that goo was, they began to surge out of his mouth. In seconds, a dozen had already landed on Aurelia's body, as she watched in horror from above, unable to physically feel them. A couple went for her face, about to enter either her nostrils or her mouth. She looked to her defenceless body and begged with all the strength she could muster to return to it. But she could not.

She contemplated a scream, but her lips failed to produce a sound.

There was barely time to react to the sound that came next. It was a sharp howl, like someone had bottled a storm at sea and unleashed it as a weapon.

She'd never heard anything so brutal, so primal, in her life.

And that wasn't all. The crow-man was dangling off the balustrade, screeching and cawing like a harpy fleeing back to its roost. The flies became black dust and were blown out of the window. The intruder clutched desperately with one hand, then just a few fingers. The wind came again, and it walloped him so forcefully he lost his grip. Aurelia heard him yelling, till his shout dissipated into the atmosphere.

With sudden tiptoeing movements, Aurelia's spirit was pulled towards the mirror, where a dark-skinned woman, large and petrifying in her stillness, greeted Aurelia with a severe stare. In her hand was a book.

Castrellus' Journal.

Aurelia knew fear. The woman was potent; she exuded a force which threatened to suck Aurelia into an oblivion of mystery. She was exactly like the women Aurelia used to dream of as a child; black and rapturous as they danced around fires and totems. Her eyes were deep like whirlpools, lurking in which could only have been some tentacled beast of legend, powerful enough to sink the mightiest of vessels. No deduction was required to recognise that this black woman was the same woman-spirit from Aurelia's visions, the same force that had sprung to life at the bottom of Lake Mesita, and the same voice that had sounded from within her mirror earlier today. Aurelia started to think of her as the Visitor, as that was what seemed to be her bizarre purpose.

"You're welcome," spoke the Visitor. This time, her lips moved.

"I can't believe this. What just happened?"

"Someone tried to murder you." The words whirred in strangely high pitch frequencies, lingering in Aurelia's ears.

"What... who?"

"They cloaked themselves in the guise of a plague-infested crow," replied the Visitor. "I saw nothing of their true form, but shapeshifting is one of the powers of those who hunt our people."

Why did she sound so nonchalant, as though this wasn't the most outrageous turn of events imaginable? Aurelia went cold. "Shapeshifting?"

"Magic is complicated."

"Magic," Aurelia said again. "That's what this has all been about."

"You act as though you didn't already know."

Aurelia's head sank slightly. "I'm so confused. Please, tell me what's going on. What I'm up against."

"They were similar to us once," the Visitor began. "Those monsters were wielders of magic too. They had their place in the world, as all do, but they were led astray. I know that you have heard of the book our people feared. You saw our ancestors speaking of it when you stole into the Ankasa. We never figured out how, since we never located the book for ourselves, but the ruler of the Kaspician people turned his most loyal and most powerful followers into monsters. What they became, we called the Menyr. They took on many different powers and various forms because of the unpredictable dark sorcery that created them. Many centuries ago, we succeeded in keeping them at bay and defeated them. But in those days, there were hundreds with the magic to oppose them. Now, you stand almost alone against them."

Aurelia's thoughts came and went without her knowing. She moved from one to the next so quickly. Menyr. A war. Kaspicians. The Ankasa. She didn't know what was going on anymore. "Are these Menyr like the creatures that came out of the ground when I saw you in the Ankasa?"

"If only," answered the Visitor. "Those beasts are mindless husks. Your enemies are demons who have powerful magic, strong bodies and cunning minds."

"You aren't very reassuring."

She gave a half-shrug. "There isn't anything reassuring about a supernatural war that has lasted for thousands of years."

"It took hundreds of you to win, and now all that's left is me. What about you, can't you fight?"

"I've been dead for centuries," she laughed. "What power I have to interact with your world is a blessing from our ancestors. I draw upon their strength constantly and even still, my power to help you is limited."

"And what about these ancestors you keep bringing up?"

"Dead too, of course," smiled the Visitor. "But you know them. Their magic flows through your hair, and your skin. The things that others resent you for."

"You're talking about the people from the meeting, with the strange accents?"

The Visitor produced a slight chuckle. "That's them," she said.

"I don't understand why you didn't go to Elfine. She is the warrior, not me," Aurelia protested.

Sharpening her gaze, the Visitor said, "I'm here for you — no one else. Unless you want to stay stuck idle in this meaningless life of luxury."

"I'm not idle and my life is not meaningless," Aurelia retorted.

"What exactly were all those times spent frolicking at dinner parties and playing with herbs at the Academy, then?" the Visitor asked.

"You could try asking Savas, if I'm no good," Aurelia went on.

The Visitor grinned. "Good one, Aurelia. You need a lot of training, though some of it will come naturally to you."

"Magic training, you mean?"

"One of the first things you should know is that magic is not an outlet for your emotions. When war comes, you must be ready to use your power to fight for more than just the ones you love."

"This is because of how I reacted to that ludicrous Cornetta and her bullying, isn't it?"

"The word is full of ungrateful sorts who will hate you no matter what you do for them," the Visitor said. "Those who came long before me arrived on these shores, black and dreadlocked and lathered in paints and odd symbols. It was only when the locals realised they could exploit our people for their magic that they chose not to ostracise them. Even still, when we had won their battles for them and exhausted our power to the point of death, they evicted us because we were not entitled to be a part of the peace that we had won. Cornetta and those like her? Even after thousands of years, their noses still wrinkle at you, because you reek of me. There will always be some who refuse to accept that you were granted power, while they were granted none. You are not someone that many Gaminians would want to have as their champion, but I am here to tell you that that is exactly who you are, and there are many battles ahead for you. Soon, there will be nothing here for you, and the only thing that will call to you is the thing that has always set you apart from this world. You must embrace it."

"Embrace you, you mean?"

"It is what you have sought your whole life," the Visitor said.

Aurelia bowed her head in thought. "You're right. I don't feel like I belong in Northcrest. I never have. It's not that I thought I was special or something, but everyone else thought I *wasn't* special." She paused, and shook her head lightly. "The suffering of my ancestors makes my own seem pathetic. I don't want war. I don't want to fight Menyr. But I don't want my life to be idle or meaningless in Northcrest either. I want to learn. If there's something I can do to make a difference, for everyone, I will. Where do we go from here?"

Behind the Visitor's form, something began to take shape in the mirror. A river, surrounded by natural beauty and life. The picture moved. Further along the river, darkness loomed. A great hand in the sky choked the clouds of life and hissing rain sizzled as it met the earth. Aurelia looked further ahead. There was an overgrown thicket, leading to the mouth of a cave, out of which seeped its black, hazy breath.

"You see something," said the Visitor. Her eyes went upwards into her skull, leaving only a whiteness. She seemed to whisper in conversation to herself. "The ancestors speak. This cave. I have been there before. What is it that I overlooked, after all these years?"

"Is it some sort of message?" asked Aurelia.

"Indeed. I know this place all too well. It is where our enemy slumbers. The one who the Menyr serve. You have read about her; she is Princess Onaxia. The magic that has held her captive is beginning to weaken, and soon it will only require a fraction more power to tip the scales in her favour. You already know how vast her power is — she created a disease that wiped out hundreds while still trapped in the spirit plane. What she is capable of in the physical world is even more terrifying. But there is one who met her, fought her and whose spirit endured."

"Castrellus," ventured Aurelia. "But those things in the library said his Journal was written by filthy hands."

The Visitor's eyes came back to focus and she squinted. "What things?"

"I don't know. Perhaps they were spirits like you. When I got angry at them, they disappeared," she replied.

It seemed that the Visitor was weighing up several responses. "Castrellus remains connected to many who died without proper burial, because of the circumstances of his own death. These lost souls are the remnants of what Onaxia did to Northcrest's people. Ignore their trickery, for now."

Aurelia wasn't sure if she trusted the Visitor's answer. The spirits seemed convinced of Castrellus' malevolence, or at least that of his writing. "Fine. But how do we find him?" Aurelia asked.

"You have read about the House of Noul by now, I assume. It is where he died. The place is hidden from me. My theory is that only a living being can find Castrellus."

"So, that's what you want from me, to find Castrellus and the House of Noul?" Aurelia said.

Something uninvited arrived suddenly. Aurelia picked up on it, even from her side of the mirror. A sinister force gathered between them, ricocheting off their bodies. There was a crackle, and the vision of the river and the cave in the mirror immediately dispersed. Lights flashed and peals of thunder clapped behind the Visitor. There were howls and hisses and growls of strange animals. Chants of men and women in alien languages followed.

Behind the Visitor, Aurelia saw the most peculiar of giants. It was a four-legged thing with a leathery, grey hide and sharp tusks. Aurelia had read about elephants with Tutor Fark, but she didn't remember any like this, nor did she recall people riding them. There was a strange looking man atop the beast, wide and broad shouldered, fair-skinned and red-haired. He didn't look like much, but the glistening whip in his hand, fashioned perhaps of some kind of metal, looked deadly. Stranger still were the band of lifeless things in chains, trailing behind the elephant-rider. Where were they going? Suddenly, the man with the whip looked right at the Visitor, and his elephant roared; out of its trunk came flying a giant gob of green fluid that sizzled like acid and ate up the ground where it landed.

"We have been here too long," the Visitor shrieked, looking behind. "They are here. Remember to keep the Journal close — it will have answers."

Aurelia tumbled down, as if pushed off a cliff. She came to, disjointed, like she had been sucked out of a grisly nightmare. Her interdimensional dialogue was over; the Visitor disappeared into the Ankasa, where it seemed she would remain unsafe.

Aurelia's eyes seemed to close all by themselves, and though the bedsheets were sticky with sweat, she sank into a deep slumber.

Chapter 11

A Secret Unburied

Elfine had spent much of her childhood playing in the Esterwood with Aurelia and Savas. It was a special place for her, but its charm was lost on Sigun. He hadn't remarked on any of the birds, the grunting boar with her piglets, or the crystalline waters of Lake Mesita. Nor did he say anything about the coppices of apricots and walnuts, or the glades that were home to massive stones, dyed green by layers of moss. A general reverence for the natural world was common in the north. Despite the tide to push back old-fashioned beliefs, Northcresters had remained fairly superstitious and devoted to nature. The most interesting to Elfine were the numerous spirits, said to cause mischief in the forest. Her favourites were the tales of Pugis, the butterfly-winged pixie and Mukele, the wasp witch-spirit. Mukele, it was believed, hunted and ate Pugis' caterpillar offspring for their ambrosia-like blood.

The snapping of a brunch under Sigun's foot disturbed a fox. The creature sped off into the distance, startling him.

"Careful you don't fall into one of Mukele's traps," said Elfine.

"What's that now?" Sigun was taken aback.

"The wasp witch-spirit. She sets traps for Pugis' children."

"*Spirits?* Such nonsense belongs in the reactionary past. No surprise you Gaminians have clung on to these tired inventions."

"Knowledge of the spirits is compulsory, especially since they kill so many hapless wanderers. Siladrian flesh is the sweetest."

He flinched, then looked all around. There was nothing. "You jest."

"*Boo!*" She screamed right at him and a little spittle wet his cheeks. Terrified, he fell backwards onto the grass and was breathing rapidly. Elfine watched him for a moment, then laughed.

He got back up on his feet in a huff, unimpressed. "Don't do that again! Siladrian women of my mother's echelon do not dabble in humour with such leisure."

"And what a delight she seems."

"She could teach you a few things!"

Elfine bit her lip playfully before leading Sigun to a coppice. There, they both sat upon two stumps and looked ahead, already bored of each other. Elfine began to pick the grass, only to glance at the dead blades then discard them over her shoulder without any thought.

"Do you remember when we first met, in Dinaea?" She asked, after a while had passed.

"Of course," he replied.

"You knew we were to be wed then, didn't you?"

"Father told me of his plan only recently," he said.

She didn't expect that to be the case. It had been easier to think of Sigun as instrumental to this whole ordeal, but perhaps he wasn't as guilty as she thought. "They say Siladrians hate the north. Do you?" she asked.

"There is history here, but I can't say that Northcrest is superior to Dinaea in any way," he said.

"But this city is the birthplace of all modern Gaminian culture. It has more than just history — Northcrest's spirit runs through the veins of all Gaminians."

He squinted at her, mockingly. "Sunhold was only built at the end of the First Great War. Before that, Dinaea was Gaminia's sovereign city. And, I should add, the only city that the Kaspicians could not conquer all those years ago."

"Because it was so far away, hidden in the south. Northcresters fought hard for years, and that's where the final battle was won."

Sigun wore a smug grin. "Our records speak of many decisive battles and skirmishes in the south that were just as important to the war effort."

"Maybe, but in the end, your people rejected us. When the first king, a Northcrester, was crowned, the Siladrians fled, saying a northerner had no right to rule them."

"What right did he have to rule our people? There's no proof he ever even set foot in the south!"

"He ended the greatest threat to ever oppose us. He was wise enough to rule Gaminia *and* Siladria."

"Yet he wasn't wise enough to conquer *my* ancestors. When he sent his wearied troops to intimidate the ancient Siladrians, the remnants of his army were battered," Sigun crowed.

"I bet you take a lot of pride in that."

"About as much pride as you take in your wasp-witch."

Elfine was surprised to find herself laughing at his curtness. She stood up, and began to walk towards Lake Mesita; Sigun trailed closely, looking around constantly. He was uneasy in nature, but the lake seemed to captivate him for a moment, and he stopped to observe. Under the crepuscular glow, the surface of the water was haunting, and with little doubt, hid something unearthly.

"You won't last a day in the Myriad. I hope you know that," Elfine warned, standing by the water's edge. Above, she spotted a vibrant blue and orange kingfisher perched on the bough of a willow. The bird watched the water with its keen eyes, waiting to catch its dinner. As she studied its long bill and imagined it swallowing a fish in one, Elfine realised that she'd forgotten about Benthrin, the Menyr who she was to assassinate this evening with Lorcan.

"I can survive the Myriad. I'm tougher than I look."

"It's not about how tough you look," she replied, looking his weakling body up and down. "The Myriad is a closed circle. People, least of all 16-year-olds, don't just waltz on in. Aren't you at all suspicious as to why they've offered you a seat?"

"My parents say that I am the most gifted student the Republic has ever seen. I've passed all my exams in law, strategy, statecraft, diplomacy, finance — there's no aspect of politics that I haven't mastered. What's suspicious is that the Myriad didn't want me sooner!" He boasted, slapping his upper thighs.

"Oh, well if you've passed the teenager tests, you're obviously fit to advise the King."

"Such an astute, northern *lass*." He looked to her with that thin, small-toothed smile as if what he'd said was meant to sound sweet. But she knew he'd done it to wind her up. "Perhaps in a few hundred years, they'll even admit women to the Myriad."

"One can but hope," she said, drily.

He turned to face her sharply; something about his tight lips spoke of disquiet. Slowly, he reached to touch her arm, but as she instinctively recoiled, he pulled his hand away and placed it behind his back. "Is my touch so poisonous?" he said, then drooped his head. "There is something I want to share with you."

She looked at him wide-eyed, feigning interest.

Sigun gulped; his prominent Adam's apple stuck out as though it was a goose egg he'd swallowed, and not his fear. "You must repeat this to no one, but 250,000 taigs — that's official Siladrian coin — are missing from the Republic's coffers. That's enough—"

"For the army that your father promised King Thenris," interrupted Elfine.

"No — it's enough for three. And that's not the weirdest part. I haven't even seen this army."

Elfine took a step back and looked at the lake, an odd sense of dread slinking along her neck. Pivoting back to Sigun, she realised her face was tingling, as if Mukele had finally caught her with her stinger.

Inside the Great Hall was a hellish assault on Elfine's senses. The stenches of ale, roasted meats, and the sickly-sweet wine formed a particularly offensive aroma. The raucous shouting and singing were deafening too.

Over a hundred people were squeezed in, so there was barely room to manoeuvre. Many of the faces were strangers to Elfine, though she recognised the usual nobles and courtesans from her childhood, including that rotund girl, always in pink, who Aurelia despised. There were important members from entities like the Myriad and the Northcrest Institute, as well as Protectors and clerics from the Yotanite Church.

As Elfine and Sigun drew near to the high table, a trio of bards strummed on mandolins with enthusiasm and sang loudly. Elfine's ears naturally closed, forgetting that the words of the song were about her. She caught the last part of the song only:

With battle concluded and Gaminia restored,

Shall follow the birth of our spring,

White koondi, briarsbane and leaf of life abound,

And upon Mount Numanich do foretell,

Light's triumph over the Hateful Tsar.

It made her shiver that people were singing about the war, as though there was any joy to be derived from it. The people of Northcrest not only believed that this wedding was the first step in combatting the Kaspicians, but also that it meant that they would win the war. Elfine didn't share such optimism yet, and the zealous energy of the hall overwhelmed her; she managed to fake a smile as she took her seat. For the first time, she sat on the same side as the monarchs: next to Dame Leneare, then Mother, and then the Queen herself.

Sigun was glowing brighter than ever with all the attention. Father looked annoyed at having to shake Sigun's hand; the boy beamed back at him with a sycophantic smile that made Elfine shudder. The Chancellor said nothing, only continuing to eat his food with his mouth open, surrounded by pools of grease.

Only then did Elfine realise that Aurelia and Savas were absent. Her brother not being present came as little shock, but it was unusual for Aurelia to not honour a commitment, especially something as important as this.

"You missed the first course," said Mother, wiping the corner of her mouth with a serviette.

The Dame looked uncomfortable in the middle of the two. "I hear we've braised ox cheeks to come," she said. Elfine had forgotten the sound of Dame Leneare's voice. It conjured the image of a leaf falling onto the forest floor: a crisp, quiet rustle, almost inaudible amid the merriment.

"Don't people ever tire of eating? I ate more than the average hamlet does in a year this afternoon," Elfine said. She reached for a silver pitcher and poured herself a modest glass of ruby-red wine, downed it, then poured a second, larger glass.

Mother's nose twitched. "Ishanaia have mercy! I'd worry more about how much of that poison you imbibe. And with such liberty!"

Elfine smirked; she wondered if her lips and teeth were already slightly red. Father seemed to be entranced by whatever boorish drivel was spewing out of the Chancellor's mouth. The pair kept staring at one another with the oddest of expressions, then grimacing and shaking their heads as if propositions were constantly being rejected.

The long, craning neck of the Queen stuck out all of a sudden; her hair dangled over her plate, picking up bits of gravy. "Dear Elfine! You sit among ladies now and are encouraged to drink wine. With this marriage, your name will be recorded in history forever. Your mother and I are so very proud of you."

"It's an honour to marry Siladria's most gifted and wonderfully handsome gentleman," Elfine said, forcing a smile.

The Dame cocked her head to the side. "You two have such a long future together," she said.

The next course arrived, and whilst everyone seemed to resume enjoying their meal, Mother became agitated. She was constantly looking at the door, a slight frown having settled permanently on her face.

"Where are Savas and Aurelia?" she said.

"I always know where Sigun is," crowed the Dame, who then waved to her son. "Surely, Trinne, you have that special sense too. You can't lose a child."

Elfine ignored the Dame and spoke up before Mother might have said something pointed. "Would it calm you down if I went to look for them?"

"Yes, and I'll come with you," Mother replied. Not wasting a moment, she stood up. There was something frantic about the way she moved; she seemed desperate to get out of the Great Hall.

"Where are you going?" Father said, irritated.

"We'll be back shortly," replied Mother, who then bowed her head before the King and Queen.

Elfine followed suit, then, as politely as she could, went to Sigun and explained the situation before excusing herself.

"Are you sure you'll be back soon?" He whined.

"Yes. Father will keep you entertained. He's a wonderful conversationalist," she said with a grin. She didn't bother to check if Father had heard her comment, and made straight for the door. Mother set off in such a hurry it was hard to keep up with her.

*

The hanging torches along the corridor crackled like autumnal leaves underfoot. Elfine looked back constantly. Ever since her encounter near Numanich, newfound fears of the long hallways of her home corroded her confidence at night. She half-expected to find that same monster waiting behind every corner, ready to whack her in the belly again.

Mother's face had a look of urgency as she grabbed Elfine.

"Something is not right," Mother started, squeezing Elfine's hand tightly. Mother often over-thought things, so Elfine wasn't expecting anything important to come out of her mouth. "On my way to the Great Hall, I noticed an owl perched in one of the Queen's fig trees in the bailey. It screeched thrice; that means a close relative will die soon."

Elfine contemplated laughing, but chose not to, out of respect. "With any luck, it'll be my husband. Or yours."

"You mock the wisdom of our ancestors. Fool. That owl bore a message for me: either Savas or Aurelia is in danger."

"You don't really believe that, do you?"

"Through prayer, Ishanaia grants me wisdom. Your myopia astonishes me sometimes."

A loud commotion erupted from downstairs. Elfine rushed to check the corridor balcony. It was just a few of the wedding guests stumbling out of the hall, clearly drunk. One of them squealed as he tripped and fell into a bush.

"But how do you know the message was about Savas or Aurelia?" Elfine asked.

"Because only they are missing!" Mouther shouted, following her to the balcony. She pulled Elfine in closer. *"Where are they*? I won't waste any more time — we're checking Aurelia's room right away."

Once Mother reached the door, she knocked with vigour. But there was no answer.

"Aurelia, are you inside?" Elfine called. From within not a sound could be heard.

Elfine eased the door open.

They were relieved to notice Aurelia sleeping on the bed, but there was a mutual gasp of horror when they saw the shattered mirror. Elfine's first instinct was to get Mitenni so she could help Mother make one of her special tonics, but Mother stilled her with a stern look in her eyes.

Mother gestured to the shattered mirror. With Aurelia's desk lantern, she illuminated the peculiar scene. The light revealed the cracks in the grand mirror, as well as the hazardous shards all around it.

Aurelia stirred, then shot up, awake.

"Aurelia! Are you alright?" Mother cooed.

She grumbled faintly as she came back to life. "I don't know," she said.

"What happened?" Elfine asked.

"It's hard to remember," she replied, scratching her forehead.

"Be patient and let the memories flow back into you, child," Mother said.

With a furrowed brow, Aurelia said, "A monster was here. It attacked me."

Elfine was starting to get sick of hearing about monsters. "What are you talking about?"

"The Visitor saved me. The thing came here to murder me but she stopped him."

Mother's expression soured. "Ishanaia have mercy... a monster? And what Visitor?"

"Yes. A Menyr. That's what the Visitor calls them. She's some sort of ancestor of ours," explained Aurelia.

"What does this Visitor want from you?" Mother asked, shaking her head with despair.

"I think she wants me to find someone. Another spirit," said Aurelia.

Mother buried her face in her hands, overcome with some form of sadness, or fear.

Elfine took another glance at the shattered glass, hoping to find some new clue. She couldn't even begin to wonder what the connection was between her sister and the Menyr, indeed, she didn't dare discuss it. That would have to wait till she next saw Zatela — the only person who might be able to explain this.

"A Menyr came for you," Elfine said, worried. "This is grave. I shouldn't be telling you this, but I've been investigating these Menyr. They're connected to the Kaspicians somehow. They aren't human, Aurelia — you're lucky this spirit came and saved you, otherwise you'd be dead."

Her sister's eyes shrunk into a squint of quiet dread. "Then you should know, the spirit also spoke of the one who leads the Menyr. Princess Onaxia is her name. She is locked away somewhere, but that's about to change soon. The spell holding her is weakening."

"Ishanaia, we need you now more than ever," Mother prayed aloud. "Please, Supernal Goddess, widen our eyes so that they may see further, expand the reach of our souls so that we know your edifying wisdom, so that we may take it like the fruits of your Eternal Grove!"

Elfine shuddered hearing Mother's prayer. What good had that ever achieved? Things looked bleaker than ever, and prayer certainly wasn't going to change anything. "What are you going to do, Aurelia?"

"I don't know what else the Menyr are capable of, or this queen of theirs. But the Visitor seems to think that this lost spirit might know how to fight Onaxia," Aurelia said.

Mother scoffed. "You aren't seriously considering getting involved in this? Elfine is right, this Visitor of yours may have saved you this time, but what about the next? What if she cannot find you? I did not raise you to be so foolish as to throw your life away for somebody else's cause!"

"That's your reaction to this?" Aurelia retorted. "You of all people should know that life in Northcrest has never suited me. You made me enrol in the same school as that stuck-up troll Cornetta when you knew I didn't want to be anywhere near her! Dreams have always been my gift, but something is changing now, and I'm not going to ignore it. I want to run with it."

"If you'd have told me, we could have prayed about it and figured something out. What if this Visitor is some kind of demon?!" Mother shouted.

"Prayer is not the answer to everything! And she is not a demon, Mazin told me as much," Aurelia said, angrily.

Mother's jaw fell. "You went to that charlatan as well?"

"I'm sorry," Aurelia muttered. "I didn't know what else to do."

"If word got out in Sunhold about any of this you'd be ostracised!" Mother warned. "Mazin is not family. You should never have told him these secrets."

The atmosphere in the room was stifling all of a sudden, like the heat of the day had returned to exact its sweltering retribution. Elfine's skin tingled and became uncomfortable; she wanted to peel it off and bury herself in snow.

"Mazin has helped me more than you or Ishanaia ever has," Aurelia said.

"What help could one so low in Ishanaia's eyes render?" Mother went on.

"You're completely obsessed with Ishanaia! If it weren't for Mazin, I'd never have been able to travel into the spirit world or start on this journey at all."

"My god, your redemption is yet far away," Mother said, then leaned in closer. "This is not the right path." A frown emerged on her face, then ebbed shortly after. "Wise women who could pierce the veil with their dreams, Aurelia, were once Ishanaia's chosen. They were the leaders of our faith, but they did not achieve their power with trinkets and tricksters like Mazin. Our people had power because they loved and worshipped Ishanaia. You were connected to her long before this Visitor showed up."

"There's no end to your ability to find fault with good things, is there?"

"Yes, and that is the greatest gift Ishanaia gave to me — to sense things that do not come from her, and are therefore unholy," Mother countered. "If it is not by

Ishanaia's hand that this Visitor, or Mazin have touched your life then I don't want them around."

Elfine had endured similar sorts of arguments with Mother before. She was impossibly difficult to argue with because no one could bear her stubbornness long enough to try and convince her of their opinion. Everything to do with her faith or her goddess belonged to an untouchable realm of infallibility, where Mother's vision was constricted, like a frog stuck at the bottom of a well, only able to see the lone halo of light above.

"Not everything is about Ishanaia, Mother," Elfine said. "Aurelia isn't even a person of faith. None of us are really, except you."

"Oh! But she will be when Ishanaia comes, you all will be. And Ishanaia *is* coming for her people. This much has been revealed to me through dreams of my own," said Mother, passionately.

"Are you talking about the Yotanites? I thought you didn't even like them," Elfine said.

Mother laughed, mockingly. "Those faithless fools believe in nothing but taxes and saving their own skin. I'm talking about *us*. The real people Ishanaia chose. If you knew the things that the Supernal Goddess had revealed to me you would fall to your knees in reverence. My child — you have suffered in this city for your looks, deemed too dark, but did I not tell you that those who came from that distant continent and worshipped Ishanaia were black? There was never any Aseg or Zerkal either. The people of this land made them up to make their religion more pleasing, because Gaminians could never worship a woman for being anything more than the mother of a great man." She bent down, gingerly picked up a shard of glass from the mirror and glanced at it with a serious look about her. "When you look at your reflection, do you not see that part of us connected to those who came from where Ishanaia's feet treaded, and marked the ground for eternity?"

Aurelia was stunned. "I don't know why I didn't think of that myself. The Visitor is the darkest person I've ever seen. She's my ancestor."

Knitting her brow in deep thought, Mother paused. "Can it be? Ishanaia. Please, reveal the truth to your servant." She shut her eyes, nodding to herself and muttering quietly for a moment, before asking, "What else did this Visitor speak of?"

"A lot," Aurelia answered. "She spoke about her black ancestors' arrival in Gaminia, how they used their magic and their gifts, how they fought in wars. She said in the end they were rejected."

"Oh my… Ishanaia's words edify me always," Mother said. "I see clearer now. I am sorry for being suspicious. It was my first instinct as a mother to protect you. I have always known your dreams were a sign of something special. All the premonitions you had as a child, no matter how small they were, made me certain that you had a special bond with Ishanaia. Do you know why she has asked for your help in finding this spirit?"

"It's because of my powers. I did something bad earlier. To Cornetta. I made her vomit… and soil herself. By accident."

Elfine tittered in the back, then covered her mouth when she saw Mother's sudden grimace. "Was she wearing white?"

Aurelia pinched her lips together and nodded.

Mother moved to the window. She opened it and let some air in, which, along with Elfine's humour, calmed the atmosphere. With her fingers resting on the ledge, she stuck her head out for a moment, then quickly retracted it like a tortoise.

"In my dreams have seen a land where people like your Visitor live," she said. "They perform miracles with their magic, under a purple sky. My spirit tells me that they were Ishanaia's chosen, and perhaps they still are." Mother relaxed her tense shoulders. "I must tell you something. In the northernmost reaches of Lyrel, that spindly country above Cragmoor in the southwest, there is a place called Rivane. To reach it requires a treacherous journey through mountains and snow. When I turned 14, my parents became too ill to take care of me. The next thing I remember, they'd packed my stuff up and I was on my way to Rivane. Melindra didn't care, if anything, she was glad to see me gone. My mother's older sister — before she became Queen — reluctantly agreed to look after my parents, but not me. She said they already had enough maids in her King's Respite townhouse," Mother's lips twisted scornfully.

"Great-auntie Horse-face was always a bitch then," Elfine joked.

"Just because you're a married woman now, doesn't mean you can swear in front of your mother," Mother shook her head with disapproval. "A distant relative by the name of Ayrn lived in Rivane, and he had agreed to take me in. As I remember it, Ayrn's home was a sort of castle, built into the face of a mountain."

"A castle? All the way up in the mountains?" asked Aurelia.

"The location wasn't the oddest part: the settlement of Rivane proper lay below, but it was all abandoned. Ayrn was completely isolated in the freezing vastness of those mountains."

"I can only imagine what such a person was like," Aurelia said.

"Over the years I forgot his face gradually, but I'll always remember how fascinated he was with my dreams. I had to recite them to him so he could scribe them down in a tome. Time went by peculiarly in that castle, but one day, he said that he'd filled the whole tome with all of my dreams, and that every single one of them was precious. *Precious…*

"There must have been other things after that, but the only other thing I remember with any clarity is the day I left Rivane. On that day, Ayrn took me to the tome and showed me some of my dreams. I still remember his words clearly: first you will bear a son, he said, and his soul will have two aspects, but you will only know one. There will come a girl. She will carry a terrible burden; a sword strong enough to split Ysa in two will always be within her grasp. One more daughter will you have, he said, and to her, nothing will be unknown, for her eyes will see all things. Their father will be a powerful figure. When your blood rises to the throne, he will also ascend, but it will only be in his absence that you will know freedom."

Mother paused to wipe her nose and teary eyes, before continuing, "'I have seen great sadness too,' Ayrn said. 'The sickness of your parents cannot be cured, but know that Ishanaia's light surrounds you and she will take care of you.' Even though I'd been raised as a Yotanite, I'd never given Ishanaia much thought before that day. He left me with that prophecy and the knowledge that a goddess was on my side. I've revered Ishanaia every day since."

"Mother, I'm so sorry! Why did you keep this to yourself for so long?" Aurelia burst out.

"I didn't think you'd believe me," she replied.

"There has to be more," Elfine said. "Did your parents ever elaborate on their connection with Ayrn?" she asked.

"Prickly lung killed my parents shortly before I returned home; I never spoke with them about Ayrn."

"What about Melindra? Did you ever talk to her?" Aurelia asked.

"When I came back, she at least let me live with her. I wish there were other Tillensises, but ours has always been a small family. The year after I came home, it was announced that King Thenris had selected my aunt Melindra to be his new wife, in the wake of the sudden death of Thenris' wife Janira. After Melindra became Queen Consort, months, if not years passed where we didn't speak. It took several years for her to sell the family home in King's Respite and convince King Thenris to let me move into Sunhold," said Mother.

"Maybe the old hag has magical powers too," Elfine suggested.

Mother stewed, thoughts seeming to curl along her furrowed brow. "The fact that she was able to replace Queen Consort Janira — a descendant of one of the families who retook Northcrest from the Kaspicians after the First Great War, always astonished me. Our name certainly doesn't carry that sort of weight," she said.

"The Visitor has said nothing of Melindra and we've never been close to her. I wouldn't trust her with any of this," Aurelia said.

Mother concurred with a curt nod. "I didn't bring up my story now to overshadow you, but from what you have said of this Visitor, it sounds like she can be trusted. Now that you know what strange things have happened to me, I hope you will be able to better understand the nature of Ishanaia. But I don't want you fighting any battles, Aurelia. You're a dreamer, and a warrior in a spiritual sense, perhaps, but not of the flesh. If you are asked to pick up a sword and kill, I ask that you do not do so. There will always be others for that."

Elfine knew that Mother was talking about her with that last part. *Others.* That was what she was next to Aurelia. It didn't make her jealous of her sister. Elfine had her own path already, despite whatever this marriage might try to change. She didn't care that Aurelia was the favourite child, Mother's special one.

"We've been here far too long," Mother said. "Everyone will be wondering what's happened. Elfine, you should return to the Great Hall."

"Is someone expecting me there?" Elfine smirked.

"Go on now," Mother enjoined. "I will stay with Aurelia until she can get some rest."

"I'm sorry, Elfine. I feel awful, but I'm exhausted," Aurelia said. "I'll see you tomorrow."

The wedding had not turned out how Elfine had expected. The revelation that her younger sister had a numinous bond to an ancient deity was the only exciting thing to come of the day. It was hard not to think there was a connection between what she was doing with the Chicane and what Aurelia was now going through. The Menyr, Princess Onaxia, lost spirits — something was coming, and Elfine doubted that anyone in Northcrest, save for maybe Zatela, knew what it was.

She began to spiral down the stairs, but before she even reached the bottom, a terrible pain arrived.

Something had grabbed her by the throat. She couldn't breathe. Her tiara clattered as it met the floor.

An ambush.

Elfine's eyes roved desperately around in search of some sort of weapon, but she saw nothing. The predator had caught her in a dark, empty corner, and the ludicrous wedding attire, which she now hated more than ever, had slowed her down. She tried to scream for the Protectors, but she found she had no voice.

A thousand dreadful thoughts surfaced at the same time and Elfine couldn't separate a single one. Vague whispers, flashes and faces came and went.

The creature's claw of a hand was tightly clasped around her neck, and its other hand shoved a rank cloth in front of her mouth and nose. It felt like her lungs were being dragged through lava, singed and battered relentlessly.

In the next moment, it was all over. There was no sensation in her hands to raise a fist, nor could she even attempt a kick.

Before long, her vision ebbed into a thoughtless void.

Chapter 12

Your Power Runs Deeper than Dreams

Savas admired the way his people treated a celebration. Northcresters were well-known for their love of alcohol and food. They, just as Savas was, were pleasure-seekers, prone to hedonism. He claimed an odd pride as he observed his inebriated countryfolk in the packed Angel's Hovel, bantering, beaming and belching. Some were already spilling out onto the streets to sop up the alcohol in their bellies with a greasy snack; squirrel kebabs doused in a sticky blood sauce was the most popular dish.

In the tavern, the smell was unbearable, but Savas pretended not to be bothered by it. This was a proper man's watering hole, after all. He aimed to blend in, and given the recent addition at the table, he was concerned. Lei Jia, although male-identifying, gave off the same nonconforming energy that Temek had recognised in Savas. Maybe it was due to his years of service at the Temptress' Parlour, but Lei Jia's hair was slick and swept back in a fashion that no Northcrester would ascribe to; his round, khaki-coloured face was unblemished by facial hair or marks of any sort, and his shirt and trousers, both red, were tight.

"You really must be an atrocious sibling to desert your sister on her wedding day," said Lei Jia, his voice overriding the din.

"It's not even a real wedding — she hates her husband," Savas replied.

"How few 'real weddings' there must be then," said Lei Jia, smiling as he looked to Temek. "Temek has told me a lot about you."

"She's told me about you and your revolution too," said Savas, hoping to sound prepared, but all he received was a swift hush.

"Imbecile! Don't speak that word in public — we say the North Wind," he chastised Savas. Then, to Temek, "I thought you'd made the rules clear?"

"I did!" she retorted, then shrugged. "Look, I asked you here because we need a favour: there's something we need you to acquire." She hesitated for a moment and swirled her frothy ale around listlessly.

"My ears will close if you make me wait any longer. What is it you want?" asked Lei Jia.

The way he enunciated some of his syllables confused Savas, who couldn't tell if Lei Jia was annoyed or being sassy for the sake of it. "Enough poison to kill something that may or may not be human," he supplied.

Lei Jia emitted a short-lived chortle, then his expression became severe. "I require a few more details if you expect me to aid an assassination plot."

"The Wraith," answered Temek. "He — it... I don't know, he started showing up at the Parlour after you joined the North Wind. He wanted us to peddle this thing called Viska to certain 'special' clients. When I refused, he did something to me and then had his men beat me up. He thinks Savas and I are working for him, but we've been looking for a way to kill him."

One of Lei Jia's eyes began to twitch whilst he scratched his chin. "I have heard of this Viska very recently," he said. "It is connected to something that my people are afraid of. You're telling me that the person responsible for this Viska concoction came to the Parlour, and I never knew?"

"You left, remember?" Temek said. "The rest of the Parlour were completely taken in by the Wraith. Even if you saw anyone you knew, I doubt they'd have told you what happened."

Lei Jia shuddered and made a queasy face. "Is there anything else you can tell me?"

"I think he was looking for something underground, I just don't know what. Something connected to the Parlour maybe?"

"If I can get to the bottom of whatever is going on there, the leaders of the North Wind will be very impressed," said Lei Jia. "There's a deal we can come to here: I can get you what you need, but he has to join our movement as well. I'm not trusting something as important as this to an outsider, least of all some castle-dwelling nationalist."

"Me?" said Savas, pointing at himself in astonishment. "I never get picked for anything."

"Don't worry — you won't have to out yourself," Lei Jia quipped, fluttering his lashes. "Come to our next meeting and we'll make the arrangements there." He stood up, ready to leave. "And please, don't do anything outrageous before." After an affected smile, he made for the exit.

There was something about the way that Lei Jia drew in so many stares from the pub's patrons as he left that made Savas question what he was doing in this place. He knew who he was now; and he felt more like himself with Temek, and even with Lei Jia, than with the blokey sorts around him. But then he looked up and remembered.

The thing that had kept him infatuated with the Angel's Hovel for so long was at the bar. He'd been there for a while, but Savas had been too engrossed in Lei Jia to commit to his usually staring and daydreaming. The man looked impatient, as if he was waiting for something. He wasn't particularly striking to look at: average height, broad chest, dark, slightly messy hair, square jaw and thin lips, like a pink gash. The man was tapping his fingers impatiently on the counter. When the man finally caught Savas staring at him, he glared, then disappeared around a corner. That was about the same as all their other interactions. Savas hoped the man would come back around so he could catch another glimpse of him, but he didn't.

"Does he really want me in the North Wind?" said Savas, after a pause.

"This is clearly bigger than we thought if Lei Jia knows about Viska. But this is my way to make progress. I don't want to be a vee coin slave hunting squirrels for the rest of my life; together, we can do this."

"I worry that these revolutionaries won't want us around if they find out we're, you know, queer."

"Lei Jia seems to be doing just fine, and he's much gayer than either of us," Temek teased.

Savas let out a little laugh. "Was he born with that confidence?"

"You two have met before, or did you forget?"

It was loneliness that compelled Savas to go back to The Temptress' Parlour that day, around six months ago. Friendships rarely began in such a place, but it was there that Savas had first spoken with Temek. When she used to work there, she had her own room, far superior to the ramshackle box-room she had in Endvil now.

"You keep coming back here. Haven't you figured yourself out yet?" Temek had spoken lightly. She was different when she used to work in the whorehouse: sultry, red lingerie, the long hair, which she constantly had to have groomed and oiled and the sweet, floral scent she had to wear. Savas couldn't help but notice these things, but it was never out of a place of sexual desire; rather, he was envious.

"What's that supposed to mean? I like it here," he replied, fiddling with the silky sheets.

"But it's not a place you're supposed to *like*. You know I'm not here to just talk to people, right?"

His face went warm and prickly. "I know that! We're talking though — and I like that."

"Here, let me get you some water." She helped him sit properly and gave him a big swig of ice-cold water mixed with sugar and salt: her apotropaic potion for dispelling drunkenness.

"Alcohol helps me forget things," Savas said.

"One of my clients is a physician from Chapel Heights. He says alcohol wrecks our insides and we don't even feel it till it's too late." She spritzed a touch of perfume to her wrists.

"Is that a bow and arrow?" Savas pointed to the contraption, placed by the curtains.

"Oh — I've always had that. It's the only thing my father left before he went away."

"Where did he go?"

"I told you already. My parents left me for work. They went sailing on some expedition and never came back. Don't make that face; I'm not sad about it. They were awful parents anyway."

Savas scratched his eyebrow. "My parents have never been all that interested in my life. I still think it'd be weird if they weren't around."

"Who's this loquacious specimen?" came a voice by the door.

"Lei Jia!" Temek cried. "You can't just barge in whenever you like."

"I can hear your tedious drivel next door. You've a client waiting in the lobby. Has this chatterbox finished, or does he need my special touch?"

Late on Elfine's wedding night, the Angel's Hovel remained noisy and smelly.

"He has an unusual accent," Savas said.

"His parents were migrants from Yenhai, I think," Temek replied.

"Yenhai?"

"Somewhere south, very far south. I seem to remember him saying something about the Son of Heaven getting sick, his wife taking control of the empire and all sorts of problems following, like this rebellion started by a load of peasants with magical powers in their kicks and punches."

"Sounds like a place worth visiting," Savas laughed.

"Good luck getting there. Lei Jia said his parents took no fewer than six ships to get here."

"He's…"

"Beautiful? I know — but don't tell him that. He knows it. And he's way better looking than that Northcrester you're so obsessed with," said Temek.

"What Northcrester?" Savas cried.

"Oh, you know. Lorcan, or whatever his name is. If I hadn't slept with him at the Parlour before and told you about his, you know, you probably wouldn't have gotten so obsessed," Temek giggled.

"Am I that easy to read?"

"When one's as desperate as you are, everything is pretty obvious," she joked.

He frowned. "No man will ever love me, will they?"

She pouted, in thought. "You'll have to open up about who you are eventually, Savas. Have you thought about telling your sisters?"

He didn't expect his face to get so warm and prickly with nerves. "These things aren't really spoken about in my world. Gay people are scorned by Yotanites, and Mother believes every word of their scripture. I don't know how my sisters would react either. We've never spoken about love or anything like that before."

"Skrak. What on Ysa?" Temek cried, all of a sudden in a panic.

A bar fight was starting behind Savas. In mere moments, drinks were thrown onto the floor and hurled at other people, worsening the bready stench of lager that already filled the tavern. Someone flung a chair, sending a group tumbling back into the bar and knocking a row of frothy pints over. At least half the bar was involved now, with others making a desperate bid for the doorway. Drunken hooks and jabs were deployed like some sloppy boxing match for rookies. The noise elevated rapidly, reaching a cacophony of cussing and roaring, while folks egged on their brawling friends. This sort of scene was reasonably common at the Angel's Hovel, but it wasn't something Savas wanted to unwittingly get sucked into.

Better to run now, he thought.

Just then, a sudden grip took hold around his neck. Seconds later, he found himself on the floor, being dragged by his collar out of the bar. Savas squealed, shocked at the pain and confusion, but no one dared to help; most just stared for a moment, too absorbed in their own fighting. Some chanted drunken slurs of encouragement. Others were even laughing.

"Savas!" Temek cried, attempting to move through the path that Savas' aggressor had forged.

Thrown over his attacker's shoulders like a ragdoll, Savas saw Temek race after him into the streets outside, where she lashed out at the brute, screaming and kicking.

But her attempts were powerless. The man was a giant — a colossal creature that Savas remembered: one of the Wraith's bodyguards, the one with the ponytail.

Savas cried out as his captor leaped forwards and kicked Temek in the chest.

She collapsed, holding her ribs.

As much as Savas thrashed and wailed, there was nothing he could do.

*

Aurelia woke up around midnight to the sound of rain crashing into Sunhold. Outside her window, trees rustled vigorously. A horse-drawn carriage clattered through the soaked, cobbled paths. Although she wanted to return to Castrellus' Journal and reflect on the Visitor's message, the ceiling seemed to yawn at her as if opening a portal into an endless nightmare. A faint sickness wended through her stomach, and she knew she had to get out, despite the weather. But there was more: Savas was on her mind, and it was vague concern for him that then impelled her to depart Sunhold and wade into the soggy night. Fuzzy as her thoughts were, she bobbed like flotsam downstream, meandering through the wet city, and after a short while, she came to a halt.

The Angel's Hovel.

Inside, it was quiet, though an odious stink travelled along the air. Where was Savas? She caught the bartender watching her. An odd hunger dominated his expression, as though he craved some hidden delight she didn't realise she possessed. He was a stout, bearded man, nearly a full head taller than her. He busied himself drying glasses with fat, sausage-like fingers.

Aurelia approached him, with as much confidence as she could muster. "Good evening. I don't suppose you'd know if a man named Savas had been here tonight? He's a regular."

The bartender continued drying with his dirty dishcloth, before languidly turning to face her. "Savas? Posh li'l whelp from Sunhold?" He grunted, with an urban twang. "Seen him, yeah. Who's askin'?"

She bristled. "His sister."

The man's face scrunched up till his expression was unreadable.

Aurelia caught sight of several other patrons staring at her, all cheerless and deadpan.

He turned his back to put away some of the glasses. "My info ain't free. Best pay up now if you wanna find him, little girl."

There was a snigger from one of the nearby tables.

Aurelia went into her pocket and realised she didn't have any aurums. "I'm sorry, I've no money."

He frowned, revealing decades of thick, sweat laden wrinkles along his forehead. Slowly, he lowered his hand down to his crotch and he groped his manhood like a beast in heat. "Poofter got what were comin' to 'im if you ask me!"

Aurelia ran to the door, humiliated and confused. More than ever, she wanted to locate her brother and make sure he was OK. Even though the rain had intensified, she could hear a commotion in the distance. Concentrating hard, Aurelia managed to cut through the watery noise. After a few steps in the right direction, the plaintive cries of her brother were unmistakable.

She set off at a dash, a map forming in her mind to guide her to the source of the trouble. Soaked now, she splashed through puddle after puddle, knowing that she was drawing nearer to Savas. Her instincts led her to an alley, where she peered from behind the wall and saw two large figures, standing menacingly over Savas. Her brother was curled up into a ball on the ground with his hands shielding his face. A new height of anxiety set Aurelia's heart to explode as she helplessly observed, racked by dread.

"You better still be awake princeling — wouldn't want you passing out and missing the pain," said one of the giant brutes.

Aurelia looked on in horror as the man kicked Savas' wilted body.

"That bald freak is gonna get it even worse when we find her!" the other man threatened.

"He is weak now. Enough that I might enter his thoughts, and take the thing that I want," said a slow, calculating voice. It was a wretched and gangly looking thing that then crept into view. Aurelia shook with fear as she saw it hovering ominously close to her brother.

"Again," hissed the gangly thing.

The two men delivered another round of kicks and Savas gurgled and whined in agony, spitting blood onto the cobbles. One of the men unsheathed a hefty-looking machete and the second man took out a large baton.

"Do you think he's enjoying it?" said the one with the baton. He put it between his legs and stroked the weapon up and down, laughing wildly.

"No," said the creature. "This boy is devoid of any joy. I see his thoughts clearly, like the sad love letters of a desperate child. But Winnik was wrong. This boy is not the one. He knows nothing of our plans, and he will open nothing. If those *things* are communicating with one of them, it is not this boy."

"What do we do?" asked the one with the machete.

"Break him, but return him to me, alive," the creature ordered.

The brute with the machete closed in on Savas. Time was running out. Flustered, Aurelia had barely noticed the ghostly woman reflected in a large puddle of water by her feet.

"Your power runs deeper than dreams, girl," said the familiar reflection. "Are you going to use it, or watch your brother die?"

Aurelia's eyes whipped between Savas and the Visitor, whose words commanded Aurelia into action.

"Stop! Don't touch him you snakes!" Aurelia screamed, rushing to Savas' side.

"What on Ysa?" growled the one with the machete.

"Who's this harlot?" yelled the other.

"Au-Aurelia...?" Savas' voice was weak, and the sight of his bloodied face did not make Aurelia weep, but gush with vengeance.

The two attackers looked to their leader for direction, hesitant to attack now.

"The little witch escaped," murmured the creature, who then took a few steps back.

The two brutes grunted at each other like hogs. Their thirst for bloodshed mounted; she sensed that they had tasted blood before, and longed for it now. There was something monstrous about the way their vast chests rose and fell. As if totally fearless of the law, these men acted without compunction. Were they Menyr?

While Aurelia cradled Savas in her arms and washed the blood off his face with rainwater, a potent current began to seep into the air around them. She could sense the enormity of the Visitor's power in each droplet of rain that met her flesh. At that convergence of water and skin, something immaterial rocked Aurelia's body, imbuing her with magical power. It swelled rapidly. The wind joined in: a timely breeze came, carrying incantations of great force into the atmosphere. Before long, it was as though the might of a tsunami had strengthened Aurelia's power.

When the hulking frame with the machete edged closer, there wasn't a whisper of fear inside her.

"What are you anyway, some sort of half-cast hodgepodge?" He spat a yellow gob at the ground by her feet. The devouring hunger in his eyes could not make a dent in her resolve.

A frothing white torrent formed a flashing image in Aurelia's mind, and she reached out towards it with her spirit, colliding with its magnitude. The Visitor's voice reverberated around her skull, whispering arcane words of empowerment, and in a strange moment, a tune whistled faintly about her: the sound of her ancestors' magic.

The brute swung the machete around, about to slice open Aurelia's face, when all of a sudden it was stopped in mid-air. His face was petrified with confusion, like a hideous mascaron. Vapours hovered around his body. She felt it: the slowing down of his bloodstream, and the cold laying waste to his insides. His mad killer's delight dropped, supplanted with the terrified look of a lost child. Soon, his flesh was pink and blue in places it should not have been. Death called to him, and Aurelia beckoned it closer; the power within her was far from exhausted. Globules of rainwater amalgamated into a writhing mass, which snaked from his feet up to his neck. Like boundless pythons, the soaking vines constricted his every body part. His eyes bulged as the grip tightened around his veiny neck, and from out of his mouth, his last words wheezed forth.

"*Oja-...*"

Distancing itself from the action, the gnarly creature stepped back, then squealed with something that was either glee or fear, because the watery monstrosity Aurelia had commanded now sought new blood. As she directed it towards the other of Savas' aggressors, he dropped his baton in a panic, whimpering.

"Skrak!" swore the man. He lunged forwards trying to reclaim his weapon but gave up when Aurelia's spell lashed out at him like a cobra. A call to action came from the dishevelled leader in the back, but it was too late. Mesmerised by the choking ropes of water, and overcome with fear, the baton-wielder missed his chance.

Whoosh.

A single arrow struck him, launched from the shadows. It made a subtle, rending sound as it pierced his thick body, causing him to lurch forwards and fall. Blood splattered the streets, but was quickly washed away.

With her concentration broken, whatever magic Aurelia had summoned subsided. But it was of no consequence. The machete-wielding brute collapsed, near frozen solid. He might have been dead. She didn't care. When she looked up, she saw the scrawny creature speeding off into the night, followed by the wounded marauder, an arrow embedded in his side.

A sharp pain rushed through her head. All of a sudden, fatigue overtook her, but she remained determined. "Savas! How badly are you hurt?" She asked, forgetting the mystery archer.

"I'll be fine," he mumbled. "What just happened?"

From afar, the archer stepped forward. The person's small body moved quietly through the downpour and the darkness till they were beside the two siblings. In their hand was a small, poorly fashioned hunting bow.

After removing a thick, black hood, Aurelia recognised Temek.

Temek knelt down by Savas' side and inspected his face. "Are you OK?" she asked.

"Let's just get out of the rain," he cried.

Together, Aurelia and Temek moved Savas under a nearby shelter. Aurelia watched Temek closely; she remembered their brief encounter. Could she trust her, even after she helped save her brother?

"What about you? Are you OK?" Temek asked Aurelia.

"I'll deal with myself later. I feel fine." She lied; her head pained her greatly. "Will you help me get him back to Sunhold?"

*

The streets were devoid of life. They made for the quieter back entrance. Circumspectly, they proceeded to Savas' chambers.

They sat him on his bed and gathered a sponge and some water to clean his wounds. He was badly bruised and had a serious cut on the face, which Aurelia had to wipe several times before it stopped bleeding.

Temek helped Aurelia and Savas out of their drenched cloaks before removing her own, then hung them by the door. After rummaging through several drawers, she unearthed a few warm blankets for Aurelia and Savas, and as there were only two, she chose to go without. Instead, she lit the fireplace then pulled up a chair next to it for warmth. The splashing flames brought immense comfort after a night in the wet dark.

"Thank you," Aurelia said. "Just wait here a moment, I have healing supplies in my room." A moment later, she returned with a restorative concoction that was intensely herbal-smelling. Although she didn't have the exact recipe for whatever Kistig used on Temek's arms, she'd experimented before and made something similar. She gave the paste a final grinding with her pestle and mortar before it was ready.

"I'm so sorry Savas. This is all my fault," Temek sighed.

"I didn't have to pick this battle. I got involved because I wanted to," Savas replied, with a weak smile.

"You could've died because of me!"

"Who cares? Tonight, we won."

Temek looked to Aurelia. "Thanks to your sister."

"And that arrow," said Aurelia. "I'm guessing your arms have healed?" she asked Temek, then prepared to administer the medicine to Savas.

Temek's gaze shifted slowly towards Aurelia. "Yeah," she said, surprised herself. "Whatever you gave me last time worked quickly." To Savas, she said, "If she's your doctor, you've nothing to worry about."

Regarding the sea-green paste, Savas' nose twitched. "The more it smells like cat poo the better, isn't that what they say?"

Aurelia smiled thinly. "Stay still, it'll sting." She scooped out a dollop of the viscous paste onto her fingers and massaged it into the cuts on his face, as well as ones on his arms and stomach. He winced a few times in pain but didn't make too much noise. The paste absorbed into the skin with little effort, till only a fine layer remained visible on the surface.

"You should feel a lot better in the morning," Aurelia said. She wiped her hand on a cloth and sat beside Savas. "Which of you is going to explain what happened tonight?"

"Judging by the way things went down, I was wondering if you'd be the one with the answers," Temek said.

Aurelia arched an eyebrow.

"Scumbags got what was coming to them." Savas attempted a laugh, but what came out was more of a pipe-addict's wheeze.

Aurelia shook her head, then looked to Temek by the fireplace. "I'm as confused as you are. What do you two know?"

"Those men…" Temek began, "That *thing* you saw behind them is their leader. We know him as the Wraith. He sells something called Viska. He's a drug dealer, and only the Three might know what else. Your brother and I got caught up badly with them. I'm sorry that this ended up involving you. You should know, that Kistig from the clinic, he is one of the Wraith's clients."

"Kistig?" Aurelia said, shocked. "He's my supervisor. What could he want with some bizarre drug?"

"I don't know," Temek replied. "But I'd avoid him if I were you."

Aurelia could not believe that the Savas she knew was involved in something as deep as this, but somehow, it reassured her that she wasn't the only one being drawn closer to the jaws of peril and uncertainty. "After the wedding, something attacked me in my room," Aurelia stammered.

"Are you serious?" Savas cried. "Have you told anyone?"

Aurelia nodded, solemn. "Just Mother and Elfine. Both of us nearly died tonight. Does someone want all of us dead?"

"You just did something I didn't even know was possible. That could make you a target, but me? I can't do anything," said Savas.

"They didn't take Temek, Savas. You were the one they wanted," Aurelia pointed out.

"But why? I don't understand," he said. "At least Elfine will be fine. She's tougher than either of us."

"Right," said Aurelia. "I suppose we can't take any of this to the Protectors?"

"General Tonsag and his oafs aren't good for much," Temek said. "Anyway, you'll be safe up here in this castle of yours."

"You're welcome to stay a while," Aurelia offered.

Temek chuckled to herself. "That's kind, but I have some friends who should be able to look out for me," she said, smiling at Savas. "It's really late — I should probably get going."

"Are you certain?" Savas asked. "I'm sure there's a spare bedroom in this castle somewhere." He eased himself onto his back and made a silly face at her.

"Don't worry about me. Take care of yourselves, and Savas, I'll see you soon, yeah?" She bid them goodnight and left.

Aurelia shuffled closer to her brother and lay flat next to him. The two stared at the dull ceiling in silence. "Are you in love with her?" she said.

"We're good friends, that's all."

Aurelia thought of the bartender, who had called Savas queer. She'd never heard the word before, but had guessed the implication. "She's quite manly. Is that why you get on so well?"

"What do you mean she's manly?" Savas countered. "We just understand each other."

"OK." She sighed. "You should be alright for tonight, but I'll need to make a fresh paste in the morning. Before I go, I need to properly explain what happened earlier. There's some stuff about Mother too. I didn't want to say everything in front of Temek, but it's important, so please listen."

Aurelia recapped her mother's story and what had happened earlier today in her room. Soon after, Savas slept, exhausted from the night's trauma. She gave the room a cursory glance before returning to her own chamber, where she slept fitfully.

Each time she forced her eyes shut, they opened again. Eventually, she gave up, compelled to study Castrellus' Journal at her desk. She flicked through the pages with greater zeal and hunger than ever, tracing the magnitude of the ancient history contained within and hoping to find some clues about the magical powers burgeoning inside her.

After tonight, she wanted nothing more than to be with the Visitor; she wanted to talk to her, question her and learn from her. A second thank you was also in order — Aurelia knew that they'd only survived because the Visitor had been watching over her.

Having grown up in a world where she didn't always feel she belonged, the mystical pull of this being, who no one else could lay claim to, was the greatest reinforcement of her identity she had known. Aurelia was finally beginning to see herself in the likeness of this black woman — this Visitor.

And she loved it.

Chapter 13
A Dark Gambit

Sigun squirmed with a pounding headache in bed. The dawn rolled in and an auroral glow crept through the cracks between the curtains, exposing the listless dust that hovered in the room. He swivelled to face the wardrobe, away from the light. Hoping to relieve some of the pain of his headache, he moved his hand to cover his forehead and applied pressure, though it was to little avail.

An excess of wine, spirits, beers and fatty foods surged through his body — all part of a necessary performance. To lose face before his new peers would have been shameful, so he had obliged every offer to drink, or eat, all night. Now he paid the price. The hazy hangover made it difficult to recall the wedding at all, though if his father were to be believed, the event was only of peripheral importance, and his wife was equally irrelevant.

Yet Elfine was rather pretty. She didn't look too much like the noblewomen of the Republic: her nose, ears and lips were delicate, her skin smooth like silk. Her looks were just one thing that had captivated Sigun. Elfine was also sharp, incisive. Sigun didn't realise how attractive a smart woman could be until he'd met her. Indeed, he'd been taught that intelligence was not to be desired among women.

A moment went by, and the feeling of spinning began to wane, allowing him to recall the ceremony. The horse-drawn carriage through town, the priests at the altar, the mountains of food and oceans of drink, his walk with Elfine through the Esterwood. And then... nothing. His memories of Elfine ceased in the Great Hall, where he recalled her departing with her mother, and never coming back.

"Women and their late-night ablutions," he said aloud. "Elfine. Are you well?" Reaching out with his hand to the other side of the bed, hoping to meet her in a post-marital embrace.

Empty.

In seconds, he had leapt to the curtains, opened them and laid the entirety of the room bare in the light of dawn.

"Elfine? Are you hiding somewhere? You better not be playing one of your silly tricks on me!" Flustered, he turned the room upside down, searching for her in all places, but she was nowhere to be found.

So many questions flooded Sigun's thoughts: had they consummated their marriage? At what point had she vanished? Had she even slept here at all? He tried to force some deep breaths, desperate to convince himself nothing that serious had happened. Surely, they had had sex. The servants had left several buckets of water for bathing, and he decided to have a wash to calm himself down. He filled the wooden tub with the cool water, and after submerging himself, it pleased him to imagine all the excesses of last night being washed away. And yet, that patter of anxiety remained. Elfine was a diplomat, a respectable woman; what could steal her away from him, on this most important of mornings?

He decided he would set to finding her, if only to scold her for such wilful behaviour. After drying off, he put on an extravagant, orange robe and marched into the corridor.

"I grow weary of these games Elfine!" he shouted aloud, not caring that he was disturbing the rest of Sunhold. Sigun continued in much the same manner, stomping and screaming like a disgruntled child.

"Stop right there you! Yes, you there!" he barked at a maid. "Surely you — or one of your 'class' has seen Lady Elfine?"

"Sorry, milord. I haven't," she murmured, head hanging down.

The interactions that followed were all equally fruitless. Nobody confessed to having seen Elfine all day, or knowing where she went after she left Great Hall. How useless were all these servants! After some time, Sigun happened upon a cook, who directed him to Protector General Tonsag, a man who had been present at the wedding. Conveniently, General Tonsag also resided on Sunhold's grounds. Sigun and the General had not been introduced yesterday, but his father had painted a clear picture of General Tonsag — the son of King Thenris' eccentric younger sister, a princess, who lived in Gladehill, southeast of Northcrest.

Sigun strode towards Tonsag's quarters, expecting the matter of Elfine's absence to be resolved in moments. The corridors were unnervingly quiet, as though they had witnessed an unspeakable sin.

"Protector General? Are you awake? I require your assistance at once! It's of the utmost importance!" He knocked furiously at the door. There was a slight stir from within. Sigun impatiently thudded the door again.

"Quit knocking, I'm coming! Who the hell is it anyway?" bellowed the General.

Sigun pursed his lips together and pointed his chin high. "*Lord Sigun*!"

The portly Tonsag burst through the door. Black smudges under his eyes made the tiredness of his face dramatic and upon his forehead, undulated row after row of wrinkles.

His large, mannish features caused Sigun's lip to quiver into a slight sneer. "You must help me right away!" he screeched. "Elfine is nowhere to be found!"

The General's nostrils flared with indignance and a flash of panic sent his face corpse-grey. If he wasn't fully awake before, he was now. "A Siladrian marries Northcrester nobility and can't find her the next day," Tonsag mused. "I hope for your sake that this turns out to be a simple misunderstanding."

Watching General Tonsag, who looked to be considering all sorts of macabre possibilities, Sigun's distress started to spiral. "Surely, she's just hiding somewhere in Sunhold. Elfine likes to play tricks and make jokes."

"Give me a moment." The General slammed the door in Sigun's face, then re-emerged in his costume. It was only slightly superior to what the average Protector wore: a combination of leather and steel, adorned with black and green markings. Sigun found it hideous, though he chose to keep his opinion to himself at this time.

"Well, what should I do now?" Sigun's voice cracked under the heat of Tonsag's pitiless gaze.

"I don't expect you'll be of any use in this matter." Tonsag rearranged his breastplate and started to walk away from Sigun. "Go and see your parents. It was your father who put you to bed last night; he might be able to help piece things together."

Sigun marched off in a huff, just about remembering where his parents had been put up for the duration of their stay.

"Father, mother? Sorry to wake you," he called, outside their door. There was a sudden rustle and crackle of paper racing through the air, then a frantic dash. A familiar face appeared in the crack of the door.

"Are you alone?!" His father shrieked, sounding hoarse. "Get in quickly, you stupid boy!"

Sigun glanced back along the corridor, which appeared empty, then inched his way through the door. His father's anxiety was palpable. As soon as Sigun stepped foot in the room, he felt uneasy. Articles of clothing were randomly strewn about the room that looked to have been forgotten in a hurry. The remnants of a broken ceramic jug near the window had left a cloying aroma in the room. Only a thimble of light permeated the slant between the curtains.

Chancellor Rorstein was famous among Siladrian nobility for his ice-cold disposition: the unflinching leader of the Republic who never panicked and whose hatred of King Thenris was legendary. Whoever stood before Sigun now was not that man. Not a trace of his father appeared to be present. A quick glance around the room, and Sigun was doubly concerned when he saw a packed knapsack by the table.

"Where is mother?" asked Sigun.

An irate vein bulged on his father's forehead. "Your mother's waiting in the carriage — we're going back to Dinaea."

"You're leaving? Father, Elfine is missing!"

"The Kaspicians will breach Northcrest soon, we must protect ourselves first and foremost! Forget the stupid girl!" He raced around the room packing various items into the knapsack.

Sigun's head started to spin all over again, but it wasn't because of a hangover this time. Something toxic wended around his stomach till he was almost ready to vomit. "This is about that awful Benthrin isn't it!" screeched Sigun. "I told you I didn't want him at my wedding."

"He got what he came for, and so have we. Now it's time to leave," retorted his father.

"I can't just go back to Dinaea. My life is going to be here with Elfine, working for the Myriad," Sigun carried on.

Chancellor Rorstein slowly turned his head to face Sigun and then marched right up to him and slapped him in the face with such force that the boy crashed to the floor. Before he had time to think, he was then lifted up by the collar and shoved into the door. Sigun's throat welled up with fear as rivulets of tears trickled down his hot, smarting cheeks. A final, callous glance was all his father gave him, seeming to decide he was not worth the effort.

"Imbecile. You're not coming." Rorstein released Sigun from his grasp. "Benthrin wanted you here, and I happily obliged. Your mother will be upset when she realises you aren't coming, but she'll get over it quickly — she is pregnant with one who will exceed you in every way."

Sigun couldn't breathe. His whole body was caving in on itself. All he wanted was to scream that he hated his father, but instead, the only thought that surfaced was the overpowering, paramount feeling of disgust he attached to himself. He hated himself more than anything in that moment, and his face crumpled with self-loathing.

"Mother is pregnant? But I th—"

"Thought what, fool?" Sigun's father filled his lungs with pride. "The witch cured her. We don't need you anymore."

Sigun crumpled, like a fallen, dead leaf, trodden on till his resolve was all but crushed. "Then leave me. I will find Elfine on my own."

"They're coming for you, boy. Those bloodsuckers. You won't last a week." Rorstein rushed out of the room and swung the door shut behind him.

Helpless on the ground, Sigun curled up into a ball on the floor and bawled, praying the gods would show mercy. But he had never called on them before. He knew they would not answer, and indeed, they did not.

*

Physical and mental exhaustion ate away at Elfine, tearing away chunks of her vitality like carrion. She was stuck in a nightmare. Her head lolled from side to side and her eyes twitched as she attempted to wake herself.

When she came to, she felt the pain of the rope bindings, tightly wrapped around her wrists and ankles. For a moment, she longed to pass out again, if only to quell the hurt.

With her eyes finally open, she saw that the room was dimly lit by two lanterns. The space was large, but there were no windows. Elfine deduced that she was in a cellar of sorts. The walls and tables were barren save for a few typical instruments. There were no obvious signs that a kidnapper lived here: no torture instruments, mounted heads or suspicious red-brown stains, like those in the Chicane meeting house.

Then, she heard light footsteps, coming from upstairs. There was a measured quietness as they met the floor, only producing the faintest of shuffles, as if attached to the legs of a stalking arachnid. Desperate, Elfine glanced all around in search of some means of freeing herself but saw nothing. Her captor approached from the end of the room. Veiled under a black hooded robe, only the pallid, gaunt flesh of the lower half of his face was visible.

"Who are you?" Elfine rasped, her throat dry as a heel of bread.

Silence.

Beside her was a table, upon which were several vials of a dark red liquid. The man gave one of the vials a quick inspection, then began to daub some of its contents onto a ragged cloth. It took on the deep, blood-like hue almost instantly, and filled the room with a disarming scent. Her next dose of poison.

"Answer me!" she spoke as loud as she could, but it was no shout.

With a precise, chilling motion, his neck swivelled in her direction. His grey, vacant irises suddenly peered down at her: undoubtedly.

"*Tihota*," he hissed, then fixed his hood.

Tihota? The word sounded Kaspician. Before venturing to the Numanich Mountains with Lorcan, Elfine had familiarised herself with the language a little. "You're Kaspician, aren't you?" she shrieked.

"*Prata* — yes."

"Where are you taking me?" She tried to fight and shake herself free but it was futile; the strength she relied on in combat had been sapped.

"To your executioner," he said, coolly.

"I will gut you like a swine when I'm free." She struggled forcefully in the chair, causing it to wobble from side to side. "Let me go! Let me go!"

For all her courage, the unfeeling monstrosity before her did not react. Out from his mouth seeped an incantation that inveigled her to sleep. As he spoke, the room seemed to tremble with the force that rose out of him and Elfine's energy plummeted further. The pain of the poison, which she'd hoped had been consigned to memory, returned with renewed vitriol as the contaminated cloth touched her lips. It summoned the pain of a thousand stings and bites, as though her body was drowning in a noxious sea of acid. She thrashed briefly as it took hold.

Sweat beaded on her forehead; her spit pooled at the corners of her mouth, then dribbled down her chin. Elfine descended into a realm of agonising nightmares once more, stifled by whatever dark curse had been exacted upon her by this man. Right before her mind lapsed into oblivion, she heard him conversing with himself, then disappear at the top of the stairs, like a long-limbed spider, returning to its web to sleep.

Chapter 14

No Time to Recover

Aurelia meditated, only half-asleep. Her thoughts churned with concerns and possibilities. After what she had done last night, the full-body transformation was undeniable now, as was the Visitor's warning. The task before her felt terribly urgent. War with the Kaspicians, the thing that terrified Northcrest's leaders, was the least of her concerns. She had to be on the lookout for enemies, find Castrellus' spirit, and do whatever was necessary to thwart this mysterious Princess Onaxia.

And there was also the matter of her supervisor, Kistig. She'd not seen him since their last practical together; another was scheduled in a few days' time. After what Temek had said, she was suspicious. Who was he really? She knew nothing about him, only that he was a recent addition to the Myriad, and had taught at the Academy for only a handful of years.

"Healer Kistig was most delighted to have you as one of his students — his first female pupil!" Mother had once said, when Aurelia found out she'd been admitted to the Academy. Now, those words made her lip curl with distrust.

A commotion about Sunhold truncated her meditations. Curious, she directed her consciousness to waft into the corridors, like a scent carried upon a breeze. There was great fear in those panicked voices and those footsteps, urgently swallowing up the steps in the corridors. Some new horror was brewing. In truth, she could hardly face getting up. Last night's awesome feat had exhausted her and borne a dreamless sleep, but the noises grew louder. She forced herself awake by wriggling her fingers and toes, thereupon finding the means to disembark the dream plane and re-enter the waking world. She got dressed and straightaway set to making Savas' medicine before investigating the situation outside.

On her way to Savas' room, a cursory look from the ledge of the corridor revealed servants and Protectors moving frantically below in the bailey. Although Aurelia was concerned, her duty to Savas took precedence this time, and she knocked for him. He did not answer. A moment passed, and she entered uninvited. He was still asleep, faintly illuminated by the sunlight seeping through the window. Garrulously snoring with his limbs akimbo, he looked a right state. With her little stone mortar, Aurelia ferried the fresh paste to his side and proceeded to reapply a new dose. It absorbed into the wounds, which already had started to heal.

After making a slight noise, he stirred, then opened his eyes.

"Good sleep?" Aurelia asked, grinning.

"The best," he groaned, sitting upright.

"It's midday," Aurelia chuckled. "Anyway, you seem to have healed nicely." She stood up and paced towards the curtains, then flung them open in one quick movement.

Savas gasped, covering his eyes all the while. "I *was* healing nicely."

Aurelia rolled her eyes. "There's a real racket around Sunhold today."

"Doubt it's anything important. Are you OK, after last night?" he asked.

A hefty march like charging cattle came down the corridor, followed by a sudden rapping on the door. "Lord Savas, it is urgent." The voice of a Protector said. "Please, may I enter?"

"What is it?" Aurelia called back, moving closer to the door.

Savas looked at her, irritated.

"Lady Aurelia!" The Protector sounded relieved. "Please, you must let me in at once. It's a matter of urgency," he said.

Aurelia was startled. "Please, enter," she said.

The burly fellow blustered in like a tornado of pure steel. His big eyes stared dramatically at Aurelia and Savas. "Thank the Three you two are together. I'm looking for Lady Elfine. Please, tell me that you know where she is."

"No, but we haven't been awake long," replied Aurelia. She folded her arms. "What's going on?"

"It's too early to say anything for certain," continued the Protector. "But Lady Elfine was reported missing at first light this morning by her husband. General Tonsag has convened an emergency meeting of the Myriad and your father has summoned you to the Great Hall."

A sinking feeling thrust Aurelia through the floor. "Missing? What do you mean *missing*?"

"I'm afraid we've no answers yet," said the Protector. "Please, head for the Great Hall at once. Thank you." He hastily bowed, then blustered back out of the room, clanking off into the distance.

"Could you blame her from running away from her snob of a husband?" Savas joked.

But Aurelia did not laugh; she was worried all of a sudden. "Zerkal's moon Savas! Both of us were nearly murdered last night. I can't believe we didn't think to check if Elfine was alright."

His smile dropped. "Skrak. I mean, we did think of her, but surely she's fine?"

"I don't know. We should join the others at once." Aurelia made for the door and waited impatiently for

Savas to get up. He slowly got out of bed and dressed himself, but he delayed in front of the mirror.

"You don't think any of them will question my wounded face, do you?" Savas looked nervously at himself in the mirror.

"Just say you tripped, if anyone even asks. Hurry up!"

The corridor to the Great Hall was eerily quiet: the portraits on the high-reaching walls seemed to watch the two siblings with a peculiar interest. Aurelia's thoughts did not detour from Elfine once. Even though her sister kept her role in the Chicane mostly secret, Aurelia struggled to believe that her sister could be overwhelmed by anyone. Weren't the Chicane lethal warriors? And Elfine was not one to give up prematurely on anything: the fierce Elfine she knew would not turn away from this marriage and flee, no matter how much she despised it. With every conclusion Aurelia drew, she was invariably led to believing that some insidious force was at work. Someone had attempted to murder her in her own room last night, and Savas had been abducted in a tavern of all places. They had survived. Perhaps Elfine had not been so lucky.

"Remember we have to sit as far away from the King and Queen as possible: we don't have any rank compared to the Myriad, Protectors and the like," Aurelia reminded her brother.

Savas nodded. "Thanks for the reminder."

Two sentries outside opened the door to let them in. Hastily, Aurelia and Savas made for the high table, where the 20 or so members of the Myriad, as well as Mother, had already convened. To show deference, Aurelia and Savas sat far to the left of the King and Queen, who were seated in the centre of the high table. Many of the Myriad were strangers to the siblings, though there were several they recognised. Prince Zander was here, along with

Protector General Tonsag, who looked agitated as he patrolled up and down the sides of the table. Seated close to the monarchs was another familiar face, that of Master Ingrith, the head of the Northcrest Institute.

Situated at a different camp of authority was High Priest Resus, the worryingly overweight, bearded leader of the Yotanite Church. Despite his decrepit appearance, he had considerable clout among the Myriad. Mother was a frequent detractor of the High Priest. In her eyes, he was a sanctimonious con-man, whose only benedictions lay in money-making and misogyny. And they weren't the only ones Aurelia recognised. The contemptuous glare hailing from the other side of the table belonged to her supervisor, Kistig.

"Truly dreadful news brings us together this morning. My dears — our sweet Elfine has been reported missing," said the Queen, addressing Aurelia and Savas. A few indolent sighs sounded from around the table, then the room fell silent.

The General approached Aurelia and Savas; he lumbered like a pig with a sword, all red and sweaty. "I have assembled teams throughout each district of Northcrest to search for Elfine," he said, confidently. "And I will personally be leading the investigation into her disappearance. So far, our only clue is that you and your mother were the last to see her."

"Until Elfine is found, we require the input of all who may be of use," said the Queen. "You and your brother are invited to speak here on this occasion."

As the many unfamiliar gazes turned to Aurelia, she feared that the next thing she said would be some unintelligible, anxious babble. She took a deep breath to prepare herself. "I took a rest after the ceremony as I was feeling quite tired. I overslept I suppose. Mother and Elfine came to check on me in the evening." The departure from the truth came forth quite naturally. "Elfine said she was going to return to the Great Hall afterwards."

"Well, she never did," Tonsag said, matter-of-fact. "Did Lady Elfine seem alright when she left?"

"She seemed no different to her usual self," Aurelia replied.

Savas nodded in quiet agreement.

"You two are meant to be closer to her than any. There must be something useful you can share," Father probed.

"There's really nothing I can think of," said Aurelia. "I don't know what could've happened." Her father annoyed her, as usual. How could he zero in on her and Savas like that, as if to accuse them of withholding something crucial? What irked Aurelia even more were the useless monarchs; they could not muster anything beyond a little tut or an affected gasp. Under their direction, Gaminia didn't stand a chance against the Menyr.

From the right side of the room, High Priest Resus piped up. "Don't waste your time quizzing children, Thane Olsin. What we should be focusing on is the matter of the disappearing Siladrian devils!" he bellowed. "Where are the dishonourable guests of the Republic? The Chancellor and his wife have also disappeared, or are we to believe that is a coincidence?"

The gargantuan priest's raspy voice barely reached Aurelia, but his indignation aligned with the majority. Hating the Republic, it seemed was an easy way to accrue approval in the Myriad. But was there any truth to his accusation? Aurelia had straightaway suffered the Chancellor's discourtesy, and although Sigun didn't exactly make pleasant company himself, he surely wasn't capable of orchestrating something on such a scale as this.

"The boy was the one who reported her missing," said Master Ingrith, the head of the Northcrest Institute. "Let's not forget why this wedding came about in the first place — the Siladrians were just as afraid of Kaspica as we were. This match was made to appease both sides and was about ushering in a new age of cooperation. What would they stand to gain in such an ill-fated ploy as this, apart from our abhorrence?"

The High Priest's cheeks flushed with scarlet rage. There was something profound about the natural rivalry between these two in Aurelia's head: one representing the Three, the other science.

"*Appease both sides?*" mimicked the High Priest. "I certainly never had any intention of cosying up to those southern, eel-munching louts!"

Several laughed at the table, though none did so as loud as Prince Zander.

Mother looked mortified.

"The boy has remained in Northcrest," said Tonsag. "But the flight of his parents is very troubling. It was expected that they would remain in Northcrest for several days longer."

"Good riddance to them!" barked Prince Zander.

"Not if they've kidnapped my daughter," retorted Father.

"Perhaps you ought to interrogate the ugly babe of a boy for some answers, Thane Olsin," the Prince snapped. "Was it not your ludicrous idea to grant the Siladrians free rein in Northcrest? You must be devastated — look at this mess! The leadership of this council is sure to come under severe scrutiny if Lady Elfine is not found soon," he continued, arousing rumbles of support from around the table.

"What's ludicrous," began the King, "is that those Siladrian oafs were even invited here in the first place!" He erupted into a coughing fit, then cleared his throat with little decorum. "We should never have struck a bargain with them."

Aurelia wondered if the King did not recall agreeing to Elfine and Sigun's arranged marriage, or alternatively, if he had opposed it, how it had come to be.

The Queen nodded at her husband in an endearing manner. "The loss of my great-niece Elfine is a heavy price indeed. But what other options did we have?"

"The Queen speaks truly," said Master Ingrith "Our armies are scattered and out of practice. The news of potential war with the Kaspicians is not something our soldiers have taken well. I fear that we must still remain diplomatic with the Siladrians and beg for their military aid."

"What good will their armies do?" asked Kistig. "Did you not read the report from the Chicane? The Kaspicians are coming *now*, and they are far more gruesome than some mercenary force from the South."

The reminder of this report instantly quietened the room. The Myriad suddenly looked inadequate, like a pack of dogs, meek and scrawny, desperate for someone to lead them.

"And you, boy. Have you anything useful to say concerning your sister's life?" Father asked Savas.

"I haven't seen Elfine since the wedding ceremony." He replied in a hesitant monotone, fidgeting with his trousers.

"Too busy nose deep in the usual bottle of poison," snarled Father, "sharing it with your latest creature of choice."

Before Father could continue his interrogation of Savas, three sergeants burst into the room. In their company were Sigun, and another, concealed under a hood, trailing some distance behind.

"Please forgive this interruption," one of the sergeants started, out of breath, "but we have a witness!"

"And a culprit," finished a second sergeant, who then thrust Sigun towards the high table.

"Lord Sigun?" murmured Master Ingrith.

Sigun looked limp as he stared at the ground, puffy and red in the face.

"Come forth, witness," the Queen commanded.

From behind the Protectors emerged the witness. The red-bearded priest of yesterday's wedding ceremony removed his hood and stepped forward. The once fiery demeanour of this man seemed to have been extinguished and he now crept cautiously towards the high table.

"Good day to you all." The plump priest sounded nervous. "I saw Lord Sigun on my way home, loitering by those spiral stairs in the east wing."

"We searched the area," added one of the sergeants, "and made a horrific discovery — Lady Elfine's tiara," he continued, brandishing the sapphire and diamond encrusted accessory.

A series of gasps issued from the various lips at the table, and so much air seemed to depart from the room that the Great Hall became stifling.

Aurelia was not so willing to believe that the specimen before her had any involvement in this, but seeing Elfine's tiara summoned a maelstrom of angst in her gut. Now, more strongly than before, she couldn't shake the feeling that her sister was in danger.

"When I saw the Protectors around town, saying all sorts of heinous things about the Chancellor and his wife and Lady Elfine, I came to report my testimony straight away," continued the priest.

"This flooting fart-hole is lying!" bawled Sigun, through a sudden bout of tears. "If my parents were here, they'd tell you just as much!"

"Your parents have left you to our judgement, boy. Indeed, what devilry have they committed to abscond like this?" asked the High Priest.

Sigun continued to blubber, but not a soul empathised with him. "I don't know…" he said. "They left for Dinaea."

"This boy should be placed in chains immediately!" Kistig shouted.

"How abominable that your own parents left you to rot here," said Master Ingrith. "The boy's parents have conjured something foul."

"Please, I am innocent, as are my parents! They just wanted to be safe from Kaspica! Benthrin is the one you want!" Sigun wailed.

Incensed, Mother shot up. "Kaspica?!" she screamed, frenetically scanning the reactions of the Myriad. "The Siladrians knew nothing of Kaspica's intentions until we revealed them. Now, your family know more than we do? The gods will judge your people harshly if you have conspired behind our back!"

Even the slightest allusion to the enemy was enough to bring terror into the room. After a wedding that was assumed to have some sort of protective power, nobody wanted to hear the word Kaspica so soon after.

"Let's remain calm," said Master Ingrith, as Mother settled back into her seat. "The Chancellor would prove a much more fruitful quest than this child. Besides, the priest's testimony is hardly conclusive."

"Yes! The scholar sees the truth. I am innocent," Sigun whimpered.

"You wretched thing," growled the Queen. "If you are guilty, there will be no place low enough in the Nether Pits for your soul to burn."

General Tonsag put a hand on his sword hilt and gave a quick nod to the Queen before approaching Sigun. "The boy will be detained and questioned at once. We'll extract what we can from him."

"An excellent idea," King Thenris said.

Aurelia caught the fat priest smiling in a strangely beguiling fashion, and though she could not say whether she imagined it or not, his beard came to life, crackling and dancing like a fire. A moment later, three sergeants took Sigun by the arm and began to drag him away.

"No, you can't be serious! I told you everything I know!" shrieked Sigun, as he struggled against the Protectors. His resistance was pathetic. "I'm a nobleman... please, I do not belong in some *filthy sewer of a jail cell*!"

The Myriad looked on, all notion of compunction gone.

"Now that we've dealt with that, we should agree upon our plan of action," said Father. "I propose that our focus should be to locate Elfine and the Chancellor."

With their fists raised into the air, the Myriad showed unanimous support for this motion.

"I will see to it that an elite battalion of the Protectors is sent to scour the roads leading south," said General Tonsag. "I invite everyone, however, to report anything they discover about Lady Elfine's whereabouts. She could still be in Northcrest after all, alive and unharmed."

"Good. Shall we adjourn here?" suggested the Queen, looking carefully at the King.

"Adjourned!" rasped King Thenris.

The meeting came to a terse end. In a short moment, most had departed, save for High Priest Resus, who approached Father.

"Thane Olsin," he wheezed. "Would you be able to have a word with the General on my behalf and step up the patrols near my church, and perhaps arrange for a few extra guards around my home? I'm worried for my safety."

"Yes, of course High Priest Resus. Do not worry about it," Father replied.

"Many thanks, Thane Olsin," the High Priest replied, bowing before he exited the Great Hall. Now, only Aurelia, Savas and their parents remained.

"You must be devastated," Father said bluntly. "We'll be doing everything we can to find her, as should you."

"At least now you care about her," said Aurelia.

"What did you just say to me?" Father growled.

"You heard her," Savas added.

"If you two were a little less busy being unruly brats, perhaps we'd have avoided this mess. Don't you dare even try to pin any of this on me," Father said.

"Olsin, just stop it. We'll get nowhere with this arguing," said Mother, instantly calming him.

Father sighed, clearly exhausted. The silence that ensued, unnatural between people who ought to be so close, made the exchange all the more awkward. "The circumstances surrounding this are unusual. You both understand that now, don't you?" He looked to Savas in particular, then continued in a whisper, "a member of the Chicane could not be bested by *any* of those fools from the Republic. The Chancellor arrived with several others, none of whom appear to be anywhere. Do what you can to help, but be careful."

"Yeah. We will," said Savas, who then made to leave.

"Wait — Aurelia, Kistig told me to let you know that there won't be any more classes for the time being. The Myriad need him too much right now."

Aurelia had no intention of going near him anyway. "Thanks for letting me know."

She and Savas trickled back into Northcrest to retrace Elfine's steps, first looking around the botanical gardens, then along the route that the carriage travelled yesterday. Hours passed quicker than expected. They then moved into Endvil, where Savas bribed various urchins for information, but none had seen or heard anything helpful. Aurelia sensed nothing in any of the places they went either. No magical intuition came. Finally, they hoped to ferret something out back in Sunhold, but again were unsuccessful.

Defeated and tired in bed that evening, Aurelia began to wonder why she had been called to Savas' side, and not Elfine's. Something supernatural had summoned her out of Sunhold to rescue her brother, but Elfine had not been present in her thoughts at all last night. The realisation brought an intense kind of guilt, the kind that made her hate herself and feel useless; however, she convinced herself that it wasn't her fault, and there was nothing she could have done anyway. Given all that had been going on lately, there was one conclusion that made more sense: that Aurelia wasn't meant to find Elfine.

The twilight hours blanketed Northcrest in the usual lull, and any chance of finding Elfine seemed woefully unpromising.

Chapter 15

The Kidnapper's Magic

Elfine lay motionless. With each thought she conjured, her mind descended further into a cheerless oblivion. As much as she wished that Lorcan or Zatela would rescue her, she already knew better than to be optimistic. The only hope she clung to was that her captor had not killed her yet: he needed her alive. This impossibly small chance that she could survive this nightmare kindled an ember of courage inside her. That courage strengthened her enough to resist the poison and not pass out completely.

She trembled along a fine line, caught between waking and sleeping; it was an unusual place, so much so that for the first time in her life, she sensed something extraordinary. There was a presence beside her. The connection between them was faint, but she knew it was there. Elfine recalled hearing about people seeing guardian spirits and other entities when they approached death. Although she had never experienced anything like this, she had no fear. With uncanny intuition, she had the feeling that whatever it was, was something — or someone — familiar.

"You must open your eyes if you wish to live," whispered a low voice.

Not a moment later, Elfine's eyes were open. Her mouth was brutally dry, as though she'd swallowed a desert. Through hazy vision, she glimpsed the red-brown, dried blood on her wrists, still bound in rope. The skin of her palms was cracked and ashy. Then, she noticed her clothes. If she'd had the strength, she might have laughed at the fact she was still in her wedding dress. She wondered whether she deserved this: had her reluctance to live up to her obligations landed her in this mire? And what about Father and the Chancellor? Painstaking planning was required to make this wedding happen; clandestine scheming that Elfine had been excluded from. How was this the conclusion of all that hard work? As doubt settled, she wondered whether this had been the plan all along.

And then there was Sigun. She knew for a fact he would not rescue her. He would do nothing to remedy this catastrophe. Mitenni would be more likely to stage a rescue operation, armed with her broomstick.

To dwell on Lorcan, however, was torturous. The longer he lasted in her thoughts, the worse her condition became. She reassured herself that he would have been fine last night without her help, that even if he had tried to take Benthrin down, he would have succeeded with the special swords Zatela had given them. He was a competent agent, with more experience than her.

Footsteps came racing down the stairs, faster than before. The man remained hidden under a dark hood. Quickly, he slithered closer to Elfine.

"Elfine!" It was Lorcan's voice. "I'm here."

He unveiled his hood, and Elfine could not believe her fortune. "Lorcan…" she said, still weak.

"Let's go," he said. Kneeling down, he took out a small blade sheathed under his robe. He cut the ropes binding her feet, and then also freed her wrists.

Elfine tried to muster the strength to stand up but her body struggled.

"I'll help," he said.

Did he? His words caused Elfine's vision to blur. Or was it the poison? She could hardly tell, nor could she feel his arms around her, but by some force, she now found herself in a different room, with an outfit prepared before her. Her body became flaccid, as though envenomed by the hallucinatory injection of some psychic spider.

Lorcan led her to the far end of the room and motioned towards the garments on the table. There was a simple black robe, an indigo cloak and some black leather boots. "You are filthy! I brought you a change of clothes," he said.

Touching the robe, she realised it was silk, and the cloak was cotton. Their softness surprised her; she wanted to touch them more, but stopped herself.

"No, let's go straight to Sunhold," she thought. The words would not come out though. Only then did she feel the binding rope of energy, fixed around her tongue. She could not speak her mind, and instead slipped into the outfit, uncomfortable with the knowledge that his gaze did not leave her form once.

In the next instant, she was standing in a cool, squalid living room. There was an unpalatable smell, but she couldn't place it. The house looked old and dilapidated — she was probably in Endvil. A few rats scurried towards a wardrobe in the corner, out of which she noticed something was dripping.

"Keep moving," said Lorcan, his voice lower than before.

Sunhold. Must go to Sunhold.

"No," was the growl that then came out of his mouth. "Not Sunhold."

Elfine watched the face of her lover disappear. Veiled under a black hood again, her captor returned to his true form.

What sort of creature could assume the face of another, only to discard it in an instant?

"He didn't prove much of a challenge," said the man. "I enjoyed shifting into his form."

"What?"

"Your lover." His bony finger pointed towards the wardrobe.

The smell in the wardrobe. It was death. Elfine wanted to sink through the floor to an alternate dimension. She wanted to erase herself from existence. She wanted to pretend that this nightmare wasn't real, that this man hadn't just spoken those words. But she knew that it was all true. This was Benthrin. Lorcan must have tried to take him on alone. Elfine brimmed with cold anger, furious that Lorcan had not waited for her, and despondent that she had not been there to protect him.

"Benthrin," she growled. "I will kill you!"

"*Slyedas* — follow."

Leaving the kidnapper's den, Elfine saw that Northcrest was engulfed in a spectral stillness. It must have been the early hours of the morning. The streets looked bleak, as though life had come to a halt since the calamitous wedding.

They came through an alleyway pungent with the rotten waste of a nearby restaurant and stopped before coming out onto the street. The man raised his hand cautiously, causing Elfine to stop a few paces behind him. Two Protectors on patrol passed through the street up ahead, and once they were gone, the man raised his hand, inciting Elfine to follow him once more.

As they drew upon the city walls, Elfine realised that he was taking her out of Northcrest, and farther away from any chance of rescue. They arrived at the south gate, and Elfine's final chance of escape was the two sentinels who operated and guarded the large door. The pair paced up and down listlessly, chatting to pass the time. A lantern caused their sheathed blades to glimmer, and Elfine was envious as she glared at the steel that could kill her captor.

Although the gate appeared sealed shut, the man glided towards the two sentinels fearlessly. Northcrest's gates were rarely shut since it wasn't uncommon for merchants to come and go at odd hours.

The young Protectors approached the man cautiously. They exchanged hesitant glances. "Excuse me, sir. Have you business outside the city?" one Protector said, looking the man up and down.

Elfine wished desperately to remove her hood and scream. But she couldn't.

"My wife and I are headed south to Stazeg. We visited the capital for the royal wedding, but we must depart now. A carriage awaits us not far from here," the man explained.

The Protector who spoke first nodded slowly, but the other looked unsure. "Stazeg? You'll be on the road for quite some time," said the second Protector.

"The journey is not so long," the man replied. "We are tired though, and would like to be on our way." His voice was starting to sound familiar.

"No surprise," the first Protector chimed in. "The dawn hasn't even come yet! You can't have gotten much sleep."

"Will you open the gates, or not?" The man's voice sounded malicious this time.

Elfine saw that her captor was distracted as he spoke to the Protectors. The next breath she took brought a renewed sense of clarity. Her vision sharpened. Then, her arms started to twitch, finally able to fight the spell's control. She imagined flushing out all of the priest's noxious incantations from her ears, erasing their power. She saw a steel chain in her mind begin to rust. For the first time in a while, Elfine managed to move her neck and her hands.

"You travel at your own risk, sir," said the first Protector. "Lady Elfine is missing, and we've heard the

Kaspicians could be anywhere. But you are still permitted to leave. Let me open the gates for you."

"And what of you, m'lady? Did you enjoy the wedding?" asked the second Protector.

Elfine's jaw slackened as she attempted to speak. Nothing intelligible came out.

"My wife seldom says anything of import," the man interjected sharply, watching the gates creek open.

The second Protector pulled a face. He inched closer towards Elfine. "She can speak for herself, surely?" he said, attempting a laugh. "Something must have really stunned you in Northcrest!" Now right in front of her, he put a hand to his sword hilt and eyed Elfine's kidnapper vigilantly.

A sharp whirring sounded in Elfine's ears. Suddenly, the steel chain which had started to weaken in her head began to solidify again. She froze with the feeling of some intrusive horror being forced back into her ears, like a centipede crawling with hundreds of tiny legs in her head.

The man knew what was happening. He knew that she was fighting his control. But she wasn't going to let this chance go. Thinking of that little kindling of courage from before, she found a source of strength inside of her and detonated it. Like a dragon's burning breath, it caught and devoured everything of him that lingered inside her.

Elfine fell to the floor, wailing like a dying banshee. The spell was broken for just a moment, though at no small cost. Her skull throbbed and blazed with flashing images of white fire.

"M'lady, are you alright?" shouted the second Protector. "Sir, move aside!" He shoved past the man and rushed Elfine onto her feet. The other Protector came down to help, having left the gates wide open anyway.

"Lady Elfine, is that you?" the second Protector asked, then reached to unveil her face.

"Where did he go?!" Elfine screeched.

The man had seemingly vanished somewhere in the darkness.

"We have to alert General Tonsag at once!" cried the other Protector. "Who was that man?"

"Wait! He's still here," said Elfine, scanning the area frantically.

The Protectors both drew their swords, ready for combat. The three were back-to-back, gripped with a sense of something well beyond their imagination, and Elfine knew that if this thing exceeded her own skills, then these rookie Protectors would be no match. In what seemed like a slow-motion dance, she and her new allies moved around in a circle, waiting for their enemy to strike.

"This is no use, he's gone! Lady Elfine, please, we must get you to General Tonsag!" The second Protector sheathed his blade and reached for Elfine's arm, but she was enraged — she knew that he had played exactly into the enemy's hand. She had hoped to wait a while longer and perhaps exploit some undiscovered weakness of her captor's, but like this, the ambushing predator would surely win.

The tall spectre emerged from the shadows, much taller than before. Basking in strange, flickering shadows, its body resembled an insect with eight javelin-like limbs. It seemed to expand until its form rivalled the city walls in height, and many tendrils of shadow unfurled behind. This eldritch horror was surely no man, and the terror it induced was thrice that of what she had felt in the mountains.

Strange incantations departed his lips and whipped up a miasma that left the atmosphere void. The two Protectors were instantly paralysed. The creature moved closer, its voice crackling and hissing like a bonfire. He met his quarry with delight and the two pitiful men tumbled down in agony.

Elfine was right: these sentinels were ill-prepared to withstand something this wicked. Their voices became shrill as they wailed, writhing like worms on the ground, as if gutted to shreds by crows. A wicked grin moved across the man's face as he watched them suffer. His eyes moved to Elfine and stung her still with fear. She couldn't fight this time, nor could she attempt to flee.

"Agh! My mind, it burns!" The first Protector screamed.

"Stop it!" The second one gave a tortured cry.

"Please..."

"Run!"

Elfine watched, motionless. The man's hands formed strange shapes in the air. They moved fluidly, as though directing fish through water. The night became bleak and soundless. The sounds of the dying Protectors had ceased. Silence closed in around her. They were dead.

The man gradually returned to his original form. He then circled his prey, like a merciless torrent. Crouching down to meet the two lifeless bodies, he stared at them for a stretched-out moment. With ashen, emaciated fingers, he stroked their cheeks, and whispered in a foreign tongue, "*Okoromit minya, zizeni tvoii das.*" Something not of the corporeal world seeped out of the Protectors' mouths, like a breath of pale light, and was breathed in by the predator. The two bodies quickly withered, turning grey and gaunt.

"Menyr," Elfine spat. "That's what you are."

The man seized her by the neck and lifted her effortlessly onto her feet. "You will follow, girl. And you will be silent."

Elfine snarled and ground her teeth. But as his command dictated, she followed, and she did not speak a word.

Not far from the gates, he led her down a secluded path to a horse-drawn carriage. As he shoved her inside the back, he unveiled his hood and smiled grimly at her. He locked the door, then assumed the reins.

The lanky priest from her wedding ceremony was as unsettling now as he had been yesterday, now that she knew he was Benthrin, who Zatela had wanted dead; who had conducted the wedding. A devouring pit swallowed her insides as she thought of Lorcan. If only the fool hadn't attempted the mission alone, she thought. Why hadn't he just waited, or called it off when she didn't show?

There was no time to mourn his life and the love that they had shared. Elfine needed to survive. She was determined. Benthrin had shown her his power tonight to scare her. But she wouldn't give up so easily. She scowled to herself in the darkness of the carriage, wondering who this evildoer was.

Her mission was to assassinate him, and so it would remain.

Chapter 16

Visit to an Old Acquaintance

Trinne had not set foot in the Esterwood for some time. As a child, she was much closer to nature, but in adult life, she developed a suspicion for many things. The spirits that called this place home were partial to spying, she remembered reading somewhere. Trinne hated the idea that creatures were watching her, such as those hiding in the trees, or whispering by the barrabid reeds. Once, she thought that creatures like Pugis the insect pixie and Mukele the wasp-witch, had no place in Ishanaia's world. There were other things she recalled too. Her parents used to tell her stories of how ancient Gaminians held important meetings here, in the Esterwood. They told her that it was once a place where great decisions between tribes occurred, in a time where Gaminians communed with the earth regularly, and wielded power over its caprices.

Only now was Trinne starting to wonder how many of these tales were true. Magic, it seemed, was not confined to vivid dreams and intercessions of the goddess. Now that Aurelia had communed with a strange spirit of her own, Trinne was left questioning her past beliefs. And that was why, after so many years, she'd decided to pay Mazin a visit. Trinne wondered whether he knew something about Elfine's disappearance, seeing how much time he insisted on spending with Aurelia. However, she'd always distrusted Mazin.

As she neared his hut, nothing stirred, save for a pair of finches in the canopy. Her fist made little noise as it knocked upon the oak door. She thought of Ayrn as she stood there, wandering around the long, dark corridors of Rivane's castle. Clouds shrouded the sun as she waited to be invited in. The shade slowly covered her body, and the trees above became monstrous, as if they had hundreds of eyes, dozens of limbs and gnarly fists. The disembodied cackles of distant corvids suddenly overpowered the finches' warbling.

"Could it be? The Lady Trinne has come to my humble hut? I thought I'd never see the day! Do come in!" Mazin said.

"It has been some time," Trinne said.

He pulled the door back to let her in, but no light from outside seemed able to brighten the space.

Trinne watched him circumspectly as she sat on the stump by the fireplace. He sat beside her, and lit the fire. As the flames brightened the room, she noticed the glimmer of cyan in his irises, a colour she had never seen in the eyes of another living soul. She'd forgotten the way his eyes could change in different lighting.

"You look ravishing, Lady Trinne. Life in Sunhold has suited you very well."

"I don't want you seeing my children anymore."

Mazin's face didn't move. The vortexes in his eyes tugged on her spirit, threatening to suck her inside, and Ishanaia whispered at the back of her mind.

"Ishanaia for you are all that is holy and good, you protect your flock," she said in her thoughts. Aloud, she said, "You will not corrupt me as you have my children!"

Mazin's eyes bulged with some unknowable emotion. "Lady Trinne, is something the matter?"

"Apart from the disappearance of my child? Oh! Each day remains a blessing in Ishanaia's bosom," she went on. "You, on the other hand, look dreadful. I see sin etched across you in places you surely cannot even bear to look upon."

"You still think you know everything, don't you? After all this time, you can't tell good from bad." There was a change in the room as he spoke; an energy bounced between the two of them: it was a battle of wills.

"I know what sits before me — the servant of my enemy!" She snapped.

He laughed, and the sound ricocheted off the walls. Slowly, he began to recite something, "Noul's veins pulse with the black blood of dead dreamers. The congregation sleeps while the Two-spirit Queen sullies their souls. Deep, do her tendrils burrow, yet our Groom of Whispers does watch in many mirrors, and foretell the undoing of her reign."

"Silence! Stop your blasphemous chanting, Dreamist!" She screeched. "I know what you people do. No benign god would align themselves with ones such as you."

"If you had the heart to listen to my words, you'd know I am not your enemy, nor have I ever been," he said.

"You are opposed to the divine order of things. Don't think I don't know about the Codex — I see you. *Homosexual!*"

Mazin wilted. "Why have you come here, Trinne? To shame me?"

"Shame you?" She repeated. "You have done that yourself. Oh, my foolish Aurelia to have eaten and drank in this godless hovel!" Her eyes became teary. "What did you do to her? *What* did you give her?"

He grimaced. "I helped her, that is all I have ever done."

"More lies. You servants of false religions, all you do is lie!" She snarled, her voice hoarse.

"Let me speak without interruption, then, you may make your judgements freely. Magic, Trinne, is rare, but Aurelia has it. Many centuries ago, that same gift was once coveted by the Dreamists, though few in their ranks ever had the affinity for sorcery — myself included. That is why the Dreamists chose to master the earth instead: to know all the mystical properties of leaves, roots, flowers, saps and crystals. Some called us alchemists, or herbalists. The barrabid reeds that grow around the lake have many properties. Ingesting them in certain forms with certain techniques, can enhance… certain talents," he explained, haltingly.

"Her dreams were pure," she wept. "They came from Ishanaia. What right did you have to taint her with your poisonous reeds?"

"Aurelia's dreams are her own," he said. "And she was born to traverse the other side. If you would allow me, I can show you what I have seen — the thing that terrifies me, the moment that you should also dread."

She became still. "What new mendacity is this you tempt me with?"

"None, only the truth. The future, even."

"You want to take me to this other realm, the one that I see at night sometimes, is that it?"

He nodded. "You must understand that everything I have done has been to help Aurelia; I have tried to steer her away from suffering. There are many who would destroy your children. There is one in particular who seeks their death. It is the aftermath of her coming that I must show you."

"Princess Onaxia," she said. "Aurelia has spoken this demon's name before." She paused, allowing herself a moment to pray in her thoughts. "Very well — Ishanaia approves, just this once. Show me."

Mazin went into a drawer and unearthed a pouch. He sprinkled the specks of yellow powder into two cups, then added some water. "Here," he said, handing her a cup.

"You must also hold on to this so that we will not lose one another on our trip." He passed her a violet crystal and retained one for himself. Under his breath, he said something.

"The ways of your people are truly sordid." She knocked the drink back in one, then pinched her nostrils; it tasted like rotten cheese. "Goddess, forgive me…"

"*Follow my voice.*" He spoke in a soft whisper. It echoed in her skull several times before she found herself in the midst of a dead place. She looked around, and with horror, realised that she stood outside Sunhold. It had been levelled completely. Panicked, she turned around and saw that everything in view was rubble. She thought to wade through the tumbled piles of stone to see if her children were in the castle before remembering it was a dream. Behind, she saw that nearly the whole of Northcrest had been destroyed. Clouds of smoke and ash and flames rose in each corner of her vision. Mad wails of grieving mothers, the calls of desperate fathers and the shrieks of orphaned children tore through the enormous emptiness.

"Frightening, isn't it?" asked Mazin, right beside her. "There is no stopping this."

"What is this devastation? The Kaspicians?"

He nodded, glum. "Their Queen is a being of extraordinary power. Soon, she will walk free. The power that imprisons her is fading, and she will set her sights on Gaminia once she regains her strength."

"I don't understand. Why did you show me this if it cannot be prevented?"

"If there's one thing I've learned from working with herbs, roots and flowers my whole life, all forces can be balanced by another. The effects of one concoction can be undone with a different one. Every power has its rival."

"Aurelia has been touched by Ishanaia. But what can her dreams do to combat this? One child is already missing, I can't bear to lose another."

"Dreams are only the beginning, Trinne. Do not let your daughter's potential be wasted because of your own short-sightedness."

"How dare you!" She cried. "Aurelia is a fool. She's my baby, and knows nothing of the world. You just want to take advantage of her gifts."

"You are angry. It's the guilt you feel for Elfine, isn't it?"

Instantly, she was frozen in place. She searched briefly inside herself. Was it rage, dread or utter sadness that had crippled her so?

"Where were you when Elfine was taken?" He asked. "With Aurelia?"

"You know nothing. You don't know what you are saying!"

"You are a good mother," said Mazin. "Elfine's fate was not your fault, Trinne. Nor will Aurelia suffer if you let her embrace her gifts."

"Your words always come out like smoke. They seep into the atmosphere and stick to things without their consent, then before long, they are gone. Only a bad smell lingers. I will never grant you my trust, Dreamist. But I cannot deny that I believe the vision you have shown me to be true. We are approaching dark days. If preventing this catastrophe requires Aurelia's involvement, I will not stand in her way anymore."

"Then we are in agreement."

"You know, I came here because I thought it was you. I never understood what you Dreamists did, only that you fiddled with objects and things of magical origin. When she told me of the thing that came for her — that Menyr, as she called it — I was sure you were the one who'd sent it," she said nervously.

A shiver flashed through Mazin, and his face blanched white. "The Menyr are powerful weavers of magic, Trinne. They are masters of illusion and deception, and their hunger... it is legendary. Aurelia is lucky to have survived an encounter with such a creature."

"She only did because of the spirit. The one she told you about before she told me. It came to her rescue. Mazin, please, is there any more you can tell me?"

"It is because of the Menyr that I have not set foot in Northcrest for more years than you would believe. You must be vigilant."

"If we are to be pulled into the fray, and you can help, then you must act," demanded Trinne.

"I intend to," he said, smiling. "There is someone I must see now, an old friend."

"Are my children going to die? Am I?" Trinne was shocked that the words came out. Ishanaia would not approve of her asking someone like Mazin to predict such a thing.

"Ask your goddess, Trinne, not me. But if it matters, I believe you will be OK. Before I go, may I request something of you?"

She waited.

Mazin reached out his hand and touched her shoulder gently. "Thank you," he said.

Within Trinne's mind, flashbacks of an earlier time came in and out of focus: images of a different Mazin; images of her youth; a forgotten memory coming to light after so many years. Was it something about Rivane, where she saw all those premonitions of the future? No — it was at a strange place they had first met. All of a sudden, she remembered it vividly:

"What are you doing here?" Mazin had asked, around two decades ago, standing beside the Temptress' Parlour. He had hardly aged a day since.

"I was led here." The teenage Trinne spoke absent-mindedly.

"To a whorehouse?"

"Yes."

He attempted a friendly chuckle. "You don't look like the sort who would have any business here."

She folded her arms. "I saw this place in my dreams."

Mazin blinked. "A dream brought you here?"

Trinne nodded, casually. "My dreams have started to come true. My aunt is going to be Queen — I dreamt that too."

"You've an interesting life ahead of you then," he replied.

"Have we met before? You look so familiar."

"No, but Noul's reach is great. Perhaps, my god has touched you too."

She recoiled straight away. "A Dreamist… Ishanaia spoke to me of your god. You should be ashamed of the life you lead and the choices you make."

Mazin looked bemused. "Noul has always been misunderstood. We've only ever wanted to live peacefully, alongside the rest of society. Is that too much to ask?"

The night became hauntingly silent. "No, there is no place for men like you amongst the Three. Aren't you worried about your soul?" She asked.

"I have never ceased to worry about it. But what did your dream show you of this place?"

"That something wicked lurks in the air around this place," she said. "It is invisible to me now, but there is a door in that place that leads to suffering."

As she returned to her body in the present, with the memory of this moment clear in her thoughts, she saw that Mazin was gone. She realised that she had known something crucial all along: the House of Noul was hidden underneath the Temptress' Parlour.

Under the glistening sunlight of the Esterwood, she left Mazin's hovel. Ghostly winds redolent of all her fears whistled as she returned to the carriage which had brought her here. Something haunted her about Mazin, and the feeling that he somehow had some power over her terrified her; it made her question Ishanaia's love, and threatened to unravel all that she held dear. What she knew of him, and of his relationship with her children, was not enough to loathe him. However, she had always held onto the intuition that he was not who he said he was.

*

The approach to Sunhold had never been so tumultuous a journey. Something unnatural had stricken Northcrest's denizens and impelled them into chaos. She saw Protectors from out the window racing around urgently, their swords and armour clattering and their boots stomping along the stone pathways. Locals hung from their high balconies shouting at each other, desperate to gossip about Kaspica and Elfine's disappearance, and spew their rekindled hatred for the Republic and its wicked residents. Merchants and roadside peddlers were shifty, as if suddenly afraid to do business.

Yet as Trinne entered King's Respite, she sensed something graver still was at work. The roads were choked with rioting men and women, screeching at the top of their lungs. The sovereign district's lustrous veneer looked tarnished: the unmistakable residents of Endvil, in their tattered brown tunics and tell-tale pocky, soot covered faces, had spilled out like a horde of invaders. The locals of King's Respite watched them with disgust, snarling and hissing swaddled in their expensive robes.

Trinne peered out the window and saw a brawl. Cabbages and potatoes flew through the air and apricots and apples tumbled down the street; streets which were once famously white, were now sullied with smashed produce, dirt and blood. Vases shattered; pots and pans clattered as instruments of war in the hands of the Endvil rioters. Wooden signposts thudded against the ground. A passer-by lurched near to the carriage and forced his head to the window, his eyes bulging ferociously. He glared at Trinne, licked his lips and slobbered over the glass.

"Quickly, take a detour and get us away from here!" Trinne called to the driver.

In all her years, she had never seen anything like this. She was far removed from the struggles of poorer types and had no idea what had riled them. Surely, this wasn't all to do with Elfine?

After a short while, the driver dropped Trinne off safely at Sunhold. Shaken, she went to her aunt's quarters at once, even though the Queen rarely saw anyone uninvited.

"Aunt Melindra?" She called from outside the door. "Are you in?"

"Come in," said the Queen.

Trinne hadn't been in the royal bedchamber for a long time. It was easily the most impressive room in Sunhold: twice as large as her own, filled with random articles of gold and silver and jade figurines from Yenhai. There were rectangular windows taller than most human beings, and a four-poster bed that could fit eight. The third-floor suite also boasted a large balcony that looked straight over the bailey.

"Please, I hope you'll forgive me for the int—"

"Take a seat, dear," said the Queen, motioning to the large, purple chair beside the one she was sitting on. There was a small wooden table with a silver platter of wines on it. The Queen poured one for Trinne and handed it to her after she sat down.

"Have you seen what's happening outside?" Trinne said anxiously, not interested in the wine.

"Outside where?"

"In King's Respite. Everywhere. People are rioting!"

"One has to admire the Northcrester spirit, no?"

"It's bedlam out there," said Trinne. "I feared my carriage might have been toppled."

"Probably something to do with that revolution the Myriad have been griping about," said the Queen.

"It's true then. There is a revolution."

"Looks like it." A splash of wine went into her mouth.

"What does this mean? People are fighting. Blood is staining the streets of King's Respite!" Trinne cried.

"Was there something important on your mind, dear?" the Queen asked, patting her lips with a serviette.

Trinne was mystified. But something odder still caught her attention. It was a smell, or at least she thought it was. She'd never come across anything quite like it before, and even though she thought it was a scent, she could tell that it was coming from something that was not truly there. Her thoughts took her to a cold, dark place: she thought it might be a graveyard, for it reminded her of old bones.

"Have you seen this? It's from Calech. It is called a diamond." The Queen lifted her left hand slowly; it caught the light and glimmered. Trinne hadn't even noticed the ring.

"Y-yes... it's very beautiful." Trinne regretted coming. Her aunt was the same, self-absorbed harpy she'd always been. "I should probably return to the tower and check on Olsin." Trinne smiled and stood up, ready to leave.

"What were you doing in the Esterwood?" The Queen paused to down her drink, waiting for a response.

Trinne didn't want to offend her aunt, so she sat back down quickly. "You know, I hadn't been there for some time. It's really ra—"

The Queen cut her off again. "Rather dull? I can't imagine so. Speak. Tell me about your adventure." Her voice sounded uglier than ever before.

A chill crept into the room. Trinne had never felt uncomfortable around her aunt before, as much as she didn't like her much. The humongous size of this suite suddenly became menacing, as though the ceiling was endlessly tall and the walls impossibly wide. Trinne felt tiny and exposed. "I just went for a stroll," she said, finally.

The Queen sprang forwards like a cobra about to envenom its prey. She sniffed Trinne all over with cavern-like nostrils. In the next instant, she leaned back, crossed her legs and smiled. "He showed you something, didn't he?"

Only when Trinne looked down did she see that her hands had begun to shake; she didn't understand what was happening. This wasn't the aunt Melindra she knew; she even sounded different. Her voice had a deep, raspy consistency. Like the caw of a crow. "I don't know what you mean," Trinne mumbled.

The Queen glared harshly. "You always were an irritating meddler. Never known when to keep your nose out of other people's excrement, have you?"

"Excuse me?"

"You and your wretched little urchins, scurrying about Sunhold at all hours like your halfwit predecessors. I should never have brought you here. The children I had to keep, but you? What a waste of a life yours is. I wish you'd died after you had Aurelia."

"Queen or not, I refuse to be spoken to like this," retorted Trinne.

Something deafened Trinne. She had barely time to react. The room was plunged into shadow instantly and the Queen was standing tall before her, the source of the darkness. Tendrils of shadow swirled from around her and licked Trinne's face and every corner and surface around them. Two feathery wings of sheer black jutted out from the Queen's back, and upon her head sat a crown of ebony plumage. A murder of crows seemed to caw as the Queen glared, the lower half of her face growing into an elongated bill. There was the stink of something putrid.

As Trinne looked where her aunt's eyes had been, she saw the hollow spaces behind the rotten yellow irises, where maggots crawled. "You... it was you!" she screeched.

"Yes, it was. And I'm going to be keeping you here for a while. Sleep, now, Trinne."

*

Mazin had not stepped foot in Northcrest for many years. He remembered the last time he had been in the city. Northcrest was vastly different in those days, and he barely recognised it now. It had changed over the years that he had been gone, living in exile. Tonight, the city was the most chaotic he had ever seen it. He was glad for once that none could see him, otherwise he might have been arrested simply for how he looked, or attacked by a mob.

In Endvil, there were other, much more sinister things lurking than protestors. It was for that reason that Mazin had gone to great lengths to prepare himself for his reunion with the Wraith: chanting in magical languages, invoking the power of as many deities as possible and smearing himself with foul-smelling tinctures. That was all he could do, since he had no real magic of his own. To come this deep into the city was a huge risk.

He darted through Endvil like a falcon flying from perch to perch. Orphaned cats feasting on scraps in the alleys hissed when he passed by. Few of the dilapidated homes looked inhabited. Out of one home, however, with its ruby-red lantern, an eldritch chill oozed from the space under the door, and a soft, amber light glimmered inside. Silently, he approached the door; it creaked open with a will of its own.

First, he saw the strands of clumpy, white hair dangling like skeins of tattered thread — this view came as no shock to Mazin, he hadn't expected the Wraith's condition to have improved over the years. The creature was staring out its window into the pitch-black nothingness of Endvil. In his hand, there was a hefty brass cup, filled to the brim with blood-red nectar — Viska. Slowly, the Wraith swivelled around and lashings of the drink spilled onto the ground, splattering the threadbare wooden floorboards with crimson splotches.

The face was exactly as Mazin recalled: wizened and embraced by a foetid caress, as if just yesterday exhumed after centuries slumbering in an underground sepulchre. A cruel smile crept across the Wraith's face, revealing rotten teeth.

"*Bozhye.* You don't look a day over 89," the Wraith started, taking a hearty swig of Viska.

Mazin shut the door behind him. A surge of memories and past emotions came racing to the fore as he regarded the Wraith. The smell of Viska, however, was something he'd forgotten. It repulsed him as it did all those years ago, when he made it for the first time.

"I still partake in Viska sometimes, though I have tweaked your recipe over the years," the Wraith said. The same wicked smile tiptoed along the crevices of the creature's skin as he swirled his cup, causing the glass to overflow and spill again.

"So easily you weave your way into my thoughts," said Mazin. "How long has it been, Henaias?"

"Did you think I'd been counting the days as they went by?" Laughed the Wraith.

Mazin was not amused. "A girl called Elfine is missing. Which one of your wretched ilk took her?"

"Goodness, who on earth cares about that? Sit down, have a glass of Viska — it's wonderful for the skin."

"I would not dare imbibe the blood, flesh and bones of a living thing. How disgusting you are, Henaias!"

"How else can one hope to reach their 700s?"

"There is no humanity in you left at all, is there?"

"So foolish, Mazin. You remember so little." The Wraith took another sip of his drink and stood up.

Suddenly, he was threatening.

Like a serpent, the Wraith slithered closer. Mazin feared to meet his gaze; he knew what a Menyr could do if one locked eyes with its victim. The Wraith breathed down Mazin's neck, right behind him. His breath was glacial and stank of rancid meat.

"Your drug-addled brain probably can't remember how to count to ten anymore," mocked the Wraith.

"Elfine is the Queen's own blood, Henaias. Whoever had a hand in her abduction will surely suffer greatly for their misdeeds."

The Wraith burst into laughter. *"The Queen's own blood,"* he mocked. The Wraith then returned to the table, refilled his cup with Viska and had a few sips. As the red accumulated around his mouth, he wiped it clean with a tattered sleeve.

"Why do you laugh? You should fear what will happen to you when you are discovered," warned Mazin.

"Fear? I have festered in this city for centuries with no purpose, cut off from my people because of what that wretched lover of yours did to me. I fear nothing, especially not now."

"Centuries of drinking that vile potion has sent you mad. I should never have made it for you."

"And yet you did, spurred on by your narcissistic need to be morally upright. You took pity on me and how grateful my people are for it. Viska really made headlines in Menyr communities all over the world. Thanks to you Mazin, we have something that can temporarily sustain us, and be used against our enemies."

"Viska may have saved you from languishing, but you will not win the war," Mazin said fiercely.

"Soon, we won't need that concoction," said the Wraith, confident. "Do you remember the Nomos Tal, or did she take that memory from you as well? There's more power in it than any potion."

Mazin tried to move out of the Wraith's way, but found his body had become heavy. "I… I—…"

"As I thought. You are dead to the orgasmic subtleties of magic. You cannot feel it; the power that made the Menyr, the power that nearly wiped your ugly race out for good," the Wraith crowed.

"The book. I remember now. You always wanted his book. What good would having it now do?" asked Mazin.

The Wraith grinned wickedly. "The girl and her brother would make two marvellous Menyr. She'll crumble without the help of those dogs at her side." The Wraith crept closer to Mazin. "Her sister certainly didn't put up much of a fight!" He laughed.

"So, it was you who took Elfine. The Keyholder," said Mazin.

"*Keyholder,*" he parroted, with a wicked grin. "You have always been dreadfully boring." The Wraith dragged his nails across the wood of the table hypnotically.

Mazin's head started to spin. He was finding it hard to stay alert. "It makes me sick that the two of you were actually there, all those years ago, right at the heart of my people's demise."

"Two?" the Wraith sniggered.

"There's no reasoning with you, monster. You'll never find your way into the House of Noul, and you'll never find what you seek," said Mazin.

"Foolish Mazin. You think you can stop me, or that the spirit whispering from the other side can? Ah — you thought I hadn't sensed her by now. Ylestra. She won't stop us either."

Mazin smiled. "Do you think me a warrior? It's the girl you should fear. She can beat you."

The Wraith shook his head. "You'll never find out how this ends. Onaxia told me about your condition. About what happened to you over the years. *Ghost.* She told me how to put an end to you."

Mazin moved to the other side of the room and leaned against a bookcase. He placed his hand over a blade, concealed in his cloak. "I have served my purpose." He made to take out the blade, but in a blur of movement, the Wraith was right before him.

Mazin froze, as if stung by a giant scorpion.

"No, Mazin," said the Wraith. "You have never been of use to anyone in your life. Your very existence has been irredeemably meaningless, despite your freakishly flamboyant appearance." The Wraith put a single finger on Mazin's shoulder. Like a bony claw, it slid across his torso, igniting flames of fear inside Mazin's mind that left him feeble.

"*Kradu silu tvoyu*," whispered the Wraith.

Mazin's physical strength was instantly sapped and stolen.

"Whatever force has kept you going, is now mine."

Wearied to immobility, Mazin collapsed towards the floor. As his vision faded, he watched the blade roll out of his hand and clatter onto the ground.

The Wraith knelt down, made a grab for the weapon and plunged it into Mazin's stomach. At the sight of the stream of warm blood, the Wraith doused his hand in it and licked each finger clean. In moments, he began to transform. No longer was he a hideous abomination, but the Henaias that Mazin had met all those years ago in the House of Noul. Henaias was a young man of haunting beauty: the ashen, creased skin gave way to a dazzling complexion, and the greasy wisps of white hair now gleamed midnight black.

As a parting curse, he planted a life-draining kiss on Mazin's forehead with his newly pink lips. "You should never have lived this long to begin with. Farewell, Mazin."

Chapter 17

Glimpse of the Enemy

The dawn brought no respite from yesterday's turmoil. There had been scant progress in finding Elfine, and the morning streets were already noisy with rioters and protestors, their grievances still unaddressed. On their way out of Sunhold, Aurelia and Savas had heard servants and Protectors gossiping. Some feared that Elfine had been kidnapped by the Siladrians, others believed that she had been murdered by the Kaspicians; others still discussed the riots, casting all blame on the brown-skinned Hellasics of Endvil. The heinous end to the royal wedding had riled many folks, and their darkest fantasies stirred. In just one night, Northcrest was unravelling. Decades of anguish had been unleashed into the now stifled city. After what Aurelia had learned from the Visitor — and what Savas had undergone with the Wraith — it didn't come as much of a surprise that the rest of the city was about to boil over.

Aurelia and her older brother had scoured the city the day before, desperate for information, but no one offered anything useful. They continued much the same today, but it seemed that Elfine had dissipated into smoke. They took themselves to the Capercaillie and the Olive for a brief respite, now their preferred tavern. Even here in Brighthaven, the atmosphere was restive. It had changed since Aurelia's last visit. She'd clocked the suspicious looks, pointing and whispering from alleys on the way. A spirit of unease held the tavern in its claws.

The slow motions of Savas' hands as they swirled his mug of ale back and forth became mesmerising, weaving a web of trepidation upon the sticky table. His normally animated green eyes were fatigued, his olive skin was dry and his dark curls were greasy and unkempt.

"We'll never find Elfine like this," he said, finishing his ale. He gestured to the swarthy Piscanese waiter for another, who looked relieved to have something to do.

"She's not even in Northcrest anymore. I can just tell," said Savas.

"I think you're right," Aurelia said. She'd ordered a platter of Piscanese snacks, including deep-fried chickpea balls, sesame-coated flatbread and a lemony bean dip. She was full, but couldn't stop herself from tearing tiny shreds of flatbread to nibble on. "But what are we supposed to do, just forget about our sister?"

"Have you seen what's going on?" Asked Savas. "The city is about to boil over. Elfine is tough; she'll be OK if we don't find her."

"I can't bear the thought of giving up on her," she said.

"We're doing what we can. Remember what you told me? The Visitor gave you a task. Did you bring the book?"

She nodded, then went into her satchel and took out Castrellus' Journal. She'd been too fraught to read it since she last saw the Visitor, but she and Savas knew that if they were to get to the bottom of whatever was going on, they needed to finish reading it together.

"It looks like any other old book," he remarked.

"It's not." She felt out the surface of the tome. Unsure which page to turn to, Aurelia became absorbed by the sounds of the flapping pages. She read aloud to Savas from the page she landed on:

Sage Era 2391, 4th Moon, 12th Sun

The air reeks, my people are coughing, dizzy, suffering headaches, fatigue and nose bleeds. They are breaking out with lesions on their skin. They can barely remember who they are. Doctors are calling this illness Spirit Rot. They say it targeted us because we opened our doors to society's undesirables — undesirables like me.

I now know that it was I who brought Spirit Rot into the world. By sealing that ill-fated bargain with the demon Onaxia, I have brought ruination to my people and Northcrest. How could I have known that this would be the price for my actions? There was one thing I have yearned for in my life above all other desires, and Onaxia offered me the solution. Yet she lied.

I, for some reason, remain healthy. It must be my punishment. The gods of all religions and all places have only ever wanted me to suffer. King Venelag has been instructed by a new astrologer — a cogent woman from the west — to lock the monastery's doors and to exile our sick into the catacombs that run beneath the monastery. The smells of the rotting dead are seeping into the city. The healthy want us expunged, out of sight completely.

Now, many seek to make their claim on the House of Noul. A band of Yotanite priests have come to minister to our dying flock and dispense their unfeeling requiems. They skulk around us, their bodies draped in black robes and cloths covering their mouths to protect them. They wear gloves too, for to touch us is death. But I wonder, why are they here, if to be near us is so deadly?

Not only them, but a man who calls himself Henaias also arrived not so long ago. He claims to be a researcher from the White Academy, looking into a means to cure us. Although he has promised us help, the bodies continue to pile up each day, especially now that we are quarantined together. Henaias is very peculiar: he comes each day and wanders aimlessly around the monastery, going in and out of rooms and troubling the sick with odd questions. It is *clear that he is looking for something. Perhaps the Haruspex sent him to find what I stole from her.*

That book, which she ordered me to steal before I fled Pisca, has brought me nothing but misery. She only wanted it for herself. I have done my people a good deed by ferrying it overseas. The thing should be destroyed, but perhaps I can use it to my own ends before that day. Our leader has fled, and the congregation now look to me to lead. They know of my secret, that my kin are gifted with magic. I have not used my powers for many years, but it is said that within the Nomos Tal is stored the power to do anything, even banish an ancient demon.

Aurelia flicked ahead to what appeared to be Castrellus' final entry:

Sage Era 2391, 5th Moon, 8th Sun

The Dreamists are all dead. I too am approaching death, but I have won. The dark magic of that book of spells showed me what to do, even if things didn't go as I had planned: an intruder came to destroy me. That wretched Henaias found his way back in here, even after King Venelag's advisor had the entrance to the catacombs sealed off. But he was too late. I trapped Onaxia's curse inside myself, and had he not charged me as he did, like a rabid beast, the spell would not have touched him. And so, half of her curse will live inside of him, bound to me in this spirit-body until I am able to cross into the world of spirits. None shall ever find the House of Noul now; the wickedness of the Nomos Tal has ripped the very fabric of our dimension, and this place has become hidden from all eyes. The doors to the House of Noul will not open without the Nomos Tal. For that reason, I have cast a veil of illusion over the book, rendering it inseparable from my diary. I hope that no one ever finds their way to this defiled place.

What a fool I was to not to see that Henaias was a Menyr — as was that Yotanite priest. Those creatures that lurked in the deserts of Pisca, picking travellers off the roads. I never used my magic for much good after I rejected the ways of my people, just as they rejected me for who I loved; however, I will rest easily in my exile knowing that I sentenced that creature to a lifetime of suffering. It lies deathly and cadaverous before me; I will sleep now, for my body is becoming immaterial, and pray that wraith of a man never wakes again.

Aurelia looked at her hands. Suddenly, they were covered in sticky black goo, and the whole room began to plummet into darkness. Only the book remained visible. The Nomos Tal. This unfathomably evil work of dark sorcery her ancestors had feared for centuries had been in her possession this whole time. How could she have known? The black goo was so strong and tacky she couldn't pull herself away. The book was reeling her in with its viscous grip.

Thousands of keening wails resounded in her ears.

"Didn't we tell her not to read that book?"

"She picked it up anyway. Now we just have to see if she'll turn into a monster."

"Oh, she will. Have you seen her? At least the last guy had some training. This idiot won't last a month, I reckon."

"Hah! You're right. Look at her! Just like the monkeys that came before her."

"What kind of moron just picks up a book that wasn't there before, and thinks it's an ordinary book?"

"I wonder if she knows how many people have died because of this book."

"Like us?"

"Aurelia? Are you OK?" Savas' voice sliced through the pandemonium.

Aurelia gasped, inhaling the room's supply of air. She exhaled all her anxiety when she saw her brother sitting in front of her.

"I can't believe it. This is the book our ancestors were so afraid of," said Aurelia

"And this Henaias," Savas said. "Castrellus called him a wraith. Could he be one of the Menyr in Northcrest?"

"We should consult the Visitor."

"How do we reach her?" asked Savas.

Aurelia frowned. "I don't know. Normally, she comes to me. Mazin gave me something once that took me to the Ankasa. To her."

"Should we go to Mazin then?"

There was a hubbub outside suddenly. A few scrawny looking youths ran past the window. The hurried stomping of Protectors came next, three of whom barged into the tavern, looking around urgently. Whoever they were, they weren't normal Protectors. They looked more distinguished than any city patrol Aurelia had ever seen. Two of them donned gilded plates of armour, which looked impervious to any blade or arrow. The third seemed to hop with webbed feet like a frog. Rested on his back were an ornate longbow and a quiver of white arrows.

When the rest of the patrons filtered out, it was clear that the men were looking for Aurelia and Savas.

The one with the bow rushed over to their table. "We've been looking for you all morning," said the man. "Your father sent us to find you; he wants you back at Sunhold immediately." He leaned in closer, and continued quietly, "We arrived this morning from Frostfoot Keep with Marshall Morovig. The Kaspician army is less than a day behind us."

"As if things couldn't get any worse," Savas snorted.

"We shouldn't tarry," the guard enjoined, motioning to the door.

The day became overcast and humid. With each tavern or restaurant that they passed, Aurelia heard people praying for the North Wind to come, to free them from an oppression she didn't even know existed. The crackdown on the protests had begun swiftly. But there was something about those words that caught her attention. The North Wind. She couldn't recall anyone ever saying those words together before.

King's Respite remained in a shambles. The rioters had done considerable damage. There were spillages and destroyed goods everywhere. Windows were smashed and doorways splintered. Blood stained the white pavements.

Aurelia watched a young girl with an older man, perhaps her father or uncle, lament the pigsty her street had become. Down an alley to her left, she saw a couple of young protestors being discreetly ushered into a shanty doorway. There it was again, those words.

The North Wind.

*

In the Great Hall, the officious Marshal Morovig was instantly recognisable, even though Aurelia hadn't seen him for nearly a decade. To her knowledge, he was the oldest and highest-ranking military commander in Gaminia. Not only that, he was the younger brother of King Thenris. The Marshal was taller than any man Aurelia had ever seen, and his aura was similarly large, filling the entire room. It seemed that his chair, too frail to bear his greatness, could collapse at any moment. Despite his years, he did not look nearly as old as his brother in age and exuded strength and wisdom. Draped over the back of his chair was an enormous bear hide cloak. It was a ludicrous addition in the current weather, but Aurelia knew a little about Frostfoot Keep. It was the sole vestige of Gaminian architecture in the Numanich Mountains, where temperatures were well below freezing most of the year. If Tutor Fark had spoken truly, then there was no worse a place to live, and Morovig was Lord over that Keep.

After a pause, someone began to shuffle noisily to the far side of where Aurelia and Savas were sitting. Aurelia zoned out as silence entered the room. Wasn't coming here a matter of urgency? Nobody was speaking.

Then she saw the Visitor.

She stood up from the table, seeming like she had been waiting for Aurelia. With one look, her dark eyes tore Aurelia to shreds and restored her at the same time.

"Marshal Morovig," said the Visitor. The Great Hall blurred out of focus and the others seated at the table seemed to turn into clay figurines, motionless.

"Can the others see you? Can they hear me?" Aurelia fretted.

"When have any of these fools ever seen or heard anything useful?" The Visitor grinned.

"Savas and I made a discovery. The Journal that I've been reading is the same book that our ancestors mentioned — the book you said we should be terrified of!"

The Visitor began moving about the Great Hall at a sedate pace.

"You already knew..." Aurelia ran her hand through her curls.

"I suspected."

"And you entrusted it to me, knowing how dangerous it is?"

"Would you rather I had given it to your brother?"

Aurelia turned her gaze downward and shook her head lightly. "Castrellus wrote that you need his Journal — the Nomos Tal — to open the House of Noul's doors."

The Visitor paused, touching the surface of the wall, underneath one of the stained-glass windows. "Did Castrellus reveal nothing about the House of Noul's whereabouts?"

"No," Aurelia answered quickly. "Only that it became hidden from the world after whatever he did to that Henaias."

"Clever, Castrellus," said the Visitor, as if the man was right in front of her. "It is in the Ankasa."

"What? How is that possible? I thought the Ankasa was a spiritual world."

"There are infinite secrets to the Ankasa, and being able to hide a real thing in there is not out of the ordinary."

Aurelia then looked to Marshal Morovig, frozen mid-speech. "OK, but the Kaspicians are advancing. Elfine is already gone. We're running out of time to act. We need to find this place now"

"Do you remember when we spoke in your mirror on the night of Elfine's wedding, and an image came to life?" Asked the Visitor. "It was a memory, but not one of my own."

"I remember seeing a river, a forest, some soldiers, a cave too," Aurelia replied.

"There is something we must seek in that memory, something the ancestors wish for us to know. Come." In a matter of seconds, she repositioned herself by Aurelia's side. The Visitor's touch connected them intimately, and Aurelia tasted a portion of her wisdom and power. Her grasp on the present vanished quickly, and she entered somewhere new.

The sound of a gentle flow of water was the first thing she noticed. Then colours and shapes took form around her. She was a fish swimming downstream. Sunlight filtered through the leafy lochs of weeping willows. White butterflies flew among the long wisps of grass, and dragonflies skittered by the purple barrabid reeds.

A band of men appeared to her right. She counted at least 20 of them. They had bivouacked near the water and were roasting fish over an open flame. Swimming closer to the bank, she watched them with caution. They were Gaminian; she could tell straight away from their chatter and their dress. Although all had basic weapons, less than half had proper armour, and the rest were wearing rudimentary leather. They were visibly fatigued, with saggy, lumbering bodies and hoarse voices: they'd been fighting a losing battle.

Among this sorry platoon, there was one man who stood out. He wore an ink-black leather costume with green patterns, an ornate breastplate and a hooded black cape. In his scabbard was a long, silver sword and on his back was a shield of pure oak, with the Owl of Providence etched upon it: the emblem of Gaminia, and also Ishanaia. Although younger, Morovig's face was easily distinguished.

Just above, resting on the reeds, a vibrant kingfisher peered down at Aurelia. The Visitor could no longer mask her presence around Aurelia. There was always a warmth emanating from her, but it was unstable, like it could instantly become destructive and terrifying.

"This was the mission that made him a legend," warbled the Visitor, through her beak.

"How are we even seeing this?" asked Aurelia.

"This memory is a gift to us from the ancestors," the Visitor explained, "but to see it, one of our people must have been present."

"I thought you said all of our people were gone?"

"I did not lie, most of them are. But I am bound to you alone; I know little of any others who still live."

"Incredible. Memories can be shared across time?"

"Even the spirits of those with whom we share blood can be recalled; their essence may linger centuries after death."

"Like the spirit of the lake, though I have never seen her."

"Have you not?"

Aurelia resumed watching the men. Some ate ravenously, three writhed in pain on the ground far away, clearly too sick for food and already ostracised for their illness. A handful practised combat, swinging wildly in the air with their swords. Morovig must have given an order, though Aurelia didn't hear it: all of a sudden, the warriors began to move out.

"They're leaving the sick behind. Why are they so ill?" Aurelia asked, looking at the pitiful men, lifeless on the ground. On closer inspection, she saw that the sick were pocked with lesions and welts; their skin was also taut and pale, as though they hadn't taken a decent meal in months.

"Spirit Rot — Onaxia's gift for us all," said the Visitor. "Didn't you read about that?"

"But I thought the disease was quarantined in the monastery."

"King Venelag didn't foresee that the disease would touch the warriors that his people idolised. They thought it only affected those who he considered the dregs of society, those with Castrellus'… inclinations."

The kingfisher left its perch and, in a breath-taking display, assumed the Visitor's form exactly as Aurelia remembered her from the Great Hall. "We should follow Morovig," she said.

As Aurelia moved closer to the river's edge, in an effortless transition of her own, she found herself back in her own skin and clothes, completely dry. The Visitor looked at her impatiently, but Aurelia could not resist the urge to touch her flesh, hair and clothes, all of which felt completely real. She dropped to the ground to touch the water, but her hands passed through it as if it were imaginary; the illusion was only so strong.

The two rushed to keep up with Morovig, who marched ahead with his troops. The woods suddenly become denser. Sunlight scarcely reached where they trod, and on the floor was the decay of the sylvan giants above, causing each footstep to produce a foreboding crunch. Aurelia looked back and saw that the riverbanks already looked impossibly distant, and in front, a low mountain loomed at the edge of the woods.

After cutting a path through ropes of branches, the warriors, under Morovig's direction, ascended the mountain; Aurelia and the Visitor followed. The way up was a steep, craggy path, strangled by thorny vines and roots. Upon the rock face was a mouth-shaped entrance, out of which seeped the cave's black, cloudy breath. The soldiers gathered wood and lit a fire, then prepared torches.

"The Menyr have plagued our lands and murdered our people!" Shouted Morovig. "We are all that is left of the band of warriors sent to rout this enemy. We cannot fail now. If we do, they will continue to defile Gaminia." He paced up and down, his furrowed eyebrows looking more austere than ever. "The Chicane have tracked them to this place, and now, it is up to us to finally expunge these beasts."

"Tracked who?" Aurelia asked the Visitor.

The Visitor said nothing.

Aurelia shot her a quick frown, but she didn't want to lose the men as they all hurried into the cave. Their torches lit the path, but the narrowing passageway induced a feeling of claustrophobia, and Aurelia feared she'd end up stuck between the walls. Worse still was the putrid stench, carried along by a biting draft.

They halted where the path forked in three directions. Quickly, the soldiers decided who would go where; Aurelia and the Visitor went straight ahead, following Morovig and five of his men. She was grateful that the chosen path soon widened, but this relief was short-lived. Goosebumps formed all along her arms, and her breath became frosty. Spiders and centipedes crawled along the walls, in and out of tiny holes, perhaps stalking one another. The smell of rot seemed desperate to incapacitate her. Suddenly, she had a terrible sense of the evil lurking in this cave. Whether she was really in this place or not, she could not say, but all her instincts told her to turn back.

The path led to a precipice inside an enormous cavern. Fine rays of sunlight percolated through small gaps in the ceiling, which was adorned in lattices of ivy. The site looked to have once been a mine: there were disbanded carts, pickaxes and human skeletons, still in their mining rags. Wooden ramparts and bridges, visibly atrophied over time, still hung in the space above to connect the passages. What really alarmed Aurelia was something else: past the short incline down, there was a settlement. Small edifices of wood, coarse stone and cloth tarpaulin had been erected to serve as what seemed to be people's homes. There was at least a dozen of these primitive structures, and dotted around the area were several lanterns, quietly burning.

Morovig and his men tossed their torches into the shadow behind, crouched onto the floor and begin to sneak towards the encampment. While his men seemed sluggish on the ground, Morovig slinked forwards with feline finesse.

"We shouldn't lose them," said the Visitor, descending.

Aurelia followed her. On closer inspection, the settlement was threadbare. An eerie noise whirred. The flea-ridden bedrolls, ramshackle tables and chairs and pungent stinks of carrion and excrement were grim indications of what sort of creature could eke out a living here. In a butchery, there were bones and the old, greying meat on the counter was mobbed by flies, fat from drinking the oozing rivulets of blood.

The soldiers' abandoned their stealthy approach all of a sudden. They began to ransack the settlement, overturning every stool and flipping tables. Aurelia conducted her own investigation, though she wasn't sure what she was looking for. She waded through collapsed beams of wood and filthy cloth awning, drawn to something in the rubble heap. The men regrouped to discuss their next move, but Aurelia was fascinated by a sheet of crumpled parchment, upon which were written the words: *Istori Kanyazhna Ogonyana.*

The Visitor cocked her head, as if in anticipation of some great paroxysm of emotion from Aurelia. She was still though, and nothing moved save for a passing salamander.

"Have you found something?" Came the Visitor's voice, incisive in this cavernous space.

Aurelia had never seen the Kaspician script before, yet somehow, the words translated into her thoughts as she read them: *The Tale of the Banished Princess.*

She skimmed through a couple of the pages, but was surprised to see that the writing described Onaxia quite differently to how the Visitor had. Here, someone had spoken of Onaxia as a victim, and not an oppressor; a girl, taken away from her family against her will, forced to live in a foreign land until she could bear it no more. Onaxia was imprisoned in this cave on the grounds that she was mad, because she was dangerous. But all she wanted was to go home and be with her family. Aurelia could read no more; the rest of it had been lost to decay.

"Why can I read Kaspician? And who is Princess Onaxia, really?" She asked.

The Visitor linked her arm through Aurelia's and directed her to look ahead. She did not appreciate the Visitor's touch this time; she sensed something egregious in the solemnness of her face. There was a silence that lasted too long, so much so that it felt planned. Then, a piercing howl swept through the cavern that near sent Aurelia stumbling backwards onto the ground.

A vaporous shadow descended, blotting out the crevices of light in the ceiling. Suddenly, the cold was unbearable, gnawing at Aurelia's flesh. The men felt it too — she pitied their shivering forms and chattering teeth.

"What wicked sorcery is this?" Asked one of the warriors.

"Remain strong. They will not overwhelm us!" Ordered Morovig.

The predators emerged.

Despite their human appearance, they certainly were not mortal men or women. They edged closer, like the souls of the damned coasting through the black mists of the Nether Pits. Aurelia counted four, but could discern nothing in particular about them, as they were swaddled in shadow. She knew what they were now. Menyr. Morovig and his men huddled close together. The faint light from the lanterns was all but worthless in this level of darkness. They drew their swords. Aurelia could sense their hands shaking.

The next breath she drew, the Menyr had launched their attack. Shrouded in mist, they mauled and clawed like the centipedes of the cave. With flurries of deadly kicks and punches, Morovig's men were battered to pulps in seconds. None so much as tried to resist.

In the next instant, the thick shadows receded, and a scarcity of light illuminated the four Menyr. Although they were hidden under hooded robes, Aurelia saw their pallid, scrawny bodies; they all had the same unkempt black hair, save for one, tall man, around whose shoulders were grey locks. What disturbed her was the air of grandeur about them. Somehow, despite their wretched appearance, they stood tall, their backs poised with pride and their chins pointing to the ceiling.

A statuesque woman stepped forward. "Another man, come to kill us. You loathsome thing." Her voice, though bearing a distinct accent, was captivating.

Morovig released a gob of bloody spit as he tried to sit up. The grey-haired man pounced on him and kicked his chest back to the dirt. Morovig wheezed in pain, then rolled onto his side like a wounded dog. The dying screams of the rest of the warriors reverberated around the central chamber.

"You animals. Will Onaxia not even show her face before you kill me?" Morovig roared.

The cave-dwelling aggressors began to tip-toe back. Were they laughing? From out of the darkness, a fifth being emerged. The first four immediately stepped aside and struck the ground with their foreheads in reverence. Aurelia clung tighter to the Visitor.

"Onaxia," whispered Aurelia. In the same instant, Onaxia glared in her direction, immobilising Aurelia with fear. Only as she moved closer, did it become clear that she was looking at Morovig. Onaxia appeared to be made of neither skin nor bone, but an ethereal substance, fluctuating between spirit and flesh. She was encased in a mist that emitted an amethyst light. Her eyes were grey and irresistible; they seemed to expand and recede as though two vortices that led straight to the cosmos. As she drew up to Morovig, the atmosphere started to whistle and hum uncontrollably.

"Invader. You dare to challenge my people, when you live on land that you stole from us?" Onaxia's voice was faint, like an echo from another world. There was not only anger in her tone, but melancholy. Yet her words were bewitching, and Morovig squirmed in pain, unable to stomach her presence.

"Get out of my head, witch!" Screamed the Marshal, covering his ears.

"Your crusade ends here," Onaxia ordered, moving closer. He sat upright, suddenly stilled. For a moment, the willowy form of a woman was visible, but the ghostly mist quickly shrouded her again. She reached forwards and took his face into her shadowy hand, and said, "You will tell your brother, the King, that you slew each and every one of us. While your comrades died heroically, you alone were able to survive. The Menyr are defeated, and you will forget about us, believing that whatever threat we posed to you, is now vanquished. You will go to Frostfoot Keep, where you will be far from the capital and your allies, and your memory of me and this place will never return. Age will slowly wither you there, and by the time you return to Northcrest, you will be grey and powerless. Soon, my people will come for you and the rest of the Chicane. I have foreseen my freedom: one who bears the mark of the one who imprisoned me will be born in Northcrest, and she shall liberate me from this tomb. The Keyholder is coming."

Morovig could do nothing but nod in agreement without breaking eye contact with Onaxia. Then, he stood up and turned around, and was gone.

"*Slava Kanyazhna!*" The four creatures chanted in unison, marvelling at their mistress' power. They came together around Princess Onaxia, and Aurelia wondered whether she ought to be happy for them. From the other passageways, more Menyr began to appear. There were at least a dozen of them.

To the original four, Onaxia said, "It is time to act. The four of you are my most loyal followers. Until I am free, you must lead our people."

The Visitor nudged Aurelia, then led her closer to the scene.

The woman took down her hood. "What is it you require of us, princess?"

"No. That is impossible," Aurelia murmured, awash with horror.

"There is a young girl with the name Tillensis living in Northcrest," said Onaxia. "That is the name of the woman who put me here. You must find her and insinuate your way into her family. From her bloodline, the Keyholder will be born. When the child is ready Melindra, you must do whatever it takes to get her to me."

"Yes, princess."

"Benthrin — you must go south. We must infiltrate the Republic too. The Siladrians will be brought to their knees as well. I see it now, all of them burning. A great event will bring them together, and we will wipe them out overnight," Onaxia went on, ardent. "Kaspica will be restored under my name."

"Yes," said Benthrin. "Your wisdom is legendary."

"My power will be at your disposal in Northcrest," Onaxia said. "Henaias has not yet been extinguished. My curse lives inside him, and you will be able to draw upon its might from afar, but if you get too close to him, there is no telling what it could do. You must keep your distance from him until he is revitalised."

"Understood, Princess Onaxia," Melindra said. "I will make sure the Tillensis girl is brought before you when the time comes."

"There is one more thing you should know. They will not be powerless. Have you ever faced one of their kind before? Come. I will show you how to fight them. How to cloud their view."

Aurelia and the Visitor watched the Menyr split up. Some of them began to sort through the rubble and restore order to their settlement.

"How can this be?" said Aurelia. "How can the Queen be a Menyr?"

"Onaxia sent her to Northcrest to find your grandparents. She's been watching you ever since, waiting for this Keyholder. Her powers of illusion must be far greater than the average Menyr to have gone unnoticed for so many years."

"I've known this woman my whole life. I've lived in the same place as her, sat across from her, eaten with her. My powers are nothing, but surely I would have felt *something* off about her?"

"If she was able to draw from the vestiges of Spirit Rot in this Henaias, her will could have been much stronger than yours."

"Was there ever a great-aunt Melindra?"

The Visitor paused to consider the question. "Yes... I can see her, faintly. Her name was not Melindra, originally. The Menyr completely replaced her. I dare not think what became of your mother's real aunt, or what she did to your grandparents."

"Mother said they died of a disease. Prickly lung. I bet Melindra did that too. I can't believe this. I've been living with a monster my whole life!" Aurelia shrieked.

"Understand this, Aurelia. The Menyr are moving quickly now because of the weakness in the ancestors' plan. The destruction of the one who built this prison, it seems, can collapse it. My theory is that all those centuries ago, when Onaxia found Castrellus, she wanted to use the power of the Nomos Tal to break her chains, but Castrellus fooled her. So, she found another way out. It must have been since then that she's been following your bloodline and waiting for the Keyholder," the Visitor explained.

"Elfine is the Keyholder, isn't she?"

The Visitor nodded, conveying no emotion.

"But she didn't create this prison. You did," Aurelia surmised.

"I did not. My sister did," said the Visitor, frowning. "When the ancestors finally saw reason, they thought I was too invested in Onaxia's life. They feared that I might even show her compassion because I knew her story so well. I was sent elsewhere — to the place of my death — and my sister worked the spell that ensnared Onaxia. Just as you and I are connected, it is possible that my sister has a connection to Elfine, which likely makes her exactly what Onaxia needs."

"Sister." Aurelia had forgotten the woman of one of her earlier visions, who had called Ylestra her sister. "I saw her spirit in the Ankasa. Where is your sister now?"

"I have not felt her presence for centuries. But there was an echo of Velir when I saw Elfine. I can say nothing more; in the years I have spent here, not once have I been able to communicate with my family, until you came."

"I don't know what to say. Elfine had no part in any of this," Aurelia said. "Is she going to die? Is my sister is going to be OK?"

The Visitor's face tightened.

"Answer me!"

"It is my belief that Onaxia desires to kill Elfine."

Aurelia wiped the sudden tears away with the back of her hand. "My sister deserves life. Why go on if she must perish?"

"You must fight so that her efforts are not smudged into insignificance. If her death is what fulfils the enemy's plans, then we must find strength in her life."

"I want all of these Menyr dead," said Aurelia. "I want them gone. I want this Onaxia to be ruined. I will not let her have her way and destroy my family."

"Their magic comes from a place of evil," spoke the Visitor, "but it can be purified and washed away, like dirt. Do you see what I mean?"

The Visitor reached to touch Aurelia, and through their connection, Aurelia sensed a relic of her ancestor's power: it was the magic to dispel the shroud that the imposter queen had foisted over her supposed allies.

"Sometimes, your mind is enough to fight dark magic, but we use words of power when that is not enough. Words of the Ubija. Come, it's time you learned some real magic."

Chapter 18

The Light of the Moon

Aurelia's arrival back into her body was an uncomfortable experience, but she was glad to see that in the time she had been gone, only moments had passed in real-time. The meeting hadn't even started. Although, compared with the wealth of secrets she'd just been shown, the threat of the Kaspician invasion seemed of peripheral importance.

General Tonsag's sunken expression, bearing into her with its rife despondency, quickly grounded her back in the present. "Commander Anek," he said, addressing the man with the bow who had escorted Aurelia and Savas here. "Thank you for bringing these two here."

Commander Anek replied with a curt nod as he sat by Morovig.

"Now that *they're* here, things can get underway," grumbled Prince Zander.

"We will be civil in this hour," said the Queen, who was sitting only a few seats down from Aurelia. "Aurelia, Savas. I'm afraid that Marshal Morovig has arrived with the gravest of news: the Kaspicians are on their way. Not only this, two sentinels guarding the south gate have disappeared."

Tonsag began his usual, ominous pacing. "There was a report of a disturbance just before sunrise. People heard screaming by the south gate. We found two Protectors, mutilated and withered beyond recognition."

Aurelia couldn't help but steal a glance at the Queen. Likely the work of one of her kind, she thought. Only then as she looked around the table did she realise that Mother was not here.

"Good to know that our first line of defence is so capable," Prince Zander jibed.

"Boy, when you're strong enough to pick up a sword, then you can be the judge of a warrior's worth!" Tonsag reprimanded.

Zander turned red with embarrassment, frowning to himself.

"All gates were ordered sealed last night," continued General Tonsag. "No one was allowed to travel in or out of Northcrest without proper authorisation."

"Then they are already here," interjected Marshal Morovig. "Have we made contact with the other shires? Staghorn and Gladehill are close. We need their armies here right away," he ordered.

"I have sent word to Staghorn, Gladehill, Pelling and Cragmoor already," said Father, quieter than usual in the presence of the Marshal. "We hope to receive support from the other four shires as soon as possible, now that we have lost the Republic as an ally."

"They cannot refuse the King's demands," said Master Ingrith. "The other shires will not fail us. But what of your forces, Marshal Morovig?"

"We evacuated Frostfoot Keep a week ago," Morovig said. "My battalion is around 400 strong, and is camped on the eastern edge of the Esterwood. Their experience dealing with the Kaspicians counts for something, but we are fewer in number. What can Northcrest offer, Tonsag? Have any of your men clashed swords outside of the sparring arena?"

"Our barracks has no fewer than 1500 warriors," General Tonsag said, proudly. "Together, that puts our force at nearly 2000. Northcrest has a chance, even on its own."

Morovig sneered. "Your soldiers are pampered infants compared to the enemy. They are well over 5000 in number."

Aurelia caught a whiff of a smile on the Queen's face. She wondered if the King would say anything, then finally understood that his habitual silence was probably a symptom of Melindra's Menyr trickery.

"*5000?!*" Master Ingrith burst out. "The other shires combined would barely bring our number to that."

"Besides, Cragmoor and Pelling are over a week's ride from here," added Father. "We can't throw all our forces at this fight. Is retreat an option?"

"Retreat?" hissed the Queen Consort. "No. I want everyone here. All of our forces must rally in Northcrest. We absolutely cannot let the capital fall. If we flee our sovereign city, the enemy will know that we are weak."

Morovig dared to snort at the Queen Consort's response. "5000 says nothing of the true terror at the enemy's disposal," he said. "You all act as though the Menyr never existed, as if my crusade with the Chicane and the Protectors against them 50 years ago never happened. Did none of you read the Chicane report, or guess at what had befallen these two dead sentinels? The Menyr are leading the enemy into battle, and you want everyone to sacrifice themselves in the first fight? If the preservation of our country and our way of life is what we want, then we should be evacuating people already!"

The Queen scowled

Aurelia watched her closely. There was something in the way her jaw moved that made it seem like she was concentrating. No — she was casting a spell, just as the Visitor had said she would. Aurelia could hear it, sense it on the air like a rotten stink.

I know what your kind do. You get into people's heads and control them. Make them think how you want them to. Not this time.

Focusing for the first time in Melindra's presence, the thick fog around the table became visible to Aurelia. She could see it clinging to and obscuring the minds of everyone seated. The Queen had cast a veil of illusion over the Myriad's eyes and shrouded their view. Just as the Visitor had instructed her, Aurelia reached deep into each and every crevice of her core until she found the power to dispel what Melindra had summoned. Strong as the Queen was, it was obvious that she had not expected to be challenged here, and the fog quickly began to disperse because she had been caught her off-guard.

"The Marshal is right," said Father, rubbing his temples. "If none leave, and the Kaspicians breach Northcrest, what then? We know little of their ways. They could execute us, burn our homes to the ground with our children still inside, enslave us even. Given how strong their army is, I agree that we should evacuate."

"Agreed," added Master Ingrith. "We should have everything in place to evacuate the city by sundown. Civilians can be sent either west towards the capital of Staghorn, or southeast towards Gladehill."

"We should not flee immediately," said Prince Zander. "We have lost vision of the enemy's movements. They could have diverted their forces. Some could already be heading towards Staghorn or Gladehill. We should notify the city and make preparations for an evacuation, but not commit to it until we know what the Kaspicians are doing."

The Queen stole into the moment of silence after Zander's comment. "Northcrest is the strongest of all of Gaminia's cities," she said, passionately. "Its walls are taller and stronger than anywhere else. There is nowhere safer than here. The shire of Gladehill is nothing but farmland and small-minded villagers! There is no citadel there that can withstand an enemy invasion."

"The Queen speaks the truth," said Kistig. "We would be foolish to send people to the idyllic and indefensible Gladehill."

"What good will high walls do when the enemy has catapults and trebuchets?" Morovig insisted.

"Westiz, the capital of Staghorn, is capable of resisting an attack, yet the city is three days from here on foot — many would not survive this journey," added General Tonsag. "The Ridge of Staghorn is famously difficult to cross. It only takes one bout of rain for the terrain to become treacherous."

"Then it is a risk we must take; rain this season is rarely severe, and it hasn't stormed in months," reminded Highpriest Resus.

"Northcrest is defensible," said Tonsag. "But if Morovig speaks truly — that the enemy is led by the Menyr — who knows what dark power lies within their arsenal? We have forgotten our ancient enemy, and know little of their current capabilities."

"Menyr!" hissed the Queen. "What nonsense is this. Those creatures were eliminated decades ago. Morovig himself slew them. If one man could best them, what do we have to worry about a few more?"

Aurelia couldn't believe the irony of the Queen underplaying the danger she posed to Northcrest and its survival. How long had she and Onaxia been planning this invasion? The Myriad never considered that the threat would return, when all along, the Menyr have been ruling Gaminia, silently waiting to make their move.

"Their power lies in deception and seduction," said Morovig. "If what I know is true, they cannot destroy the city's walls any faster than an ordinary human. Yet, the effect they could have on the Protectors, and my battalion, is another matter. The Menyr rail a person's confidence, they destroy one's resolve. They can do this from afar. I've seen it before. We absolutely cannot sacrifice everything we have to protect Northcrest. I agree that some must stay behind, but my brother, the King, and a few select others should be the first out of here."

"And then what? The King cannot abdicate his throne out of fear!" shouted the Queen. "Northcrest answers only to King Thenris, or would you put yourself in charge of matters here in his absence?"

"My brother can speak for himself," snapped Morovig, looking to the King.

The King seemed barely awake. Aurelia detected the slightest jitter in his hands. Melindra grasped hold of his shaky wrist and caressed him.

"King Thenris has been very tired of late," said the Queen.

It is clear that she has him spellbound, Aurelia thought to herself. A simple touch was all Melindra needed to control the King's mind.

"We must," uttered the King, slowly, "not let the Kaspicians take Northcrest."

"A wise remark, my King," crowed the Queen.

"But my brother is right. Some of our people, along with two of the Myriad should go with them to lead. My wife and I must stay here," continued the King, apparently cutting through Melindra's befuddling fog.

"Then who should travel to Westiz?" asked Kistig, nervous.

"High-priest Resus, your words of godly wisdom would comfort our people along the journey," said the King. "And my son. Zander. You are well-connected in Westiz, you too must accompany this evacuation."

The Queen looked distressed. The idea of an evacuation had her all riled up.

"A sound plan, King Thenris," said Master Ingrith. "Perhaps, General Tonsag, you can arrange to send one of your trusted commanders also."

"That shouldn't be an issue," said the General.

"Fine, then," conceded the Queen.

"What about the Menyr?" asked Father.

Master Ingrith cleared his throat. "We never had the chance to study them, so even at the Northcrest Institute, we didn't figure out their weaknesses. I will make it my mission to go over all the old files and scour our library's resources."

They can be blasted off a balcony quite well, Aurelia thought, but even that doesn't seem to put an end to them.

"We shouldn't waste any time, then," said Morovig. "The sooner we prepare, the better. I will make my way to my men's encampment and brief them. Tonsag, you need to prepare our warriors in the barracks. The rest of you know what you have to do."

He seemed about to get up but the Queen Consort delayed him. "Are you excusing yourself already, Marshal Morovig?" she asked, pointedly. "There's still the matter of these rioting blackguards to decide."

"There is no time to punish those involved," said Prince Zander. "The Protectors must be committed to defending Northcrest from the Kaspicians."

"Agreed," said Master Ingrith. "We should only arrest those who are severely disruptive. The rest will be just as stricken with fear as we have been when they hear what is coming. Their grievances will have to wait."

"Sound advice," said General Tonsag. "Hopefully, they'll put their energy to good use in defending the city, rather than destroying it."

"Good," said Morovig, "We'll return after dusk, brother, OK?"

"Yes, we can adjourn," said the King.

Elfine's disappearance had shaken the Myriad enough, but the urgency with which they scattered this time was beyond palpable. It was apparent that they were terrified. Only Father stayed. He approached Aurelia and Savas, weary and crestfallen. Suddenly, the stark emptiness of the Great Hall was crushing.

"I never thought it'd come to this," said Father. "But don't be afraid, I'll make sure that the two of you and your mother are first in line to leave the city, even if I have to stay behind."

"Where is Mother?" asked Aurelia.

Father squinted. "The Queen saw her earlier, apparently, and said she was resting," he said. "I know I've been distant lately, but I didn't want either of you to be worried about this war. And I should have told you about the Menyr sooner," he said. "But the truth is, Morovig battled them when I was still a boy. I don't know a lot about them, other than that they hunt and kill humans for food."

Aurelia thought back to her vision with the Visitor of the butchery in the cave, where slabs of greying meat were dribbling all over the counter. She'd never considered that it could have been human flesh.

"We know about the Menyr," said Savas.

Father recoiled slightly. "How?"

"There's a lot we haven't told you," Aurelia said.

"What do you know? Did they take Elfine? Do they have your sister?!" demanded Father.

"Yes," answered Aurelia.

Father looked furious, but too sad to surrender fully to anger.

Aurelia had never seen her father well up like this. "There's a cave somewhere far from here where the leader of the Kaspicians is trapped. Princess Onaxia. The Menyr are taking Elfine to her as some sort of barbaric sacrifice," she continued.

Father grabbed her by her collar and glared deeply at her. "This isn't another of your mother's ludicrous fantasies, is it?!"

"Get off her!" Savas shouted.

Startled, Aurelia leapt back. "No! These are my own fantasies," she said. "And Melindra is a poor source of information. She is a Menyr."

Both were stunned straightaway. They stared at her, their expressions formed of pure fear.

"How did you come to this conclusion?" asked Father.

"I have seen it, and that's all I can say," she replied.

"I have been suspicious of the King's condition for some time, but Melindra is so cogent it's hard to doubt anything she says," Father added, his voice low.

"She's had you in her pocket the whole time! You need to focus on helping the city right now. That's the first step to redeeming yourself after bartering away Elfine to the Chancellor. Savas and I will deal with the Queen."

Father's expression wilted. "You can't be serious. If you go after without evidence, even I won't be able to protect you. What proof do you have?"

"Nothing tangible, so you'll just have to trust me. Are you on our side, or hers?"

"If she's a Menyr, she'll kill both of you," Father warned.

"No," said Aurelia. "When I get the chance, I'm going to break every bone in her body."

Father was suspended in disbelief. He didn't know anything about Aurelia's new powers. "I will not let you face her alone," he said.

"Have you ever been to this part of the Castle before?" Savas asked, rushing to keep up with Aurelia and Father as they made for the royal chamber.

"No," she answered.

"What are we going to do if the Queen is actually in there? Are you even ready to face her?"

"I don't know yet," she said.

"Shush, Savas!" Father snapped.

He had armed himself with a knife. Aurelia hadn't wanted him to come along; she was concerned that he'd get hurt, or make matters worse in some other way. But he'd been intent on helping, and she was pleased to finally see him doing some good. It was about time.

"It's through here," said Father, who then led them down a long corridor, at the end of which was a grand entrance. "I sincerely hope you're wrong about this, but if you aren't, stay behind me, and say nothing."

"Queen Consort Melindra?" called Father, cautiously easing the door open. "It's urgent. Are you in there?"

A breeze whistled as the door opened. The windows to the balcony were open, clattering against the wall and allowing a stream of leaves to enter and rustle along the floor.

"There's no one here," said Father.

Savas tottered by the door, but Aurelia strode in. She'd never set foot in this august chamber before. Her eyes searched exclusively for Mother, uninterested in the opulent décor.

"Something's not right," she said quietly.

"We need to get out now. If we are caught trespassing in here, only the Three will be able to save us," said Father, making for the door.

"Wait!" Savas burst out. "Aurelia's right. I sense something," he said, stepping further in.

"What is it?" asked Aurelia.

"It's right in front of us." Savas stood next to Aurelia and reached forward into the empty space in the centre of the room. "Ow!"

A fleeting flash of black lit up in a circle and made a clapping noise like a peal of thunder before it vanished.

"What on Ysa was that?" cried Father.

"Give me your hand," Aurelia instructed her brother. "She's covering everything in fog so we can't see."

Savas looked at her, unsure, but he put out his palm.

"I can see it clearer when I hold your hand. I know how to get rid of it," said Aurelia.

Similar to what she had seen in the Great Hall, Aurelia witnessed a dark cloud come to life before her. As though it were possessed by a demonic vitality that gave it strong limbs to lash with, it flailed and hissed. It was far greater than what she had seen in the Great Hall. Melindra had conjured something very powerful in here.

"It's fighting us," said Savas.

"What are you two grappling with? I see nothing!" Father exclaimed.

Aurelia's body began to quiver with a chill. A miasma of black magic in the room was doing its utmost to snare her, but like a beacon of strength, she clung tightly onto her brother and leeched a portion of his magic. With Savas' support, she struck back at the evil presence, and it produced a vile screech in its pain. Its strength declining, a glimmer of what the dark magic concealed on the floor suddenly appeared.

"Was that Mother?" said Savas.

Father rushed in between the two of them, hoping to see something. He looked distraught. "Trinne!? Trinne, are you in here?"

Aurelia held on, but she knew that her will alone was not enough to exorcise whatever this was. The shadow-quilted cloud endured, constantly trying to push her back. As if caught in a windy tunnel, she, Savas and Father began to slide back towards the door. Father grabbed hold of both of them in a panic, but the force pushing them was too strong.

"What's happening?" shouted Father.

A horrid whirring noise entrapped the chamber as the wind picked up speed. Melindra was close. But Aurelia hadn't come this far unprepared; the Visitor had shown her how to battle this dark magic of illusion, how to make it flee. She had seen the spell already in the Ankasa when that thing had come for her. The language should have been alien to her, for it did not resemble anything she had ever come across, but the words of the Ubija flowed naturally out of her mouth, as if she had spoken them countless times before, as if this language was her own.

"*Ki sata wavesti!*"

The shrouding nebula's horrid face, complete with a long mouth and bone-white eyes and scrawny limbs became visible. It hissed and squealed all the way to the window, where it exploded into a fine, black powder.

Father dropped to the floor instantly to embrace Mother, who was curled up like a child on the floor, her eyes two tired slants and her complexion robbed of its usual glow. "Trinne! Are you OK? Say something!" he cried.

Savas helped Father prop her up onto the bed before starting to snivel with tears.

Aurelia glanced at Mother with dread, but she couldn't consign herself to sorrow yet. Melindra could have been anywhere, plotting something even more nefarious. "We need to get out of here. Let's take her to your quarters," Aurelia said to Father.

"I can walk... just," Mother managed to say. "Mitenni... bring Mitenni too."

The tower that Aurelia's parents lived in never seemed so chilling a place. Aurelia hadn't stopped shaking since arriving. Mother was lying on her bed, severely ill, tended to by Mitenni, who had quickly made a restorative potion after being summoned by Savas.

Aurelia and her father were stood by his desk.

"We need to leave Northcrest tonight," he said. "If the Queen has done this and we are the ones standing in her way, there's no telling what other treachery she has readied. The whole council could be working for her!"

"I can't leave yet," Aurelia said. "I've been given a responsibility, and I intend to see it through."

"You've kept so much from me. Are you going to tell me what's been going on?"

"I don't know," she said. "Can you be trusted?"

He scowled. "You have no respect for me at all! I am your father. You should be able to trust me with anything."

"And yet I cannot, because of what you did to Elfine! I don't know whose side you're on," said Aurelia.

"I have only ever been on the right side," he retorted. "I will never forgive myself for Elfine, but the pressure was too great. Did you really think, after all this time it was my idea? The Queen was the one who encouraged me to meet with Chancellor Rorstein and offer this in exchange for his support. Only now do I see how much of a fool I was to listen to her. I feel filthy having worked for her!"

"She encouraged you, but it was you who did it. You could've chosen to fight Melindra's suggestion, or at least tell us about it. Savas and I would have had the sense to talk you out of it," Aurelia argued.

"I'm so sorry, Aurelia," said Father. "I want to do everything in my power to put things right. What are we dealing with?"

"I hope so, because you have a lot of work to do," said Aurelia. "Remember Princess Onaxia, who I mentioned earlier? The Menyr serve her. She is imprisoned with magic in the cave where Morovig's crusade ended. Onaxia enchanted his mind and made him tell everyone in Northcrest that he had killed all the Menyr, but he didn't kill any of them. Melindra was in that cave; she could be one of Onaxia's most loyal followers. They have been trying to set her free for years, and conquer Gaminia. Now that they have taken Elfine, they will finally be able to unlock the doors of Onaxia's prison. They can't be stopped, but we can slow them down. There used to be a place called the House of Noul; its entrance is now hidden by magic, but inside, there is a person who can help us fight Onaxia and her army. I have to reach him."

Father's mouth quivered, unable to produce a sound.

"I was lost for words too when I started to experience these things," Aurelia said. "But I don't need anything from you, only your trust."

"No Aurelia, it's not that I have nothing to say," he said. "I have come across the name Onaxia before, when I was a student at the White Academy. There are extremely rare works in there that only the most privileged of eyes get to read. There was one tale about the birth of Kaspica, how it became a country some 2000 years ago. The people were led there by a man called Hessiern who claimed to have mystical powers because of a book, said to be a gift from the gods. Onaxia was his daughter, but something happened. He disappeared, and she never took the throne after his death. In the end, Kaspica became divided into fractious oblasts, no longer a kingdom. How can his heir still live after all this time?"

"She must be some kind of immortal, I don't know," said Aurelia.

"Could be something to do with the book," Savas added.

"Do you remember anything else about the book?" Aurelia asked.

Father ran his fingers through his hair. "Only that it was not written by humans, and that it did not originate in these lands. It was believed to have arrived in the possession of some sort of monk from the Southern Continent, who said that the gods of his religion intended for Hessiern to be master of the book. There was a whole, ridiculous prophecy ascribed to him wielding the book's power. Naturally, the madman believed it."

"If Onaxia is no ordinary human, perhaps it was written by her kind," Aurelia hypothesised.

"We'll probably never know," said Father. "I want to know how this all began. I've never seen anything like what you did to that thing."

"It started with dreams," Aurelia replied. "Visions. Spirits. Then, something awoke inside me, and now, I have special powers."

"I think we might have died in there if you hadn't done what you did."

"We would have, if Savas hadn't helped me," said Aurelia.

His gaze shifted to the ground for a moment, then made its way back to Aurelia. "We must anticipate that

Melindra knows we have foiled whatever she had planned for Trinne. Menyr are cunning and deceptive beasts. If she's powerful enough to have not aged in four decades and infiltrate Sunhold so easily, anyone who is not around you or your brother could be susceptible to her domination. Your mother is in no condition to travel; she'll need at least two days—"

"I'm fine," Mother called, standing by the railing of the open second floor. "And we aren't going anywhere, not until Aurelia and Savas have done what they have to do. Ishanaia has called them to this. We can't run yet. And we can't give up on Elfine."

"Trinne! Are you alright?" Father asked.

Mother came down the stairs, helped by Mitenni.

"That monster that has pretended to be my aunt all these years, she took something from me," said Mother. "She entered my mind whilst I was incapacitated and watched my dreams. My memories. She saw what I had seen of our ancestors in the Ankasa. I don't know what she was looking for, but she found it. Something Ishanaia must have shown me that I had overlooked. Whatever it is, Melindra now thinks that she has the advantage. I doubt she will return to Sunhold until her aspirations are achieved."

"But what are her aspirations?" asked Savas.

"To wipe out our leadership, for one," said Mother. "She almost had all of the Republic's and our most important people in one place, had the Chancellor and his wife not fled." Mother paused, and took a breath. "When Melindra tunnelled into my mind, I saw a memory of hers. Do any of you remember a tall priest from Elfine's wedding? Melindra met with this man and several others in Endvil the night before the event."

"Several others? Just how many Menyr are there?" said Savas.

"There were five, maybe six with her," replied Mother. "I fear we won't know their plans until they know ours. We have to be proactive. Aurelia has to do her duty, and Savas must help her. Our one advantage is that they probably never imagined we could fight them, and yet the two of you are looking stronger by the day."

"Dispelling that fog was one matter," said Aurelia, "but I've seen the Menyr in a vision and they are fearsome fighters. We know that Elfine was bested by one and she is a warrior. Savas and I cannot fight them alone. We don't know their weaknesses."

"Lady Aurelia," interjected Mitenni. "If I may offer some advice, the Menyr, as your people call them, are known to my people also. There are many tales told by the haruspices about them."

"Haruspices?" Savas interjected.

Aurelia remembered reading that an unnamed haruspex had bidden Castrellus to steal the Nomos Tal. He must have belonged to similar people as Mitenni.

"My people are nomadic," said Mitenni. "They follow the wisdom of a haruspex, or haruspices — someone who can divine the future," she explained. "I have never seen a Menyr, but the haruspices knew that moonlight was their weakness. The creatures would never come to us at night if the moon was in full bloom. That is why the moon is one of our greatest deities."

"You expect us to weaponise the light of a floating rock?!" cried Father. "Please, Mitenni, don't bother unless you have something useful to offer."

Her face flushed with embarrassment. "I did not mean to suggest that we do this ourselves Thane Olsin — one has already done it for us," Mitenni said. "Before her wedding, Lady Elfine carried home a sword. I do not know who gave it to her, but I recognised the Sygecian symbols on it at once. It is a haruspex's sword, imbued with the moon's power already."

"If only she'd had it with her when she was taken," Savas lamented. "I'll take the sword. I can't do any magic tricks, but I'm sure I can lop someone's head off if I have to."

"Are you sure, son?" said Father, graver than ever. "No one should go up against a Menyr with that sort of confidence."

"I'm ready for this," he said. "And I'll have Aurelia to protect me if anything goes wrong."

She nodded. "But we still don't know where the House of Noul is."

"The place you seek is underneath the ungodly hollow in Endvil known as the Temptress' Parlour," Mother said.

"The Parlour?" Savas said. "That's why the Wraith kept going back. He was probably looking for the way in."

No sooner had Savas reached the doorway, when a deafening noise rocked the whole room. Father tumbled into his desk and several of his books fell off the shelves.

"What on Ysa was that? Ishanaia have mercy!" screamed Mother.

Aurelia bolted to the window and couldn't mask her horror. Racing to her mouth, her hand tried to suppress the scream. "Morovig said they were a full day away," she stammered. "But they're here. The Kaspicians are here."

Chapter 19

The Fire Woman and her Lover

The Chicane meeting house had been barren these past few days. At least Zatela knew where Rhyslan was: headed towards that cave, hoping to link up with the force General Tonsag had recently dispatched. Terig's fate remained a worry, Elfine had been kidnapped, and Lorcan hadn't been seen since the night of the wedding. There were no other members of the Chicane left; so many had died since Zatela first joined.

There wasn't time to go and look for Lorcan. The enemy had already begun its barrage of the city, and several boulders had been catapulted into Northcrest and levelled a number of houses. The city was in a state of panic. None had expected the enemy to arrive this soon. Yet it wasn't the bulk of their force. From the battlements by the east gate, close to 500 Kaspicians could be seen. So far, they had barely dented the city walls because of Morovig's army, who were desperately fending them off in the Esterwood.

Everywhere Zatela went, Protectors were clattering like dazed flies doing nothing but buzzing aimlessly around. She knew she was needed out there. Morovig's men were good, but they were nothing compared to someone who had served in the Chicane for four decades. As a leader, she had a duty to find Lorcan, and that was what had impelled her to Benthrin's house, where she had sent Elfine and Lorcan.

Once inside, the smell was a sensory violation. Ordinary cadavers didn't stink like this. But she knew well what the Menyr did to their victims. Sucking the life force out of a human being quickly turned it putrescent. She took one look then closed the doors to that gruesome wardrobe; what remained of Lorcan was not worth burying.

"This happened on your watch," said Okim, the oldest serving member of the Chicane.

About a decade ago, Okim had instructed Zatela to keep his identity a secret from the Chicane's newer recruits, as over time, his path directed him away from the life of a monster-hunting spy. The ailing King and the scheming Queen, along with the fact that the Menyr had seemingly vanished, rattled Okim. Thus, Zatela had kept his secret and left him to do what he thought was the most effective way of helping Northcrest and its people. She wasn't sure how much of a difference he'd made, but she knew that through clandestine meetings, he had amassed quite a following.

"How could you be so negligent to send him here like this, when he wasn't ready?" Asked Okim.

"They should've been able to handle it together." She retorted. "I gave them Hermesian weapons. I trained them for years to be able to do this."

"The Menyr outsmarted us. And now they are here with an army. Northcrest will last a month at best, even if our allies arrive. Two of our most promising recruits have been wasted before the war has even begun. Where does that leave us? Only you and I remain in Northcrest with any power to oppose this army."

"We still have time," said Zatela. "They are not all here, only a fragment of their army is on our doorstep. Your mission can still succeed, and so can mine. I have made the journey before."

"What new idiocy is this!" snarled Okim. "Don't tell me you mean to go back there, while they are toppling our walls and Chapel Heights burns?"

"If Terig is still out there, alive, I need him," Zatela said. "We need to explore every avenue available, and there are things his people could offer that we won't get anywhere else. You know it's true, it's the only reason why you ever agreed to let a Kaspician into our ranks."

Okim grumbled. "What help could his kin provide at this stage? They are a broken lot, wandering endlessly around the Taiga."

"They are broken *because* of Onaxia. They want her dead just as much as we do. The Gaminians may have stolen Northcrest from the Kaspicians all those years ago, but Kaspica wasn't theirs for the taking either. Those people are now strangers in their own land. They would do anything to see Onaxia dead, and Terig is our key to getting them on our side."

"Northcrest will not be standing by the time you return, that is *if* you survive the journey back."

"Okim — the Chicane have served you in secret for years. What you have achieved is monumental. You started something that's going to change the world. I need one last, epic quest in my life. My powers are still strong, even after all these years have gone by. The Sygecian sun still blazes through my blood; the cold winds of Kaspica will not claim me."

"If you leave, the Chicane is no more," Okim said.

"Lorcan has been butchered and Elfine has been kidnapped. Rhyslan, I hope, will succeed, but otherwise, Terig is the only hope we have left. There is no reason for the Chicane to exist anymore."

"We failed Lorcan. He was an orphan, but Elfine has Ojanti blood, like you. If Rhyslan catches up to her, there's a chance that they might survive still."

Zatela sniffed, but there were no actual tears to wipe away. "I should have done more for Elfine. But what do I know of the Ojanti? I was born a slave. I know nothing of who my parents were, or why I can summon devastation into the world with my mind."

"Don't act the fool now, Zatela — you know more of the Ojanti than I. Is it not true that they can speak to you from a spiritual plane, hidden from mortal eyes?"

She looked away.

"Morovig recruited you for your connection to the Ojanti: those magic-bearing people from that dark, forgotten continent. You know that."

"Morovig was a fool. He brought me into the Chicane because he wanted to have sex with me."

Okim sighed. "Despite his shortcomings, you found Elfine. Her family could be the only Northcresters left with Ojanti blood. You know that the Menyr took Elfine because they figured out the same truth as we did. That family must be related to—"

"I can't stay in this skragging pit of a house any longer," she snapped, heading to the door. "Morovig is waiting for us in Endvil."

"Zatela — wait," Okim said. "I understand why you must go. Terig and you are bonded by love as much as oath. I will not stand in your way. Come, let us find Morovig and show the Kaspicians what we do best."

Zatela had always moved with a certain lethality, as though at any moment she might pierce the heart of a passer-by with a concealed dagger. That's if they even saw her. Most never did. In the 38 years she'd lived in Gaminia, her enemies who had laid eyes on her had only done so just before she killed them.

She arrived in Northcrest at the age of 16 after escaping from the illegal ring of slavery in Sygecia, a terrible legacy that she was born into. Buying and selling people as property was outlawed across the Southern Continent, but it remained legal in the country Calech, the originator of slavery on the continent. The Calechians, unfortunately, being richer and more powerful than the Sygecians, often were able to purchase unwanted Sygecian children as slaves, like Zatela. That was until she accidentally projected enough fire out of her fingertips to burn down the manor of the warlord who bought her. A few days later, after stealing his Hermesian swords, she hid as a stowaway on a cargo vessel bound for Gladehill and never returned.

She hitchhiked to Northcrest, survived on the streets for a year, then got a job as a barmaid. As the years wore on, she earned a reputation as a fierce fighter, able to batter any of the drunkards that frequented her bar. By the time she was 19, Morovig Helig, then leader of the Chicane, recruited her into his enigmatic organisation. Almost four decades ago, that was a much more powerful version of the Chicane, one that was loyal to King Thenris.

When it was understood that Morovig was to be made Lord of Frostfoot Keep, and step down from his role in the Chicane, the organisation was completely transformed under Okim; he realised that if the Menyr were the true enemy, then the entire political system needed to be revamped, with an end to the current corrupt monarchical system being pivotal to his plans. In a secret ceremony, King Thenris swore in Okim as the new leader, but Okim directed his efforts elsewhere, and after he recruited Zatela, he made her the unequivocal face of the institution, meaning that she would report to King Thenris and the Myriad, and that she had the right by law to recruit whoever she wanted into the Chicane. Under Okim's guidance, the identities of Terig, Rhyslan and Elfine were never publicly revealed to the Myriad.

Towards the southern edge of Endvil, close to the south gate, Zatela, Okim and Morovig convened in a quiet alley.

She had not laid eyes on Morovig, her old mentor, for over thirty years, but his presence was just as unmistakable now as then. Age had not wilted him too gravely, though the glacial winds of Frostfoot Keep had turned his skin paler and tauter.

"After so many years, you can't imagine how happy I am to see you both," Morovig began.

"And what delightful company you've brought with you," said Okim, with a smile.

"I'm leaving, Morovig," Zatela cut in tersely. "I'm going to Kaspica to find Terig." Saying it aloud this time, she started to remember what Kaspica was like: the endless winter, the enormity of the Taiga, filled with so many eyes and the bleak towns, set in the steep mountains.

"To Kaspica?" said Morovig.

"I need to find Terig. He can help us," she said.

"That's if he's still alive," Okim added.

Morovig beheld her solemnly. "Even you cannot survive there. The Menyr... can you face so many of them?"

"For a time."

"I fear you are sacrificing yourself."

"Afraid that the former slave girl is braver than you?"

"You are fiercer than any of I have known."

Zatela squinted sharply.

"It's not my fault, you know," Morovig said.

"That the Menyr besiege us, or that you abandoned us?" asked Okim.

Morovig shrank backwards slightly, humiliated. "Something happened in the Great Hall. Memories started to return to me, ones that I never knew I had. Onaxia... she had me spellbound. I never wanted to go to Frostfoot Keep and leave you, or lie about the Menyr. I don't know why, but I have been recently freed from her chains."

In the distance, something rattled, like bottles or jars being knocked over.

"We haven't time for this," said Okim. "Zatela intends to leave and we must help her on her way. Your men need all the help they can get out there before darkness falls."

Footsteps approached in the distance and Zatela switched to high alert. She wasn't sure if the others sensed the threat. They weren't as sharp as her. She shot Morovig and Okim a look of concern and both reached for their swords.

She jumped and climbed upwards onto a roof, where she hid to observe the full spectacle. Crouched low on the weak tiles, she waited. Morovig suddenly looked old and weak from here, but Okim's wide-legged stance was threatening as he stood back-to-back with the Marshal.

In a sudden display of movement, a flash of shadow, skittered towards the two warriors, striking in the centre of them and splitting them apart like a knife through bone. The shadow disappeared. Zatela could not trace it, though her eyes looked for it desperately.

"Menyr!" screeched Okim.

"Where is it?" called Morovig, struggling back onto his feet.

Zatela still saw nothing, although she was frantically searching. A strong wind began to blow her forwards until she lost balance. She made to grip onto the edge of the roof, but it was too late, and the force had already brought her to the ground. Quickly rising to her feet, she saw the foe at last. It reached from behind Morovig and grabbed him around the chest with a fierce grip. In an instant, the Marshal looked sapped, but Okim leaped towards him and shoved the hooded assailant back.

As the two continued to challenge their attacker, Zatela realised that a second Menyr was after her. The strong wind returned with renewed vigour and thrust her into the door of the house she had been on top of. She crashed into it, grateful for the protective leather which shielded her from being badly winded. A figure, hooded and disguised behind the same black robes now stood before her.

"Did you think we weren't watching you?" asked the one in front of Zatela. Its voice was razor-sharp.

She looked up and saw that whoever was to her left was fending off both Okim and Morovig well enough with a much less impressive sword than theirs. The way the Menyr moved mesmerised Zatela — they were enviably deft.

"Aren't you arrogant," said Zatela. "You don't know how many have been watching you." She reached around herself and took out her weapons of choice: a slender axe, excellent for throwing at people's heads, and a short Hermesian sword — the kind of blade that can send a Menyr to its grave for good.

"Don't listen to it Zatela; it'll get in your head!" cried Okim, mid-parry.

Zatela heard residents screaming from their homes, doors locking and windows bolting shut. She wasn't intimidated by one Menyr though. Her weapons readied, she launched into a brutal attack, swinging both blades and manoeuvring around her opponent with twirling, dance-like flourishes. Although the creature moved nimbly with a dagger in its hand, it was not quick enough to best her. Zatela placed blow after blow into its blocks, and after each strike, she felt her opponent's strength weaken, until she was able to plant a grisly kick into its chest, sending it tumbling down into a wall.

"Cut off its head, Okim, unless you've a Hermesian blade?" She heard Morovig say. A dying keen followed; the others must have beaten their opponent.

Zatela looked at the hooded fiend on the ground, suddenly no longer so frightening. "No more tricks?"

"The more time you waste here, the easier the road to our goal becomes," spluttered the creature. "*Navist menye selit!*"

As the Menyr thrust out its palm, Zatela was sent skirting backwards towards her companions. She managed to get back up onto her feet in time to react as the creature tried to make an escape. Taking aim with her axe, she threw the weapon, and it produced a conclusive crack as it embedded itself in the thing's skull. After a second of wobbling on its feet, the monster fell to the floor, dead.

She dislodged her axe from its head and unveiled its hood, revealing the blood-drenched face of a familiar man. "Kistig," she spat. "One of the Myriad."

"I don't recognise this man," Morovig said, as Okim took off the other's hood.

"Ysa be damned," Okim said. "Isn't this the priest who testified against the Siladrian boy — Sigun?"

"That's him, yes," Zatela answered. "There must be more, working on some greater evil."

"You can't fight every battle, Zatela," Okim said. "Morovig and I will still be here in the days to come. We should join the soldiers in the Esterwood so that you can depart safely."

In the distance, Zatela heard another boulder crash into part of the city. She'd heard five since the enemy arrived, and each one shook the city worse than the last. But it was what followed that was the most unsettling: the screams of fear and wails of those crushed, the knowledge that the Protectors could do nothing to defend the city and the guilt that she had not done enough in her role as leader of the Chicane to protect Northcrest.

The three ascended up to the battlements as dusk approached, and from there, took a clear view of the situation in the Esterwood before embarking into the fray. It didn't take long to draw up a conclusion: things were dire. Morovig's force had thinned already, while the Kaspicians seemed to have lost far less. No one expected things would go differently. The enemy had the Menyr at the helm, and could find confidence in the fact that they had thousands more on the way.

As darkness drew near, both sides would inevitably seek shelter and rest instead of blindly flailing at one another. There were few with vision which could penetrate shadow like Zatela. That was another mystical gift she knew she had inherited from her predecessors, and one which meant she was not afraid to venture towards Kaspica as night was about to fall.

Standing before the east gate now, there were around a couple of hundred Protectors on the embattlements above, trying to aim their arrows and crossbow bolts through the trees. On the ground, they were guiding locals and doing their best to keep as many people as possible safe. The rest of Northcrest's army was spread around the city, with a few hundred tending to the ruin in Chapel Heights, where several of the catapult shots had landed.

"Marshal Morovig!" called a sergeant by the gate, who then saluted. "Are you planning to head into the Esterwood? We could use your expertise here."

"I'm needed out there," he said. "Get the gates open."

"Yes, Marshal," said the man.

Zatela hurried past him. She reminded herself where her weapons were and how they felt, instantly priming herself to attack the next Kaspician she saw. As much as she'd hoped the fighting might have slowed down, the nearby cries, clashes of steel and hisses of arrows portended that it could go on all night. Zatela had forgotten the stench of the battlefield too. Even moments after dying, a human body could stink. That didn't stop her from advancing through the Esterwood, straight to Morovig's men. The sight of the Kaspicians, so close to Northcrest, was abhorrent. Their sheer size and brutish bodies were enough to scare most; often covered in tattoos all up and down their bulging arms and bare chests, they were grisly.

"I will cut a path that way!" Zatela called to Morovig and Okim, pointing ahead as she did so. There was a road that led north — the same one that the Kaspicians had travelled along. It was the way she intended to take, though she would move discreetly.

"Come then," said Okim, "let us clear the path of muck for you."

"Bonus points if you kill a Menyr," said Zatela, lightly.

"There'll be no scorekeeping on the battlefield, just cut off as many heads as you can," Morovig said, drawing his sword and following Zatela.

"You aren't the boss anymore, remember? I rather like the idea of keeping a tally," Okim tittered.

"Try to keep up with me — and don't die. I won't go back to bury either of you," Zatela said, freeing her sword from a Kaspician's massive forehead. She hadn't fought in battle alongside Okim or Morovig for years. The last time she'd fought with Morovig was in that cave, where she had hidden when the Menyr proved too much to deal with. She still remembered the sight of Onaxia; that was when Zatela fled, using all the magic she could to make herself undetectable.

Now, there was something intensely gratifying about dicing off arms and lodging her axe into enemy shoulders with these two at her side. While she had come to enjoy the relative peace Gaminia had fostered in the last few years, it had made her complacent. Amid war, death and darkness, she thrived.

"Zatela!" Morovig called from behind.

She turned around quickly and saw him signalling that a slim pathway had opened up through the enemy forces. Three Kaspicians came for her, thinking she was distracted, but she balled her first and summoned the fire that had lived within her since she escaped Sygecia and a hissing wave of flames gushed out of her, setting the enemy soldiers in front ablaze. The smell of burning flesh always made her nose twitch for a few seconds. By the time they'd fallen down, charred and unrecognisable, it was time to leave. One glance back was all she offered to Okim and Morovig as she stole away, ready to reunite with her lover and gather an unlikely army.

Chapter 20

The North Wind Rises

For the first time ever, Savas and his sister had slept in the tower too, albeit uncomfortably on the floor. The noises that continued to sound from both beyond and within Northcrest's walls had kept Savas up most of the night. Nothing, Savas thought, could match the horror when that first catapult had hurtled straight into a high-rise in Chapel Heights, but now, the spectral screams and wails in the dark seemed the most frightening of all.

He looked out of the tower's slim windows, glum. Smoke was rising in grey plumes out of Chapel Heights and Endvil. They'd been fortunate that the ballistae hadn't landed in King's Respite yet. Many Protectors had amassed around Sunhold while others patrolled the streets. Yet even as they did so, Savas was unconvinced that they would be enough. After just one night of defending the city, a sad, exhaustion proliferated in the air. Savas doubted that anyone in Northcrest believed that victory was possible.

"Sleep alright?" Aurelia asked at the first light of dawn. She'd crept up on him. "We should get a move on. You know where this Parlour is, I'm assuming?"

"I can't go straight there," Savas said. "I need to find Temek and make sure she's OK."

"Northcrest is being razed to the ground — we've wasted enough time by sleeping this long. We need to find the House of Noul now," she said.

"How can you even say that? I can't go about my day as though my only friend doesn't exist because you have some supernatural calling."

"Don't you realise that we don't have any time to spare?" She argued.

"Saving a life is not a waste of time," he retorted.

"Be quiet! The both of you!" shouted Father, suddenly at the top of the stairs. "We can't think up here with your racket."

"Sorry," Savas muttered.

"Are you ready to go? Have you got the Journal?" Father asked.

With pursed lips, Aurelia said yes, motioning to her satchel.

"What are you going to do while we're gone?" asked Savas.

"I will try to get word to Queen Hildra of Lyrel and King Zakaria of Pisca," he said. "And I need to meet with the Myriad, without Melindra finding out. Pray to the Three for safety, and don't forget Elfine. You may find information about what has happened to her on your way."

"We haven't forgotten Elfine; we'll keep our eyes peeled," said Savas. "Will Mother be alright?"

"She'll be fine. Go on now, your sister needs you. We all do."

As Savas waved from the doorway, he wondered what it would be like to not see his parents again. He stopped along the bridge to take in the full view of Northcrest for a moment.

It was worse than the Nether Pits.

Savas didn't share his sister's newfound courage to march right into the hell that was taking over their world. Then again, he also had not found himself in possession of a host of new supernatural powers to actually make a difference. He wasn't surprised by Aurelia's confidence — he knew his little sister was the kind of person to change the world for the better if she could. But what was he supposed to do? It was more than just the anxiety of Northcrest being destroyed, it was the fear that he would eventually have to follow Aurelia somewhere new. Somewhere even worse perhaps. In a way, he hated himself for his cowardice. He didn't even like Northcrest. Even his parents, the two people he'd known the longest, rarely showed him any affection. He had nothing going here, apart from Temek, and that wasn't exactly going anywhere. Somehow, he sensed she was about to be swallowed up by a destiny of her own too. Savas wasn't ready for everything to change like this, but he did his best to seem unfazed by it all.

"We'll find her, but after that, we've got to get to the House of Noul," Aurelia said.

"I'll get the sword from Elfine's room and meet you outside."

The air in Elfine's room was cool, like what one might find in a crumbling, uninhabited house. The feeling of a sudden, inexplicable emptiness was palpable. It was as though Elfine had been gone for years already. He rifled through her things and guilt gnawed at him. If Elfine was dead, would he suffer for disturbing her possessions?

Stop it, he thought. Elfine was alive. He fumbled through a drawer with shaky hands and a glimmer caught his eye under the bed. Somehow, the fact that she'd slept with the sword under her bed made him feel worse: had she kept it there out of fear that something might stalk and attack her while she slept? As he lifted the weapon and took it out of its sheath, its lightness surprised him. It didn't seem like there was anything special about it, until the sunlight caught the steel and illuminated the foreign inscription along the blade. They were symbols and pictograms, like nothing he'd ever seen before. Immediately, he sensed that they were arcane and older than any language he knew. He struck the air a few times to practise; though he had never wielded any sort of weapon before, it didn't feel so unnatural to have it in his grip. The feel of the hilt was entrancing, and Savas could've sworn he heard whispers as he held it. He strapped it around his waist and headed out.

"What took you so long?" asked Aurelia, standing in front of Sunhold, where close to a hundred Protectors were gathered.

"Are we in a rush?" said Savas, simpering at a cloud of smog. "We won't get past them without a good reason. Come on, let's sneak out the back."

On the journey to Endvil, they passed only chaos and destruction. Sunhold remained a distance from the devastation, but here, it was altogether horrific. Savas had never smelt, heard or seen death on this scale. War was thought to be a thing of the past. It was something that Tutor Fark might have lectured about, but it wasn't supposed to become a reality. That was what Savas had grown up believing. And yet Northcrest's streets were inundated with the cries of screaming children, separated from their parents, and bewildered Protectors doing their utmost to rescue people crushed under fallen buildings. Worst of all was the air, filled with smoke and the aroma of burning human flesh.

It came as little relief that the Kaspicians hadn't breached the city yet — they were doing more than enough damage from beyond the walls with catapulted projectiles.

"Temek lives just down this alley," said Savas, pushing past a couple of teenage boys, looking for their lost sister. But Savas immediately stopped. There was nothing. Were his eyes mistaken? He hoped it was not true. All of the buildings on Temek's side of the path had been crushed. A cracked boulder gloated amid the rubble, its dirty deed done. Savas' stomach felt barren, as though his insides had been gobbled up by ravening maggots. His lips and jaw quivered.

"Savas..." Aurelia uttered.

He ignored her and bolted towards the ruins. It was impossible to tell if anyone had been in there. The whole house had been flattened to ruins. He tried to manoeuvre the debris, calling Temek's name all the while, but he saw no evidence of a body.

"She might not have been in there," Aurelia tried to reassure him. "Savas — don't break down. Think. Temek wouldn't have been sat idly in her house at a time like this. Where else could she be?"

A woman close to Mother's age darted past Savas and Aurelia and fell to her knees screaming as she saw the ruination of the alley.

"The North Wind," Savas said, finally. "I know where to go."

They crossed a small bridge and passed into the part of Endvil that bordered Brighthaven, where the atmosphere was less dire. There were fewer people on the streets. Most had sequestered themselves in their homes, perhaps hoping for an update on the evacuation procedure. It was fortunate that Temek had explained where this place was before. The site where the revolution met surprised Savas — it was a moderate manor, easily more impressive than the average Brighthaven home. Like the rest of the area, it had managed to avoid the onslaught of the catapults, which had so far only struck the eastern part of Northcrest.

A few revolutionaries were standing by the property's side entrance; the front was boarded shut. As Savas and Aurelia approached, the revolutionaries became cagey.

"Why are you here?" asked one of them.

"The North Wind," Savas said urgently.

The man eyed him up and down cautiously, then looked to his companions for direction.

A second stepped forward. He looked to be a little older than the first to speak. "Which of these four books contains the most wisdom: *A Farmhand's Guide to Udders, Hooves & Snouts; Stop Hiring Hellasics!: A Completely Non-racist Reflection;* or *On Revolutionary Matters: The Green Book?*"

"Be quick about it! There's only one answer," barked the third doorman.

"*On Revolutionary Matters: The Green Book,*" Savas snapped.

The second man to speak slapped Savas on the arm enthusiastically. "Good! So, you're a revolutionary!"

"Just let us in," Savas bayed.

"The Helm is about to speak, hurry up and head inside. You won't want to miss this."

"Aurelia? Come on," he called back to his sister, who seemed to be in a world of her own, mumbling at the air.

The doormen directed him down the stairs into an airy basement. There were around 30 people seated, with more standing around the room. Who they were was anyone's guess: some of them looked poor, some old, others fat and well-fed. On the wall were posters with Sunhold burning, or depicting Protectors being hung to their deaths; yet the most zealous was one which showed King Thenris decapitated, his crown beside his boots. The only revolutionary Savas knew until now was Temek, a vee coin labourer from Endvil, and it was that sort of person he expected to find here. But to his surprise, Savas saw that this wasn't some slipshod uprising of impassioned peasants and workers, but the combined efforts of a whole range of folks, some of whom looked educated and capable beyond measure.

The room fell quiet. One man stepped towards the front of the room and all eyes were at once transfixed by him. With his arms outstretched, he said, "Friends of the revolution, welcome again."

"Do you see Temek anywhere?" Savas whispered to Aurelia, looking all around on his tip toes.

She stretched her neck out, but then shook her head. "There's someone up there," she replied quietly. "He's got a sack over his head."

The speaker continued, "The Protector pigs keep arresting us, but we will not stop until our message is heard. Those devils in the Myriad think that by offering vee coins we will settle down, as if our demands are so easily appeased, but they are wrong! Do these bastards think we are so worthless, that we can be bribed with fake money and left to rot, while they plan to evacuate themselves? Our city is burning to the ground under the watch of King Thenris, Queen Consort Melindra and their corrupt Myriad! What are the Protectors doing? We only still stand because of Marshal Morovig and his men, dying in the Esterwood. The monarchy has failed Northcrest. It has failed you."

The man was clever, and definitely not from Endvil; his accent was not noble, like the sort Savas was accustomed to in Sunhold, and the peculiar twang in his accent suggested that he was not from elsewhere. Savas got on his tiptoes again for a good look and saw that the speaker didn't have the air of a great leader: he was fairly short and slim, and didn't seem to take up much space or exude the vigour one might associate with the leader of such a movement.

Someone tapped Savas on the shoulder. "Hi ugly."

He turned around and greeted her with a beaming smile. "Temek!"

"How's your face?" she asked.

Savas smirked. "You know your house has been cracked open like an egg?"

"Not my four square metre shed! Did you rescue my wigs?" she asked, patting her stubbly head with a smirk.

All he could do was hug her.

"Temek. It's good to see you," Aurelia said.

"You too," she said. "That's Okim by the way," she pointed at the speaker.

"King Thenris and his Myriad think that we shouldn't care that Lady Elfine was abducted in Sunhold — the pinnacle of our country's strength," Okim continued. "They say that Protectors who disappeared the night after her kidnapping is no concern of ours. They demand that we cease to riot. Why? Because they do not wish to hear our voices. They do not wish to admit that their whitewashed halls could ever be fallible; they do not desire to see people like us have any power. They fear that if we point out their mistakes, it'll be as though we're taking the reins away from them. Taking the whip, even. Do you not know how this country came to be, how Gaminians built this land with the help of the Elder Tribes and then betrayed them? Sunhold is filled with the same evil colonisers as those who stalked this continent thousands of years ago. We must struggle against the evil elite, and speak our heart's bitter truths about these people. They care for nought but wealth and power. We cannot win this war with such greedy hands steering us. Power must return to the people."

Okim signalled to a couple of ushers near the front, and they brought the sack-covered man to the front and unveiled him.

"It's High Priest Resus," Aurelia mouthed. The High Priest was red and swollen in the face, clearly having been roughed up.

"Sometimes I forget you grew up in Sunhold," Temek remarked.

"I... knew he wasn't the best sort, but how did he end up here, the target of the revolution?" Aurelia pondered, in shock.

"This reactionary element has had his villainous claws digging into the backs of Northcrest's people for far too long. He calls himself a priest, but I know who he really is: a money-grabbing landlord with homes all over King's Respite and Chapel Heights, filled with his servants who live like slaves. This man who claims to serve the Three is the same priest whose doors do not open for people of colour; his congregation is exclusively for the white Northcrester. But your racism hasn't stopped you from having your way with the women from the Southern Continent, has it, you filthy swine?"

"*Ang wasara unti bessa!*" screamed a Sygecian mother. "The scumbag had my daughter kidnapped when I couldn't pay his rent!"

"Empty the bitterness of your hearts as you look upon this monstrosity," said Okim. "Come — let he who was a mouth speak out against this felon!" The crowd surged forward in great numbers, unleashing their anger at the High Priest.

"It's getting intense," Temek said. "Can we go outside? There's something I need to talk to you about."

On his way out, Savas passed a tall, slender figure that he recognised on the stairs. He turned back, only catching a glimpse of a hooded figure with a bow and arrow strapped to their back. It was Commander Anek, who had turned his neck, and held Savas' gaze for a moment that was both too long and not long enough. Savas thought about what sort of life he could have at the side of someone like Anek. Someone strong and beautiful. He would have done anything in that moment to forget about this war and have that life.

"Listen, Temek," Aurelia began, "since we last saw you, things have gotten dire. Savas and I need to get going."

"Not until I tell you what I've learned," she said, sharply. "After what happened the night we were attacked, I told Okim everything I know about the Wraith. He wants me to kill him."

"Did you tell him about me?" Aurelia asked.

"I couldn't leave that part out," Temek replied.

"And he actually believed you?" she continued, mouth agape.

Temek nodded. "Turns out the revolution is just as interested in politics as it is in the supernatural. You know about the Menyr already, don't you?"

Both nodded.

"The leaders of the revolution say the Menyr have been infiltrating courts and governments for centuries," Temek said. "Okim wants them gone. I said from the beginning I wanted to kill the Wraith, but now I know I can't do it alone. Will you two help me put him in the ground?"

Savas imagined the sound of the sword he now held, piercing the Wraith's flesh and gutting his belly. Mitenni was right: the weapon was made to destroy those beasts. It hungered for their flesh. Ecstasy overtook him for a moment as his thoughts lured him to a sanguinary dimension, where all he saw was the spilled blood of Menyr and their shrivelled, grey bodies piled up around him. He shuddered when the vision ended.

"Underneath the Parlour, there's a place called the House of Noul. We need to get there immediately, but I think the Wraith might already be there, along with the Queen," Aurelia explained.

"Skrak. The Queen? Lei Jia was sent to the Parlour this morning. If the Menyr are there, we need to help him," Temek said, urgently.

"Know any shortcuts?" Savas asked.

Temek gave a curt nod. "Follow me."

Chapter 21

The Ojanti

Aurelia had never noticed the Temptress' Parlour before. It seemed strange that underneath it could be the historic House of Noul she'd read so much about, where Onaxia's dark magic had poisoned hundreds of innocent people. In fact, it looked quite salubrious compared to the average Endvil structure. It was a tall, slender building, almost as if the walls that enclosed it on either side crushed it to shoot upward.

"Didn't think I'd be back here so soon," said Temek, easing the door open with her boot. The lanterns burning along the walls were embossed with gold flicks. Dancing flames revealed a long, narrow corridor, adorned with sultry works of art, vibrant, patterned rugs and numerous purple curtains, leading to private quarters.

It was silent.

"How are we supposed to look for him if the Menyr are already here?" Savas whispered.

Aurelia stilled him instantly with a stern regard. They continued cautiously, following Temek. There were odd scents that seemed to come and go at random. In one moment, Aurelia was tickled by the scent of roses, the next she smelt orange, then something smoky. Distractions, she decided.

Savas almost tripped over something and Temek swivelled round, bow and arrow suddenly in hand.

"Skrak. No…" Temek whined. She knelt down to examine the severed hand on the floor that had caused Savas to stumble. It was peering out from a slant in a velvety set of yellow curtains; so small and already pallid, as if it belonged to some ancient corpse.

Temek readied her bow, then gave Aurelia a nod, signalling her to pull back the curtain.

With one terse flourish, Aurelia laid the room bare, and before her hands even released them, she staggered backwards, unable to contend with the rancid, metallic stench emanating from within.

Temek collapsed to her knees in shock.

Aurelia couldn't tell if Temek was really crying, or just whimpering like a dog. She didn't know how to react herself, but she could tell there was nothing she could say to console Temek. A quick count of the corpses revealed at least 15 bodies, most in a heap, with a couple strewn about randomly. They had been discarded in the most heinous and pitiless way, half-naked and bloodied beyond recognition. Beyond the aroma of fresh blood, a noxious stink stalked the room, reminiscent of iron. Aurelia sensed it was not to do with the hapless victims, but the monstrosities that had consumed them, and the atrocious way in which they had done it.

"I'm so sorry," Savas said to Temek. "We won't let them get away with this."

Temek got herself together and went further in, with one hand shielding her nose. "Do you see Lei Jia anywhere?" she asked, inspecting the bodies as much as she could bear.

Savas helped her search, but it was clear that both of them were about to be bowled over with disgust. "I can't see him. We have to carry on. We'll come back."

"You're right," Temek whimpered.

It was too difficult to look back at that room of senseless death and misery. Days ago, Aurelia would never have thought to encounter a scene so grisly. The Visitor had readied her in some small way for what was to come, but as Aurelia had come to expect, her guide did not go into any great detail regarding what this war would do to those caught in its indiscriminating grasp. Cadavers should not have been so uncommon to a student of medicine and healing, seeing as she had witnessed sketches and diagrams, and indeed, several real ones in the company of her supervisor. But this was something else, something desperately evil and unnatural. Although she battled with the idea of turning back, they only went deeper into this baleful mire, guided by Temek, who now looked more determined than ever to fight.

Temek paused at the end of the corridor then led them down the path to the left, where she stopped again. "There didn't used to be a door here."

"Didn't you say that the Wraith mentioned a door, that night he came for you?" Savas asked.

Temek's stance slackened as she burrowed into her memories. "I can't believe I forgot about that. You're right. That's exactly what he said. It's anyone's guess as to where it leads, though."

"Or who's waiting for us," Savas added.

"Yeah, and after what Okim told me, there's no way we can charge the Menyr with brute force and expect to win," she added.

With a quick motion, Savas unsheathed the Hermesian blade and displayed it in front of Temek. "We have this. It can kill them."

"You might kill yourself trying to wield that," Temek smiled. "I'll do my best to weaken them with arrows so you can go in for the killing blow. The rest will be up to you," she said, turning her eyes to Aurelia.

"I don't know what we'll face down there, but these things are deceptive. They can get into your head and cloud your judgement. If we stay together, we'll be fine,"

Aurelia said. "My magic — the Visitor's magic — will protect us."

A gust of dusty, cold air blew in their faces as Aurelia opened the door. The stairs down led them to a massive realm; it felt like it spanned the entirety of Northcrest's underbelly. Only a little light dared enter such a pit, but the bashful glints of yellow and orange along the paths below revealed that the Menyr had lit lanterns. It came as a small reassurance that these supernatural monsters could not see in the dark.

Aurelia led the way. Guided by her spiritual insight, she traced a faint path, as though she could see footprints left behind in the ground to follow. It soon became apparent this was a set of catacombs. There were strange statues along the way and insignias propped upon the walls with antiquated inscriptions and unusual carvings. The statues were not figures that she recognised, not the usual renderings of the Three. Whoever these figures were, they had no connection to the Yotanites, but perhaps some other religion, like the Dreamists. Even that seemed unlikely, as the ornate sarcophaguses she saw did not match what she had read of the Dreamists: an unlikely collection of Northcrest's most undesirable and wayward souls.

Whoever was interred here, their murmurs drifted softly along the air. The voices were delicate and ethereal. There was no malcontent in the sounds, but they began to grow louder, until it seemed that the lips that shaped them were right by her ears. When the sound was no longer a whisper, but as loud as any ordinary voice, Aurelia's vision blurred for a moment and she drifted to a sarcophagus on the corner of the path. She brushed its dust-laden surface; it was smooth, fashioned from limestone with representations of people and ships carved into it.

"What are you doing?" Savas said, impatient.

Her vision stabilised, Aurelia read quietly aloud, "Hermine Tillensis, slain in battle, Crucible Era 1498." There was a pause as the magnitude of her ancestor being buried in this place over a thousand years ago sunk in. The voices returned, louder and clearer, with a warning of what was ahead.

"The Menyr are around the corner," Aurelia whispered.

There was a gentle lavender glow emanating from the end of the path. Aurelia knew that hue well: it was the telltale sign of the Ankasa, where the sky bloomed with shades of violet and purple.

"Savas," Temek said quietly, then gave him some sort of signal. It seemed she intended for them to backtrack, go around the other side and create some sort of flanking manoeuvre.

Aurelia wasn't well-versed in the tactics of combat, but Temek had been exposed to all sorts through her connection with North Wind. She trusted that the revolutionary fighter knew what she was doing. Aurelia stood alone, and the immense pressure of being the only one with the power to oppose the Menyr punctured her thoughts. Savas had a special sword, Temek had her bow and arrows, but she knew that it fell to her to go in first and draw the enemy's attention. After all, she was the one with the Nomos Tal.

Coming around the corner, Aurelia spied the enemy in the distance. Queen Consort Melindra was instantly recognisable, but the other was a man she did not know. He stood triumphant next to a withered and discarded body, with a face that looked too beautiful to be reduced to such a wretched state. Behind the two Menyr was a luminous gateway: the source of the lavender glow filtering through the pathways. Aurelia had never seen anything like it, even in the countless books of history and legends she had devoured over the years. It was crafted of roughly-hewn stones, with antediluvian symbols etched on the surfaces; some of the stones hovered in mid-air, and the ground seemed similarly suspended around the gate, where flecks of dust and stone gathered to form a faint cloud.

"You're late," squawked Melindra, in an ugly and piercing voice.

"Is she alone?" The man beside her rasped, sinister and scornful.

"You look ill," Aurelia said.

The atrocity of Melindra's true form was stark beside the glint of the mystical gateway. Although she wore the mask of an ordinary woman, Aurelia saw the fissures in her guise, where black feathers and putrid shadows burned a sickly green.

Melindra snorted with a rancid contempt. "You brought the Nomos Tal, I take it?"

She had. It was safe in her satchel. "What is it, really?"

Melindra cocked her head to the side in condescension. "The Nomos Tal sits at the pinnacle of what is known of all magic in Ysa; it is the greatest device ever invented. And it is an egotist at heart. A sensitive artefact. It was not made to be shared, like the cheap harlots upstairs, though they won't be troubling anyone ever again."

The man sniggered. "The magic of this book was not designed for a lesser being, like yourself, or even us," he said. "It longs to be in the hands of someone... worthy."

"The book is tied to Castrellus still," Aurelia said. Finally, she understood why the Menyr's plan had demanded so many centuries of waiting. "You waited all this time for me, or someone like me, to open the door, for what? So you could kill him and bring the book to your Princess Onaxia?"

Melindra beamed, but the aspect of a crow was stalking her every movement, along with the fluttering sounds of feathers, as she hopped closer. "Exactly," she said.

"None of this makes any sense," Aurelia snapped. "You endured year after year without it, but I managed to stumble upon this book simply enough. You can't have been looking very hard."

With her lip curved into a mocking smile, Melindra said, "I would never dirty my hands looking for a book. Did you, Winnik? No, I didn't think so. Why would we, blessed with long life, look for the Nomos Tal? That book is more powerful than you can fathom, but it did not want to be found by us. It sought you first, because we cannot open this door."

"You speak of it as though it is alive," Aurelia interjected. Her ear twitched as she heard Temek and Savas moving into position down the path ahead and to the right of where the Menyr were.

"It has a will, in a sense, and it is defined by its desire to be used," explained Melindra. "It seeks to be reunited with its true owner, not that imbecile imprisoned behind me. That's your part to play, my dear: to find it and bring it to those who will do right with it."

"And Elfine, the Keyholder?" Aurelia continued. "Isn't she part of your wicked plans as well?"

Melindra should not have been able to twist her lips with yet more scorn, but she managed to. "Oh, poor Elfine! Onaxia is known for her hospitality, so I'm sure she will treat your sister well, until she does not."

"You sicken me. Elfine is not some pawn for you and your corrupt cause to toy with! There is no reasoning with a monster," Aurelia said coldly.

"Blind, like the rest of her kind," said Winnik. "She cannot see our prowess, our beauty, our majesty!"

"No, and she never will," said Melindra.

Before Aurelia could turn back, Winnik took out a delicate bowl and began to beat it with a small instrument. He proceeded to swirl the instrument around the inside, which produced a soft whirring noise, that escalated into an overwhelming ringing sound that filled the expanse. Aurelia dropped to her knees with her hands covering her ears, screaming. When she looked up, she saw a fleeting vision of the Visitor: the one who had guided her to this place, the one she had become so attached to after only days. Moments after appearing, the spirit fizzled out into sparks of white and blue, unable to even utter a parting snippet of wisdom or mouth the words to a decisive spell. Aurelia felt their bond, which had grown across dimensions, dreams and visions, grow weaker and weaker, until the Visitor was fully out of reach. The Visitor was gone. Now, the only power Aurelia had left in this fight was her own.

"Goodbye, Ylestra," Melindra crowed.

Aurelia stumbled back onto her feet, trying desperately to reach for her magic. But it was nowhere. It was gone, just like the Visitor, like Ylestra. Without the Visitor's presence around her, she felt helpless, as though all she had learned and come to know was slipping through her fingertips like rainwater. As Melindra and Winnik lurched towards her, a volley of arrows from the side came hissing through the air. While none managed to land a fatal blow, two ere embedded in Winnik's shoulder.

In the brief moment that followed, Savas charged forwards, brandishing his moonlight-enchanted sword. The sword lit up with the ethereal glow of a full moon, activated to an even greater extent at the sight of those it was designed to destroy.

Melindra gasped then covered her eyes with one hand. With quick reflexes, she struck Savas with a backhanded slap, launching him towards the gateway. "You move stealthily, boy. But your form is sluggish." The treacherous Queen then turned her gaze to Aurelia and grinned with macabre delight. From out of her back erupted two wings of rotten black down, pocked with yawning holes and flaccid feathers. To complete her transformation, her face became something between woman and bird: nestled below the pair of flitting yellow eyes and in place of her nose was a long black beak, which opened wide with a shrill caw.

More arrows came, but Melindra froze them with her hands mid-air this time and redirected them in Temek's direction, who quickly dodged into cover. At least she and Savas had managed to lure Winnik away from Aurelia. The Menyr chased the two of them around the narrow space in a tense melee.

"Did your mother survive, Aurelia?" mocked Melindra, taking another step closer.

"She'll be fine. Your tricks were easy enough to undo," Aurelia countered.

"With a 2000-year-old Ojanti strumpet to draw from I'm sure I could achieve great things as well," Melindra's beak attempted a smile, but her mouth was now lined with black ooze and leaking flies. "I sense how weak you are without her."

"Why have you done all of this?" Aurelia asked, defiant.

"Because Northcrest doesn't belong to you," squawked the winged Menyr. "It doesn't belong to any Gaminian. Certainly not *you*."

"Onaxia said as much, when I saw you all perishing in that cave," Aurelia said. She stole a glance at her brother, locked in a swordfight with Winnik, who had armed himself with a blade of his own. To her surprise, Savas moved with precision, as though he had held a sword many times before. He stood his ground well enough, meanwhile, Temek continued to provide support from a distance with her arrows, though they did not seem to impede Winnik at all.

"Northcrest belongs to the Kaspicians," Melindra argued. "The people who live here now are imposters. They stole this land from us and banished our people to live beyond the Numanich Mountains in the cold, where nothing grew and our people could never prosper. But that is not why I, and many of my kind hate you and your interfering ancestors. I hate them because of whose side they took in a feud that did not concern them. They disembarked on our shores and tried to resolve centuries of tension with their powers. They did not even hear our side of the story, and instead, opted for our obliteration. The Kaspicians lost everything because of the Ojanti, and they had no right to be here."

"But you turned your people into monsters to fight back. How are you better than the Gaminians, or the Ojanti?"

"Gaminians!" Melindra bellowed a laugh. "Be quiet with that nonsense. No such thing exists, dear. There were no Gaminians in those days. Yours is a made-up nation, a false word written on maps and a lie that overcrowds tomes of history and culture. We Kaspicians were at least a real race of people. And we did not beg the aid of those refugees who arrived on our shores! The Ojanti came here drained and anaemic, but even still, the magic of our people could not match the power of those who had fought decades of battles. What we did to stand up was a necessary sacrifice. When the Nomos Tal came into our possession, we sacrificed ourselves freely. All our people with magical blood who offered themselves were reborn as

Menyr. We became strong because the alternative was oblivion."

"I see you now. Why you wormed your way into my family and lurked in the darkness for so long, unable to show your true self. You were afraid of the Ojanti in me. Terrified that I could out you to the world. That I could destroy you."

"Arrogant dog," hissed the Queen. "I will silence you here. Forever."

As Melindra readied her talons to slash Aurelia, an energy surged into the atmosphere. Aurelia heard the sound of a fierce river. Her many encounters with the Visitor replayed in her thoughts. But Aurelia could not feel her ancestor's presence. No hum, whisper or murmur to accompany the bold eddies of the water she knew.

The Menyr lurched closer and made her move. Tendrils of feathery, black shadow lacerated the air and clawed their way to Aurelia's torso as the phantom flapping and cawing of crows blared. The attack was like being strangled by bladed vines, whose leaves, at the sound of a malicious incantation, constricted Aurelia tighter still.

Without the Visitor to come to her aid, Aurelia's whole body was in agony. Although her senses started to fade, the clashes of steel and fighting ahead hummed faintly in her thoughts, like raindrops of sound. Had she been wrong? She'd marched in here overoptimistic, thinking that the Visitor would take care of everything. But now, dread closed in around her. If she did not rise against her oppressor, the three of them would die and achieve nothing. Her home and family would die, and Onaxia would win. That was a future she could not allow.

And so, she held on.

The image of the river returned to Aurelia's thoughts. In her mind, she raced into the water and plunged her arms into it till she met Ysa's core. Her reach went deeper still; it penetrated the fabric of the whole universe. She absorbed something into her flesh more enigmatic and potent than what could be contained in a mere river, supernatural or not. She stood at the ultimate confluence of power, ferried to the depths of the greatest ocean imaginable; once there, she pitied the meekness of the water as it shrank from her. It lent her its power, perhaps out of fear, and it made her spirit bubble over with magic.

No time seemed to have passed, yet Melindra receded; her wings looked shrivelled and her shadows bashful. "What is this poison you command?" She shivered, her flesh almost blue. "I should've known. Even when I killed your mother's family, I felt the fight in them. The power. It was stronger even than the kings I enchanted. They will use you girl. They all will. Even your beloved Ylestra. She's no saint. If I were you, I'd run far away!"

Aurelia was on the verge of bursting with power. The strength that she'd invited into her body travelled out of her and crashed straight into the crumpling Menyr. The atmosphere seemed to imbibe Aurelia's will and Melindra could do nothing to stop it. A glacial clinch summoned by Aurelia bound the deposed Queen, petrifying her from head to toe. The body that was once swathed in darkness and foul magics turned a frosty blue; like a statue, she fell backwards and shattered into feathers and ice — the sum of her being — and the dust that remained was diffused into the ghostly carpet of the catacombs.

So entranced had she been by her duel, Aurelia hadn't noticed the spectacle ahead. Temek lay strewn across the floor like a broken doll, her bow seemingly having been of little use against Winnik, in whose flesh several arrows were lodged. Meanwhile, Savas maintained a display of skilful swordsmanship with the Hermesian blade in his hand. As the sword's moonlight essence struck the Menyr with the sharp blade, he stumbled back, and finally saw the ashen remains of his companion.

"No!" he screeched. "This cannot be!" Winnik rushed towards the fallen Queen, dropped to the floor and ran his fingers through her powdery remains.

Savas was right behind the Menyr in a trice. The Hermesian sword glowed, joyful, as it went through Winnik's body and came out of his mouth. Blood dribbled along the blade's tip and splattered onto the ground; in just a second, his flesh withered and sagged, until all that remained was a robed cadaver.

Savas kicked the centuries-old corpse and it clattered into a pile of brittle bones — a fitting end in this underground manor of the deceased.

With his face a canvas of muck and sweat, he gave Aurelia a nod. He looked exhausted, but he leapt towards Temek to help her.

But she was already busy aiding someone else. "Lei Jia!" Temek shrieked. "Are you alright?"

The languishing man Aurelia had mistaken for a corpse turned out to be Temek's friend, Lei Jia. He didn't look like he'd make it.

"*Tian ah.* Skies above. What are you doing down here, Temek?" he rasped, his voice fainter than a whisper.

Aurelia reached into her satchel, took out the Nomos Tal and presented it before the luminous gateway. The gate beckoned the book closer and it drifted upward, opening onto a page Aurelia had never seen before; a page that had not existed until this moment. No longer did she hold the innocuous ramblings of a persecuted wizard, but some arcane relic of an abominable world, probably best forgotten.

"What about the Wraith?" asked Temek, her wearied voice faint amid the whirring coming from the gate. "He's not here."

"Go and get Lei Jia stitched up," Savas hollered. "Aurelia and I will find the Wraith. I promise."

"Open," Aurelia commanded, and the gateway ate her words greedily, giving way to a direct channel to the House of Noul.

Chapter 22

The Steward of the House of Noul

When Aurelia had imagined the House of Noul, she saw it as immense, replete with murals of ancient divinity, gilded striations woven into a roof, and giant columns, tinted amethyst from the atmosphere. Yet the world the two of them stepped into was bleak. The vivid sky, warm yet merciless with a pale purple hue, hid nothing; from the very stone of the House of Noul, histories seeped forth, begging to be recalled. The decaying approach, peppered with tombstones and run-down, religious statues, snaked at an incline towards the aged door of a monastery.

"At least we know where the exit is," Savas remarked, looking back at the gateway.

"There is so much magic in the atmosphere," Aurelia said, engrossed in her surroundings. The iron handle of the door gave little resistance as she twisted it open. Whispers fled high into the corners of the ceiling as they entered, made to scarper like mice.

Stained-glass windows portrayed religious scenes that must have been related to the faith of the Dreamists. One displayed many people, sleeping on the ground in a circle. Another showed two identical men staring at each other, enclosed by a black box. A third showed a man holding a torch to an engraved tablet under a starry sky. The longer Aurelia stared, it seemed that the images began to distort and speak to her. She looked away and realised that hollow as this place was, it was not truly empty. They were not alone.

The murmurs of the departed had trailed behind them closely in the catacombs, yet here, the keens of the forgotten were shrill. They weren't exactly voices, for what Aurelia experienced was well beyond the realms of her senses; the elegy humming around her was not heard, but felt. The victims of Spirit Rot, Onaxia's fatal curse, thronged, and their sorrow roiled. A moment's concentration was all it took for the entire congregation to materialise.

Each pew was suddenly filled, and easily a hundred souls were present, their eyes all fixed on the one Dreamist who spoke from the central pulpit.

"That can't be," Savas said.

"You see them as well?" asked Aurelia, but he was too fixed on whoever was speaking.

"How long ago did you say this book was written again?" Asked Savas.

Aurelia couldn't believe her eyes. Mazin was lecturing, preaching by the pulpit. His words, along with all other sounds in this hallucination of the dead, were formless. She wished desperately to know what he was saying. "The book was written over 400 years ago," she whispered. "How is Mazin standing there?"

The head of this monastery has taken a liking to me too. He is not of fair-skinned descent like the Gaminians. Aurelia recalled the words she had once read when the book was nothing but memories of a persecuted man, etched on parchment.

"But Mazin never said anything good about religions or gods. I don't understand. Is he a Menyr, or a spirit?" Aurelia pondered, still transfixed by her friend's ghost.

"Mother always went on about the idea of him being a bad influence. Are you sure he's on our side?"

The thought became heavy in her hand as she weighed its likelihood. Mazin had been nothing but an ally over the years, the possibility that he had been working for the enemy bled Aurelia grey with worry.

"Mazin is my friend. I won't hear anything else," Aurelia said, dismissively.

Savas huffed. "Look," he said. "The people are moving. Something is happening."

The congregation dispersed. As they passed Aurelia and her brother, their faces were rendered indistinct and cloud-like; they moved as air in human form, making no impact on the unyielding Ankasa that entombed them.

"This must have been during the outbreak," Aurelia realised. "The doors are closed. The Dreamists are all staying here." She watched the spirits disappear down various corridors, but Mazin remained up front. Three figures suddenly crowded around him, one of whom was instantly recognisable.

"That's Melindra," Aurelia said. "Maybe if you give me your hand again, we can give voice to this memory."

"If you think it'll help," Savas shrugged.

Just as before, their symbiosis gave form and coherence to new magics in the air, though the power as their flesh met and spirits entwined was subtle this time. No words or special tricks were required — the will alone to transform their surroundings sufficed, and after a moment passed, the four beings in front could hide nothing of their true selves. Mazin stood poised before Melindra and two others. One was a lanky, gaunt sort of man; the other possessed a deceptive beauty, with glistening black hair and sharp features.

"What a pleasant sermon," Melindra crowed. "You give these people such hope, Mazin." Her eyes roved across him with a corrosive condescension.

"You are foolish to speak of hope here," said Mazin. "Six more are dead today. Castrellus and I are doing our best, despite the quarantine you encouraged King Venelag to enact."

"An awful, yet necessary affair," Melindra re-joined, with tightly pursed lips.

A man approached from behind and came by Mazin's side. "Again, you are here. Who are these men with you, Melindra?"

"Castrellus," Mazin said, taking Castrellus' hand.

"It's him," Aurelia said, her eyes trained on Castrellus with curiosity. His form was distinct to a fault: there was neither blemish nor scar in his crystalline form. For all the years of his harrowing vigil in this unyielding prison, he looked well. Dark, though nothing in the vein of the Visitor, his skin was crisp like a sheet of parchment, but within his mesmerising, pale-yellow eyes the might of a sandstorm loomed. The absence of hair on his head invited a soft glint of orange to bloom on the smooth surface, and draped over his shoulders was a set of black ceremonial robes, patterned and adorned with fine threads of gold and green. The sight of him shook Aurelia; her insides simmered with an amalgam of nerves, some formed of excitement, others fear: fear that she drew close to the end of her journey, and news of Elfine was so far non-existent.

Melindra produced one of her most insincere smiles. "May I present to you Warden Henaias, a researcher from the Republic, and Benthrin of the Yotanite church. The King believes that the presence of a devout Yotanite in these... unsavoury halls, may have some sway in remedying this catastrophe, and young Henaias here is committed to researching the illness to find a cure."

"You send the priest of a false religion and some upstart, fresh out of college, to treat the dying? King Venelag's words should hold no power here. We care nothing for his whims, nor do we seek the counsel of his latest ill-fitting bride," Mazin hissed.

"I assure you," said Henaias, "I am here with the purest of intentions. My team and I believe that the key to a cure could lie within the monastery itself."

"A cure?" scoffed Mazin. "It is funny that the three of you have no fear of this malaise that they are calling Spirit Rot. Tell me, have you already found a cure? It would not surprise me if you kept it for yourself."

"No cure exists for *your* breed," growled Benthrin, "but perhaps some can be saved."

"You've a strident tongue for a man of the Three," retorted Castrellus. "I will return to the people, Mazin. They need me."

"Walk in whisper's stead," Mazin said.

Something changed as Castrellus departed. Melindra looked to her two accomplices eagerly. They repositioned to form a triangle around Mazin, who looked confused as to what they were scheming. The monsters seemed to present their hideous forms all of a sudden, no longer interested in hiding their visages. Melindra took on the guise of the plague crow, the priest exuded something akin to an arachnid, and the researcher, who Aurelia now realised was the Wraith, did not change at all.

"Menyr," sighed Mazin, "I should've sensed you sooner."

"And yet, you did not," Henaias flashed a wicked grin.

"You have hidden much over the years," Melindra said. "But we will extract your truths now, like sap is drawn from a birch."

The atmosphere began to sizzle, as though cold water was being flicked into a vat of scorching hot oil. It was deafening and invasive. Aurelia and Savas covered their ears with their palms as Mazin staggered to the ground. Everything shook and trembled as the Menyr burrowed their way into Mazin's mind.

Aurelia looked around, but Castrellus was gone. Where were the others? The congregation were not coming to Mazin's aid. Nobody here had the acuity to sense the Menyr. Even if they had seen, there was nothing any of them could have done.

"His thoughts are nebulous," Benthrin said.

"Give me your strength, Henaias," ordered Melindra. She took his palm into hers, and at once, Mazin began to whimper like a frightened dog, doing his utmost to resist them. These sewers of shadow and tainted power were strong enough alone, but united, their strength was magnified. They chipped away and slashed at the foundations of Mazin's being, desperate for whatever secret he had buried.

"Magic of the earth," cawed Melindra. "You impress me." She released him.

The three Menyr all took a measured step back at the same moment.

"There is much of magic you do not understand, crow spawn!" Mazin wheezed.

A sideways cock of her head was all Melindra could muster. "Perhaps. But I know what I shall do to you." She stalked closer towards him and rested her bony fingers close to his neck, which all of a sudden looked so delicate and easily broken. "How does a lifetime of banishment sound? Will you thrive, or wilt, after the first few centuries of exile? Will you forget all that you are while you rot in the extremities of this cesspit of a city? That is what I sentence you to: a life between realms, to live as a ghost — a spirit without purpose. All you had to do was tell us where they imprisoned her, and you could've lived. Just like those before you, you have chosen the wrong side. Fool. *Udyavai, idii sotusa nasegdav!*"

Quiet began to sluice through the monastery like a trickle of rainwater. Mazin had ceased to react, and the Menyr paused in place, their forms wafting uncontrollably as though shaped of some heated, noxious kind of air. The vision came to an end. All was still.

"The Menyr destroyed Mazin," Aurelia said, distraught. "They took everything from him in their hunt for the Nomos Tal. He didn't even remember any of it happening."

Savas offered comfort by reaching his arm around her shoulder, something which he had not done in a long time. "I'm sorry," he said.

Down the corridor to the right, where Castrellus had gone, the doorway, looming at the far end, opened in invitation. The man whose persecution had begun all of this intrigue and mystery at last stood but a few steps away. Having lost her connection to the Visitor and seeing what the Menyr had done to Mazin, Aurelia's conviction wavered. The doorway did not look alluring. A brusque shiver rippled through her body.

"He's waiting for us," she said. Her words had become less and less distinct, as though they were traversing the silt-covered depths of a river. "Do you think he'll be able to tell us anything about Elfine?"

Savas rested close to her hip, sword in hand, poised to attack. "I don't know, Aurelia. I hope so."

"I miss her. A lot."

"I know. I do too. Are you ready?" Asked Savas.

Aurelia nodded. "Castrellus?" she called, standing outside the door.

Inside was an unimpressive chamber, but in the centre was a blazing pyre, where knives of purple fire hissed as though being ground on a whetstone. The flames resembled the Ankasa's skies, manipulated for some occult purpose.

"You saw the memory, didn't you?" Castrellus said, standing by the flames.

"Yes," said Aurelia. Her mind throbbed with questions, like the sensation of a twinging wound, pulsing endlessly. "What was Mazin doing here, and *how was he here*?"

"The House of Noul was his charge before it became mine," he spoke softly, his words a cool caress, like mist. "He was our leader, and my lover."

Savas perked up. "Your lover?"

"For many years," Castrellus smiled, pensive.

"But such long life, how has Mazin survived so many centuries?"

"Even before Melindra robbed him of his corporeal form, Mazin had Ojanti blood, like you do. It is not uncommon for your people to be able to extend their lives beyond what is normally possible," Castrellus said.

"Ojanti…" Aurelia tasted the strange word in her mouth. "Melindra spoke of these people. So, Mazin is also a descendant of theirs."

Castrellus' emotions were veiled. Centuries immured in this foreboding realm had made him hard, unreadable. "They came from somewhere distant. A dark continent, I believe. Thousands of years before my time."

"But Mazin doesn't have any powers," Aurelia said. "Not like the Ojanti I have seen. How can this be so?"

"Mazin is the only Ojanti I ever knew, and he never spoke of his family. He was born without any powers of his own. Indeed, that is what drew him to the alchemy of the Dreamists; those who could tap into the magical properties of the earth itself were of great interest to him. At some point, he became the leader of the House of Noul in Northcrest." Castrellus paused to inhale, then inspected the fire. An inconsolable tear pooled shyly in the corner of his eye, but it did not fall. "H... h-how is he?"

Aurelia's jaw shook a little. She didn't think Mazin would still be his weakness, after so many years. The thought of this strange love, separated by dimensions and marred by dark, interfering sorcery, disarmed her. Her own emotions shuddered, uncertain, like a flimsy tree trying to stay grounded in a storm. "I always believed he was well, though now I am not sure," she said, at a stammer. "Why did you come to Northcrest?"

"I did not have a choice," he answered. "My people decided to exile me because I loved a boy. The Haruspex used me to find the Nomos Tal, because I was our strongest sorcerer. She betrayed me upon my return and outed me to our tribe. I took the book, ran and never looked back, but I could never have predicted the immensity of what followed thereafter," he sighed.

"I can't believe your tribe turned their back on you because you loved another man," said Savas. "That's so cruel."

Castrellus' gaze wafted over to Savas, looking him up and down with an indecipherable form of scrutiny. "I wonder why *you* came here, when your sister would have ventured into this place without you," he said, his words laced with frost.

Concerned that her brother was not ready to be quizzed, Aurelia checked her brother and pulled him closer to her.

"I came here because my sister needed me," Savas answered.

"So servile. Always doing what others ask of you," Castrellus spoke louder, with more authority than before. "You have brought pain into this place, and it is a pain that I know. Do you know that it makes you powerful, your sadness, that thing you have hidden for so long?"

Castrellus dipped his hands in and out of the flames, and then, as if something of arcane significance had come to life on them, seemed to read his own palms.

Aurelia shuffled closer to her brother. This strange room, despite the burning pyre, had grown cold in the moment she had been distracted by Castrellus' voice. The walls seemed smaller. Castrellus was closer than before.

"We're here for you. To talk about Onaxia. Not me," Savas said.

Castrellus tilted his head, his brows knitted together. "Who are you?"

Savas huffed. "My name is Savas."

"And who hides beneath Savas?" Castrellus said, enticing.

Aurelia squeezed her brother's arm tightly. She didn't understand Castrellus' goal.

"What do you want me to say? That I'm gay?" Savas snapped.

A murmur, issued from the crackling fire, echoed throughout the room, clinging softly to all it collided with. The flames flickered from purple to blue, red to white and back to purple again. As their transformations went on, words of magical origin wafted above the pyre and percolated into the atmosphere. Were they the Ubija, those words of ancient power the Visitor had started to teach Aurelia? No, Aurelia was gifted with languages, and she did not recognise this one at all. The spell began to roil with a timbre, mighty enough to send vibrations of unease through her body. All the hairs on her arms jolted upwards, petrified with fright. Something festered in the atmosphere, a thing that had not been called upon for a long time.

"What did you just do?" Aurelia shrieked.

"Making sure my desires are also fulfilled," the old spirit sneered.

"Aurelia — I was going to tell you." He stopped to watch Castrellus, looming by the flames. "What's going on?" Savas asked, with fear in his voice.

Castrellus looked grave, inhaling the fumes of the pyre as though they were plain air. "It was both my despair and the power of the Nomos Tal that fuelled my passage into this plane, but Noul clung to me, the last of his herd, and hid me from Onaxia. I have passed four centuries here, with him whispering in my ears constantly. This place has become precious to him. He will not allow it to be deserted. The Groom of Whispers must be appeased, but I will not be his pawn any longer."

Aurelia recalled Castrellus' Journal once again. This time, they sliced through her thoughts like daggers: *Tonight, our leader will initiate me fully by way of an ancient rite. I must speak my darkest secret into the spirit fire of Noul, then, the Groom of Whispers and I will be bound.*

The sound of Savas' hyperventilating overtook the room quickly. "What the bloody skrak are you saying, ghost? What have you done to me?!" He bellowed.

"He's made you a Dreamist," Aurelia interjected, panicked. "A servant of Noul."

Castrellus made a menacing smile. "Much more than that. You are the steward of this plane now."

"Aurelia," Savas panted. "What is he saying? What does that mean?"

Her thoughts were a formless cloud; she reached deep over and over for any intuition to solve this, but there was nothing to grasp hold of. Aurelia didn't have the answers her brother needed. Castrellus had tricked them, and she couldn't even guess at what he had truly done.

"You are his now, and bound to this place. I died by the time I arrived here, yet since you are alive, the House of

Noul will be like a fine sheet of water, always before you, permeable, but not a prison. Noul will draw you in, and perhaps other times, you will enter freely. It is not so harsh a sentence, but the Groom of Whispers is a ravenous god. You must feed him with knowledge; where he lies dormant, not even the brightest ray of new wisdom can reach him."

"You might as well have sentenced me to death!" Savas cried. "I don't want to be stuck in the service of some decrepit deity my whole life."

"There will be a way to undo it, Savas," Aurelia tried to reassure him, but she was lying — she had no clue if there would be a remedy for this or not.

"Is that so?" Castrellus spoke mockingly. "Perhaps after a few decades, Noul will allow you to trade places with another, just as I have done with you."

Savas' head slumped low and he buried his face in his hands, fighting back his emotions. "You're evil. And selfish," he snarled, glaring at Castrellus. "So, tell me, if this greedy god of yours is so hungry, how have you kept him sated all this time?"

"I was once in line to be a Haruspex of the Hermesian people. My magic sustained a connection with the Nomos Tal since I first bound myself to it and allowed me to see more than enough of the world to satisfy Noul, even from here," Castrellus replied.

He was Hermesian, like the people Mitenni spoke of who fought Menyr in the deserts with the kind of weapon now in Savas' hands, Aurelia realised. She shouldn't have been surprised; it made sense. But the fact that his magic had somehow installed a pair of eyes into the Journal that she had been carrying around unsettled her. He had been spying on generations of people for centuries from his jail cell. "You've seen everything that's happened to me these past few days. You knew we were coming. You've had this escape planned for a while, haven't you?"

The near indiscernible curl of his lip was as close to a yes as she would get. "There were others who could have opened this door. I did not command the book to find you, if that's what you are implying. I merely watched and waited. Do you think you were the first with veil-piercing eyes to walk past it and see it there? Witches, warlocks and sorcerers from many places have seen it over the years. But you were the first in four centuries to not be dissuaded by the demons that surround the Nomos Tal."

Savas regarded Aurelia sharply. "What's he talking about? What demons?"

"I should have told you," Aurelia replied. "There were spirits that spoke to me twice. They told me not to take the Nomos Tal," she paused, fixing a critical gaze on Castrellus. "They said that everyone who used it turned into a monster."

Castrellus ignored her. He looked up abruptly, and the fire cast a haunting reflection in his eyes. Turning to the side, he did not look in their direction, but side-eyed them with a studied reproach.

"Sounds like they were right," Savas bemoaned.

Aurelia shook her head, rife with disappointment. "Our sister is missing, kidnapped by Menyr. We fear for her life. I know that her disappearance is connected with Onaxia and her plans. There has to be at least something you can tell us about this evil Princess."

"There is no power any human magician can summon to oppose the will of an immortal. Onaxia is not diminished by old age, nor is she constrained by fragile bodies as we are. Her magic is near infinite."

"What on Ysa is she?" Asked Savas.

Castrellus shrugged. "I spent barely 30 years out in the world. What wisdom I can impart is inadequate. You would have to dig deeper than this place to find the answer to that question."

"What hope is there then, unless the book can be used against her again?" The desperation in Aurelia's voice slowly became palpable.

"I used it once and ended up tearing into an alternate dimension as a prisoner for four centuries," said Castrellus. "Do you dare to use it yourself?"

"Our world will be destroyed if we do nothing," Aurelia retorted.

Castrellus rubbed his chin. "The Nomos Tal is bound to me alone, and I do not wish to use it for your cause."

Aurelia was furious. "The price of your freedom is my brother's servitude, and you offer nothing in return. What will you do when you leave this place? Our ancestors have made a compelling case that Onaxia and her minions will ravage everything in their path."

"My sister is right. How can you have become so self-serving and apathetic after all this time?" Savas added, his voice raised with frustration. "You were persecuted for your sexuality and endured hardship. The world hasn't been kind to you — we see that. But it hasn't been kind to us either. You're supposed to be on our side, not trying to dupe us. We risked our lives to reach you and all you've done is tarnish me with some curse. You better offer something worthwhile in return."

Lips pursed with contempt, Castrellus turned sharply to face the pair. The cogitations of his mind were clear as he chewed the side of his mouth and shifted his unfocused gaze limply around the room. "Do you really believe you can stop her?"

"I don't know," Aurelia responded. "But we have to try."

"You are brave. I'll give you that. Foolish, but brave." His head drooped, pensive and overburdened with thought. "I don't share your optimism," he said, finally.

"You're afraid?" Savas barked. "So are we. Me especially. That doesn't mean you get to walk away from this without helping us. Do something. Anything!"

Castrellus sank deeper into contemplation, and a moment later, his cold exterior gave way to reconsideration. "It is possible that the Nomos Tal could be bound to another," he suggested.

"Go on," said Aurelia.

By some act of sorcery, the Nomos Tal found its way into Castrellus' palm. He stared at it, his intentions veiled. "Come. Let us see." He moved like air, wafting down the corridor, appearing to take tens of steps at once. As Aurelia and Savas followed, they saw that he was now by the central pulpit, where the memories of Mazin and the Menyr had now vanished.

"This was the seat of all power in the monastery once, where Mazin preached. If I dig deep enough, that strength could be mine temporarily," Castrellus said, the book in hand. He ran his fingers along the stony pulpit, eyes closed in meditation. His lips twitched, as if in a dialogue with some invisible being. "Ahh," he said, after a while, nodding to himself. "Neither of you is suited to the path the Nomos Tal offers, though there is a third that I see: one who lusts for strength and has the will to command it, one who is poised to oppose Onaxia and her allies," Castrellus continued.

Aurelia regarded him, mystified, as Savas came up behind her, the Hermesian blade still in his hand. There was an acute discomfort as Castrellus then began to worm his way into her thoughts without invitation. As though stinging nettles had taken up residence in her mind, spheres of a smarting pain throbbed, sending her onto her knees with a groan.

"Are you OK?" Savas asked, helping her up.

She was not. Castrellus' strength was incontestable. Aurelia tried to conjure an impregnable stone wall in her thoughts to halt his advances, but each time she summoned it, he toppled it. What he sought, he found with little difficulty, then plucked like a ripe, gilded fruit.

"There will come a girl," started Castrellus, smug. "She will carry a terrible burden: a sword strong enough to split Ysa in two will always be within her grasp."

"Zerkal's moon, he's talking about Elfine," Aurelia sighed deeply.

"She's alive?" Savas asked. "What do you know about Elfine?"

"I see that she is strong," said Castrellus.

With clenched fists, Aurelia said, "But what of the demons' warning, that those tied to the Nomos Tal in the past lost their minds? I could shoulder this burden myself, but I won't let you force it upon my sister," she growled. The image of the gushing river flooded her thoughts again, begging for her to soak up all of its essence. In seconds, she was back at the bottom of the sea, at that terrible confluence of magical power and ancient secrets, where the strength to topple Castrellus could be gathered. Savas crept by her side with his blade drawn, but everything suddenly lagged. Inflicted by a spiritual torpor, their bodies could advance no further. Something heavy amassed around their spirits and subdued them. A slow, hostile incantation drooled from Castrellus' lips like wax from a hot candle. They were not the words of the Ubija, but those same unknown utterances that had skittered upon the flames earlier. Hermesian magic, different to the Ojanti and the Menyr. His power surpassed Melindra's, easily. Aurelia sensed her connection to her spiritual power slip out of reach and she knew that she had no means to fight back.

"At last, freedom." With his gambit concluded, Castrellus whipped up a whirlwind about him and vanished into the air, followed only by a fizzling display of flashing lights.

He was gone.

No words found their way onto Aurelia's lips. No sound was simple enough to produce. Instead, she breathed those quiet, seemingly airless breaths of shock and dismay. It didn't seem plausible for this to be the culmination of her meeting with Castrellus. For a moment, she watched and waited, half-hoping that a second mystical being might appear and deliver the news that everything was going to plan, that Aurelia had done exactly as she was supposed to. She longed for the Visitor to appear and reassure her. But there was nothing, save for the cadaverous caress of the Ankasa, unending in its gloom.

Savas scratched his temple. "That could've gone better."

"I don't know what happens now," Aurelia said, dejected. "Elfine has become part of his plans, and we've lost the Journal."

"Elfine will be OK," Savas said. "She spent years training with the Chicane. I don't know what she is capable of, but if we can survive the Menyr, so can she."

The two returned to where they had entered and saw that the glowing door they had once stepped through was gone.

"Perhaps if I pray to Noul, he'll open the way?" Savas joked, already seeming to have come to terms with his sentence of lifetime servitude to Noul.

Aurelia managed a faint smile. "You are the steward of this hell pit. Maybe that counts for something."

"Well, I certainly don't feel like a steward."

"Concentrate, otherwise we're both going to be trapped here," Aurelia said, worried.

He looked far too tense. His whole body went stiff, like he was trying to combust every vein in his body at once.

"Calm yourself," she said. "Now, try again."

This time, he allowed himself to relax. The rise and fall of his chest became hypnotising with its measured rhythm. His face softened and eyes closed, it appeared that he found his way into the necessary meditative state.

"Sometimes, I find myself in deep water," Aurelia whispered, so as not to disturb his concentration. "It is a powerful place for me. There must be something similar for you. Find your strength and think of the fine sheet of water Castrellus spoke of. Then, open a way through that sheet to get us home."

Savas wobbled, like a slight flower in the wind. If he found a place like Aurelia had described, he made no mention of it. The pulsating vortex of blue and white that appeared in front of them appeared quite suddenly.

The gate made a strange noise as it swirled, whirring and humming like something of pure, unbridled magic. Aurelia felt as though she was next to a cyclone.

"Young lady!" shouted a voice. "Before you go, you should take this."

A hand reached for Aurelia from behind and thrust something into her hand.

"Mazin?" she said, dumbfounded as she regarded her friend.

"I think this is for you," said Mazin, presenting Aurelia with a letter. "That man. He left it."

"How can this be? How are you here?"

"To have returned here, I suppose I am finally passing on," he replied, solemn.

"Aurelia," Savas said, urgent. "I don't know how long this will stay open for."

She realised it didn't matter; nothing made any sense here. As she took the letter from Mazin, the spirit fizzled into nothing, seamlessly coalescing into the atmosphere.

Chapter 23

Dreaming the Way Forward

As Savas stepped through the portal, he'd expected it to feel like being submerged underwater for a long time, but the whole experience concluded in a matter of seconds. The door returned them to the grisly scene they had left behind earlier, where the skeletal remains of Winnik and the dust of Queen Consort Melindra remained. Temek and Lei Jia were gone. Although he wasn't surprised, Savas had hoped to see her on the other side. He was worried about her injuries — and Lei Jia's, who looked in a terribly bad way. In truth, they were all lucky to be alive, given that Aurelia had not been able to help them with her magic. The Hermesian sword felt natural in Savas' hands during the fight. Something came intuitively when the threat of the Menyr was before him; wielding the blade's power into deadly strikes and swings came to him without much effort. But the high of that battle was quickly eclipsed by the dreadful conclusion of events in the Ankasa. This Castrellus that his sister had longed had done nothing useful for them, and had orchestrated their arrival to the House of Noul to shackle Savas to the hellish graveyard of reality in his stead. Savas couldn't even contemplate this unwanted stewardship yet, not until it actually affected him. That wasn't all, he had outed himself in front of Aurelia. They hadn't had time to discuss it, but the fear that she might oppose his sexuality terrified him. He wondered how she would use the knowledge that he was gay, if she would tell their parents, or disown him. Perhaps even she would never speak to him again after this day, and she would leave him to rot, either in Northcrest, or trapped in the House of Noul, like Castrellus.

Leaving the Parlour, the first few steps back in the city were sobering. The brief flight into the spirit world, where everything seemed mercurial and colossal made Savas forget what was going on in the real world, where things had only gotten worse. In the short time that they had been gone, the sun had still not returned. Even the cover of night could not stifle the ruination of Northcrest: death abounded, along with its merciless smells and the ethereal screams of the bereaved, robbed of the right to mourn. The stones of yet more buildings lay strewn in the streets, some of which had become impassable.

"We need to go this way to get back home," Savas said to his sister, directing her through rubble.

"Are you sure you're OK with not checking on Temek and Lei Jia?" Aurelia panted, rushing to keep up.

"I'll look for them later," he said. "We need to make sure Mother and Father are OK. They'll want to know if we found out anything about Elfine."

They raced through town to reach Sunhold, where Protectors patrolled with such agitation that they mistook Aurelia and Savas for intruders, only to realise their error after Aurelia wiped the thick layer of dirt off her face. The Queen Consort has not been seen for some time, one of the Protectors had also said. Savas' anxiety whispered that they already knew that it was he and Aurelia who were responsible for Melindra's death. But he was sure it would not be possible for them to know, unless she had cast some sort of spell on the guards even before the confrontation. His heart raced with all the questions and fears that rattled at the back of his mind like broken glass. The Protectors could not take action against his family, Father would protect them, Savas thought. Besides, the Queen had been a puppet of Onaxia — a Kaspician spy, and a sorceress.

She had deserved to die.

Quickly, they moved across the bridge and drew upon the door to the tower. The room was empty, save for Mitenni, who was sitting at Father's desk.

"You're back," she said.

"Mitenni?" Savas said. "Where are Mother and Father? Are they OK?"

"They are sleeping," she said, quietly. "How did it go?"

Savas watched his sister suspended in thought, desperately searching for the right words. But it appeared that she could not.

"It didn't go how we hoped," Savas said, stepping further inside. "The spirit in the monastery played us for idiots. He put some sort of spell on me, stole the book and vanished." It sounded worse when he said it aloud.

"And the Menyr? What of Melindra?" Mitenni continued.

"She's a pile of ash under the Parlour now, along with her friend," Aurelia said, cold.

Mitenni made an incredulous noise. "At least you survived. I would call your mission a success."

"Maybe," Savas said, unsure.

"You two must be exhausted," Mitenni said. "Come, I have prepared your beds."

*

Aurelia was walking across the desert. The sand was prickly and scorching hot. Her bare feet blistered from the pain. Flicking her tongue around her mouth, she found that it was void of saliva and lined with cracks from dehydration. She'd never known thirst like this, or fatigue. Many days passed and blurred into one long nightmare under this same, wretched sun. She looked up at it, filled with scorn. The sky was dazzling blue, somehow more vivid than the sky over Northcrest, which was always smeared with clouds.

For the first time, she saw something new. Upon a lone tree was perched a falcon with slate grey streaks across its breast.

Its head swivelled to face Aurelia, but it made no noise.

Aurelia collapsed under the tree and quickly forgot about the bird. The shade was as a long-awaited respite from the incessant beating from the sun. Her eyelids quivered, desperate to stay open, yet she was dying.

The raptor departed, squawking noisily, and Aurelia jolted back to life. She wiped her sweaty brow, and only then noticed the crude, obsidian structure in front of her. It was like nothing she'd ever seen or read about. Upon its many stones were runic etchings, pictures and symbols from a world she knew nothing of. From out of the building, a low murmur of magic seeped into the desert air, enticing her in.

With the fraction of strength that she had, she arose and staggered towards the strange edifice, climbing up the long steps into a chamber that the desert sun was unable to penetrate. Darkness loomed for only a moment, quickly dispelled by the hissing blue flames that came to life along the walls and lit the way. The passage was far wider and taller than it had seemed on the outside. Markings similar to those that were inscribed upon the outer stones, appeared on the high ceiling, glowing blue. Hesitant, Aurelia continued down until she reached a spiral of stairs. She followed them down and entered a vast chamber that must have been the heart of the place.

Only one thing occupied the room. She crept towards it, battling nerves and fatigue. In an instant, her eyes were heavy with tears. Her body pricked all over with dread.

Fear came close to paralysing her, but as her hands reached forwards, she saw it. A sarcophagus.

Inside it, the Visitor lay dead.

Aurelia should have collapsed with emotion. That was the reaction her mind told her to perform, but a sound distracted her, straightaway sobering her. It was not the sort of sound she had expected to hear down here, but the sound of eating was unmistakable. Not just any kind of eating, but a distinctly loud, lip-smacking noise came from behind.

With a quick pivot, Aurelia turned to face the source of the sounds.

"Red pea soup and dumpling. You did eat already, child?"

"What on Ysa is going on?" Aurelia retorted. "Where am I? Who are you?"

It was a woman, sat on a tiny stool in front of a pot of boiling soup. She was a short, rotund lady, with a head and nose to match her width. Her eyes were like two chestnuts dented into her cocoa-coloured face, with bushy, caterpillar eyebrows. The hair on her head looked dry like the desert outside, with thick tousles of black and grey seemingly poking out at random like some sort of thorny fruit.

"Eat first, aks question later," said the woman, who then spooned a mouthful of the soup into her mouth.

Aurelia took a few tentative steps forward and the woman unveiled a second stool from behind her.

"Sit, please!" she continued.

Reservedly, Aurelia did as the woman asked. "What is th—"

"Yuh try red pea soup before? One o' di speciality dem from we home. Tek it — nuff dumpling, yuh see?" The woman handed Aurelia the hot bowl and a spoon.

It was delicious. But Aurelia had had something similar before. Mazin made food like this often, though she never thought to ask where he learned such recipes, or if any of the dishes had names. "Thank you," she said.

The woman smiled, then took another loud slurp of soup.

"Will you tell me where we are now?" Aurelia asked.

"We in di Black Cairn," the woman replied. "Inna di desert round Calech, in di Southern Continent. A fi yuh friend dat dead 'uman over deh so?"

The accent was a struggle to grasp, but it didn't take too long for Aurelia to piece together the deviations from the Gaminian that she spoke and figure out what was being asked of her. Besides, she was familiar with this dialect.

"That's Ylestra," Aurelia said. "She is my friend, yes. What happened to her?"

"Dead," the woman giggled. "Long time already. She never tell you?"

"She did mention her death, once," Aurelia replied. "But I can't feel her anymore. A Menyr did something to me. Cut me off from her."

"Dem deh tings always up to no good," said the woman, scraping her bowl clean.

"You speak like Ylestra's ancestors. My ancestors. Are you?"

"Me?" the woman chuckled. "Maybe. Me lef' plenty pickny inna dis world."

"I see," Aurelia said, swirling her spoon in the soup listlessly. "What is this Black Cairn, anyway?"

The woman paused to consider. She went for a dumpling this time and bit it in half. Her lips continued to battle each other in a contest to make as much noise as possible. "Dis a mi first time in 'ere so. Some kinda prison, me tink."

"Prison? For who? Ylestra?" Aurelia asked.

"Down below fulla evil," the woman replied. "Yuh don' need fi know who down deh so yet."

"For a strange woman eating soup in a prison by yourself, you aren't very forthcoming," Aurelia said, putting her unfinished soup on the ground. "I know I'm dreaming. But I can tell the difference between dreams now. This isn't some vision of the past like others have been. We're talking right now — in the present. You smell more like your stew than magic, but I can tell you are Ojanti. I'm guessing you want something."

The woman burst into laughter, dropping her bowl on the floor. "Ishanaia have mercy. What a smaddy!"

"Well?"

The woman flashed a toothy grin, stood up and invited Aurelia to follow her as she walked towards Ylestra's sarcophagus. Her small hands stretched outwards, she caressed its smooth surface and let out an indecipherable sigh. "Onaxia. Yuh did see her, no 'chu?"

Aurelia nodded, hesitant. "I've seen Princess Onaxia in a vision, yes."

"So, yuh did see how powerful she be. Mekka aks yuh sumting: how yuh a go beat her without di book, while Northcres' a bun' to di ground?"

Aurelia's thoughts stuttered, caught at the sealed gate that was her lips and unable to emerge with any clarity. "I don't know," she said.

"She got 'nuff tricks fi fool yuh. Plenty bad people on Ysa done throw in dem lot with her. People who mek even Ojanti sorceress scared. Yuh need help, child," the woman said. "And I want fi help yuh."

"I don't even know who you are," Aurelia said.

"Dat don' important," was the reply. "Yuh magic strong already. I trus' yuh can find dis place inna di real world, because yuh nah go nowhere without dis 'uman 'ere so. Dis Ylestra. She a call out to yuh, her cry dem loud. But she can't reach yuh. Yuh ear dem don't strong enough fi hear her."

"Are you saying there's a way to get her back if I come here?" Aurelia asked, hopeful.

"More than what yuh did have before. Mi a tell you say, if yuh come 'ere, yuh can resurrect her real body. Not just some duppy fi follow you round, a real guide."

"Resurrect her?" Aurelia was astounded. She was doubtful that she'd even be able to restore the connection she once had with Ylestra, but to give her ancestor her corporeal form back seemed too tempting an opportunity to overlook. "Are you serious?"

"Mi look like a liad to you?" she beamed, revealing several misshapen teeth.

"But what about the war? My family? I can't just leave everything I know behind in the middle of this chaos. Who will fight the Menyr if not me?" Aurelia asked, suddenly feeling guilty about the idea of leaving Northcrest.

"War? No war deh a Northcres' yet," the woman said. "Lef' dem deh eeedyat fight dem little battle. Ojanti yuh be, not soldier. Di war yuh mus' fight neither with Kaspician, nor Menyr, because Onaxia gon' wake up whole heap o' old demon."

*

The morning arrived in a hurry. Outside Sunhold was the same cruel picture as yesterday, only the bombarding had picked up again. Smoke rose up into the sky from what looked to be Chapel Heights, where several more catapults had hit their mark and left people's homes in heaps of stone and dust.

Aurelia didn't manage to sleep too long. She woke to the sight of Mitenni, who had retrieved some food from the kitchens and now busied herself laying the table. There was an assortment of brown bread, cheese, smoked fish, pickled vegetables and hot tea at the table. For a moment, it looked like it could have been any other morning, but the smouldering stink of Northcrest and its people wafting through the embrasure quickly eroded that fantasy.

Without inviting anyone else, Mitenni took a seat at the table by herself, took a bite out of some bread and discreetly spat it into her palm, then wiped it on the leg of her seat.

"Was it stale?" Aurelia asked, coming up behind her.

Mitenni's face bloomed bright red. "Oh," she squeaked, embarrassed. "Just not to my liking, that's all."

"Finally, something to eat," Savas said, his morning voice a tired rasp. He walked over to the table and took a seat.

Aurelia sat next to him, though she did not have much of an appetite this morning.

"You're back," Father said, coming down the stairs. "And Elfine is not with you."

When Mother surfaced, the family came together to eat. After it was relayed that the mission into the catacombs was a failure, the table fell silent while the thoughts and fears of what was to come coagulated in everyone's minds. Mother and Father made shallow attempts to eat their breakfast, if only to regain a bit of strength, or create a bit of noise at the otherwise silent table. Mother's face was stretched out with sadness, her face sunken and sapped of its joy, meanwhile, Father had pursed his lips into a pensive grimace, exacerbating the austerity of his regard.

Aurelia's gaze roved over towards the window, where the devastation went on unchecked, occasionally punctuating the silence of the room with the harsh sounds of war. It drew her closer, as though the pain and suffering that was going on outside was able to latch onto her spiritual power and suck it in so they had an audience to pity them. Each time she blinked, she found herself walking the streets of Northcrest, either blessed or cursed with the gift to see its lost souls, many of whom were children, waiting for safe passage into the spirit world, or even the Nether Pits. That was the first time Aurelia wished she didn't have magical powers.

"Your mother and I have been speaking," Father said, after making a little cheese sandwich, and breaking a long silence. "We agreed that if you did not discover any news of Elfine, we would leave Northcrest."

"You really saw nothing of Elfine where you went? None of the spirits gave you some clue as to what has befallen her?" Mother interrupted Father.

Aurelia felt her nose twitch as a tear sped down her cheek. "No," she sighed. "But Elfine is alive." She could not bring herself to reveal what Castrellus planned to do, that he intended to take the Nomos Tal to Elfine. The thought made Aurelia sick. But her parents would not have been able to bear this knowledge.

"How do you know she is alive?" Mother asked, her voice soft with melancholy.

"I just do," Aurelia said. "I can't explain it. It's something magical."

"You've never lied to me before," said Mother. "You aren't now, are you?"

"The spirit we saw said Elfine was alive," Savas said. "He said she was strong, and well. But we don't know anything else, Mother. I'm so sorry."

"At least we have some hope of seeing her again," Father said. He took mother's hand in his and gave her a comforting smile. Aurelia had never seen him show so many emotions.

"You're right, Olsin," Mother said. "And I believe you, Aurelia. I can feel her too. She's not lost to us, not yet."

Father looked back to Aurelia. "There is safe passage waiting for us this afternoon out of the city. We've horses, food and supplies to make it safely to Staghorn. The people there will receive us warmly," he smiled, then wiped the breadcrumbs from the corner of his mouth.

"Staghorn?" Savas said, unenthused. "That's just farmland. What will w—?"

"I had a dream," Aurelia interrupted. She affected a calm tone, but it was not enough to conceal her apprehension.

Mother's teacup made a sharp noise as she rushed to set it down. She held Aurelia's gaze for a moment. "A dream?" she said.

"I saw a place in the deserts of Calech. The Black Cairn. I spoke to someone there. She told me to come to her. I think I have to," continued Aurelia, struggling to make eye contact with anything but the table.

"The Black Cairn?" Mitenni choked on her tea, unable to mask her shock. "Forgive me, I did not know it was a real place."

"What is it?" asked Father.

"I am not sure," said Mitenni. "Some kind of prison for the Southern Continent's worst criminals is what I was told."

Father sighed and shook his head. "You've already made your mind up about following this dream, haven't you?"

"If we want to stand a chance at stopping Onaxia and finding Elfine, we're going to need allies. Strong ones," Aurelia spoke with conviction. "Who knows what demons she is going to wake? Even if we beat her, only the Three know who or what might come after."

"There's no hope for Northcrest. We are set to lose this war. But why are you already thinking about fighting more?" Father quizzed her, his brows tightly pinched together.

Aurelia looked at the smoked fish and her nose wrinkled at the smell of it. "I don't want to fight any wars, but I'm not convinced that Onaxia is the cause of our problems. There's more to all this, and we won't beat her without the spirits who have guided me on our side. I need to find them. To bring them back, even."

"This place you intend to go to, do you expect to save your sister in going there?" Mother asked.

Aurelia frowned. "I don't know. I want to do whatever I can, but I don't know where to look for Elfine. All I have is this dream of the Black Cairn. Maybe along the way, Savas and I will be able to help Elfine."

"Northcrest will fall soon," Mother said matter-of-factly. "We received word from General Tonsag while you were in the catacombs that the enemy is expected to invade the city today. A spy has seen the Kaspicians preparing ladders, long enough for their soldiers to breach our walls. We will be overrun in a matter of hours once they are inside. The two of you have been positioned to play pivotal roles in this conflict. You are not meant to travel with us to Staghorn. I knew that before you said this. If these ancestral spirits are calling you elsewhere, then you must follow their voices, and trust that they also have Elfine's best interests at heart. We will prepare everything. You will leave before midday."

Aurelia stood on her balcony overlooking her home. Her feelings as she prepared herself to say farewell to

Northcrest were unclear. A lot had changed in the past few weeks, and a part of her was afraid. She feared that she was not ready to embark on this quest, but somehow, she knew that she did not have a choice. A slight breeze rustled her dress as she leaned across the balustrade, and the letter that the spirit of Mazin had brought before her tumbled out of her pocket. With so much on her mind, she'd forgotten about it. Quickly, she reached for it, before the wind blew it away, and read:

To My Love,

I found a witch to help me send this to you. I hope it reaches you, but I'll never know if it does. I'm sorry that I cannot be with you. I don't know what those Menyr did to me, but I don't know if I'll ever be able to reach you again. Nobody can see me, apart from people with magic in their veins. I am a ghost, I suppose, but cannot move past this world. I have lived many years, so death does not trouble me, though, I am lonely.

There is something you should know, Castrellus. I have learned of what you did. I know what Onaxia did to you. What she took from you. I know how much you suffered with your sexuality, and I will never blame you. I cannot. It is not my nature. I will not. Many years ago, I might have done the same thing. Even Noul's champions could not have stood against Onaxia. It is a testament to your strength that you encountered her and lived. You are more powerful than I ever was, and if anyone can survive where you are, it is you.

I have renounced my connection to Noul. I want nothing to do with a god that imprisons his loyal followers. I know that there is a way to rescue you. There must be. In my research, I have come across a strange word: the

Keyholder. I have read that a Hermesian Haruspex once gave a prophecy to Princess Onaxia's father about this thing. They say it is someone who has the power to open any door. I am not sure what kinds of door exist, apart from the ones of the real world. Even in all my years, I have never really understood magic that well.

Don't give up, Castrellus. I am preparing to travel to Rivane. We haven't seen each other for a long time, but my brother Ayrn has always been far wiser than I. I hope that he will help me figure out what to do.

Know that I always love you and keep you in my thoughts,

Mazin

A tear fell down Aurelia's face and splotched onto the centuries-old letter. Surges of emotion broke over her and she struggled to place what each of them was. Was it sadness, grief, regret or some other consuming fear that assailed her? The idea of destiny nauseated her, but the deeper she burrowed into these supernatural mysteries, the more she knew she was an active player in this grand puzzle. Melindra's treachery had led Mother to Ayrn in Rivane, but centuries prior, Mazin had also been there. Mazin, who had been a spiritual ghost this whole time, was Ayrn's brother — the man Mother described as a distant relative, and a deeply enigmatic character. Was Mazin also a distant relative? Aurelia wondered what advice Ayrn had given to his brother. Had Mazin also been waiting all these years for Aurelia to open the doorway into the House of Noul, and be reunited with Castrellus, the deceitful Hermesian? A mass of anxious thoughts whirled in her mind as she considered them. Aurelia could not bear the burden of not knowing. She desperately wanted to see

Mazin before she left Northcrest, but her spirit led her to the conclusion that he was no longer here. With only a moment's concentration, she sensed that Mazin was gone, and that the apparition of him in the House of Noul was likely the last she would ever see of her friend. His words echoed in her thoughts: *To have returned here, I suppose I am finally passing on.* Whether he had made it to the spirit world out of choice, or against his will, Aurelia did not know. As much as she hoped to see him somewhere, somehow, she doubted that it would be possible.

Turning from the morning sun on her balcony a final time, Aurelia stepped back into her room, where Temek had been helping Savas pack. Aurelia had packed her bag hurriedly, filling it with food, healing equipment, supplies and other essentials.

"Do you need to take that? There's hardly enough room as it is," Aurelia remarked, watching Savas do his best to fit a large bottle into his bag.

"Fig tonic is an essential," Savas said, lightly. "If you expect me to accompany you on this ludicrous quest, I need to have amenities."

"You can't be a warrior and a drunk, Savas," Temek bantered. "And besides, all that alcohol will make you fat," she scoffed, then passed him a little blanket to pack.

Savas squeezed it into the already bulging rucksack. "I wish you were coming with us," he said to Temek. "Then again, the city looks beautiful this time of year — I can see why you want to stay."

She chuckled. "I think I'll be OK. If all the smart people leave, who'll be left to rebuild the city?" She stomped her boot on the top of Savas' bag, allowing him to properly close it.

"Are you calling me smart?" Savas was smirking.

"Not you," Temek replied, then regarded Aurelia. "So, what's your plan then?" she asked.

"We're going to the Black Cairn. It's somewhere in the deserts around Calech." Aurelia realised that her plan was far from solid. She was literally following a dream.

"Doesn't sound like an easy place to find. You know 'the deserts around Calech' are vast, right? You also know, I'm guessing, that people speak different languages and use different currencies and have totally different beliefs where you're going?" Temek went on, with a borderline parental tone.

"Savas and I will manage on the Southern Continent; we learned Piscanese and Sygecian with Tutor Fark," Aurelia said.

"Right," Temek said, sharply, "but how many Piscanese or Sygecian friends have you ever actually practised with?"

Aurelia swallowed a glob of anxiety. Temek had a point — her knowledge of the Southern Continent didn't go past books and quiet seminars. She'd never even practised Sygecian with Mitenni, like Savas had; she'd always been too afraid to embarrass herself in case she made a mistake. "I'll learn quickly. And Father has promised us some Piscanese coins. That's where we're headed there first," Aurelia did her best to sound confident.

Temek sighed. "I don't know if I envy your bravery, or want to cry at how stupid you both are. You could just join the revolution and help us here, you know."

"The revolution doesn't need us — it has you," Aurelia said, smiling brightly.

"But what are you going to do in Pisca?" Temek probed.

"Find the way to the Black Cairn and get the support of our ancestors. The Ojanti. I hope they will have answers about Elfine. But we also won't win what's to come with only me and Savas' sword. We need people who understand Onaxia and the Menyr on our side," Aurelia explained.

"Is this what you want, Savas, to go to the Black Cairn?" asked Temek, squinting.

"I wish we could all stay together." He paused, then allowed his gaze to sag to the ground for a moment before returning to Temek. "But you have the North Wind. Aurelia will have no one if I don't go with her. The two of us have to stay together, and I need to learn more about what Castrellus did to me. My guess is the best place to find answers about that is with the Hermesians."

Temek nodded, though it was palpable she wasn't happy about Savas leaving.

"What's the next move for you and Lei Jia?" he asked.

"I told Okim what happened. He was impressed. I think I'm due a promotion," Temek giggled, then continued, "He's getting ready to evacuate and make for Westiz, the capital of Staghorn"

"Really?" Savas interrupted. "Mother and Father are heading there tonight."

"Perhaps they can join the revolution," Temek joked.

"Can you keep an eye out for them, and maybe Elfine too, when you eventually get there? I know we won't be able to communicate or anything, but just for peace of mind," Savas asked.

"Of course," Temek replied. "And as for Lei Jia, he's recovering, but he and I are going to be working together from now on. I'm kind of excited. I've never been as passionate about something like I do about the North Wind."

Aurelia smiled, though quickly found herself doubting whether there was anything to smile about at all. "What will your people do about King Thenris? And the Myriad?

Even with everything going on, they won't allow you to set up a democracy and overthrow them without a fight."

"If Okim's plans go ahead, they'll be dead before we make a play for the throne," Temek retorted, determined.

"Well, I won't stand in your way. I couldn't care less about the Myriad or King Thenris," Savas sighed.

Aurelia wasn't sure if she shared that sentiment. Things outside had never been more dire. Whether or not Gaminia could survive a war and a political revolution remained to be seen. She had read about incidences in history where invaders had allowed certain leading figures to retain their positions only to relay the wishes of the new occupiers. The Kaspicians would be willing to keep some of the Myriad around, Aurelia assumed. On the other hand, if they sensed the determination of the North Wind, they'd straightaway seek to crush any chance of resistance it could muster.

"I'll send you King Thenris' head by carrier pigeon," Temek joked.

Savas laughed, but it was a rueful laugh, masking a wave of sadness. "You don't know how much I'm going to miss you," he said.

"Don't do it. You look ugly when you cry," Temek smirked.

"Stop pretending you don't care for a second, will you?" Savas snapped. "Being apart from my only friend is going to be tough."

Temek bit her lip. "I'm sorry. Don't worry about our friendship though. We're both going to do amazing things. Think of all the stories we'll have to tell each other when we next see each other."

"You two will be together again sooner than you think," Aurelia said, and though she hadn't expected to find herself there, she met the arms of Temek and her brother in a gentle farewell embrace.

*

As they journeyed across to the tower, Aurelia spared a glance below and realised that she and Savas had been too leisurely with their time, labouring over what to pack and getting teary eyed over goodbyes. Ladders, like sets of tracks, had appeared around some of the city's walls, providing multiple routes straight into Northcrest's vulnerable belly. The last Aurelia had heard was that Marshal Morovig, along with several other commanders, had been battling with the enemy in the Esterwood, pushing them back despite the odds, yet now, it seemed that the city's keenest defenders might have been routed.

She stopped for a second and watched the tiny splotches of dark, clad in armour and wielding menacing swords and halberds as they clamoured onto the walls. Even from here, she could hear the clashes of steel and the cries of the warriors in battle. It filled her with the keenest sense of dread. There was no time to spare.

"Why haven't you asked me about what I said in the House of Noul?" Asked Savas.

"What are you talking about?" Aurelia replied, impatient.

"Have you forgotten what Castrellus did to me already — how he was able to do it?"

"No," she said.

"And?"

Words did not come to Aurelia straightaway. Nothing stirred in her for some time, and only a blank void without a single thought loomed in her mind. She had suspected this, after what happened at the Angel's Hovel, and his sudden befriending of Temek. Even still, she had not prepared for this moment at all like she should have. Her brother's eyes were deep and pleading, lined with emotions he must have carried his entire life. All Aurelia knew of love came from the culture she had known since her childhood, that of Gaminia and of her parents. But the Visitor had made her challenge everything she knew, and she liked the person she was becoming much more than the person she had been.

"This is unspeakable by Gaminian standards. Our parents will never understand this. Mother and Father were both raised on the same Yotanite diet, and their belief systems forbid this behaviour vehemently. You know this." She paused, watching his eyelids expand with tears. "But I suspect you know I don't give a damn about Yotanites or tradition anymore. Who you choose to love is of no concern to me, neither does it impact the road ahead of us. I can't say I have much interest in marriage, or relationships with men — or anyone — so who am I to judge? You are unchanged in my eyes."

A smile touched his lips for a brief moment, and a tangle that was both joy and sadness spiralled through his face as his dissimulation was finally over. "If I'd known you'd take it like that, I would've told you sooner," he smiled.

"I know I don't show it often, but I love you," Aurelia said. "Nothing will change that. Come on, let's go."

Back in their parent's bedroom, Mother and Father were frantically pacing, while Mitenni sat on the floor, pounding something herbal with her mortar and pestle.

"You've packed all your things?" Mother said, in a state of panic. "Quickly! They have breached the city. The horses are waiting at the west gate. I will lead you there."

Father rushed to steady Mother with his hand. "You absolutely will not. The enemy are already making their way inside. We must prepare our own evacuation. The children know the way."

She slapped the hand away and turned to him, scowling. "I can survive a short walk to the gate. Say your goodbyes — you can get ready to load our things."

"Come, son," Father said, gentler than ever before. He reached out his arm to his son and gave a fleeting embrace, then extended the same to Aurelia. From his desk, he picked up a weighty jute pouch and a folded map, both of which he handed to Savas. "This is a map of the two continents; it'll help you get to Pisca and find your way around the Southern Continent when you get there. And there are enough coins in here to last you a few months in Pisca. When you start to run out, use your brains. Look for work, do what you can, and stay safe. Most importantly, don't give up on Elfine."

"Yes, Father," Savas said. "I'll look after Aurelia, too."

"Good boy," Father said. "You two both look out for each other. We'll watch over Gaminia, so you have a home to come back to."

Mother started to cry. "Mitenni? Say farewell," she enjoined.

Mitenni shuffled closer, leaving her paste of herbs on the ground. Her eyes were blank, lacking the emotion Aurelia expected. "Goodbye. I will take care of Lady Trinne and Lord Olsin. I hope you know some Piscan, or Sygecia, for when you reach Helassion — that's what we call the Southern Continent."

Mother hurriedly led them away from Sunhold. Aurelia had never spent much time in the west part of town. Now, Aurelia stood before the west gate, about to leave Northcrest with no notion of when or how she would return. She spared a glance back at Sunhold, whose towers were more visible than ever, with several gaps in the skyline. Aurelia envisaged her home come tumbling down in her thoughts a couple of times, but Mother snapped her out of the hallucination when she hoisted her up to the horse's saddle.

"Savas, here, let me help you onto the other one," she said, the sounds of anxiety and panic in her voice.

A catapult struck a tavern at the other end of the road and a low ringing besieged Aurelia's ears. It seemed to go on forever. Suddenly, the whole tavern collapsed, along with half of the house next to it. Disembodied screams of those inside blared. The vision of Mother in front started to blur. Slowly, Aurelia turned her head and saw flames rising up all over Northcrest. There were no Protectors in sight, save for a few dead ones, strewn along the streets. The North Wind was the country's last hope, while she and Savas were gone. Aurelia hoped that more would join the revolution.

"There is only one route to where you are headed," Mother said. "You must reach Gladehill to the east — Savas has the map — and get the ferry to the port of Misala. It's the capital of Pisca, and the best place for you to start your journey. You will find the Black Cairn if you start there." She reached out both of her hands, one for Savas and the other for Aurelia. Tears formed in her eyes, and her face scrunched up into the saddest, most pitiable expression Aurelia had ever seen on her mother. "Please, pray for us here. Pray for Elfine. Pray that we will survive what is to come. And pray for yourselves when you can."

"We will, Mother, don't worry," said Savas.

"I hear them," said Mother. "They are getting closer. Go, and don't look back."

Chapter 24
Blood Red Sky

Elfine couldn't tell how much time had gone by. Being imprisoned and handcuffed in the back of the carriage had left her mental faculties deteriorated. The constant bumping up and down in her seat and the fact that the poison made her constantly want to vomit, left her in a dazed stupor. So far, she had only been let out of the carriage a couple of times to void her bladder, or bowels. The only two other travellers they passed on the way fell victim to Benthrin's sorcery and became his dinner. There was one thing that Elfine had come to appreciate in this sludge of vicissitudes: the isolation with her thoughts. The patter of the horse's hooves hypnotised her into deep trances and took her to a place where she was free from the agony of the present.

She gazed out the dirty window wistfully. That square of the outside world connected her to something spiritual. The splendour of the countryside was undeniable, but there was a savageness that drew Elfine in with a stronger pull: the red centipede coiled around rotten bark, the tiny ants that lugged dismembered thoraxes to their colony, the droplets of blood that spilled onto fallen leaves and the thunderous heartbeat of a murdered hare, waiting to be eaten alive. Her spirit's eyes drifted from thing to thing in the forest, suddenly able to see the smallest of creatures or occurrences, and these things captivated her; this inert cruelty that was rife in the natural world. Each time she happened upon it, a fleeting ecstasy strengthened her, and it was the chase that kept her awake. She bounced between sites of death and wilting as though an integral part of nature's will to destroy.

The priest's presence was easily distinguished in this place. She could sense him from where she sat. Her projected spirit saw clearly the Menyr riding the carriage, like a noxious cloud of smog and bilious intentions. She watched him closely in the same fashion that one might become engrossed in the movements of a venomous serpent, not out of fear that it would bite, but in quiet awe of its power, and secretly wanting to dismantle it. At times, she found herself wondering what next feat of magic he might conjure, or who would be his next victim. He had spared her the nausea of watching him eat the travellers that he had killed and feasted upon, but she resented him for this. It was her wish to see and understand everything that a Menyr did, so that she would have a better chance at killing him. She had learned that he was not invulnerable: occasionally, when she reached out, she sensed limitations in the shadows that cocooned him. Benthrin's appetite was bottomless, and she figured that when his hunger grew, his power became weaker.

These weren't the only things that Elfine distinguished. Under the carriage, buried beneath the forest floor, she heard the echoes of those long dead; in the forest, she heard what seemed to be dialogue between oak, elm, ash and birch. Never before had she felt so attuned to her surroundings, and the countless dead, whose spirits lingered and brought voice to things ordinarily mute. It gave her the impression that her passage was marked with great interest.

The day wore away and the journey's descent came to an end. Elfine projected her spirit eyes outward and saw a bridge, on the other side of which was a small glade in the woods. Once they arrived in the glade, Benthrin stopped the horse and opened the doors to let her out.

As she stepped out, she took a deep breath and savoured it in her lungs for a few, long seconds. Around the cinders of a fire was a tree trunk, an apple core and a tattered bedroll. Others had camped here recently. A glance ahead showed that the only path was overcrowded with trees and uphill; Elfine realised that they'd be walking for the remainder of the journey. To the side of the glade was also the River Essen, a snaking squiggle along the country that terminated at the Piscan Strait. Along the journey, she had seen its current in her mind. It looked mundane now, despite its great breadth and the masses of purple barrabid reeds on either side, teeming with life.

"Sit down," ordered Benthrin, pointing to the tree trunk. He proceeded to rummage through his satchel and pull out a few slivers of dried beef, which he shoved in Elfine's face.

"No vegetarian option?" said Elfine.

He scowled.

"Where are we?"

"Between Staghorn and the Republic of Siladria," he said, moving over to the cinders.

"I need water," she wheezed.

"Then you will thirst. There is none."

Elfine heard the high-pitch bellow of a deer. The rustles and murmurs issuing from the trees grew louder. As Benthrin sat by the dead campfire, her vision was transformed. Everything became slow and quiet.

Rhyslan.

How was it that he was sitting beside her? An intense heaviness stopped her from moving or speaking, but she watched the Chicane warrior stand up, dust himself off and then head forwards. A moment later, her sight returned to normal. She questioned whether Benthrin had witnessed the same vision. She knew now that Rhyslan was the one who had camped here earlier. He was looking for her, but ahead of her. That meant he knew where she was going, before even she did.

"Why did you call me Keyholder?"

Before Benthrin could respond, a noise in the distance startled him. Elfine barely noticed it. She presumed it was just the snapping of a branch, or an overweight bird landing clumsily in a tree. But she had come to expect much more from her surroundings now. Not a moment after opening her spirit eyes, she was transported out of her body and found herself standing close to the River Essen. Her gaze fixed on the water, she sensed something manifest beside her.

"Who are you?" Elfine asked.

The entities that glowed in front of her were translucent, fluctuating between hues of blue and green. If it weren't for the two hollowed out, glistening slants she took to be their eyes, Elfine would've never guessed that the things had ever been alive at all.

"You are close to where it happened," said one of them.

"Many died here once. You will die too," said another one of the other spirits.

"What are you talking about?"

Suddenly, the spirit that spoke first took the shape of a young man. The other radiant entities assumed similar forms. They were warriors once, from Gaminia. Elfine could tell by their look and the style of their equipment.

"How is it she sees us? We've been here for decades. None have noticed us before," voiced another.

"Must be some kind of witch," said the first.

"Like the fire woman?" asked the second. "She saw us."

"Maybe. She travels with wicked company," said the third.

"What are you?" asked Elfine.

"Wanderers, caught between worlds," said one of them.

"Surely, you must know something that can help me?" Elfine pleaded.

Their drawn expressions hardened as the three spirits turned to face one another, as if remembering a primordial secret that they were too afraid to repeat.

"The Menyr fear the Ojanti. They always have," said the second spirit.

"But their princess only fears the one who can seal her," said the first spirit.

"Who is that?" Elfine asked.

"Can't you tell? She's right there."

Elfine's hands rushed to her ears to protect them from the hiss the spirits then made. They started to collapse on themselves until all their light was reduced to a glowing sphere, and then nothing. They were gone, and Elfine was back in her body, sitting on the stump.

"It's time to leave," Benthrin snarled. He was stood right in front of her, glaring with his callous eyes.

"Who are the Ojanti?" Asked Elfine. "And why are you afraid of them?"

"To waste the paucity of strength you have left on pointless chatter would be unwise," he hissed in response. He faced his palm towards her and began to whisper an incantation under his breath. Fumes of black smoke seeped out from between his lips. The forest went silent as he began to work his foul magic.

Elfine didn't use her hands this time, but imagined a shield over her ears, with the power to block out the evil intentions of his spell. "I know about Onaxia," she growled. "That's where you're taking me, isn't it, to see the great hallowed bitch?"

Benthrin's face contorted with wrath. His magic's attempt to control her had failed this time. Instead, he seized her by the throat and proceeded to drag her towards the path. His grip seemed to soften briefly, only then to shove Elfine into a tree. "The next time you speak, I will remove your tongue!"

"You won't. I'm the Keyholder," Elfine flashed a smile, unfazed by the blow against the tree trunk.

He was upon her in seconds again. Around his hand shards of black grew out of nothing; they were like ice, draped in shadow, and they begged to impale her. They skittered frightfully close to her face. "Such gall," he said. "When Onaxia is finished with you, I will leave you an empty husk. Or perhaps I will carve you up like a hog. Like Lorcan."

Elfine blanched, her face transformed by grief. The pain of losing Lorcan to this monster came back, raw and torturous.

"You will be silent. And you will follow," he ordered.

Elfine heard the horse whinny behind as they left it there, alone. She pitied it for a moment. It would be easy prey for a pack of wolves. More than ever, Elfine wanted to break out of her handcuffs and crush her captor's windpipe. There was something she had learned that would help her achieve that. When he raised his hand against her the first time, she felt his magic's attempts to inveigle her, as it had done so before. But this time, she had somehow been able to resist it — she wasn't defenceless, and maybe even had some of the same gifts that Aurelia had. That wasn't all either; she was right about him needing her alive. All she had to do was kill him before they reached Onaxia, and she would have vengeance for Lorcan and herself.

*

After a few hours of journeying on foot through a wooded glen, a squall of heavy downpour broke. The rain made each footstep an arduous task, and Elfine had to tread carefully so as not to lose a boot to the mud. As they continued to progress, the trees became denser and the path tighter. Any semblance of human life was far gone. Elfine had seen neither farm, home, nor tavern, and the winding, soggy path gave her the impression that it led somewhere desperate. With her sight blurred from the rain, she struggled to make out the way ahead, but her spirit's eyes remained strong. Mapped out in her thoughts was a complex image of the whole ecosystem around her. She felt the vibrations of each life form, the reaction of each leaf as it collided with the rain, the minuscule brooklets of water that had taken form on the ground and the beating wings of the crows above.

The rain perturbed everything, but it colluded with all that it touched too. Elfine had sensed the conversations among the forest's inhabitants once before, so it wasn't bizarre to imagine that the rain now spoke to her. To make out specific words was too big a challenge, but she was certain of one thing — contained within each droplet of water was the forest's desire to blot out the Menyr's reign of terror over Elfine. Suddenly, the torpor in her legs began to fade, allowing her to move comfortably; her breathing became normal, no longer a slow wheeze and as she glanced at her palms, she saw that her skin was no longer wan. Finally, the rain did not obscure her view anymore, but enhanced it, and indeed, all of her senses.

Up ahead, Benthrin came to a halt. For a long, ominous moment, he stood alone, as one dark entity amid ochre and viridian. He moved to conceal himself behind a large tree, then turned to face the motionless Elfine.

"You will not move, nor make a sound," he ordered. His hands took on that terrifying, icy black form and traced a deathly path across his throat to intimidate her.

Like a predator studying its next meal, Benthrin skulked behind a second tree, hidden by its thick trunk. He looked searchingly into the distance, wiping the rainwater from his eyes and brow. Elfine had not picked up on the thing that had disturbed him so, but her heart pattered with nerves. She didn't know whether to be afraid or excited, but when he turned to check on her, his usual grimace was distorted, and it dawned on her that there was something new in his expression: weakness. He didn't look angry, but afraid. With the strength that the forest had bestowed on her, Elfine succeeded in propelling her spirit far enough ahead to finally see what Benthrin had spied.

It was the Northcrester accent that she noticed first. Then came the sound of a campfire, crackling plaintively against the weather, followed by the smell of the fish roasting upon its flames. Camped under the bivouac was a platoon of warriors from the capital, around 15 in number. Their outfits were tell-tale Gaminian. There were archers, clad in leather overcoats and hooded robes woven with green patterns, as well as a selection of stockier characters, shrouded in steel and equipped with swords and lances. Aloft in the flagbearer's arms was the symbol of Gaminia — the Owl of Providence — and it was this that gave Elfine genuine hope.

"We are close," said a familiar voice. "I need to know that all of you are ready to face whatever comes."

Rhyslan. He was standing in front of the soldiers, pacing up and down like their General. Zatela must have somehow given him emergency powers over the Protectors to command them. Most Protectors had no clue the

Chicane even existed. Elfine had to get his attention if she was going to escape with her life.

"Rhyslan. Rhyslan, please, help me!" she implored aloud, in spirit form. But he did not hear.

"Something awful is trapped in that cave. We must ensure that she has not escaped, and take out any of the Menyr who follow her," continued Rhyslan. "This is your chance to make a difference in the war."

"Rhyslan!" Elfine bellowed.

There had to be a better way to reach him. Her eyes darted all around, hoping to land on some overlooked device that might manipulate the fabric of reality into performing a miracle. But there was nothing. Panicked, Elfine watched Rhyslan carry on with his words of encouragement to the young warriors. Even though she remained disconnected from her body, she sensed Benthrin advancing forwards, his eyes constantly looking back to check on her movements. Time was running out. Elfine could see no other option but to will her spirit to go right up to him and grab hold of Rhyslan. She hadn't expected the leather garment to feel as real as it did, and by the time she'd finished shaking him, a realisation dawned on her.

"Elfine?" he spoke in a low voice. It didn't seem as though anyone else perceived her presence.

"You can see me?" She shrieked. "There's no time! The Menyr. He's coming. He has me hostage and handcuffed. You need to act now and together we can stop him!"

"What pathetic attempt at sorcery have you contrived?" Benthrin's voice came out of Rhyslan's mouth.

Thrust back into her body sharply, Elfine saw Benthrin stood before her. His jaw was set in a deep glower, as if it took all that he had to stop himself from tearing into her flesh.

"It's too late. They cannot save you from your destiny." His soulless eyes became two whirlpools of darkness; streaks of shadow rippled across his visage like coiling worms and his gaunt body went corpse-grey. He rose in his fury, expanding in size and might, and returned to his true form, resembling the arachnid that burrowed out of him by the south gate. Elfine wished she could shut her eyes, but it was impossible. Her spirit's gaze revealed him in his grotesque entirety: appendages and limbs of all manner seemed to dance and skitter around him like the spectre of a long dead spider, and shards of dark ice erupted across his torso.

Benthrin punched the air and a deathly potency swelled around his fist, instantly toppling Elfine. An invisible hand held her neck as a blood-curdling incantation seeped out of Benthrin's lips. The spell inflicted her with the pain of a thousand wasp stings, and she collapsed in the rain, paralysed.

"I think she's over there!" A voice shouted.

Benthrin scowled. He closed his eyes and clenched his fists tightly. A silent communion began, and Elfine got a sense of the magnitude of his power. He was channelling everything he had now. Onaxia was coming to his aid. Fine tendrils spiralled into the air above him and tickled the clouds, still bursting with rain. In the next instant, Benthrin had taken out a small blade and plunged it into his own stomach. If he knew pain, he did not make it obvious. Instead, he beamed, observing the trickle of dark blood spill onto the ground.

Faintly, he spoke, *"Vrok omoya dalos Kanyazhna, dojota ragrethai, ragrethai dojota."*

When the warriors drew upon Benthrin, they broke into laughter. All they saw was an old man, muttering madly to himself. But the Menyr did not regard them, instead continuing to speak his evil into the air. As the blood spilled forth from his self-inflicted wound like crimson drool, Elfine saw his words lingering above, waiting to bring about something heinous. It took more than a moment for his spell to take effect, and when it did, Elfine curled up on the forest floor, still handcuffed and struggling for air. The first peal of thunder wasn't as bad as the next few, but it was the sky, turned scarlet and seething with anger, that had everyone terrified.

"He's turning the sky red with blood!" Elfine heard one of the soldiers shout.

Looming in the corrupted clouds was red lightning, which tore through the heavens in rapid, snaking streaks. Before long, the whole sky had been engulfed in the Menyr's dark vitality, dotted and sprayed with an infectious red hue. Seconds passed and the air became thick and stifling, as the reek of dark magic bordered unbearable.

From where she lay, desperately shielding herself, Elfine glimpsed Rhyslan begin to back away. Thunder and lightning continued to ravage the atmosphere, but that was not where the Menyr's power ended. Suddenly, the rain turned wrathful, bombarding a path through the thick canopy and sizzling as it hit the ground. The rain had been imbued with the power of burning acid. Above, a great pair of shadowy hands choked the dark power out of the clouds, as though baiting venom out of a cobra.

Their confidence depleted, the soldiers froze before Benthrin, awaiting their death. When the rain struck them, they were quickly overwhelmed. Desperate, they clawed at their skin hoping to relieve the itching and the pain, but as red lightning struck, it was clear that their resistance was hopeless. Elfine's hopes dissolved as she watched the warriors, now writhing in pain on the ground, their skin cooking and armour crackling. She stayed close to the tree trunk beside her, grateful for its vast reach, which had so far kept her safe from the rain.

Despite their lithe movements and the protections afforded by their hoods, many of the archers also fell victim to Benthrin's spell. Although it was becoming a strain on her, Elfine continued to exert her spirit eye to keep track of the few who remained safe.

"Follow me! Quickly!" Commanded Rhyslan. Under his guidance, the surviving bowmen rushed to hide under the protection of a similarly colossal tree to where Elfine was.

"Someone, take the shot! I can't, my hands are shaking!" cried one of the archers

Rhyslan leapt out from behind the tree nimbly, with an arrow nocked and ready to launch, he trained his bow on his target. "Zerkal, make my aim true and my strike deadly."

The upkeep of his sorcery left Benthrin vulnerable. He was caught off-guard. A single arrow of devastation pierced his shoulder, and his power began to ebb. The Menyr produced a delayed shriek as he realised what had happened. His hands, once the conduit for his power, seemed unable to maintain the spell, or reach for any new magic. The strangling hands in the sky fizzled, and Benthrin fumbled forwards, clutching his wound.

A ghostly hum shook the atmosphere and the strident magic fell into disharmony. The acid burn of the rain dissipated, and the clapping sounds of thunder soon became but a memory.

Rhyslan stepped back into cover, perhaps preparing the fatal strike that could lay the monster to rest.

But Elfine had travelled with the Menyr for such a long distance. She had endured this priest's presence far too long. This nightmare had to end, and she wasn't about to leave her fate to chance. Seizing her opportunity at last, she charged forwards and made a grab for the blade Benthrin had stabbed himself with. Quickly, she wedged the blade between her thighs and cut through the bindings around her wrists.

Benthrin pivoted to face her, grimacing. Elfine barrelled into him, but he deflected her easily, then dislodged Rhyslan's arrow from his shoulder. In a show of strength, he tossed it on the ground nonchalantly.

Elfine wasn't fazed yet. She moved quicker than he had expected; the forest's blessing still ran through her. With vengeful intent, she lurched into him again with all the force of an ox and delivered a spinning kick into his face. She followed up with a flurry of blows to the stomach and a second kick to the jaw. He barely flinched. She paused to regather her strength, all the while her eyes did not leave him, and as she waited, something else entered the arena.

The dark whirlpools of chaos and boundless magic that coalesced in the monster's eyes came out in a jet, but for once, Benthrin seemed in pain. A malignant thing, encased in licking flames of shadow, climbed out of Benthrin's form and thwarted Elfine with a single look from the two, red vortexes of agony that were its eyes. Elfine was hurled all the way to the edge of the wood with a thunderous glance that left her vision distorted and her head ringing.

Elfine didn't dare meet her attacker's gaze again, or whatever foul magic that had seeped out of him. Despite a sharp pain in her chest, she raced towards the River Essen planning to cross it, but in a moment of hesitation, the river grew wider, and its waters began to gush violently. There was no chance that she could make it across. She heard a commotion on the trail behind her, and wondered whether Rhyslan or his archers had made another move. She wasn't going back into the fray yet though — she could barely see, let alone fight. There had to be some other place to go, somewhere to escape or hide. With her spirit eyes scanning the area urgently, she finally uncovered it: the mouth of an obscure cave on a low mountain.

Dashing over rocks and fallen branches, Elfine leapt higher and higher, running quicker with each breath. The forest floor was damp and muddy, like a graveyard for all the canopy's fallen leaves and rotted branches. Her shoes nearly became stuck in the thick mud, but she freed herself and continued. Where she found herself was a place where the forest's abundance could not penetrate. The calls of neither beast nor bird, nor the chirp of an insect could be heard and the trees were gnarly and withered.

The rocky incline up towards the cave's mouth did not slow her down. Now, beginning to recover from that earlier attack, she raced on.

Inside, only the dark and the cold greeted her. The passage ahead was a lightless stretch and the echo of an eerie breeze whistled through, upending the slight hairs of her neck.

"Right into my web," echoed a voice.

Footsteps came shortly after, and Elfine pivoted in a hurry.

Benthrin.

"You didn't think I'd fall so easily, did you?" He mocked her. His stomach wound was already healed, and he held the blade Elfine had used to free herself in his hand.

"All things fall," said Elfine, catching sight of Rhyslan coming up behind the Menyr. Flying in mid-air was a dagger that Rhyslan had launched over Benthrin's head. Elfine reached to catch it. She hadn't felt a weapon in her hands for so long. It was ecstasy to run her thumb across the grooves of the hilt. With the blade pointed to the right, and her left hand formed into an open palm, she was armed and ready.

Rhyslan drew the silver sword that he had used to murder the Chicane's enemies for almost a decade.

Benthrin swivelled his head back and forth to watch Rhyslan and Elfine, beginning a slow dance on his toes as they moved around him for the attack.

Rhyslan swung first. He and the Menyr were quickly drawn into a one-on-one of limber flicks, parries and deft footwork. Elfine revelled oddly in the sounds of their steel clashing while she formed her strategy. They were evenly matched, but she knew what Benthrin was capable of, and this was barely the extent of his power. Rhyslan squinted at Elfine mid-strike, urging her to make a move. She understood that the Menyr's body was weaker than its mind; he was old, and while he had brute force, he was not as nimble or as fast as Rhyslan. His strikes were slower, his feet heavier and his hips stiffer. In a battle of stamina and speed, they could beat him.

Rapidly, Elfine dived into the battle, placing her dagger to parry Benthrin's before it could reach Rhyslan.

"Keyholder, you dare strike me?" He taunted her.

She channelled her strength into her next move, and redoubled her efforts to overwhelm him. With the two of them to contend with, Benthrin was outmatched. He pivoted and twisted and thrashed as best he could, but the two of them bullied him towards the ledge of the craggy cliff. The sky remained tinged with red, and for a second, Elfine thought she smelled the burnt flesh of the fallen warriors.

They were all breathless from the fighting, but the Menyr was waiting for something. His dark intentions oozed out of him and Elfine sensed them now with little effort. Just as she turned to warn Rhyslan, he launched himself forwards in an attack. But Benthrin, as wily as ever, dodged out of the way and thrust Rhyslan to the side, slicing his belly with his dagger as Rhyslan fell and taking him out of the fight.

"And now for you…" he hissed.

In an instant, something with the weight of a boulder started to close in around her. His magic was doing everything it could to crush her. The bones in Elfine's arms and legs were close to snapping, but as she let out a terrible scream, her lips emitted a rolling wave of pale energy that rocked Benthrin backwards, undoing the spell he had weaved.

Elfine stood strong, her composure regained, and said, "I resisted you once. You were a fool to doubt I could do it again."

But he only scoffed. "Insolent!"

Like being whacked by the end of a hammer, Benthrin's magic intensified its efforts to bring her down. Shards of withering darkness shot out of his hand like claws of ice. They struck, scratched and shredded. But Elfine wasn't defenceless. Around her, a fine shield that resembled a bubble protected her. She heard it like a watery drum being pounded as it endured Benthrin's onslaught. As hard as he tried to break her, she did not yield to his sorcery. When the moment came, instinct guided her to draw her power inwards, where it became pliable to her intentions. For days, all Elfine had wanted was to ruin this ravenous thing before her, and only now did she realise that the power to do so had been within all along. The energy inside teemed, like a spinning sphere of scorching hot energy. Deep in her mind, she sensed the vibrations of power undulating in places within she did not know existed. There was no need to gamble, because she knew exactly when to strike: she seized hold of the magical power as though it was a serpent slinking in the grass, and thrust its venom into her enemy's face.

At once, his face went milk white and the blade clattered onto the ground, his hands too weak to hold it. "This means nothing," He hissed in pain. "She will devour you."

He'd always been gaunt and skeletal, but death overtook him quicker than Elfine had expected. Like two pieces of a puzzle coming together, she heard a faint click as her magic understood her ultimate will, and Benthrin's neck snapped in the same instant. Her oppressor lay dead and shrivelled like a spider's carapace.

Whatever power she had conjured left her weary, and Elfine could only sigh with fatigue as she regarded his pallid corpse.

"Elfine," Rhyslan croaked from behind.

She rushed to check on him. "Are you OK?" she asked.

"I'll be fine," he groaned.

Elfine examined the knife wound; it wasn't deep enough to be fatal, so she covered it and helped him back onto his feet.

"I didn't believe her, you know," he said. "That you could do that. But she always believed."

"What are you talking about?"

"Zatela. She said you were Ojanti, like her," said Rhyslan.

Elfine paused, her arm still around his shoulder. "Ojanti?" she repeated. "Who are these Ojanti?"

Suddenly, he looked a lot worse than she had realised. "Let's get back to the—"

But she'd forgotten all about the cave, and what was lurking inside it. The whole point of this wretched journey. The vulgar thing that the Menyr called their princess. There was nothing Elfine could do. Rhyslan was lifted up into the air, levitating as though he was weightless. Elfine did her best to jump and pull him down, but a burst of energy shoved her out of the way. Was Rhyslan trying to speak? His words could not outmanoeuvre the strangling force around his windpipe. All of a sudden, his face went red and bloated, pocked with tracks of bulging veins. Then, that same humming noise assailed the atmosphere.

A glow of amethyst filtered lit up the cave's walls. Elfine was stunned with fear as Onaxia emerged. The hooked claws of her fiery purple wings gripped onto the sides of the cave, and the enemy princess slowly exited her ancient prison. Before Elfine's eyes was the winged thing of Yotanite scripture her mother had warned her of. The thing that had dared to challenge even Ishanaia.

Princess Onaxia waved her shadowy wrist and Rhyslan was engulfed in amethyst flames that swallowed him in a flash.

"You're here," Onaxia cawed.

Elfine wanted to scream, but she couldn't. She thought quickly on her feet, hoping to drain the reserves of her magic and defend herself. Defiant, she got up and channelled a telekinetic burst straight at the princess.

Save for her hair falling slightly out of place, Onaxia was unaffected. "Almost 2000 years ago your ancestors chained me to this hollow, and you greet me with a slap?" she said, her voice piercing yet not quite fatal, like the pinpricks of a hot needle.

"I'd shove you back in there, if I could," Elfine said, trying to mask her nerves as she regarded the burning wings.

"The Keyholder," said a man's voice, hidden behind Onaxia.

"Yes," said Onaxia. "She is here. My people have succeeded."

Onaxia dragged Elfine back into the cave with a spell. Purple letterings materialised along the cave walls, illuminating the way, and Elfine was dragged along the floor by Onaxia's magic until they reached a yawning, central chamber. The princess clenched her fist and dozens of flames, radiant with that same, captivating amethyst, came to life, exposing the cavern in its entirety. A dais rose out of the ground with an altar on it, where a purple candle burned brighter than all the other flames.

"Bring me the Nomos Tal, Castrellus," Onaxia commanded.

A meek shadow of a man appeared behind the Princess, and placed a weathered tome in her hands.

"Rise, Elfine," Onaxia ordered, freeing Elfine from her magic's grasp.

As Elfine stood up, she took in the ancient enemy's form. Onaxia was tall and statuesque, her shoulders draped in thick black hair, like that of a horse, and her complexion a greyish hue, likely from her time trapped in this hovel, with so little sunlight. Her clothes were simple; the frock she wore could have been found on any peasant girl in the countryside, but her sharp features and proud expression confirmed her royal heritage. Two thick eyelids covered her black eyes, while the rest of her face was adorned with a thin pair of lips, a slender, up-turned nose, and the jewel of her visage — two striking, high cheekbones, which caught the amethyst glow of the cave with haunting effect.

Onaxia opened the book; the fluttering of its pages sent murmurs and cries around the cave. She stopped on a specific page, then traced the odd symbols with her finger.

She turned to Castrellus, and commanded him to read. At once, the reserved man began to speak the incantation aloud. Elfine did not recognise the language, though it sounded deeply guttural, comprised of various tones and short, abrupt sounds.

"What's happening?" Elfine asked. She glared at the Princess, desperate for the truth.

But Onaxia did not answer. She reached towards Castrellus, who then ceased to chant, and relieved him of the book.

"It no longer answers to you," she said, smiling. Onaxia inhaled, with her eyes shut, then extended her palms out, facing up. The cave was assailed with a thunderous noise, until it seemed that the room could no longer contain Onaxia's prison, and the gates which had sealed her were broken. Above, the roof of the cave burst, and hundreds of rocks and pieces of debris hung in mid-air, listlessly hovering. The blood red sky was more potent than before, and ripples of scarlet lightning lacerated the clouds.

Onaxia rubbed her thumb and forefinger together in a practised motion, and a reflective, purple oval emerged in front of her. At its base were stones, and its flickering centre reflected the three figures like a mirror. She snapped her fingers, and the oval shattered like glass, giving way to a portal, where an ominous world beckoned.

"Keyholder," she said, "did you think your purpose was to open just one locked door? The Ojanti imprisoned many entities in the Ankasa. You and I are going to free every last one of them."

"Why do you have to set them free?"

"Because my father's throne has been empty for too long, and I want to see your world burn."

Acknowledgements

What a journey! I can't believe how long it took me to finish my debut. This project has been ongoing for so many years, so it's amazing to finally see this huge part of me out in the world. The question I've been asked the most over the years is why I chose to write a book, and it's because of the little red journal my dad gave me as a gift when I was about ten, which he rescued for me from our family's charity shop. It was slightly worn, and I had no idea what I'd end up using it for. Before I started writing, I was much more into art. I spent a lot of time as a child sketching — another thing I picked up from dad, who was pretty much always working on some sort of picture with his vast collection of pastels. My artistic talent was nowhere near as good as his, but I loved to think up fantasy worlds in my head and fill them with characters. I couldn't explain them to other people, so for my family to understand, I drew all of the individuals and wrote down their stories. Over time, I filled all the sketchbooks dad got for me. It was there that Aurelia was first conceived, along with her family and their universe. Eventually, those drawings turned into a story called The Gemini Girl, which I wrote with a pencil in the little red journal. It was about 60 pages or so, and my most prized possession until we moved house and I inevitably lost it, as well as several of my sketchbooks.

    I didn't really think about The Gemini Girl in my teenage years. I was too busy battling all the complexities of being gay at an all-boys school and coming from a Pentecostal family. My weight also generated its fair share of mental health issues, some of which have persisted to this day, despite losing a drastic amount since my high school years.

Getting accepted to read Modern Languages at Durham University was when my life started to change for the better. Finally starting to get over my high school angst, I found my people and blossomed. As a Mandarin Chinese major, my third year took me to Hangzhou, China, where I was expected to complete a one year language course as a part of my degree. Two months into what had started out as the best time of my life, my mum phoned in the middle of the night to tell me that my dad had suddenly passed away. He'd died alone in our flat from a heart attack. My brother found him the following day.

My mental health plummeted. Although I made it home for the funeral, I could not keep up with my academic commitments when I returned to China, and the Dean of the university decided to revoke my visa and send me home.

When I returned to the UK, my brother, a long-time writer, said to me, "Why don't you get back into writing?" And that was when I decided I'd set to rewriting The Gemini Girl, albeit a much more fleshed out, adult version. It was to be my catharsis, in a sense.

I did my best to write something that reflected a range of the experiences I have had over the years, and *Dreamer in the North* was born. So, a big thank you is in order to my brother for his encouragement — and for his unflappable willingness to read every single chapter I ever sent him for critiques!

Likewise, Amelia Kyazze is an eagle-eyed editor, who has helped me to grow immensely as a writer. My earlier manuscript was certainly a lot rustier before she went over it. I am also grateful for the words of encouragement I have had from my friends over the years, especially those who took the time to read my rubbish earlier drafts and give me insightful critiques.

Lastly, thank you to both of my parents. To my mum for her continual support (particularly with the Patois translations!) over the years in all matters, and to my dad, who always thought each and every creative work I produced had some merit, no matter how little.

Continue the adventure with Aurelia, Savas, Elfine and Temek next spring…

When Dreams Lead South

Follow Aurelia's journey deep into the deserts of the Southern Continent as she seeks to resurrect the Visitor, and see the truth about her dreams and her purpose in the war finally come to light. Savas will be put to the ultimate test as the scale of the war intensifies. Meanwhile, in Gaminia, how will Temek fare as the revolution continues to gain momentum? As for Elfine, there is more than just horror waiting for her in the Ankasa. When she understands the truth about Onaxia's father and the history of the conflict between the Ojanti and the Kaspicians, there's no telling how she'll cope.

If you'd like to keep up to date with the author's progress, please follow @tsgough on Twitter, or @tommygough_ on Instagram!

Printed in Great Britain
by Amazon